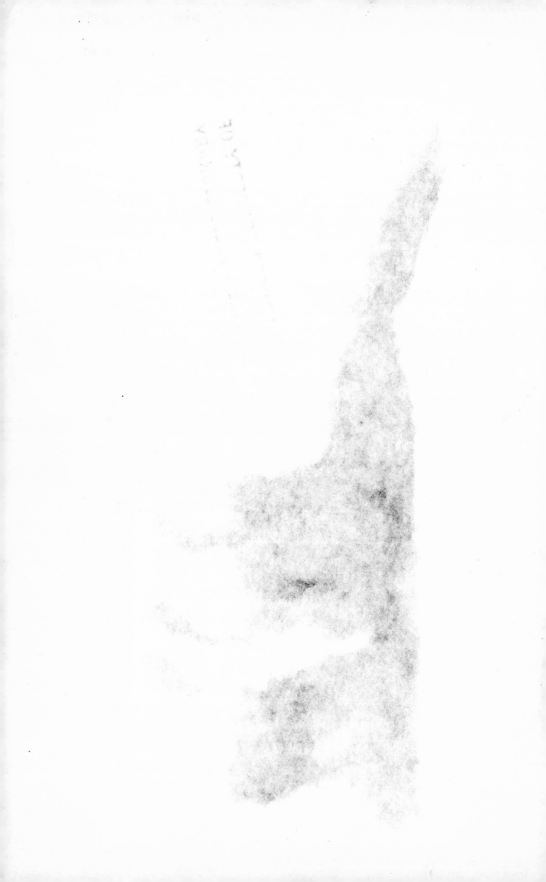

THE ONLY VICTOR

In February 1806 the frigate carrying Vice-Admiral Sir Richard Bolitho drops anchor off the shores of southern Africa. It is four months since the resounding victory over the combined Franco-Spanish fleet at Trafalgar, and the death of England's greatest naval hero. Bolitho is still brooding over the loss of his flagship *Hyperion* and at home he has to deal with the scandal aroused in London society as a result of his relationship with Lady Catherine Somervell. He is now under instructions to assist in hastening the campaign in Africa, where an expeditionary force is attempting to recapture Cape Town from the Dutch. Even after Cape Town there is to be no peace for Bolitho. The French are using every pressure on Scandinavia to close their ports to British trade; and the Danish fleet becomes the richest prize of all. But the men who follow Bolitho's flag into battle are to discover, not for the first time, that death is the only victor.

THE ONLY VICTOR

Alexander Kent

CHIVERS PRESS
BATH

First published in Great Britain 1990
by
William Heinemann Ltd
This Large Print edition published by
Chivers Press
by arrangement with
William Heinemann Ltd
and in the USA with
the author
1991

ISBN 0 86220 442 9

British Library Cataloguing in Publication Data available

For Maurice and Geraldine FitzGerald,
with our love and thanks

CONTENTS

'We few, we happy few, we band of brothers;
For he today that sheds his blood with me
Shall be my brother . . .'

Henry V

CHAPTER ONE

'IN THE NAME OF DUTY'

Captain Daniel Poland of His Britannic Majesty's frigate *Truculent* stretched his arms and stifled a yawn, while he waited for his eyes to accustom themselves to the darkness. As he gripped the quarterdeck rail and the dim figures around him took on identity and status, he was able to accept the pride he felt for this command, and the fashion in which he had moulded his company into a team, one that would react to his wishes and orders with little room for improvement. He had been in command for two years, but would not be fully 'posted' for a further six months. Then, and only then, would he feel safe from disaster. A fall from grace, an unfortunate mistake or misunderstanding of some senior officer's despatches—any of these could hurl him down the ladder of promotion, or worse. But once a post-captain with matching epaulettes on his shoulders, little could shift him. He gave a brief smile. Only death or some terrible wound could do that. The enemy's iron was no respecter of the hopes or ambitions of its victims.

He moved to the small table by the companion way and raised its tarpaulin hood so that he could examine the log by the light of a small shaded lamp.

Nobody on the quarterdeck spoke or disturbed him; every man was well aware of his presence and, after two years, his habits.

As he ran his eyes along the neatly written comments of the most recent officers-of-the-watch

1

he felt his ship lift and plunge beneath him, spray whipping across the open deck like cold hail.

In an hour all would be different. Again he felt the same twinge of pride, *cautious* pride, for Captain Poland trusted nobody and nothing which might bring displeasure from his superiors, and which in turn might damage his prospects. But if the wind held they would sight the coast of Africa, the Cape of Good Hope, perhaps at first light.

Nineteen days. It was probably the fastest passage ever made by a King's ship from Portsmouth. Poland thought of the England they had seen fall into a rain squall as *Truculent* had thrust her way down-channel for open waters. Cold. Wet. Shortages and press gangs.

His gaze fastened on the date. The first of February, 1806. Perhaps that was the answer. England was still reeling from the news of Trafalgar, which had exploded less than four months ago. It seemed people were stunned more by the death of Nelson, the nation's hero, than the crushing victory over the French and Spanish fleets.

Even aboard his own ship, Poland had sensed the change, the damage to morale amongst his officers and seamen. *Truculent* had not even been in the same ocean at the time of the great battle, and to his knowledge none of the people had ever laid eyes on the little admiral. It irritated him, just as he damned the luck which had taken his ship so far from a fight out of which only glory and reward could result. It was typical of Poland that he had not considered the awesome lists of dead and wounded after that memorable day off Cape Trafalgar.

He peered up at the pale shape of the bulging

2

mizzen topsail. Beyond it there was only darkness. The ship had rid herself of her heavy canvas and changed every sail to the pale, light-weather rig. She would make a fine sight when the sunlight found her again. He pictured her rapid passage south, with the mountains of Morocco misty blue in the far distance, then south-east across the Equator with the only landfall the tiny island of St Helena, a mere speck on the chart.

It was no wonder that young officers prayed for the chance to gain command of a frigate, where once free of the fleet's apron strings and the interference of one admiral or another, they were their own masters.

He knew that to his company a captain was seen as some kind of god. In many cases it was true. He could punish or reward any soul aboard with impunity. Poland considered himself a just and fair captain, but was sensible enough to know that he was feared rather than liked.

Each day he had made certain that his men were not lacking in work. No admiral would find fault with his ship, either her appearance or efficiency.

His eyes moved to the cabin skylight. It was already sharper in the gloom, or maybe his eyes had become completely used to it. *And there would be no mistakes on this passage*, not with such an important passenger down there in the captain's quarters.

It was time to begin. He walked to the rail again and stood with one foot on the truck of a tethered nine-pounder.

The ship's second lieutenant appeared as if by magic.

'Mr Munro, you may muster the Afterguard in fifteen minutes, when we shall wear ship.'

The lieutenant touched his hat in the darkness. 'Aye, aye, sir.'

He spoke almost in a whisper, as if he too were thinking of the passenger, and the noise of the Royal Marines' boots above his sleeping cabin.

Poland added irritably, 'And I don't want any slackness!'

Munro saw the sailing-master, who was already at his place near the big double-wheel, give what might have been a shrug. He was probably thinking that the captain would blame him if the dark horizon was as empty as before.

A burly figure moved to the lee side of the deck and Poland heard him fling some shaving-water into the sea. The passenger's personal coxswain, a powerful man by the name of John Allday. One who seemed to have little respect for anyone but his vice-admiral. Again, Poland felt a sense of irritation—or was it envy? He thought of his own coxswain, as smart and reliable as anyone could wish, one who would take no nonsense from his crew. But never a friend, as Allday appeared to be.

He tried to shrug it off. Anyway, his coxswain was only a common seaman.

He snapped, 'The vice-admiral is up and about, apparently. Call the Afterguard, then pipe the hands to the braces.'

Williams, the first lieutenant, clattered up the ladder and tried to button his coat and straighten his hat when he saw the captain already on deck.

'Good morning, sir!'

Poland replied coldly, 'It had better be!'

The lieutenants glanced at each other and grimaced behind his back. Poland was usually realistic in his dealings with the people, but he had little sense of humour, and as Williams had once put it, divided his guidance evenly between the Bible and the Articles of War.

Calls shrilled between decks and the watch below came thudding along the glistening planking, each man bustling to his familiar station where petty officers stood with their lists, and boatswain's mates were waiting to 'start' any laggard with rope's end or rattan. They were all aware of the importance of the man who wore his reputation like a cloak, and who for most of the lively passage had remained aft in Poland's quarters.

'There she comes, lads!'

Poland snapped, 'Take that man's name!'

But he looked up nevertheless and saw the first frail glow of light as it touched the whipping and frayed masthead pendant, then flowed down almost like liquid to mark the shrouds. Delicate, salmon-pink. Soon it would spread over the horizon, expand its colour, give life to a whole ocean.

But Poland saw none of these things. Time, distance, logged speed, they were the factors which ruled his daily life.

Allday lounged against the damp nettings. They would be packed with hammocks once the ship lay on her new course. Landfall? It seemed likely, but Allday could sense the captain's unease, just as he was aware of his own private anxieties. Usually, no matter how bad things had been, he was glad, if not relieved, to quit the shore and get back to a ship again.

This time it was different. Like being motionless with only the ship's wild movements to give the sensation of life around them.

5

Allday had heard them talking about the man he served and loved as he loved none other. He had wondered what he had really been thinking as *Truculent* had ploughed through each long day. *Something apart.* Not their ship. He let his mind explore the thought, like fingers probing a raw wound. *Not like the old Hyperion.*

October 15th, less than four months ago. Was that all it was? In his heart he could still feel the crash and roar of those terrible broadsides, the screams and the madness, and then—The old pain lanced through his chest and he clutched it with his fist and gasped in great mouthfuls of air, waiting for it to ease. Another sea, a different battle, but always a reminder of how entwined their lives had become. He could guess what the stiff-faced Poland thought. Men like him could never understand Richard Bolitho. Nor would they.

He massaged his chest and gave a little, private smile. Yes, they had seen and done so much together. Vice-Admiral Sir Richard Bolitho. Even their paths had been spliced by fate. Allday wiped the spray from his face and shook his long pigtail over his collar. Most folk probably believed that Bolitho wanted for nothing. His last exploits had swept the seaports and taverns of England. A ballad had been composed by Charles Dibdin or one of his fellows: *'How* Hyperion *Cleared The Way!'* The words of a dying sailor whose hand Bolitho had held on that awful sunlit day, although he had been needed in a hundred other places at once.

But only those who had shared it really knew. The power and the passion of the man behind the gold lace and gleaming epaulettes, who could lead his sailors, be they half mad, half deafened by the

6

hellish roar of battle; who could make them cheer even in the face of the Devil and the moment of certain death.

And yet he was the same one who could turn up the noses of London society, and invite gossip in the coffee houses. Allday straightened and sighed. The pain did not return. Yet. They would all be surprised if they knew just how little Bolitho did have, he thought.

He heard Poland snap, 'A good man aloft, Mr Williams, *if* you please!'

Allday could almost feel pity for the first lieutenant, and hid a grin as he replied, 'Already done, sir. I sent a master's mate to the foremast when the watch came aft.'

Poland strode away from him and glared when he saw the vice-admiral's coxswain loitering.

'Only the Afterguard and my officers—' He shut his mouth and moved instead to the compass.

Allday stamped down the companion ladder and allowed the smells and sounds of the ship to greet him. Tar, paint, cordage and the sea. He heard the bark of orders, the squeal of braces and halliards through their blocks, the thud of dozens of bare feet as the men threw themselves against the tug of rudder and wind and the ship began to change tack.

At the door of the great cabin a Royal Marine sentry stood near a wildly spiralling lantern, his scarlet coat angled more steeply as the helm went hard over.

Allday gave him a nod as he thrust open the screen door. He rarely abused his privileges, but it made him proud to know he was able to come and go as he pleased. Something else to gall Captain Poland, he thought with a grim chuckle. He nearly

7

collided with Ozzard, Bolitho's small, mole-like servant, as he scuttled away with some shirts to wash.

'How is he?'

Ozzard glanced aft. Beyond the sleeping quarters and Poland's swaying cot the cabin was almost in darkness again, but for a single lantern.

He murmured, 'Not moved.' Then he was gone. Loyal, secretive, always there when he was needed. Allday believed Ozzard was still brooding about the October day when their old *Hyperion* had given up her last fight and gone down. Only Allday himself knew that it had been Ozzard's intention to stay and go with her to the seabed, with all the dead and some of the dying still on board. Another mystery. He wondered if Bolitho knew or guessed what had almost happened. To speculate why, was beyond him.

Then he saw Bolitho's pale figure framed by the broad stern windows. He was sitting with one knee drawn up on the bench seat, his shirt very white against the tumbling water beyond.

For some reason Allday was moved by what he saw. He had seen Bolitho like this in so many of the ships they had shared after that first meeting. So many mornings. So many years.

He said uncertainly, 'I'll fetch another lantern, Sir Richard.'

Bolitho turned his head, his grey eyes in dark shadow. 'It will be light enough soon, old friend.' Without noticing it he touched his left eyelid and added, 'We may sight land today.'

So calmly said, Allday thought, and yet his mind and heart must be so crammed with memories, good and rotten. But if there was bitterness he gave

8

no hint of it in his voice.

Allday said, 'Reckon Cap'n Poland will cuss an' swear if there ain't, an' that's no error!'

Bolitho smiled and turned to watch the sea as it boiled from the rudder, as if some great fish was about to break surface in pursuit of the lively frigate.

He had always admired the dawn at sea. So many and such different waters, from the blue, placid depths of the Great South Sea to the raging grey wastes of the Western Ocean. Each unique, like the ships and men who challenged them.

He had expected, hoped even, that this day might bring some relief from his brooding thoughts. A fine, clean shirt, one of Allday's best shaves; it often gave a sense of well-being. But this time it eluded him.

He heard the shrill of calls again and could picture the orderly bustle on deck as the sails were sheeted home, the slackness shaken from braces and halliards. At heart he was perhaps still a frigate captain, as he had been when Allday had been brought aboard as a pressed man. Since then, so many leagues sailed, too many faces wiped away like chalk off a slate.

He saw the first hint of light on the crests, the spray leaping away on either quarter as the dawn began to roll down from the horizon.

Bolitho stood up and leaned his hands on the sill to stare more closely at the sea's face.

He recalled as if it were yesterday an admiral breaking the painful truth to him, when he had protested about the only appointment he could beg from the Admiralty after recovering from his terrible fever.

'You *were* a frigate captain, Bolitho . . .' Twelve years ago, maybe more.

Eventually he had been given the old *Hyperion*, and then probably only because of the bloody revolution in France and the war which had followed it, and which had raged almost without respite until this very day.

And yet *Hyperion* was the one ship which was to change his life. Many had doubted his judgment when he had pleaded for the old seventy-four as his last flagship. From captain to vice-admiral; it had seemed the right choice. The only choice.

She had gone down last October, leading Bolitho's squadron in the Mediterranean against a much more powerful force of Spanish ships under the command of an old enemy, Almirante Don Alberto Casares. It had been a desperate battle by any standards, and the outcome had never been certain from the first broadsides.

And yet, impossibly, they had beaten the Dons, and had even taken some prizes back to Gibraltar.

But the old *Hyperion* had given everything she had, and could offer no further resistance. She was thirty-three years old when the great ninety-gun *San Mateo* had poured the last broadside into her. Apart from a short period as a mastless stores hulk, she had sailed and fought in every sea where the flag was challenged. Some rot in her frames and timbers, deep down in her worn hull, undiscovered by any dockyard, had finally betrayed her.

In spite of everything Bolitho had witnessed and endured during a lifetime at sea, it was still so hard to accept that she was gone.

He had heard some say that but for his judgment in holding and defeating the Spanish squadron, the

10

enemy would have joined with the Combined Fleet off Trafalgar. Then perhaps even brave Nelson could not have triumphed. Bolitho had not known how to react. More flattery? After Nelson's death he had been sickened to watch the same people who had hated him and despised him for his liaison with *that Hamilton woman* sing his praises the highest, and lament his passing.

Like so many he had never met the little admiral who had raised the hearts of his sailors even in the squalor most of them endured on endless blockade duty, or firing gun-to-gun with an enemy. Nelson had *known* his men, and given them the leadership they understood and needed.

He realised that Allday had padded from the cabin, and hated himself for bringing him out here on a mission which was probably fruitless.

Allday would not be moved. *My English oak.* Bolitho would only have hurt and insulted him if he had left him ashore at Falmouth. They had got this far together.

He touched his left eyelid and sighed. How would it torment him in the bright African sunlight?

He could recall the exact moment when he had faced the sun and his damaged eye had clouded over, as if a sea-mist had crept across the deck. He felt the chill of fear as he relived it: the Spaniard's sharp breathing as he lunged forward with a cutlass. The unknown sailor must have realised the fight was over, that his own shipmates were already flinging down their weapons in surrender. Maybe he had simply seen Bolitho's uniform as the enemy, *all authority everywhere*, which had brought him to this place of certain death.

11

Jenour, Bolitho's flag-lieutenant, attempting to defend him, had had his sword struck from his hand, and there was nothing to stop the inevitable. Bolitho had waited for it, his old sword held out before him, and unable to see his would-be assassin.

But Allday had been there, and had seen everything. The Spaniard's cutlass had gone clattering across the blood-stained deck, his severed arm with it. Another blow had finished him. Allday's own revenge for the wound which had left him almost constantly in pain, unable to act as swiftly as he once did.

But abandon him, even out of kindness? Bolitho knew that only death would ever part them.

He pushed himself away from the window and picked up the fan from his sea-chest. Catherine's fan. She had made certain he had had it with him when he had boarded *Truculent* at Spithead.

What was she doing now, all those six thousand miles astern? It would be cold and bleak in Cornwall. Crouching cottages beyond the big grey house below Pendennis Castle. Winds from the Channel to shake the sparse trees on the hillside, the ones Bolitho's father had once called 'my ragged warriors'. Farmers making good damage to walls and barns, fishermen at Falmouth repairing their boats, grateful for the written protection which kept them safe from the hated press gangs.

The old grey house would be Catherine's only sanctuary from the sneers and the gossip. Ferguson, the estate's one-armed steward, who had originally been pressed into naval service with Allday, would take good care of her. But you never knew for certain, especially in the West Country.

Tongues would wag. *Bolitho's woman. Wife of a*

viscount, who should be with him and not living like some sailor's whore. They had been Catherine's own words, to prove to him that she did not care for herself but for *his* name and *his* honour. Yes, the ignorant ones were always the most cruel.

The only occasion when she had revealed bitterness and anger had been when he was called to London, to receive his orders. She had stared at him across the room they shared which overlooked the sea, that constant reminder, and had exclaimed, 'Don't you *see* what they are doing to us, Richard?'

In her anger she was beautiful in a different way, her long dark hair in disorder across her white gown, her eyes blazing with hurt and disbelief. 'It is Lord Nelson's funeral in a few days time.' She had stepped back from him as he had made to calm her. 'No, listen to me, Richard! We shall have less than two weeks together, and much of that time spent on the road. You are worth a hundred of any of them, though I know you would never say it ... *Damn their eyes!* You lost your old ship, you have given *everything*, but they are so afraid that you will refuse to attend the funeral unless you can take *me* with you, when they are expecting Belinda!'

Then she had broken and had let him hold her, his cheek in her hair like the time they had watched the first dawn together in Falmouth.

Bolitho had stroked her shoulders and had replied gently, 'I would never allow anyone to insult you.'

She had not seemed to hear. 'That surgeon who sailed with you—Sir Piers Blachford? He could help you, surely?' She had pulled his face to hers and kissed his eyes with sudden tenderness. 'Dearest of men, you *must* take care.'

13

Now she was in Falmouth. Despite all the offered protection and love, a stranger nonetheless.

She had accompanied him to Portsmouth on that cold blustery forenoon; so much to say still unsaid. Together they had waited by the old sally-port, each aware that these same worn stairs had been Nelson's last contact with England. In the background, the carriage with the Bolitho crest on its doors waited with Matthew the coachman holding the horses' heads. The carriage was streaked with mud, as if to mark the time that they had spent together in its secret privacy.

Not always so secret. Passing through Guildford on the way to London, some idlers had raised a cheer. 'God bless you, Our Dick! Don't you mind they buggers in Lonnon, beggin' yer pardon, Ma'am!'

She had watched his reflection in the carriage window and had said quietly, 'See! I am not the only one!'

As the frigate's gig had pulled strongly towards the sally-port she had clasped her arms around his neck, her face wet with rain and drifting spray.

'I love thee, dearest of men.' She had kissed him hard, unable to release him until the boat had hooked on with a noisy clatter. Then, and only then, had she turned from him, pausing just briefly to add, 'Tell Allday I said to take good care of you.'

The rest was lost as if darkness had suddenly descended.

There was a sharp tap at the screen door.

Captain Poland stepped into the cabin, his cocked hat jammed beneath one arm.

Bolitho saw his eyes flit around the shadows, as if he expected to see his quarters completely changed

14

or gutted.

Bolitho sat down again, his hands on the edge of the bench seat. *Truculent* was a fine ship, he thought. He pictured his nephew, Adam, and wondered if he had yet accepted the greatest gift, the command of his own frigate. His ship was probably commissioned by now, even at sea like this one. He would do well.

He asked, 'News, Captain?'

Poland looked at him squarely. 'Land in sight, Sir Richard. The Master, Mr Hull, thinks it is a perfect completion.'

Always the caution. Bolitho had noticed it before when he had asked Poland to sup with him a few times during the voyage.

'And what do *you* think, sir?'

Poland swallowed hard. 'I believe it to be true, Sir Richard.' He added as an afterthought, 'The wind has dropped—it will take most of the day to stand close to the mainland. Even Table Mountain is only plainly visible from the fore-topmast.'

Bolitho reached for his coat, but decided against it. 'I shall come up. You have performed a fast and exceptional passage, Captain. I shall say as much in my final despatches.'

It would have been comic at any other time to see the swift changes of thought and expression on Poland's sun-reddened features. A written compliment from the vice-admiral, *the hero*, which might facilitate an even quicker advancement for the captain.

Or might it be seen differently by those in office? That Poland had found favour with the same man who had flouted authority, left his wife for another and tossed honour to the winds...

15

But it was not *any other time*, and Bolitho said sharply, 'So let us be about it, eh?'

On the quarterdeck Bolitho saw Jenour, his flag-lieutenant, standing with the ship's officers, and marvelled at the change he had seen in him since his flag had been hoisted above *Hyperion*. A keen, likeable young man—the first in his family to enter the navy—Bolitho had once doubted if he would survive the campaign, and the battles they would have to share together. He had even heard it said that some of the 'hard men' of the old ship's company had taken bets on how long Jenour would live.

But survive he had—more than that, he had come through it a man, a veteran.

It had been Jenour's beautiful sword, a gift from his father, which had been parried aside and jerked from his grip as he had run to Bolitho's aid, before Allday could bound forward and deliver the fatal stroke. Jenour had learned from that experience, and many others. Bolitho had noticed that since *Hyperion*'s last fight, whenever the young man wore his sword, it carried a strong lanyard for his wrist as well as its decorative knot.

It was interesting, too, to see the respect with which *Truculent*'s officers treated Jenour, although most of them were older and by far more senior. The thirty-six gun frigate had been on constant patrol and convoy duty since Poland had taken command. But there was not a member of her wardroom who had ever been in a major fleet action.

Bolitho nodded to the officers and walked to the larboard gangway which, like the one on the opposite side, joined the quarterdeck with the

16

forecastle. Beneath it the vessel's main armament was already being checked and inspected by the gunner and one of his mates. Poland was certainly thorough, Bolitho thought. He was by the rail now, his eyes on the bare-backed seamen as they packed home the hammocks in the nettings like neat lines of pods. Some bodies were already brown, some showing a painful rawness from too much exposure to the unaccustomed glare.

The sun was rising as if from the ocean itself, the lines of low rollers curling away like molten copper. *Truculent* was already steaming, despite the lingering chill of night. She would look like a ghost-ship when the heat really enfolded her and every sail dried out in its intensity.

Bolitho pitied the officers on watch in their hats and heavy coats. Poland obviously believed that there was never a proper moment to relax any show of authority, no matter how uncomfortable. He wondered what they thought of his own casual rig. There would be time enough for pomp and tradition when he made contact with the fleet, which was allegedly assembled off the coast. For all they had seen on passage they could have been the only ship afloat.

Immersed in his thoughts, he began to walk slowly up and down, a measured distance between the wheel and the taffrail. Sailors working on the ever-necessary repairs and maintenance, splicing, replacing frayed cordage, painting and washing down, glanced up as his shadow passed over them. Each man looked quickly away if their eyes chanced to meet.

Mr Hull, the frigate's taciturn sailing-master, was watching three midshipmen who were taking turns to prepare a chart. Beside him, as officer-of-the-watch, the second lieutenant was trying not to yawn, with his captain in such an uncertain mood. There was a smell of cooking from the galley and the lieutenant's stomach contracted painfully. It was still a long wait before the watch changed and he could be relieved.

Hull asked quietly, 'What d'ye reckon 'e thinks about, Mr Munro?' He gestured shortly towards the tall figure in the white shirt, whose dark hair, tied to the nape of his neck, lifted in the light breeze as he strode unhurriedly up and down.

Munro lowered his voice. 'I know not, Mr Hull. But if half of what I hear about him is true, then he has plenty to choose from!' Like the others, Munro had seen little of the vice-admiral, except for one meal together, and once when he and the captain had summoned the lieutenants and senior warrant officers to explain the purpose of his mission.

Two strong forces of ships had been ordered to the Cape of Good Hope with soldiers and marines for the sole purpose of landing and laying siege to Cape Town, with the intention of retaking it from the Dutch, Napoleon's unwilling ally.

Then, and only then, would the shipping routes around the Cape be safe from marauding men-of-war and French privateers. There was also a dockyard which, once repossessed, would be vastly improved and expanded, so that never again would English ships be forced to fend for themselves, or waste valuable months beating back and forth seeking other suitable anchorages.

Even Captain Poland had seemed surprised at Bolitho's open confidence with subordinates he did not know, especially when most flag-officers would

18

have considered it none of their business. Munro glanced at the flag-lieutenant and recalled how Jenour had described that last battle, when *Hyperion* had led the squadron and broken through the enemy's line, until both sides had been broadside to broadside.

You could have heard a pin fall, he thought, as Jenour had described the death of the old two-decker, the ship which Bolitho had twice made into a legend.

Jenour had looked down at the wardroom table and had said, 'Her stern was rising all the time, but at her foremast the admiral's flag was still close-up. He had ordered them to leave it there. A lot of good men went with her. They could have no better company.' Then he had raised his head and Munro had been shocked to see the tears in his eyes. 'Then I heard him say, just as if he was speaking to the ship, *There'll be none better than you, old lady*. And then she was gone.'

Munro had never been so moved before by anything; neither had his friend the first lieutenant.

Poland's voice cut through his thoughts like a dirk.

'Mr Munro! I would trouble you to cast an eye over those idle roughknots who are supposed to be working on the second cutter—they seem more intent on gaping at the horizon than using their skills! Maybe they should not be blamed if the officer-of-the-watch is day-dreaming, what?'

Mr Hull bared his teeth in an unfeeling grin.

'Got eyes everywhere, 'e 'as!' He swung on the midshipmen to cover Munro's embarrassment. 'An' wot d'you think you're a-doin' of? Gawd, you'll never make lieutenants, nary a one o' ye!'

19

Bolitho heard all of it, but his mind was elsewhere. He often thought of Catherine's despairing anger. How much of what she said was true? He knew he had made enemies down the years, and many had tried to hurt and damage him because of his dead brother, Hugh, who had gone over to the other side during the American Revolution. Later they had used young Adam for the same purpose, so it was likely that the enemies were truly there, and not merely in his mind.

Did they really need him to come to the Cape so urgently; or was it true that Nelson's victory over the Combined Fleet had changed strategy out of all recognition? France and Spain had lost many ships, destroyed or taken as prizes. But England's fleet had been badly battered, and the essential blockading squadrons outside enemy ports were stretched to the limit. Napoleon would never give up his vision of a mighty empire. He would need more ships, like the ones which were building at Toulon and along the Channel coast, vessels of which Nelson had spoken many times in his written duels with the Admiralty. But until then, Napoleon might look elsewhere—perhaps to France's old ally, America?

Bolitho plucked at the front of his shirt, one of the elegant selection Catherine had bought for him in London while he had been with their lordships.

He had always hated the capital, its false society, its privileged citizens who damned the war because of its inconvenience to them, without a thought for the men who daily gave their lives to protect their liberty. Like—He thrust Belinda from his mind, and felt the locket which Catherine had given him. Small, silver, with a perfect miniature of her inside,

20

her dark eyes, the throat bared as he had known and loved it. In a compartment at the back was a compressed lock of her hair. That was new, but he could only guess how long she had owned the locket, or who had given it to her. Certainly not her first husband, a soldier of fortune who had died in a brawl in Spain. Perhaps it had been a gift from her second, Luis Pareja, who had died trying to help defend a merchantman taken by Bolitho and then attacked by Barbary pirates.

Luis had been twice her age, but in his own way he had loved her. He had been a Spanish merchant, and the miniature had all the delicacy and finesse he would have appreciated.

So she had come into Bolitho's life; and then, after a brief affair, she had gone. Misunderstanding, a misguided attempt to preserve his reputation—Bolitho had often cursed himself for allowing it to happen. For letting their tangled lives come between them.

And then, just two years ago when *Hyperion* had sailed into English Harbour, they had found one another again. Bolitho leaving behind a marriage which had soured, and Catherine married, for the third time, to the Viscount Somervell, a treacherous and decadent man who, on learning of her renewed passion for Bolitho, had attempted to have her dishonoured and thrown into a debtor's prison, from which Bolitho had saved her.

He heard her voice now as clearly as if she were standing here on this rapidly drying deck. *'Keep this around your neck, darling Richard. I shall take it off again only when you are lying by my side as my lover.'*

He felt the engraving on the back of the locket. Like the small wisp of hair, it was new, something

21

she had caused to be done in London while he had been at the Admiralty.

So simply said, as if she were speaking to him even as he recalled it.

May Fate always guide you. May love always protect you.

He walked to the nettings, and shaded his eyes to watch some gulls. It made him tremble merely to think of her, how they had loved in Antigua and in Cornwall for so short a time together.

He moved his head slightly, holding his breath. The sun was strong but not yet high enough to—He hesitated, then looked hard at the horizon's glittering line.

Nothing happened. The mist did not edge out like some evil disease to mock his left eye. *Nothing*.

Allday was looking aft and saw Bolitho's expression, and felt like praying. It was like seeing the face of a man on the scaffold when given a last-minute reprieve.

'*Deck there!*' Every face looked up. 'Sail on the starboard quarter!'

Poland called sharply, 'Mr Williams, I'd be obliged if you would take a glass aloft!'

The first lieutenant seized a telescope from the midshipman on watch and hurried to the main shrouds. He looked surprised: Bolitho guessed it was at his captain's unusual courtesy, rather than the task.

Truculent's sails were barely filling, and yet the stranger's topgallants seemed to be speeding down on a converging tack at a tremendous rate.

He had seen it many times. The same stretch of ocean, with one ship all but becalmed, and another with every stitch of canvas filled to the brim.

Poland glanced at Bolitho, his features expressionless. But his fingers were opening and closing at his sides, betraying his agitation.

'Shall I clear for action, Sir Richard?'

Bolitho raised a telescope and levelled it across the quarter. A strange bearing. Perhaps not one of the local squadron after all.

'We will bide our time, Captain Poland. I have no doubt you can be ready to run out in ten minutes, if need be?'

Poland flushed. 'I—that is, Sir Richard—' He nodded firmly. 'Indeed, in less!'

Bolitho moved the glass carefully, but could only make out the mastheads of the newcomer; saw the bearing alter slightly as they drew into line to swoop down on *Truculent*.

Lieutenant Williams called from the mainmast crosstrees, 'Frigate, sir!'

Bolitho watched tiny specks of colour rising to break the other ship's silhouette as she hoisted a signal.

Williams called down the recognition and Poland could barely prevent himself from tearing the signals book from the midshipman's fingers. '*Well!*'

The boy stammered, 'She's the *Zest*, sir, forty-four. Captain Varian.'

Poland muttered, 'Oh yes, I know who *he* is. Make our number—lively now!'

Bolitho lowered the glass and watched. *Two faces*. The midshipman's confused, perhaps frightened. One moment he had been watching the first hump of land as it eased up from the sea-mist, and the next he had probably seen it all vanish, the prospect of an unexpected enemy, death even, suddenly laid before him.

The other was Poland's. Whoever Varian was he was no friend, and was doubtless much senior, to command a forty-four.

Lieutenant Munro was in the shrouds, his legs wrapped around the ratlines, heedless of the fresh tar on his white breeches, and even thoughts of breakfast forgotten.

'Signal, sir! *Captain repair on board!*'

Bolitho saw the crestfallen look on Poland's face. After his remarkable passage from England without loss or injury to any man aboard, it was like a slap in the face.

'Mr Jenour, lay aft if you please.' Bolitho saw the flag-lieutenant's mouth quiver as though in anticipation. 'I believe you have my flag in your care?'

Jenour could not contain a grin this time. 'Aye, *aye*, sir!' He almost ran from the quarterdeck.

Bolitho watched the other frigate's great pyramid of sails lifting and plunging over the sparkling water. Maybe it was childish, but he did not care.

'Captain Poland, for convenience's sake, yours is no longer a private ship.' He saw doubt alter to understanding on Poland's tense features. 'So please make to *Zest*, and spell it out with care, *The privilege is yours.*'

Poland turned as Bolitho's flag broke at the foremast truck, and then gestured urgently to the signals party as bunting spilled across the deck in feverish confusion.

Jenour joined Munro as he clambered back to the deck.

'That is what you wanted to know. *There* is the real man. He'd not stand by and see any of his people slighted!' *Not even Poland*, he almost added.

24

Bolitho saw sunlight reflecting from several telescopes on the other frigate. *Zest*'s captain would not know anything about Bolitho's mission, nor would anyone else.

He tightened his jaw and said gently, 'Well, they know now.'

CHAPTER TWO

REMEMBER NELSON

'May I assure you, Sir Richard, that no disrespect was intended...'

Bolitho walked to the cabin stern windows, half listening to the clatter of blocks and the surge of water alongside as *Truculent* rolled, hove-to in the swell. This would need to be quick. As predicted by Poland's sailing-master, the wind would soon return. He could not see the other frigate, and guessed that she was standing slightly downwind of her smaller consort.

He turned and sat on the bench seat, gesturing to a chair. 'Some coffee, Captain Varian?' He heard Ozzard's quiet footsteps and guessed that the little man was already preparing it. It gave Bolitho time to study his visitor.

Captain Charles Varian was a direct contrast to Poland. Very tall and broad-shouldered, self-confident: probably the landsman's idea of a frigate captain.

Varian said, 'I was eager for news, Sir Richard. And seeing this ship, well—' He spread his big hands and gave what was intended as a disarming

25

smile.

Bolitho watched him steadily. 'It did not occur to you that a ship from the Channel Squadron might not have time to waste in idle gossip? You could have closed to hailing distance, surely.'

Ozzard pattered in with his coffee pot and peered unseeingly at the stranger.

Varian nodded. 'I was not thinking. And *you*, Sir Richard—of all people, to be out here when you must be needed elsewhere ...' The smile remained, but his eyes were strangely opaque. *Not a man to cross*, Bolitho decided. By a subordinate, anyway.

'You will need to return to your command directly, Captain. But first I would appreciate your assessment of the situation here.' He sipped the hot coffee. *What was the matter with him? He was on edge, as he had been since* ... After all, he had done it himself as a young commander. So many leagues from home, and then the sight of a friendly ship.

He continued, 'I have come with new orders.'

Varian's inscrutable expression sharpened immediately.

He said, 'You will know, Sir Richard, that most of the force intended for retaking Cape Town from the Dutch is already here. They are anchored to the north-west, near Saldanha Bay. Sir David Baird commands the army, and Commodore Popham the escorting squadron and transports. I have been told that the landings will begin very shortly.' He hesitated, suddenly uncertain under Bolitho's level gaze.

'You are with the supporting squadron.' It was a statement, and Varian shrugged while he moved his cup across the table.

'That is so, Sir Richard. I am still awaiting some

additional vessels to rendezvous as planned.' When Bolitho said nothing he hastened on, 'I had been patrolling in the vicinity of Good Hope and then your topsails were sighted. I thought a straggler had finally arrived.'

Bolitho asked quietly, 'What of *your* senior officer—Commodore Warren? I am surprised that he would release his biggest fifth-rate at a time when he might need your full support.'

He had a vague picture of Commodore Warren in his mind, like a faded portrait. He had known him briefly during the ill-fated attempt by the French Royalists to land and retake Toulon from the Revolutionary army. Bolitho had been a captain then like Varian, and his ship had been *Hyperion*. He had not seen Warren since. But the navy was a family and he had heard of him serving on various stations in the West Indies and the Spanish Main.

Varian said abruptly, 'The Commodore is unwell, Sir Richard. In my opinion he should never have been given—'

Bolitho said, 'As the senior captain you have assumed overall charge of the supporting squadron; is that it?'

'I have made a full report, Sir Richard.'

'Which I shall read in due course.' Bolitho moved his hand consciously away from his eyelid and added, 'It is my intention to hasten the attack on Cape Town. Time is of the essence. Which is why this fast passage was of the utmost importance.' He saw the shot go home but continued, 'So we will return to the squadron in company. I intend to see Commodore Warren without delay.'

He stood up and walked to the quarter windows to watch the crests beginning to ruffle like crisp lace

27

in the wind. The ship was rising to it. Eager to move again.

Varian tried to recompose himself. 'The other vessels, Sir Richard?'

Bolitho said, 'There are none. There will be none. As it is I am authorised to despatch several of the ships here directly to England.'

'Has something happened, sir?'

He said quietly, 'Last October our fleet under Lord Nelson defeated the enemy off Cape Trafalgar.'

Varian swallowed hard. 'We did not know, Sir Richard!' For once he seemed at a loss. 'A victory! *By God*, that is great news.'

Bolitho shrugged. 'Brave Nelson is dead. So the victory is a hollow one.'

There was a tap at the door and Poland stepped into the cabin. The two captains glanced at one another and nodded like old acquaintances, but Bolitho sensed they were completely divided as if by the bars of a smithy's furnace.

'The wind is freshening from the nor'-west, Sir Richard.' Poland did not look again at the other man. '*Zest*'s gig is still hooked on to the chains.'

Bolitho held out his hand. 'I shall see you again, Captain Varian.' He relented slightly. 'The blockade continues around all enemy ports. It is vital. And though heartened by our victory at Trafalgar, our own forces are weakened by it nonetheless.'

The door closed behind them and Bolitho heard the shrill of calls as Varian was piped over the side into his gig.

He moved restlessly about the cabin, remembering one of the meetings he had had with

Admiral Sir Owen Godschale at the Admiralty. The last one, in fact, when he had outlined the need for urgency. The Combined Fleets of France and Spain had been thoroughly beaten, but the war was not won. Already it had been reported that at least three small French squadrons had broken through the tightly-stretched blockade, and had seemingly vanished into the Atlantic. Was this to be Napoleon's new strategy? To raid ports and isolated islands, to prey upon supply ships and trade routes, to give the British squadrons no rest while they, the French, gathered another fleet?

He could almost smile at Godschale's contemptuous dismissal of the enemy's strength. One group which had outwitted the blockading squadron off Brest had been under the veteran Vice-Admiral Leissègues, and his flagship was the 120-gun first-rate *Impérial*. Hardly small.

The French might even have their eye on Cape Town. It was impossible to guess at the havoc they could create there. They could sever the routes to India and the East Indies as surely as the blade of an axe.

He remembered the studied coolness between Godschale and himself. The admiral had been a contemporary of his; they had even been posted together on the same date. There was no other similarity.

Bolitho was suddenly conscious of the distance between himself and Catherine. Godschale, like so many others, had tried to keep them apart, may even have plotted with Belinda to have Catherine dishonoured and lost in lies. But Bolitho doubted that. The admiral was too fond of his own power and comfort to risk a scandal. Or was he? It was

29

openly said that Godschale's next step was to the House of Lords. There might be others there who would wish to destroy them through Godschale.

Catherine's words rang in his ears. *Don't you see what they are doing to us?*

Perhaps this mission to the Cape was merely a beginning. To keep him employed without respite, knowing that he would never resign, no matter what they did.

He crossed to the rack and touched the old family sword, dull by contrast with the fine presentation blade below it. Other Bolithos had worn it, proved it, and sometimes had fallen with it still gripped in a dead hand. He could not see any of them giving up without a fight. The thought gave him comfort, and when Allday came into the cabin he saw him smiling, the first time for a long while.

Allday said, 'The whole squadron will know about Lord Nelson by now, Sir Richard. It'll take the heart out of some.' He gestured towards the nearest gunport as if he could already see the African mainland. 'Not worth dyin' for, they'll say. Not like standing 'twixt the *mounseers* and England, clearin' the way like we did!'

Bolitho was moved beyond his own anxieties and said, 'With old oaks like you about, they'll soon take heed!'

Allday gave his slow grin. 'I'll wager two o' the cap'ns will have some grief afore long as well.'

Bolitho eyed him severely. 'You damned fox! What do *you* know of it?'

'At present, not much, Sir Richard. But I does know that Cap'n Poland was once the other gentleman's first lieutenant.'

Bolitho shook his head. Without Allday he would

30

have nobody to share his feelings or fears. Others looked to him only for leadership—they wanted nothing more.

Allday took down the sword and wrapped it in his special cloth.

'But it's what I always says, Sir Richard, and every true Jack knows it.' He gave another grin. 'It's aft the most honour may be, but forrard you finds the better men. An' that's no error!'

After Allday had gone Bolitho seated himself at the table and opened his personal log. Inside it was the letter he had started when England's mist and drizzle had faded astern, and the long passage had begun.

When she would read it, or if it even reached her, he would not know until she was in his arms. Her skin against his, her tears and her joy mingled with his own.

He leaned over the letter while he touched the locket through his new shirt.

Another dawn, dearest Kate, and how I long for thee . . .

He was still writing when the ship changed tack yet again, and from the high masthead came the cry that the assembled ships had been sighted.

Bolitho went on deck at noon, and felt the sun strike his face and shoulders like fire; his shoes stuck to the deck-seams as he strode to the hammock-nettings with a telescope from the rack.

Mountains, red and pink in the harsh, misty glare, and over all the sun, which was like burnished silver, strong enough to drain all colour from the sky around it.

He shifted the glass slightly, his legs braced as the lazy offshore swell lifted the keel and rolled

31

noisily down either beam. Table Mountain, a paler wedge, but still shrouded in haze and mystery like some giant's altar.

There were the ships. His eyes moved professionally across the mixed collection. The elderly sixty-four *Themis*, which he knew was Commodore Warren's ship. Warren was ill. How ill? He had not enquired further of Varian. It would show his hand, or display uncertainty when he must soon need these unknown men to trust him without question.

Another frigate, some schooners and two large supply vessels. The cream of the attacking force would be as Varian had described, to the north-west where the ships could anchor well offshore, whereas here there was only one natural bank shallow enough to ride at their cables. Beyond the hundred-fathom line the sea's bed fell away to infinity, a black oblivion where nothing moved.

He saw sunlight flashing on glass and knew they were watching *Truculent*'s slow approach, as surprised by his flag at the fore as Varian had been.

Captain Poland joined him by the side.

He said, 'Do you think it will be a long campaign, Sir Richard?'

He spoke with elaborate care, and Bolitho guessed he was probably wondering what had passed between himself and Varian in the cabin. Bolitho lowered the telescope and faced him.

'I have had some dealings with the army in the past, Captain. They are more used to campaigns than I care for. A battle is one thing—you win or you strike. But all this drawn-out business of supplies and marching is not for me.'

Poland gave a very rare smile. 'Nor me, Sir

Richard.'

Bolitho turned to look for Jenour. 'You may signal for water lighters when you are anchored, Captain. A word of praise to your people will not come amiss either. It was an *admirable* passage.'

A shaft of sunlight like the blade of a lance swept down on them as the Afterguard hauled over the great driver-boom.

Bolitho gritted his teeth. *Nothing*. They had to be wrong. There was nothing. He could see the other ships plainly in spite of the unwavering glare.

Jenour watched him and felt his heart thumping against his ribs. Then he saw Allday coming aft, the old sword protruding from his polishing cloth.

Their exchange of glances was swift but complete. Was it too soon to hope? For all their sakes?

★   ★   ★

The two frigates rounded-up and anchored in the late afternoon considerably earlier than even the taciturn Mr Hull had predicted. As signals were made and exchanged, boats lowered and awnings spread, Bolitho watched from the quarterdeck, his mind exploring the task which lay ahead.

It was strange how the land never seemed to draw any closer, and because of the difficult anchorage it gave an impression of brooding defiance. The point to the north-west which had been selected for the first assault was a good choice, possibly the only one. Bolitho had examined the charts with great care, as well as the maps supplied to him by the Admiralty. Up there at Saldanha Bay the coastal waters were shallow and protected enough to land soldiers and marines under the cover of men-of-war, which could offer fire. But once ashore the true difficulty would begin. Saldanha Bay was one hundred miles from Cape Town. Foot soldiers, some sick and weary from weeks and weeks at sea in their cramped quarters between decks, would be in no fit state to march and skirmish all the way to Cape Town. The Dutch were excellent fighters and would harry rather than confront them every mile. When they finally reached the Cape, the enemy would be ready and waiting. It seemed unlikely that any large force of Dutch soldiers would be sent to contest the landings. It would leave them in danger of being cut off by this supporting squadron.

Bolitho felt his impatience returning. A campaign then, lengthy and costly. A war of supply-lines, to be fought by soldiers, many of whom had been confined to garrison duties in the Indies. The Islands of Death, as the army called them, where more men died of fever than under the enemy's fire.

Jenour strode aft and touched his hat. 'Your despatch to the general has gone, Sir Richard, taken by the courier schooner *Miranda* this moment.'

Bolitho shaded his eyes to watch the small and graceful schooner tacking away from the other vessels, her commander doubtless grateful to be free of other authority, albeit for only a few days.

Bolitho watched the redness of evening spreading along the glittering horizon, the masts and yards of the small squadron suddenly like bronze. Ashore telescopes would have observed *Truculent*'s arrival as they had doubtless studied all the others.

He remarked, 'You are in irons, Stephen, so why not spit out what you think?'

But for his self-control, Jenour would have

blushed. Bolitho always knew. It was pointless to pretend.

'I—I thought—' He licked his dry lips. 'I would have thought that the Commodore might have requested to come aboard.' He fell silent under Bolitho's scrutiny.

Bolitho said, 'In his place I would have done just that.' He recalled Captain Varian's tactless remark. 'Call away the gig, Stephen. My compliments to Captain Poland and explain that I am going across to *Themis*.'

Fifteen minutes later, sweating steadily in his dress coat and hat, he sat in the gig's sternsheets with Jenour beside him, and a critical Allday crouching with the boat's coxswain.

As they pulled slowly abeam of the other ships, Bolitho saw officers-of-the-watch doffing their hats, motionless figures in shrouds and rigging staring in silence, their bare arms and shoulders like parts of the bronze around them.

Allday leaned forward, his mouth just inches from Bolitho's ear.

'Y'see, they *knows*, Sir Richard. Only here an hour an' the word has gone through the whole squadron!' He saw one of the oarsmen staring at him and scowled over Bolitho's epaulette. The man dropped his gaze and almost lost the stroke. He had probably been surprised at seeing a seaman, even an admiral's personal coxswain, chatting with his master, while the latter even turned his head to listen.

Bolitho nodded. 'Lord Nelson will be sadly missed. We'll not see his like in our lifetime.'

Allday leaned back again and rolled his tongue inside his cheek to restrain a grin. *I'm not too sure o' that*, he thought.

Bolitho watched the *Themis*'s bowsprit and tapering jib-boom sweeping out to greet them. She was an old ship and had been employed on every sort of duty other than the line of battle. Originally a sixty-four, she had been stripped of some of her armament while she was carrying soldiers from one trouble spot to the next; she had even been to the penal colony in New South Wales. Transport, receiving ship, and now with the war demanding everything that would stay afloat, she was here, part of the invading force.

Jenour bit his lip and tried to relax. He had seen the assembled guard at the entry port, the glitter of red sunlight on drawn swords. An air of wariness.

Bolitho waited while the bowman hooked on to the main chains, then pulled himself up to the entry port, immediately deafened by the bark of commands, the chorus of squealing calls, which sailors termed 'Spithead Nightingales'. He no longer needed to look for Allday to know he was there, ready to reach out if he lost his footing, or if his eye . . . *No. He would not think about it.*

The din faded away and he raised his hat to the poop, where the White Ensign made a lively dance against the hot sky.

The officer who stepped forward to present himself wore the epaulette of commander. He was old for his rank and had possibly been passed over for captain.

'I bid you welcome, Sir Richard.'

Bolitho smiled briefly. Allday was right. There were no secrets.

'Where is the Commodore?' He glanced up at the curling pendant. 'Is he unwell?'

36

The commander, whose name was Maguire, looked uncomfortable. 'He sends his apologies, Sir Richard. He awaits you in his cabin.'

Bolitho nodded to the other officers and turned aside to Jenour. 'Remain here. Discover what you can.' He patted his arm but did not smile. 'I am certain Allday will do likewise!'

Maguire led the way to the companion ladder and almost bowed as Bolitho walked aft, where a Royal Marine sentry drew his heels together with the precision of a bolt snapping shut.

There was nothing slack about the old *Themis*. It was just as if she did not belong. Maybe too many tasks in far-flung stations, too long away from home. As far as Bolitho could gather, the ship had not returned to England for fifteen years, so God alone knew what state her lower hull was in.

The screen doors were opened by a black servant and Bolitho received another surprise. During her role as accommodation ship they must have removed some of the armament from aft to enlarge the officers' quarters. Now, with her gunports filled only with wooden 'quakers', the shortened muzzles of which might deceive another vessel at long-range, or even a landsman walking on a dockside, the after accommodation was huge, and contained nothing more war-like than furniture and a stand of muskets.

Commodore Arthur Warren walked from a screened-off cabin and exclaimed, 'Sir Richard. What must you think of me?'

Bolitho was shocked by what he saw. He had never really known Warren as a friend, but he guessed him to be about his own age. But the officer in the loose-fitting coat, whose lined face had

37

somehow defied the suns of so many fierce climates, was an old man.

The door closed, and apart from the watchful servant, who wore a red waistcoat above his duck trousers, they were alone. The elderly commander had taken his leave without dismissal. It was no wonder that the confident Captain Varian had seen this squadron as his own future responsibility.

Bolitho said, 'Please be seated.' He waited while the other officer beckoned to his servant and some finely-cut Spanish goblets were filled with red wine. Warren then seated himself. One leg was thrust out, as if in pain, his left hand hidden beneath his coat. He was not sick, Bolitho thought. He was dying.

Bolitho raised his goblet. 'Your health, sir. Everyone seems to know I am here, even though the news of Trafalgar has not reached them.'

The wine was rough and brackish, but he barely noticed it.

Once he had been a flag-captain to Rear-Admiral Sir Charles Thelwall in the big three-decker *Euryalus*. Bolitho had been made to work doubly hard because his admiral's health had deteriorated over the months at sea. He had admired Thelwall and had been saddened to see him step ashore for the last time with only a short while left to live. Bolitho was only glad that the admiral had been spared what had happened that year, the mutinies throughout the fleet at the Nore and Spithead, Plymouth and Scotland. No captain had ever forgotten. Nor would they, unless they were inviting disaster.

But the admiral had looked and sounded like Warren now. As he swallowed some wine he struggled to contain a deep, tearing cough, and when he took his handkerchief from his lips Bolitho knew the stains on it were not all wine.

'I would not trouble you, sir, but if you wish I could send for another surgeon from *Truculent*. He seems an excellent man from the talks I had with him.'

Warren's face stiffened with pathetic determination. 'I am well enough, Sir Richard. I know my duty!'

Bolitho looked away. *This ship is all he has. The temporary title of commodore the only triumph he has known.* He tried to harden his mind, to shut out the pity he could feel and understand.

He said, 'I have sent a despatch to the main squadron. I am ordered here to withdraw certain ships for service in home waters.' He thought he saw a small gleam of hope in Warren's faded eyes and added gently, '*Frigates*, not this ship. There has to be a strategy for taking and then defending Cape Town, without prolonging it into a siege which only the Dutch can win.'

Warren said huskily, 'The army won't like that, Sir Richard. Sir David Baird is said to be a forceful general.'

Bolitho thought of the letter locked in his strong-box aboard *Truculent*. Not signed by some senior Secretary or Lord of Admiralty; not this time. It was signed by the King, and even though the uncharitable hinted amongst themselves that His Majesty often did not know what he was putting his signature to these days, it still held the ultimate power and opened all doors.

'I shall cross that bridge in due course. In the meantime I would like to shift to this ship.' He held

39

up his hand as Warren made to protest. 'Your broad pendant will still fly. But as someone once said, I need room to bustle in!'

Warren held down another bout of coughing and asked, 'What must I do? You have my word that I will serve you well. And if Captain Varian has told you—'

Bolitho retorted calmly, 'I have been in the King's service since I was twelve. Somewhere along the way I learned to form my own opinions.' He stood up and walked to an open port and stared along the false wooden muzzle at the nearest ship, another frigate. 'But I have to tell you, Commodore Warren, I'll not waste anyone's life because we have not tried to do our best. Throughout the navy, loyal seamen and marines, officers too, will be shocked and disappointed that after Trafalgar, victory is not complete. In my view it will take years before the tyranny of France and her jackals is finally routed!'

He realised that Warren and the silent servant were both staring at him and that he had raised his voice.

He forced a smile. 'Now I must ask you to forgive *me*. It is just that I have seen so many fine ships lost, brave men dying for the wrong reasons, some cursing those who despatched them in the first place. While I direct what is to be done here, those who forget the hard lessons of war will answer to me.' He picked up his hat. 'Just as one day I will answer to God, I have no doubt.'

'A moment, Sir Richard!' Warren seized his own hat from the black servant and followed him into the shadows of the half deck.

Before they reached the entry port he said in his halting tones, 'I am *honoured*, Sir Richard.' His voice was suddenly firmer than Bolitho had heard before. 'I am unused to this sort of work, but I will do all I can. So shall my people!'

Jenour saw Bolitho's grave smile as he walked out into the strange sunlight. It gave him a twinge of excitement, like those other times, when up to now he had been expecting a dull and undemanding role for the man he had always looked up to, even before he had laid eyes on him.

When he had told his parents in Southampton that he intended one day to personally serve Bolitho in some capacity, they had chuckled at his innocence. The chuckles had gone now. There was only the concern which was the legacy of all those with young sons away at war.

Commodore Warren walked off to seek his commander; his cut-down *Themis* did not warrant a flag-captain apparently. Bolitho took his flag-lieutenant aside.

'We are coming aboard, Stephen.' He saw no surprise on Jenour's open features. 'For the present at least. Fetch the others from *Truculent* . . . I fear that Mr Yovell will be writing throughout the night. And find a good signals midshipman aboard *this* ship—it does not look well to employ strangers. Tomorrow I want all captains on board at eight bells, so warn them before nightfall. Send the guardboat if you will.'

Jenour could barely keep up with him. Bolitho seemed tireless, as if his mind were breaking out of a self-made prison.

Bolitho added, 'The enemy know we are about—they have all day to watch us. I intend to discover what is happening around the Cape where the other anchorage lies. I feel the remedy may be

41

there, rather than a hundred-mile struggle from Saldanha Bay. I do not know these captains here, and there is little time to do so. As you are aware, Stephen, in my despatch to the army I requested that the attack be delayed.'

Jenour watched the eyes, lighter grey now as he turned towards the open sea. Like the ocean itself, he thought.

He said, 'But you do not believe that the general will agree?'

Bolitho clapped him on the arm like a boyish conspirator. 'We will act independently.' His face was suddenly introspective. 'As this is a day for remembering Nelson, let us use his own words. The boldest measures are usually the safest!'

★   ★   ★

That night Bolitho sat by the stern windows of the cabin—which had once been used by no less than a governor-general, who had fled on board to escape the plague which had broken out amongst the islands he controlled—and watched the ships' riding lights with no inclination to sleep.

The air was heavy and humid, and as a guardboat pulled slowly amongst the anchored squadron, he thought instead of Cornwall, of the bitter wind on the night when she had come to him. Just over a month ago, no more; and now he was here in the shadow of Africa, and they were separated again at the whim of others.

Did they need his skills so much that they could overlook his contempt for them? Or, like Nelson, would they prefer a dead hero to a living reminder of their own failings?

42

The deck quivered as the anchor cable took the sudden strain of a faster current. Allday had not been very optimistic about shifting to the old sixty-four. The company had been aboard too long, pressed from passing merchantmen in the Caribbean, survivors from other vessels, even pardoned prisoners from the courts of Jamaica.

Like Warren, the ship was worn out, and suddenly thrust into a role she no longer recognised. Bolitho had seen the old swivel-gun mountings on either gangway. Not facing a possible enemy but pointing inboard, from the time when she had carried convicts and prisoners-of-war from a campaign already forgotten.

He thought he heard Ozzard pattering about in his newly-occupied pantry. So he could not sleep either. Still remembering *Hyperion*'s last moments—or was he nursing his secret, which Bolitho had sensed before that final battle?

Bolitho yawned and gently massaged his eye. It was strange, but he could not clearly remember why Ozzard had not been on deck when they had been forced to clear the ship of the survivors and the wounded.

He thought too of his flag-captain and firm friend, Valentine Keen, his face full of pain, not at his own injury but for his vice-admiral's despair.

If only you were here now, Val.

But his words went unspoken, for he had fallen asleep at last.

CHAPTER THREE

THE *ALBACORA*

An onlooker, had there been one, might have compared the little topsail schooner *Miranda* with a giant moth. But apart from a few screaming and wheeling gulls, there was none to see her as she came about in a great welter of bursting spray, her twin booms swinging over to refill the sails on the opposite tack.

She leaned so far to leeward that the sea was spurting through her washports, rising even above her bulwark to surge along the streaming planking, or breaking over the four-pounder guns like waves on rocks.

It was wild and exhilarating, the air filled with the din of sea and banging canvas, with only the occasional shouted command, for nothing superfluous was needed here. Each man knew his work, aware of the ever-present dangers: he could be flung senseless against some immovable object to suffer a cracked skull or broken limbs, or be pitched overboard by a treacherous wave as it burst over the bows and swept along like a mill-race. *Miranda* was small and very lively, and certainly no place for the unwary or the inexperienced.

Aft by the compass box her commander, Lieutenant James Tyacke, swayed and leaned with his ship, one hand in his pocket, the other gripping a slippery backstay. Like his men he was soaked to the skin, his eyes raw from spray and spindrift as he watched the tilting compass card, the flapping mainsail and pendant while his command plunged again, her bowsprit pointing due south.

They had taken all night and part of the day to claw out of Saldanha Bay, away from the impressive formations of anchored men-of-war, supply ships, bombs, army transports and all the rest. Lieutenant Tyacke had used the time to beat as far out as possible, to gain the sea-room he needed before heading back to Commodore Warren's small squadron. There was another reason, which probably only his second-in-command had guessed. He wanted to put as much ocean as possible between *Miranda* and the squadron before someone signalled him to repair aboard the flagship yet again.

He had done what he had been ordered, delivered the despatches to the army and the commodore. He had been glad to leave.

Tyacke was thirty years old and had commanded the speedy *Miranda* for the last three of them. After her grace and intimacy, the flagship had seemed like a city, with the navy seemingly outnumbered by the red and scarlet of the military and the marines.

It was not that he did not know what a big ship was like. He tightened his jaw, determined to hold the memory and the bitterness at bay. Eight years ago he had been serving as a lieutenant aboard the *Majestic*, a two-decker with Nelson's fleet in the Mediterranean. He had been on the lower gundeck when Nelson had finally run the French to earth at Aboukir Bay, the Battle of the Nile as it was now called.

It was too terrible to remember clearly, or to arrange the events in their proper order. With the

45

passing of time they eluded him, or overlapped like insane acts in a nightmare.

At the height of it his ship, *Majestic*, had come up against the French *Tonnant* of eighty guns, which had seemed to tower over them like a flaming cliff.

The noise was still there to remember, if he let himself, the awful sights of men, and pieces of men, being flung about the bloody litter and gruel of the gundeck, a place which had become a hell all of its own. The wild eyes of the gun crews, white through their filthy skins, the cannon firing and recoiling, no longer as a controlled broadside but in divisions, then in ones and twos, while the ship shook and quaked around and above them. Unbeknown to the demented souls who sponged out, loaded and fired because it was all that they knew, their captain, Westcott, had already fallen dead, along with so many of his men. Their world was the lower gundeck. Nothing else mattered, could matter. Guns were upended and smashed by the enemy's fire; men ran screaming to be driven back by equally terrified lieutenants and warrant officers.

Run out! Point! Fire!

He heard it still. It would never leave him. Others had told him he was lucky. Not because of the victory—only ignorant landsmen spoke of such things. But because he had survived when so many had fallen, the lucky to die, the others to cry out their lives under the surgeon's saw, or to be pathetic cripples whom nobody wanted to see or remember.

He watched the compass card steady and felt the keel slicing through the steep rollers as if they were nothing.

He touched his face with his hand, feeling its roughness, seeing it in his mind as he was forced to

46

do each day when he shaved himself.

Again he could remember nothing. A gun had exploded, or a flaming wad had come inboard from one of *Tonnant*'s lower battery and sparked off a full charge nearby. It could have been either. Nobody had been left to tell him.

But the whole of the right side of his face had been scored away, left like charred meat, half a face which people turned their heads not to see. How his eye had survived was the real miracle.

He thought of his visit to the flagship. He had not seen the general or even the commodore, just a bored-looking colonel who had been carrying a glass of hock or something cool in one elegant hand. They had not even asked Tyacke to be seated, let alone to take a glass with them.

As he had gone down the great ship's side to his own longboat, that same aide had come dashing after him.

'I say, Lieutenant! Why did you not tell me the news? About Nelson and the victory?'

Tyacke had looked up the ship's curving black and buff hull and had not tried to conceal his contempt.

''Cause nobody asked me, *sir*!' God damn their eyes.

Benjamin Simcox, master's mate and acting-master of the schooner *Miranda*, lurched along the treacherous planking to join him. He was the same age as his captain, a seaman through and through who originally, like the schooner, had been in the merchant service. In such a small vessel—she was a bare sixty-five feet long with a company of thirty—you got to know a man very well. Love or hate and not much in between. With Bob Jay, another master's mate, they ran the schooner to perform at her best. It was a matter of pride.

Usually one of them was on watch, and when Simcox had spent a few watches below with the tall lieutenant he had got to know him well. Now, after three years, they were true friends, their separate ranks only intruding in rare moments of formality. Like Tyacke's visit to the flagship for instance.

Tyacke had looked at him, momentarily forgetting his hideous scars, and had said, 'First time I've buckled on a sword for over a year, Ben!' It was good to hear him joke about it. It was rare too.

Did he ever think about the girl in Portsmouth, Simcox wondered? One night in harbour he had been awakened in his tiny cabin by Tyacke's pitiful, dreaming entreaties to the girl who had promised to wait for him, to marry him. Rather than wake the whole ship, Simcox had shaken his shoulder, but had not explained. Tyacke had understood, and had fetched a bottle of brandy which they had taken off a runner. When dawn had broken the bottle had been empty.

Tyacke had not blamed the girl he had known for most of his life. Nobody would want to see his face every morning. But he had been deeply hurt; wounded no less severely than others at the Nile.

Simcox shouted above the din, 'Runnin' well!' He jerked a thumb at a slight figure who was clinging to the companion hatch, a lifeline tied around his waist, his breeches and stockings soiled with vomit. 'He's not so good, though!'

Mister Midshipman Roger Segrave had been in *Miranda* since they had taken on stores at Gibraltar. At the request of his captain he had been

48

transferred from a big three-decker to complete his time as midshipman in a vessel where he might learn something more about practical seamanship and self-reliance. It had been said that the midshipman's uncle, an admiral at Plymouth, had arranged the transfer, not merely for the youth's sake but also for the family name. It would not look good to fail the lieutenant's examination, especially in time of war when chances of promotion lay on every hand.

Tyacke had made it clear he disliked the idea. Segrave's presence had upset their tight routine, an intrusion, like an unwanted visitor.

Simcox was one of the old school; the rope's end or a clip round the ear were, in his book, worth far more than lengthy discussions on tradition and discipline.

But he was not a hard man, and tried to explain to the midshipman what he might expect. Lieutenant Tyacke was the only commissioned officer aboard. He could not be expected to live in total isolation in a ninety-two ton schooner; they were a team. But he knew that Segrave did not really understand. In the teeming world of a ship-of-the-line everything was divided and sub-divided by rank, status and experience. At the top there was the captain, usually so remote he seemed like a god. The rest, though crammed together out of necessity, were totally separated.

Segrave rolled over and leaned back against the hatchway with a deep groan. He was sixteen years old with fair, almost girlish good looks. He had perfect manners, was careful, even shy when dealing with the hands—not like some little monsters Simcox had heard about. And he tried

49

hard at everything but, even Simcox had to agree, with very little success. He was staring up at the sky, seemingly oblivious to the spray which ripped over the deck like pellets, or the filthy state of his clothing.

Lieutenant Tyacke looked at him coldly. 'Free yourself and go below, *Mr* Segrave, and fetch some rum from the clerk. I can't afford to let anyone useful stand-down until I change tack again.'

As the youth clambered wretchedly down the ladder, Simcox grinned.

'Bit hard on the lad, James.'

Tyacke shrugged. 'You think so?' He almost spat. 'In a year or two he'll be sending men to the gratings for a striped shirt, just for looking at him!'

The master's mate yelled, 'Wind's veered a piece!'

'Bring her up a point. I think this is going to blow over. I want to get the tops'l spread if it does, and run with the wind under our coat-tails.'

There was a sound of breaking pottery and someone vomiting from the deck below.

Tyacke murmured, 'I swear I shall kill that one.'

Simcox asked, 'What d'you reckon to Vice-Admiral Bolitho, James?'

The lieutenant gripped the stay again and bent from the waist as the sea boiled over the weather bulwark in a solid flood. Amongst the streaming water and foam he saw his men, like half-naked urchins, nodding and grinning to each other. Making certain that no one had gone over.

He replied, 'A good man to all accounts. When I was at the—' He looked away, remembering the cheers despite the hell when Bolitho's ship was reported engaging. He changed tack. 'I've known

50

plenty who've served with him—there used to be an old fellow who lived in Dover. I used to speak with him when I was a lad, down by the harbour.' He smiled suddenly. 'Not far from where they built this schooner, as a matter of fact ... He was serving under Richard Bolitho's father when he lost his arm.'

Simcox watched his strong profile. If you did not see the other side of his face, he was handsome enough to catch any girl's fancy, he thought.

He said, 'You should tell him that, if you meet.'

Tyacke wiped the spray from his face and throat. 'He's a vice-admiral now.'

Simcox smiled but was uneasy. 'God, you make him sound like the enemy, James!'

'Do I? Well, there's a thing!' He touched his dripping sleeve. 'Now rouse these layabouts and stand by to change tack. We will steer south by east.'

Within the hour the squall had fallen away, and with all sails filling well, their dark shadows riding across the waves alongside like huge fins, *Miranda* responded with her usual disdain.

She had started life as a Dover mail packet, but had been taken by the navy before she had completed more than a few passages. Now at seventeen years, she was one of the many such vessels working under a naval ensign. She was not only a lively sailer; she was a delight to handle because of her simple sail-plan and deep keel. A large mainsail aft, with a forestaysail and jib and the one topsail on her foremast, she could out-manoeuvre almost anything. The deep keel, even when she was close-hauled, prevented her from losing leeway like a cutter or something

51

heavier. Armed with only four four-pounders and some swivels, she was meant for carrying despatches, rather than taking part in any real skirmish.

Smugglers and privateers were one thing; but half a broadside from some enemy frigate would change her from a lean thoroughbred to a total wreck.

Between decks there was the strong smell of rum and tobacco, and the greasy aroma of the noon meal. As the watch below scrambled down to their messdeck, Tyacke and Simcox sat wedged on either side of the cabin table. Both men were tall, so that any movement in the cabin had to be performed bent double.

The midshipman, repentant and anxious, sat at the other end of the table. Simcox could pity him, for even under reefed canvas the motion was violent, the sea surging astern from the sharply raked counter, the prospect of food another threat for any delicate stomach.

Tyacke said suddenly, 'If I *do* see him, the admiral I mean, I shall ask him about getting some beer. I saw some of the soldiers drinking their fill when I visited the flagship. So why not us? The water out here will kill more good sailors than Johnny Dutchman!'

They both turned as the midshipman spoke up.

Segrave said, 'There was a lot of talk in London about Vice-Admiral Bolitho.'

Tyacke's tone was deceptively mild. 'Oh, and what sort of talk was that?'

Encouraged, his sickness momentarily quiescent, Segrave expounded willingly.

'My mother said it was disgraceful how he

behaved. How he left his lady for that woman. She said London was up in arms about it—' He got no further.

'If you speak like that in front of the people I'll put you under arrest—*in bloody irons if need be!*' Tyacke was shouting, and Simcox guessed that many of the offwatch seamen would hear. There was something terrible about his rage; pathetic too.

Tyacke leaned over towards the pale-faced youth and added, 'And if you speak such shite to me, I'll damn well call you out, young and useless though you may be!'

Simcox rested his hand on his wrist. 'Be easy, James. He knows no better.'

Tyacke shook his hand away. 'God damn them, Ben, what do they want of us? How dare they condemn men who daily, hourly risk their lives so that *they*—' he pointed an accusing finger at Segrave '—can sip their tea and eat their cakes in comfort.' He was shaking, his voice almost a sob. 'I've never met this Richard Bolitho, but God damn me, I'd lay down my life for him right now, if only to get back at those useless, gutless bastards!'

In the sudden silence the sea intruded like a soothing chorus.

Segrave said in a whisper, 'I am very sorry, sir.'

Surprisingly, Tyacke's hideous face moved in a smile. 'No. I abused you. That is wrong when you are unable to answer back.' He mopped his forehead with a crumpled handkerchief. 'But I meant every bloody word, so be warned!'

'Deck thar!' The masthead's cry was shredded by the brisk north-westerly. 'Sail on th' starboard bow!'

Simcox thrust his mug into a safe corner and

53

began to slide towards the door.

No matter what this proved to be, he thought, it had come along just in time.

*   *   *

'Sou'-West-by-South, sir! Full an' bye!'

The *Miranda*'s deck tilted even more steeply as she responded to her rudder and the great span of main and staysails, water cascading around the bare-backed seamen while they sheeted home swollen halliards and dug with their toes at anything which would hold them.

Lieutenant Tyacke lurched up to the weather rail, and watched the surf and spray leaping high from the stem to make the flapping jib glint in the sunshine like polished metal.

Simcox nodded with approval as George Sperry, the tub-shaped boatswain, put two extra hands on the tiller. *Miranda* did not boast a wheel but had a long, ornately carved tiller bar, which took some handling in the brisk wind sweeping down on the starboard quarter.

He saw Midshipman Segrave standing in the shadow of the heavily raked mainmast, his eyes wary as he tried to avoid men dashing past to take up the slack of the forebrace.

Simcox called, 'Over here!' He sighed when the youth all but fell, as a wave curled lazily over the lee bulwark and broke around him, leaving him spluttering and gasping, water pouring from his shirt and breeches as if he had just been pulled from the sea.

'Just bide along o' me, young feller, and watch the mains'l an' compass. Get th' *feel* of 'er, see?'

54

He forgot Segrave as a line high above the deck cracked like a whip, and instantly began to unreeve itself as if it were alive.

A sailor was already swarming aloft, another bending on some fresh cordage so that no time would be lost in repairs.

Segrave clung to the bitts beneath the driver-boom and stared dully at the men working on the damaged rigging, paying no heed to the wind which tried to pluck them down. He could not recall when he had felt so wretched, so utterly miserable, and so unable to see his way out of it.

Tyacke's words still stung, and although it was not the first time the captain had given him the sharp side of his tongue, the boy had never seen him so angry: as if he had lost control and wanted to strike him.

Segrave had earnestly tried not to rouse Tyacke's ire; had wanted nothing more than to keep out of his way. Both were impossible in so small a ship.

He had nobody to talk to, really talk and understand. There had been plenty of midshipmen aboard his last ship—his *only* ship. He shuddered. What must he do?

His father had been a hero, although Segrave could barely remember him. Even on his rare returns to their home he had seemed distant, vaguely disapproving, perhaps because he had but one son and three daughters. Then one day the news had been brought to that far-off Surrey house. Captain Segrave had been killed in battle, fighting under Admiral Dundas at Camperdown. His mother had told them, her face sad but composed. By then it was already too late for Roger Segrave. His uncle, a retired flag-officer in Plymouth, had decided to offer him his patronage—for his father's memory, for the honour of the family. As soon as a ship could be found he was kitted out and packed off to sea. For Segrave it had been three years of hell.

He looked despairingly at Simcox. His rough kindness had almost finished him. But he would understand no better than Segrave's lieutenant in the three-decker. What would he say if he knew that Segrave hated the navy, and had never wanted to follow the family tradition. *Never.*

He had intended to tell his mother on that last leave, when she had taken him to London to stay with some of her friends. They had clucked over him like hens. *So sweet in his uniform* as one of them had exclaimed. That had been when he had heard them discussing Nelson and another name, Richard Bolitho.

Now the unthinkable had happened. Brave Nelson was dead. And the other name was here, with the squadron.

Before he had left for Portsmouth to take passage to the Mediterranean, he had tried to explain to his mother.

She had hugged him, and then held him at arm's length. She had sounded hurt. 'After all the Admiral had done for you and the family—' It was strange, but Segrave could never recall his uncle being called by name. He was always *the Admiral.*

'Be brave, Roger. Make us proud of you!'

He tensed as the captain turned aft towards him. If only his face were not like that. Segrave was not too immature to know how Tyacke must hate and loathe his own appearance. And yet he could not stop himself from staring at his disfigurement, even

56

when he was trying to prevent himself from doing so.

If he passed his examination ... Segrave ducked as a curtain of spray soaked into him again. *If*—he would be appointed as a lieutenant, the first real step, to share a wardroom with other officers who would see him as the weak link, danger whenever they were called to action.

But suppose—he found he was clenching his fists until they ached—he ended up with a terrible wound like Tyacke? He felt the bile in his throat, choking him.

Simcox slapped him on the shoulder. 'Let her fall off a point. Steer sou'-sou'-west.' He watched as Segrave relayed his order to the helmsman, but saw the senior hand at the tiller glance at him, not the boy, to make certain it was correct.

'Deck thar! She's standin' away, sir, an' makin' more sail!'

Tyacke tucked his thumbs into his belt. 'So he wants to play games, does he?' He cupped his hands and called, 'Would you take a glass aloft, Mr Jay?' As the master's mate hurried to the shrouds he said, 'Hands aloft, and loose tops'l, Ben!' He gave a rare grin. 'I'll wager he'll not outreach *Miranda*!'

Then he appeared to notice the midshipman for the first time. 'Go with him and learn something!' He dismissed him immediately as the topsail suddenly boomed out from its yard and then hardened like a breastplate.

Simcox eyed the set of the sails. 'We must catch him afore dusk. Sir Richard Bolitho'll not thank us for keepin' him waiting!'

Segrave finally reached the top of the quivering ratlines and joined the master's mate by the foot of the fidded topmast. Heights did not trouble him, and he gazed across the endless dark blue desert with its ranks of yellow-crested waves. The ship was momentarily forgotten; he stared wide-eyed at the spray as it drifted up from the plunging stem, felt the mast shaking and jerking, every brace and shroud catching the wind in a wild chorus which drowned out the men on the deck far below.

'Take a look.' Jay handed him the telescope before bellowing to the deck, 'Schooner, sir! Flies no flag!'

Tyacke's voice carried effortlessly from aft. 'She running?'

'Aye, sir!'

They heard the squeal of a block, and seconds later a huge White Ensign floated from *Miranda*'s gaff.

Jay chuckled. 'That'll show the buggers!'

But Segrave was peering at the other vessel as she heeled over to an angle that matched *Miranda*'s. The vessel seemed to leap out of the distance so that he could see the patched and dirty sails, even some loose trailing cordage awaiting repair, *Irish pendants* as he had heard the old sailors call them. The hull was originally black but was scored, and in places worn bare by wind and weather. It would not be tolerated in a King's ship, no matter how hard she was worked.

'What d'you think, Mr Jay?'

The man looked at him before raising the glass again. 'At a guess she's a bloody blackbirder.' He saw the uncertainty on the youth's face. 'Slaver, lad.'

Segrave looked away and did not see the other man's pitying stare. 'Will we catch her?'

58

Jay was watching the other vessel with professional interest. 'We'll *catch* the bastard right enough.'

There was a hail from the deck. 'Clear for action! Mr Archer, lay aft if you please!'

Archer was the gunner, so there could be little doubt about it now.

Tyacke's voice seemed to be right beside him. *'Mr Segrave!* Down here at the double!'

Jay watched him clambering down the ratlines, his fair hair rippling in the wind.

There was nothing to dislike about the midshipman, but Jay knew the dangers. In small ships like *Miranda* it was one hand for the King, t'other for yourself. There was no room for passengers and mother's boys.

Simcox faced Segrave as he reached the bulwark. 'Keep with Mr Archer. He will personally lay and point a four-pounder. You will do well to watch him!'

The tub-like boatswain grinned and showed him broken teeth.

'I knowed Elias Archer knock an apple off a tree at a 'undred paces!'

The other man who waited by halliards and braces grinned as if it was a huge joke.

Segrave saw Tyacke turn to speak with the helmsmen. In the sun's angry glare his face looked as if it had just been clawed away.

Then he followed the gunner to the foremost starboard side port and tried not to think about it. He felt like running below to hide, anything but being made to bare his fear before the others.

Elias Archer, *Miranda*'s master gunner, was a grizzled little man and stood effortlessly on the

59

pitching foredeck, his arms folded while he waited for his men to clear away the four-pounder nearest to the bows.

'Done much of this, 'ave yer?' He glanced briefly at the midshipman, then returned his gaze to the other vessel. She was larger than *Miranda*, and might yet outsail them until nightfall made a further chase impossible.

Segrave shook his head. His body was like ice in spite of the sun's high glare across his neck and shoulders; and each time the schooner dipped her stem the bursting spray made him shiver uncontrollably.

He replied, 'Not like this. My last ship engaged a French two-decker, but she ran aground and caught fire before we could take her.'

'This is different.' Archer took a shining black ball from the shot garland and felt it in his hard palms. 'Ships like this 'un 'ave to be quick an' nimble. But without the likes o' us the fleet would be all aback for news, an' without *that* even Our Nel couldn't move.' He nodded to one of his crew. 'Right, Mason, open the port.'

Segrave watched as other men ran to the halliards and braces and the deck canted over again. The other schooner must have headed away a point or so, but it was hard to tell from where they stood now, here in the eyes of the ship.

Archer leaned over to supervise as the charge was carefully tamped home. He said, 'Some 'otheads double-shot their guns. But not me. Not in a little piece like this 'un.'

Segrave heard the captain call, 'Signal that bastard to heave-to!'

Archer chuckled, ''*E* won't take no notice!'

Segrave was puzzled. 'Maybe he cannot read our signals?'

A seaman with the rammer grinned and pointed at the gun. 'He'll understand this, right enough.'

The other schooner was showing her bilge as she heeled over to the press of canvas. There were several heads above her bulwark, but there was no response to the signal.

Lieutenant Tyacke shouted, 'Load and run out!'

The shot was thrust down the muzzle with a wad to keep it secure. Then, with the hands hauling on the tackles, the little gun was run up to the open port.

Archer explained, 'Y'see, my lad, that bugger yonder has the wind-gage, but it will help us to put a shot down where we wants it.'

Jay, the forgotten master's mate, called from the foremast: 'They've just pitched a corpse over the side, sir! There goes another!'

Tyacke lowered his telescope, his eyes hard. 'That last one was still alive, Mr Simcox.' The sudden formality seemed to add menace to the moment.

'Beyond her if you can, Mr Archer!'

Archer was crouching like an athlete, the trigger-line pulled taut as he peered over the barrel.

He jerked the line and the gun hurtled inboard on its tackles, smoke fanning through the port even as they began to sponge out for the next shot.

Segrave saw a sudden confusion of spray to starboard and for an instant thought that Archer's aim had failed him. But the ball hit the water just a few yards from the schooner's lee bow and ricocheted across the waves like a jubilant dolphin. Segrave pointed at the other disturbance which was

61

already settling again.

'What's *that*?'

Sperry the boatswain, who had sauntered forward to watch, said harshly, 'Sharks.'

Segrave felt the nausea returning. Those two unknown people had been cast outboard like so much rubbish; torn to pieces while he had watched.

'Bosun! Stand by to sway out the boat!'

Segrave raised his eyes again. The other vessel was heaving-to, her patched sails in wild confusion as she rounded-up into the wind.

Segrave had the feeling that *Miranda*'s people were used to this kind of thing. The arms chest was already on deck and open, and Jay came slithering down a back stay with a grunt, his hands already reaching for a hanger while someone passed him his pistol.

Tyacke was saying, 'I shall stand off. Board the schooner and search her. Don't take any insolence from any of them. You know what to do.'

Simcox beckoned to the midshipman. 'You go with Mr Jay, lad. If that bastard *is* full of slaves we'll have to release him. There's no law against blackbirdin', not yet anyways, an' we'd get precious few thanks from the commodore if we return to th' squadron with a load o' slaves. Me, I'd hang the bastards an' to hell with the law an' th' right o' it!'

Tyacke crossed the deck. 'Help Mr Jay all you can. Arm yourself—they're as treacherous as snakes.'

Small though she was, *Miranda* appeared to tower over them as they tumbled into the longboat and cast off.

'*Give way all!*' Jay grasped the tiller bar and watched narrowly as the men pulled strongly

62

towards the other schooner.

Sperry was in the boat too, a boarding axe and a heavy cutlass in his belt.

'No slaves,' he said.

Jay asked, 'How so, George?'

'No bloody stench, is there? An' us downwind of 'em an' all!'

Segrave gritted his teeth and gripped the bulwark with all his strength. It was another nightmare. He saw a sudden picture of his mother when she had told them about their father's death. How would she feel about him? Proud? Moist-eyed that her only son had died in battle? He stared wildly at the other vessel, stared until his eyes watered and smarted. *Damn them all.*

Jay cupped his hands. 'We're comin' aboard! In th' King's name!'

Sperry bared his teeth and loosened the axe in his belt.

'Oh, that was *prettily* said, Bob!'

They grinned fiercely at each other while Segrave could only stare at them. At any second they might be fired on; he had heard it said that slavers were often well armed.

Jay was suddenly serious. 'The usual, lads. Take over the helm, an' disarm the crew.' He glanced at Segrave. 'You stick with me, lad. Nowt to it!'

A grapnel flew over the schooner's bulwark and the next second they were clambering aboard, the sea-noises fading slightly as they found themselves on the deck. Segrave stayed close to the master's mate. When he looked at his companions he was not surprised that this vessel had failed to stop. *Miranda*'s White Ensign was genuine but the little boarding party looked more like ragged pirates than the King's seamen.

Jay beckoned to a man in dirty white breeches and a contrasting ruffled silk shirt.

'You th' Master?'

Segrave looked at the others. A mixture. The sweepings of the gutter.

'An' wot do we 'ave '*ere*?' The boatswain's thick arm shot out and dragged one of the crew away from the others. With surprising speed for such a squat man, Sperry ripped off the sailor's shirt, then swung him round so that Jay could see the tattoos on his skin. Crossed flags and cannon, and a ship's name: *Donegal*.

Jay rasped, 'A deserter, eh? Looks like the end o' th' roamin' life for you!'

The man cringed. 'For Gawd's sake 'ave some pity. I'm just a poor Jack like yerselves!'

Sperry shook him gently. 'An' soon you'll be a poor *dead* Jack, dancin' at the yardarm, you bastard!'

Segrave had never even tried to understand it. How men who had been taken by the press-gangs as some of *Miranda*'s had, were always outraged by those who had run.

The one who was obviously the master shrugged his shoulders and shook his head.

Jay sighed. 'Don't speak no English.' His eyes gleamed and he pointed at the deserter with his hanger.

'You'll do! You 'elp us an' we'll see you escapes the rope, eh?'

The sailor's gratitude was pathetic to see. He fell on his knees and sobbed, 'I only done one passage in 'er, '*onest*, sir!'

'Wot about the two "burials"?' The point of the

hanger lifted suddenly until it rested on the man's throat. 'An' don't lie, or you'll be joinin' them!'

'The master put 'em over, sir!' He was babbling with fear and relief. 'They'd been fighting, and one stabbed t'other.' He dropped his eyes. 'The master was goin' to get rid of 'em anyway. They weren't strong enough for 'ard work.'

Segrave watched the man in the frilled shirt. He seemed calm, indifferent even. They could not hold him, although he had murdered two slaves who were no longer of any use.

Jay snapped, 'Take charge of the deck, George.' He beckoned to a seaman. 'We'll go below.' He added, 'You too, Mr Segrave!'

It was even filthier between decks, the whole hull creaking and pitching while the sailors, holding lanterns like tin-miners, crept amongst the evidence of the schooner's trade. Ranks of manacles and leg-irons lined and crisscrossed the main hold, with chains to keep each batch of slaves from moving more than a few feet. And this for a voyage across an ocean, to the Indies or the Spanish Main.

Jay muttered, 'That's why they only takes the fit ones. T'others would never last the passage.' He spat. 'Lyin' in their own filth for weeks on end. Don't bear thinkin' about.' He shrugged. 'Still, I suppose it's a livin', like everythin' else.'

Segrave wanted to be sick, but he controlled it and asked timidly, 'That deserter—will he really be pardoned?'

Jay paused and glanced at him. 'Yes, if he's any use to us. Pardoned the rope anyway. He'll likely get two hundred strokes of the cat, just to remind him of 'is loyalties in the future!'

The young seaman named Dwyer said softly,

65

'What's abaft this lot, Mr Jay?'

Jay forgot Segrave and turned swiftly. 'Th' cabins. Why?'

'I heard something, or *someone* more like.'

'God's teeth!' Jay drew his pistol and cocked it. 'Might be some bastard with a slow-match ready to blow us all to hell! Use yer shoulder, Dwyer!'

The young seaman hurled himself against one of the doors and it burst open, smashed from its hinges by the blow.

The hutchlike cabin was in darkness but for a patch of sunshine which could barely penetrate the filthy glass of a skylight.

On a littered and stained bunk was a young black woman. She was sitting half-upright, propped on her elbows, her lower limbs covered by a soiled sheet. She was otherwise quite naked. There was no fear, not even surprise, but when she tried to move a chain around her ankle restricted her.

Jay said quietly, 'Well, well. Does himself very nicely, does the master!'

He led the way on deck again and shaded his eyes in the glare as *Miranda* changed tack and drew closer to the drifting vessel, which was apparently named *Albacora*.

Tyacke's voice, unreal in a speaking-trumpet, reached them easily.

'What is she?'

Jay cupped his hands, 'Slaver, sir. No cargo but for one. We've a deserter on board as well.'

Segrave saw the man bobbing and smiling wretchedly in the background as if Tyacke could see him. But he kept thinking of the black girl. Chained there like a wild animal for the slaver's pleasure. She had a lovely body, despite...

66

Tyacke called over, 'Where bound?'

Jay held up the chart. 'Madagascar, sir.'

A seaman near Segrave murmured, 'We'll have to let 'er go.' He glared around the filthy deck. 'She bain't much but she'd fetch a few shillin's in the prize court!' His mate nodded in agreement.

Tyacke's voice betrayed no emotion. 'Very well, Mr Jay. Return on board and bring the deserter with you.'

The man in question shouted, *No! No!'* The boatswain cuffed him around the ear and sent him sprawling, but he crawled across the deck and clawed at Jay's shoes like a crippled beggar.

He shouted again, 'He took the chart below when you was sighted, sir! I seen him do it afore. He puts a different one for all to see.'

Jay kicked his hands away. 'Now, why didn't I think of that?' He touched Segrave's arm. 'Come with me.'

They returned to the cabin where the girl still lay propped on her elbows, as if she had not moved.

They searched through the litter of books and charts, discarded clothing and weapons, Jay becoming clumsier by the moment, well aware of Tyacke's impatience to get under way again.

Jay said desperately, ''S no use. I can't find it, an' that bugger don't speak English.' He sounded angry. 'I'll lay odds that the deserter is lyin' to save 'is own skin. He'll 'ave no skin left when I've done with 'im!'

There was a looking-glass leaning against a case of paired pistols. Jay picked it up and searched behind it as a last hope.

'Not a god-damned thing!' He tossed the glass on the table and Segrave snatched it as it slithered towards the deck. As he did so he caught the merest glimpse of the girl behind him, now turned slightly to watch, her breasts shining in the filtered sunlight.

He exclaimed, 'She's lying on something, Mr Jay!'

Jay stared from him to her with stunned amazement. 'By the livin' Jesus!' He sprang across the cabin and seized the girl's naked shoulder to push her across the bunk.

But her body, slippery with sweat, escaped his grasp, and she moved like lightning, a knife appearing in her left hand even as Segrave ran to Jay's assistance.

Jay went sprawling from the impetus of his charge across the cabin and as he pitched to the deck he saw Segrave fall over the girl, and heard his sharp cry of agony.

Segrave felt the blade like fire across his hip, somehow knew that she had raised the knife for another blow at his unprotected back.

There was a cracking sound and the knife went clattering to the deck. The girl lay back, her eyes closed, her mouth bleeding where Jay had punched her.

Another figure ran into the low cabin. It was the seaman named Dwyer.

Jay rasped, ''Ere, give Mr Segrave a hand!' He rolled the girl's body aside and tugged a worn leather pouch from beneath her.

Segrave groaned and tried to move. Then he saw the slash in his breeches where the knife had gone in. There was blood everywhere, and the pain was making him gasp, bite his lip to prevent himself from screaming.

The sailor wrapped what appeared to be a shirt around the wound, but it was soon soaked through with blood.

Jay ripped open the big pouch, his eyes speedily scanning the contents before he opened the chart with trembling fingers.

Then he stood up. 'I must speak with the Cap'n.' He looked at Segrave's contorted face. 'You saved my rump, an' no mistake!' He watched his agony and added kindly, 'Be easy till I come back.'

On deck the sky already seemed darker, the clouds under-bellied with deep gold.

In quick sentences Jay shouted his information across the choppy division of water. 'She was bound for *Cape Town*! There's a despatch, wrote in French it looks.'

Tyacke called, 'How badly is Mr Segrave?' He saw Jay's shrug. 'Then you had better not move him! Send the vessel's master across with the pouch—the deserter too. I will rejoin the squadron. Are you confident that you can manage?'

Jay grinned and said to himself, 'Manage? They'll not make trouble now.'

The *Albacora*'s master protested violently as a seaman seized his arm.

Jay snarled, 'Put those irons on him! Attempting to murder a King's officer, butchering slaves, to say nothing of trading with the enemy.' He nodded, satisfied as the man fell silent. 'Yes, my friend, you've understood the signal at last.'

As the boat cast off and headed for *Miranda*, Jay positioned his most trusted men with great care.

'We will get under way presently. Watch every move, even if they blinks! Shoot if in any doubt, see?'

69

With the boatswain, he returned to the cabin where Dwyer was holding the midshipman and trying to staunch the blood.

Dwyer said helplessly, 'Won't let me do it proper, sir!'

Sperry tore his eyes from the sprawled figure on the bunk and licked his lips.

'Now *there's* a thing, Bob.'

Jay was thinking of how close he had been to death. 'Later, George.'

Segrave was weaker but still tried to struggle as Sperry held him on the deck, while Dwyer and Jay began to cut away his bloodied breeches.

Sperry said huskily, 'I'll put a stitch or two in it. Just lay another dressin' on while I—'

Jay exclaimed, 'Who the bloody hell did *that*?'

The midshipman lay quietly now, like a sick or injured animal.

The whole of his buttocks and the backs of his thighs were scarred and bruised as if he had been beaten over and over again with a cord or a whip. Whoever had done this to him it was not in *Miranda*. That meant he had carried these scars for over six weeks, and without a word being said.

Jay thought of the jibes and grins, and all the while he . . .

The boatswain said, 'He's passed out, Bob. I'll fetch me gear.'

'Yeh, an' see if you can find some rum or brandy—anythin'.'

He turned back to the midshipman, who lay as if he was dead.

'You poor little bugger,' he said softly. He watched the blood soaking through the makeshift bandages. But for Segrave's unexpected courage it

70

would have been his own blood, and no second chance either.

He saw Dwyer watching him and said harshly, 'And it goes no further, see? This is *Miranda*'s business, no one else's! I reckon 'e's suffered enough in this poxy squadron.'

*   *   *

Midshipman Segrave opened his eyes and was conscious of two things immediately. The sky overhead was dark and dotted with tiny stars; he was wrapped in blankets, a pillow beneath his head.

A shadow bent over him, and Jay asked, 'How is it?'

Then came the pain, throbbing in time with his heartbeats. He could taste brandy on his lips but could only remember the sequence of events like dark pictures. Hands holding him down; sharp stabbing pains; oblivion. Then the girl. He shook violently. *That was it*. When it had happened.

'Am I all right?' His voice sounded weak.

Jay forced a grin. ''Course you are. 'Ero of the hour. Saved my skin, an' gave us cause to 'old this ship.'

He looked across at two kneeling figures. Like some natives at prayer. But he knew they were trying to peer through the dirty skylight. Sperry was down there with the girl, doing what he probably did better than anything, if half his yarns were to be believed.

Then he asked, 'Tell me, lad, who did that to you?'

But Segrave shook his head, his eyes closed with the pain and the emotion.

Jay, the hard-bitten master's mate, had called him a *hero*.

CHAPTER FOUR

SEEK AND FIND

Themis's stern cabin was like a furnace in spite of the open gunports and the windsails rigged to each hatchway, so it was difficult even to think. Bolitho sat at the table, his head resting on one hand while he scanned the contents of the pouch which had been ferried across from the schooner *Miranda*.

Commodore Warren slumped in a high-backed chair, his ashen features turned towards the nearest port, his only movement when he plucked his uniform coat or shirt away from his damp skin.

Seated beside Bolitho, his plump, round-shouldered secretary, Daniel Yovell, had to repeatedly push his gold-rimmed spectacles back into position when they slipped down his nose, as he wrote the notes which Bolitho might require later on.

Warren asked suddenly, 'You are not surprised by the army's reply to your request, Sir Richard?'

Bolitho dragged his thoughts away from the pouch which *Miranda*'s boarding party had discovered. The evidence of the chart was interesting, but the lengthy letter to some French merchant in Cape Town was far more so.

He replied, 'Much what I expected, Commodore Warren. But we have to use the proper channels. By now, Sir David Baird's soldiers will have begun their landings. It is too late to prevent it, even if I could.'

Lieutenant Jenour stood beside the stern windows and watched the *Miranda* as she swung above her reflection, a perfect twin on the calm water. Her commander had been fortunate, he thought. A few hours later and he would have lost the wind completely.

He turned as Bolitho said, 'Your French is excellent, Stephen. When you translated this letter for me, did you notice anything unusual?'

Jenour tried to shake off the torpor. Of them all, Bolitho looked the coolest. Dressed in shirt and breeches, his coat tossed aside on to a chest, he even managed to appear alert, although Jenour knew that he had been pacing the cabin since *Miranda*'s sails had been sighted closing the land. That had been at dawn. It was now high noon. In this oven-heat men trod warily; it was a dangerous time when frayed tempers brought sharp discipline, with an aftermath of resentment. Better to be at sea, with every man too busy to brood.

Jenour screwed up his face. 'If the letter *is* a code I cannot read it, Sir Richard. It is the kind of letter that one merchant might send to another, passed perhaps by one ship on passage to that particular destination. After all, it is quite possible for French merchants to be in Cape Town surely?'

Bolitho massaged his forehead. It *was* a code, and he was surprised that even the quick-witted Jenour had missed a vital clue.

It fell to Yovell, who had been peering at his papers, his fat fingers holding his spectacles in place, to discover it.

He exclaimed, 'The battle off Cape Trafalgar, Sir

Richard! The sender mentions it to his friend!'

Bolitho saw their expressions begin to change. 'Quite what you would expect, eh? Except that *Truculent* made a record passage here from England, before anyone in this squadron knew about the battle and Lord Nelson's death. So to have time in hand to pass this letter to a slaver, the sender must have been in these waters ahead of us!'

Warren dabbed his mouth with care. 'A French man-of-war?'

Jenour clenched his fists with disbelief. 'One of those which broke out of Brest?'

Bolitho tugged the chart towards him. 'Cape Town is the clue, my friends, although I fear I cannot determine what it is.'

He made up his mind. 'Make a signal to *Miranda*, Stephen. Summon her commander aboard. I would like to meet him in any case.'

As Jenour turned towards the door Commodore Warren said humbly, 'I am sorry. It slipped my mind, Sir Richard. Lieutenant Tyacke has been aboard since he delivered the pouch.'

Bolitho bit back a sharp retort. It was not now the time, but later ... He sighed. Two frigate captains who disliked one another; their commodore who showed little interest in the whole operation; and a mixed handful of vessels which had barely worked with one another before. Small beginnings.

He said, 'Ask him to come in, Stephen.'

Warren shifted uneasily. 'There is another thing about him...'

But Jenour already had the door to the cabin open, so he did not finish it.

Jenour stepped into the other cabin and looked at

the tall man who was standing by an open gunport, his hands clasped behind him.

'If you will step aft—Sir Richard Bolitho wishes to speak with you.' He was relieved to see that the lieutenant had at least been given refreshment, and doubtless some of the commodore's terrible wine. 'We were not aware that you were still ...' The words froze on his lips as the other man turned to stare at him. How could anyone live with a wound like that?

Tyacke said abruptly, 'And who are you, might I ask?' Then he saw the twist of gold lace at Jenour's shoulder. 'I see. Flag-lieutenant.'

Jenour tried again. 'Forgive me. I did not mean—'

Tyacke shifted the sword at his belt and turned his disfigurement aside. 'I am accustomed to it. But I don't have to enjoy it.' He did not attempt to hide his anger and bitterness. *Who did they think they were?*

He lowered his head between the deck beams and stepped into the enlarged cabin. For a few moments he was taken completely off-balance. The commodore he knew slightly by sight, and for some lingering seconds he imagined that the plump man in the plain blue coat must be the much-talked about Bolitho. Not an heroic figure; but then most of the flag-officers Tyacke had met were not.

'Will you accept my apologies, Mr Tyacke?' Bolitho walked from the shadows and crossed beneath a skylight. 'I was not told you had been kept waiting. Please forgive this oversight and take a seat, will you?'

Tyacke sat down awkwardly. Perhaps he had been at sea too long, or had misheard somehow. But the man in the white shirt, with the almost gentle manner of greeting, was not what he had expected. For one thing Bolitho looked no older than himself, although he knew he must be nearer fifty than forty. But for the deep lines around his mouth, and the traces of white in a solitary lock of hair above one eye, he was a young man. Bolitho was looking at him again in that strangely direct and open manner. The eyes were grey, and for a few seconds Tyacke felt tongue-tied, more like Midshipman Segrave than himself.

Bolitho continued, 'Your discovery aboard that slaver may be more useful than any of us realise.' He smiled suddenly, so that he appeared even younger. 'I am trying to fathom how it may help us.'

A door opened, and a very small servant padded across the cabin and paused by Tyacke's chair. 'Some hock, sir?' He watched Tyacke's expression and added mildly, 'It is quite cold, sir.' It sounded as if it was better wine than was usually available in this elderly flagship.

Tyacke swallowed hard. This must be one of Bolitho's men too. He drank deeply, trying to contain something he thought he had lost. *Emotion.* The little man had not even blinked; had shown neither curiosity nor disgust.

Bolitho observed him and saw the lieutenant's hand tremble as his glass was refilled. Another survivor. One more victim which the war had tossed aside, as the sea gave up driftwood.

He asked quietly, 'Where is this *Albacora* now?'

Tyacke seemed to pull himself out of his thoughts with a physical effort.

'She will be here in two days, Sir Richard. I left a

small prize crew aboard and the injured midshipman.'

Bolitho nodded. 'I read of him in your report. He sounds a brave youngster.'

Tyacke dropped his gaze. 'He surprised me.'

Bolitho looked at his secretary. 'I shall require you to write some orders for another of the schooners.' His voice hardened and he saw the commodore watching him anxiously. 'I want the *Albacora* put alongside one of the storeships when she arrives. She must be met at sea, out of sight of prying telescopes ashore, then brought to her moorings at *night*.' He waited for his words to sink in. 'Will you attend to that, Commodore Warren?'

Warren bobbed and fell into a fit of violent coughing.

Bolitho turned his back and studied the tall lieutenant. 'I wish to take passage in your command, Mr Tyacke.' He saw the disbelief, the arguments rushing into the man's eyes. 'I am used to small vessels so have no fear for my—er, dignity!'

When he looked again, the commodore had left the cabin, but he could still hear him coughing. Jenour was at Yovell's shoulder peering at the plump Devonian's neat, round writing.

For a few minutes they were alone, ignored. Bolitho asked softly, 'Where did it happen?' That was all he said, but he saw the words hit Tyacke like a clenched fist.

Then Tyacke met his gaze and said without hesitation, 'The Nile, Sir Richard. The *Majestic*, seventy-four.'

Bolitho nodded very slowly. 'Yes. Captain Westcott. A fine man. Sadly missed.' He touched his left eyelid with one finger and Tyacke imagined that he saw him wince.

Bolitho said, 'Please return to your ship. As soon as the remainder of your people arrive in the prize, *your* prize, Mr Tyacke, be prepared to weigh anchor again.'

Tyacke glanced at the others but Jenour was studying some papers; or perhaps he simply could not face him.

Bolitho added, 'I shall want you to take me to the Cape itself, beyond if need be. I am doing no good here.'

As Tyacke turned to leave Bolitho called to him, 'There is one more thing.' He walked across the cabin until they faced each other again. 'I would like to shake your hand.' His grasp was firm. 'You are a very brave officer.' For just seconds he hesitated. 'You have given *me* hope. I shall not forget.'

Tyacke found himself in the harsh sunlight and then down in *Miranda*'s longboat before he knew what had happened.

Simcox was in the boat, agog with excitement and questions.

Tyacke watched dully as the boat cast off and the seamen picked up the stroke. Then he said without emphasis, 'He wants us to take him to the Cape.'

Simcox stared. 'A vice-admiral! In *Miranda*!'

The lieutenant nodded, remembering, holding on to it. And lastly the handshake, the momentary wistfulness in Bolitho's voice.

Simcox was unnerved by the change in his friend. Something strange and important must have happened aboard the flagship. He hoped that Tyacke had not been hurt again.

He tried to pass it off. 'And I'll bet you forgot to

ask him about our beer ration, what say you?'

But Tyacke had not heard him. He repeated, 'Take him to the Cape. By the living God, I'd sail that man to hell and back if he asked me!'

They did not speak again until they reached *Miranda*.

*　　*　　*

Richard Bolitho wedged himself in one corner of the *Miranda*'s small cabin and then stretched out his legs. The motion was certainly lively, he thought ruefully, and even his stomach, which had been hardened by every sort of sea and under most conditions, was queasy.

Lieutenant Tyacke had been on deck for most of the time since they had hauled anchor, and although he could see nothing apart from the bright blue rectangle through the skylight, Bolitho guessed that once clear of the choppy inshore currents things might be easier.

It seemed odd not to have Ozzard pattering about, anticipating his every need even before he had thought of it himself. But space was precious in the rakish schooner, and in any case it might appear as a slight to *Miranda*'s people if he brought his own servant. It was probably shock enough to see him climb aboard, despite Tyacke's warning beforehand. As he had made his way aft Bolitho had caught glimpses of the varied expressions. Astonishment, curiosity, maybe even resentment. Like Tyacke, whose voice seemed to be everywhere on deck, they might see his presence more as an invasion of their private world than any sort of honour. He had asked Jenour to remain in the

79

flagship, too. His eyes and ears were as useful as *Miranda*'s.

Bolitho had seen the captured slaver alongside one of the transports, but had not gone over to her. He had heard about the woman in the master's cabin, and the deserter who was now under guard in the flagship, awaiting his fate. He guessed there were several other things which had not been mentioned in Tyacke's report.

He heard the boom of canvas as the fore-topsail filled out to the wind, and imagined he could feel the instant response while the schooner settled on her new tack.

He looked around the cramped cabin, hearing once more in his mind Allday's outspoken disapproval.

'Not fit for a vice-admiral, 'specially you, Sir Richard! A collier would offer more comfort!' He was out there somewhere, either quietly fuming or, having accepted it, sharing a 'wet' with one of the *Miranda*'s senior hands. He usually managed to settle in that way, and gain more information than Bolitho might do in a year.

The cabin was packed with personal belongings, sea chests, clothing and weapons, the latter within easy reach for any occupant.

Tyacke had left the wounded midshipman in the care of *Themis*'s surgeon. There was another story there, too, but Bolitho doubted if Tyacke would share it. The tall, powerful lieutenant discouraged confidences, apart from with his friend, the acting-master. Maybe he had always been a solitary man, and his terrible scars had only increased his isolation.

Bolitho opened his chart and moved it beneath a

swaying deckhead lantern. Even it was not spiralling now so violently. These great sails were like wings; could hold the schooner steady on her deep keel when other vessels would be pitching like corks.

Bolitho looked at the chart, the hundreds of tiny soundings, bearings and identifying marks. He found that he was rubbing his injured eye, and stopped instantly, as if someone had called aloud to him.

He could feel sweat on his spine and then knew why Allday had been so insistent about his not boarding *Miranda*.

Bolitho shook his head and peered at the chart again. It was no use. It *was* the cabin. Not so different from the one he had been using in the topsail cutter *Supreme*. October 1803, when the French had found the little cutter and had fired on her; when Bolitho's life had changed. One enemy ball had slammed into some buckets of sand and hurled him to the deck.

It had been noon, but when he had been helped to his feet he had found only darkness. His left eye had plagued him badly since. In his old *Hyperion* it had almost cost him his life. The damage had been like a sea-mist creeping over the eye, rendering him half-blind. He recalled Catherine's pleas before he had left Portsmouth in *Truculent*. Aboard *Hyperion*, at the height of her last-ever voyage, they had carried an eminent surgeon, Sir Piers Blachford, who with others of his profession had been scattered throughout the embattled squadrons of the fleet to discover at first hand what ship's surgeons had to contend with in action. As an eventual result of their findings, it was hoped by the

81

College of Surgeons in London that it would not be left to the butchers of the trade to deal with the appalling wounds and amputations which were the price of any battle.

Blachford, like a tall, reedy heron, had told Bolitho that he would lose the sight of his left eye completely unless he quit the sea for a period of time lengthy enough to afford him the proper examination and perhaps treatment. Even then, he could not be sure . . .

Bolitho stared at the chart's wavering coastline and imagined he could feel the old pain deep inside his eye. It was imagination allied to fear. It had to be. He looked desperately around the cabin again. *Allday had known*. He always did.

But it was not just a question of duty or arrogance. Bolitho did not have the conceit to pretend it was either. There were so few leaders with the experience, the understanding, that were needed so much now, perhaps even more so than before Trafalgar. With Nelson gone, and the enemy forces on land untouched by the victory and his sacrifice, it was just a matter of time before the next blow fell.

The door banged open and Tyacke, bent double, thrust himself on to one of the bench seats. He was breathing hard as if he had been personally fighting his enemy, the sea, and his shirt was blotchy with spray. Bolitho noticed that he sat in the opposite corner where his disfigurement was in the deepest shadow.

Tyacke said, 'We're running due south, Sir Richard. The wind's veered a place, but that's all to the good should we want to come about in a hurry.' He glanced at Bolitho. 'Are you certain this is what you want to do, sir?'

Bolitho smiled and gestured to the clothing which hung from the deckhead. His own sea-going coat was no better than Tyacke's and he had purposely left the epaulettes with Ozzard.

He said, 'I know you cannot always tell the contents of a cask by its label, but at least I would hope that your people will feel more at ease. It was *my* choice, Mr Tyacke, so do not blame yourself.' He changed the subject. 'Is all well with your company?'

Tyacke's eyes sharpened as he replied, 'I have one matter left to deal with, but it must wait until I can speak to the person involved.' He sounded wary. 'It is ship's business, Sir Richard. Nothing which will impair the needs of this passage.'

'I am glad to know it.' Bolitho folded the chart, feeling Tyacke watching him. All *Miranda*'s people were returned on board. But for the midshipman, who had according to Tyacke's report acted with gallantry to save the master's mate's life. *Ship's business*, he had said. He smiled briefly. In other words, *not mine*.

Tyacke saw the smile and relaxed slightly, his hands hidden beneath the table. It was not easy. For him it was more than an intrusion; it was the deprivation of his own freedom to think and act.

He said, 'There will be some food very soon, sir.' He grinned uncomfortably. 'I know you told me not to use your title aboard this vessel, but it comes a bit hard.'

'It should draw us closer.' Bolitho felt his stomach contract. He *was* hungry, in spite of everything. Perhaps Sir Piers Blachford was wrong. It was not unknown. When he returned to England

83

... well, perhaps then he would take Catherine's advice.

He recalled one of the transports he had visited while he had been waiting for *Miranda*'s return from Saldanha Bay. It had been unspeakable; and a miracle some of the soldiers had not died of disease already. The stench had been appalling, more like a farmyard than a vessel in the King's service. Men, horses, guns and equipment, packed deck upon deck, with less room than a convict ship.

And so they must wait and endure it, until Sir David Baird's artillery and foot soldiers fought their way to the gates of Cape Town. But suppose the Dutch were stronger than anyone realised? They might turn the English advance into a rout, in which case there was only Commodore Warren's small force to land soldiers and marines and harass the enemy from the rear. The wretched men he had seen aboard the transport would be no match for the difficult landing, let alone the fighting expected of them.

He heard Allday's deep voice beyond the door and knew he was helping one of Tyacke's men to fetch a meal for the officers.

Bolitho said, 'With your experience, you should have a larger command.' Again he saw the guard drop in the ruined face. 'Your promotion ought to have been immediate.'

Tyacke's eyes flashed. 'I was offered it, sir. I declined it.' There was something like sad pride in his tone. '*Miranda*'s enough for me, and nobody can find cause to complain of her performance.'

Bolitho turned as a seaman bowed through the door with some steaming dishes. A far cry from a ship-of-the-line. From *Hyperion*.

84

The old ship's name was still hanging in his mind when he saw Allday look at him across the sailor's stooped shoulders. He murmured, 'It is all right, old friend. Believe me.'

Allday responded with a cautious grin, as if he were only half-convinced.

The door closed and Tyacke watched covertly as Bolitho cut through the greasy pork on his plate as if it were some rare delicacy.

Simcox kept asking him what Bolitho was like. *Really* like.

How could he explain? How might he describe a man who refrained from probing with his questions, when anyone else of his rank and fame would have *insisted*? Or how could he begin to tell Simcox about the bond between the admiral and his coxswain? *Old friend*, he had just called him. It was like having a vibrant force in the hull. A new light.

He thought of Simcox's earlier remark and smiled to himself. He poured two goblets of madeira and said, 'I was just thinking, sir. Some beer would not come amiss, if we could lay hands on some.'

Bolitho held up the goblet to the lantern, his face serious for a few seconds until he realised that the glass and not his eye had misted over.

Tyacke, sensing his change of mood, exclaimed, 'I beg your pardon, Sir Rich—er—sir!'

It was the first time Bolitho had seen him in irons.

'*Beer*, you say? I will pass the word to the army. It is the very least they can do.' He was still holding the goblet when he asked, 'It is Saturday, is it not? So we shall call a toast.'

Tyacke took up his glass. 'Sweethearts and wives,

sir?'

Bolitho touched the locket beneath his shirt and shook his head.

'To loved ones. May they be patient with us.'

Tyacke drank the toast but said nothing, as he had no one to care if he lived or died.

He glanced at Bolitho's expression and was deeply moved nonetheless. For a moment at least he was with her, no matter the many miles which held them apart.

*   *   *

Allday wiped his glittering razor and grunted, 'That should do it, Sir Richard. About all the water *is* fit for in this ship!' He did not conceal his disgust. 'It'll be a fisherman's dory next at this pace, I'm thinking.'

Bolitho sighed and slipped into the same crumpled shirt. It was the luxury he missed the most, a clean shirt when he needed it. Like stockings; they seemed to mark his progress from midshipmen's berth to flag-officer. Even as a lowly lieutenant there had been occasions when he had but two pairs of stockings to his name. But in many ways they had been good times; or maybe they always were, in hindsight—the memories of youth.

He thought of Tyacke's brief mention of his midshipman. Something was wrong there. He glanced up at the pale glow in the skylight. Dawn already; he was surprised that he had slept without waking once.

Allday gestured to the coffee-pot and added, 'Barely kills the taste!'

Bolitho smiled. How Allday could shave him

when he could scarcely stand upright beneath the skylight was a marvel. He could never recall him cutting his face once.

He was right about the coffee. He decided to send a despatch regarding beer for the sweltering ships. It would help until they could take on fresh water.

Commodore Warren should have made some arrangements. Perhaps he no longer cared? Bolitho pushed the coffee away. Or maybe somebody wanted *him* out of the way. *Like me.*

He heard the sluice of water and the crank of a pump as the hands washed down the deck for a new day. Like everything else in the sixty-five foot schooner, the sounds were always close, more personal than in any larger craft.

'I'll go up.' He rose from the seat and winced as his head glanced off a deckhead beam.

Allday folded his razor away with great care and muttered, 'Bloody little paintpot, that's all *she* is!' Then he followed Bolitho up the short companion ladder and into the damp wind.

Bolitho walked to the compass box. How much steeper the angle of the deck seemed than when he had been below. There appeared to be people everywhere, swabbing down, working in the shrouds, or engaged in the many tasks with running-rigging and coiled halliards.

Tyacke touched his forehead, 'Morning, sir. Steady at sou'east-by-south.' He raised one arm and pointed over the bulwark. 'That's the beginning of the Cape, sir, 'bout four miles abeam.' He smiled, proud of his little ship. 'I'd not risk weathering it much closer. You have to be careful not to be deceived by the soundings hereabouts. There's no bottom according to some charts, but if you glance yonder you'll see a reef all the same!' It seemed to amuse him. Another challenge perhaps?

Bolitho turned and saw all the watching eyes drop or return to their various tasks. Like pulling on a line of puppets.

Tyacke said quietly, 'Don't mind them, sir. The highest ranking officer who came aboard before you, begging your pardon, was the commander in charge of the guard at Gibraltar.'

Simcox joined them and said, 'Sky's clearin', sir.' It was a totally unnecessary comment and Bolitho knew that he was like the rest, nervous in his presence.

'When do you become appointed Master, Mr Simcox?'

The man shifted his feet. 'Not certain, Sir Richard.' He glanced at his friend and Bolitho could guess what was troubling him. Leaving *Miranda*; taking away Tyacke's only prop.

Bolitho shaded his eyes to watch the sea changing colour in the faint sunshine. Plenty of birds this morning, messengers from the land. He looked abeam and saw the mass of Table Mountain, and another across the larboard bow still wreathed in mist, with only its high, craggy ridges bathed in gold.

Simcox cleared his throat. 'The wind favours us, Sir Richard, but I've known ships caught in a gale to the south'rd o' this point, blown all the way to Cape Agulhas afore they could fight their way back!'

Bolitho nodded. Experience? Or was it a warning? Suppose there were men-of-war around the jutting tusk of the Cape? It was unlikely they would wish to reveal themselves for the sake of one frail schooner. But *Supreme* had been small too when the frigate had run down on her.

Tyacke lowered his telescope and said, 'Call all hands, Ben.' The first name had slipped out by accident. 'We will wear ship and steer due east.' He glanced at Bolitho. 'Into the lion's den!'

Bolitho looked up at the whipping pendant. Yes, Tyacke would miss the acting-master when he was promoted to full warrant rank. He might even see his replacement as another intruder.

He said, 'It is the only way, Mr Tyacke, but I shall not hazard the ship unduly.'

The seamen ran to the braces and halliards, fingers loosening belaying pins, casting off lines from their cleats with such deft familiarity that they needed no shouts or curses to hasten them. The sky was growing brighter by the minute, and Bolitho felt his stomach muscles tighten when he considered what he must do. He could sense Allday gazing at him while he stood ready to assist the helmsmen if needed.

It had not just been stockings which had marked Bolitho's change of fortune. Once he had gained promotion to lieutenant at the tender age of eighteen, he had been freed from the one duty he had feared and hated most. As a lieutenant, no longer did he have to scramble up the treacherous ratlines to his particular station aloft whenever the pipe was shrilled between decks, or while he stood his watch with the others.

He had never got used to it. In all weathers, with the ship hidden below by a drifting mist of spray and spindrift, he had clung to his precarious perch, watching his men, some of whom had been sent

89

aloft for the first time in their lives. He had seen sailors fall to an agonising death on the deck, hurled from rigging and yard by the force of a gale, or by billowing canvas which had refused all efforts to quell it.

Others had dropped into the sea, to surface perhaps in time to see their ship vanishing into a squall. It was no wonder that young men fled when the press gangs were on the prowl.

'Stand by aft!' Tyacke wiped the spray from his scarred face with the back of his hand, his eyes everywhere while he studied his men and the set of each sail.

'Let go an' haul! Roundly there! Tom, another hand on th' forebrace!'

The shadows of the main and staysail seemed to pass right over the busy figures as the long tiller bar went down, the canvas and rigging clattering in protest.

Bolitho could feel his shoes slipping, and saw the sea creaming under the lee rail as Tyacke brought her round. He saw too the uneven barrier of land stagger across the bowsprit while the schooner continued to swing.

Allday muttered, 'By God, she can turn on a sovereign!' But everyone was too busy, and the noise too overwhelming, to hear what might be admiration instead of scorn.

'*Meet her!* Steady as you go! *Now*, let her fall off a point!'

The senior helmsman croaked, 'Steady she goes, sir! East by north!'

'Secure!' Tyacke peered up into the glare. 'Hands aloft to reef tops'l, Mr Simcox!' A quick grin flashed between them. 'With the wind abeam it'll not do the work intended, and we might lose it.'

The twin masts swayed almost vertical and then leaned over once more to the wind's thrust.

Bolitho said, 'A glass, if you please.' He tried not to swallow. 'I am going to the foremast to take a look.' He ignored Allday's unspoken protest. 'I imagine that there will not be too many watching eyes this early!'

Without giving himself time to change his mind he strode forward, and after a quick glance at the surging water leaping up from the stem, he swung himself on to the weather bulwark and dug his hands and feet into the ratlines. Up and up, his steps mounting the shivering and protesting shrouds. *Never look down.* He had never forgotten that. He heard rather than saw the topmen descending the opposite side, their work done as quickly as thought. What must they think, he wondered? A vice-admiral making an exhibition of himself, for some reason known only to himself . . .

The masthead lookout had watched him all the way, and as he clambered, gasping, to the lower yard he said cheerfully, 'Foine day, Zur Richard!'

Bolitho clung to a stay and waited for his heart to return to normal. Damn the others who had raced him up the shrouds when they had all been reckless midshipmen.

He turned and stared at the lookout. 'You're a Cornishman.'

The sailor grinned and bobbed his head. He did not appear to be holding on to anything. 'That be roight, zur. From Penzance.'

Bolitho unslung the telescope from around his shoulders. *Two Cornishmen. So strange a meeting-place.*

It took several attempts to train the glass in time with the schooner's lunges into the offshore breakers. He saw the sharp beak of the headland creeping out towards the weather bow, a tell-tale spurt of spray from the reefs Tyacke had mentioned.

It was already much warmer; his shirt clung to him like another skin. He could see the crisscross of currents as the sea contested the jutting land before surging, confused and beaten, around it. As it had since time began. From this point and beyond, two great oceans, the Atlantic and the Indian Ocean, met. It was like a giant hinge, a gateway which gave access to India, Ceylon and all the territories of New South Wales. No wonder Cape Town was so valuable, so cherished. It was like Gibraltar at the gates of the Mediterranean: whoever held the Rock also held the key.

'*Ships, zur!* Larboard, yonder!'

Bolitho did not need to ask how he could already see them without the advantage of a telescope. Good lookouts were born, not trained, and he had always respected such sailors. The ones who were first to sight the dreaded breakers ahead when every chart claimed otherwise. Often in time for the captain to bring his ship about and save the lives of all aboard.

He waited for the glass to steady again and felt his face stiffen.

Two large ships at anchor; or were they moored fore-and-aft? It would seem so, he thought, to offer greater protection, a defence against a cutting-out attempt, and also to provide a fixed battery of guns to fend off attack.

The lookout said, 'Beggin' yer pardon, zur. I

reckon they be Dutch Indiamen.'

Bolitho nodded. Like the Honourable East India Company, such vessels were usually well-manned and armed and had proved more than a match for privateers, even men-of-war on occasions.

He turned to watch the sea breaking over some rocks. It was far enough. Further, and Tyacke would be hard put to claw away into open water.

Whatever the ships were doing, they represented a real threat. They had probably brought stores and men for the Dutch garrison, and might well be expecting others to join them.

Bolitho stared down at the deck and almost lost his grip. The mast was so steeply angled to the wind that the topmast leaned right over the blue water. He could even see his own shadow reflected on the crests.

'You may come about, Mr Tyacke!' For a moment he thought he had not heard, then saw the men running to their stations again.

A tall waterspout lifted suddenly abeam and seconds later Bolitho heard the echoing boom of a gun. He had no idea where it came from, but it was too close to ignore.

He made to lower himself to the ratlines again when the lookout said hoarsely, 'There be a *third* 'un, zur!'

Bolitho stared at him, then raised the glass again. He must be quick. Already the jib was flapping wildly, spilling wind and cracking like musket-fire as the helm went over.

Then, for just a few seconds, he saw the masts and furled sails of the other vessel, her hull lower and almost hidden by the two bigger ships. Dutch or French, it did not really matter. Bolitho had been a frigate captain and had commanded three of them in his time; there was no mistaking that familiar rig.

Waiting, maybe, for the letter which Tyacke's men had found aboard the *Albacora*. Bolitho pushed the hair from his eyes as the mast bucked and swayed over again and the spar felt as if it would splinter itself apart. This was a very large bay, according to Tyacke's chart some twenty miles across, far bigger than Table Bay which they had passed before dawn.

Whatever the Dutch commander's motives might be, he obviously considered the bay and the moored ships well worth protecting. A frontal attack by the English squadron would be costly and probably end in disaster.

He touched the man's shoulder. 'Take care of those eyes!' Even as he spoke the words they seemed to come back at him like a mocking threat. He did not hear the lookout's reply; he had begun the difficult climb down to the deck.

Tyacke listened to what he had seen before saying, 'They could divide us until—'

'Until they are reinforced? I agree.' Bolitho made up his mind. 'You will close with the squadron as fast as you wish.' He found that he could look at the lieutenant's terrible scars without steeling himself. 'Then I will need to speak with the general.' He touched Tyacke's arm. 'Sir David will not be too pleased.'

Tyacke strode away, calling commands, watching the compass and rudder while Simcox scrawled his calculations on a slate.

A voice seemed to whisper inside Bolitho's mind. *Why interfere? Why not let others take*

*responsibility—or are you allowing yourself to be taken
in a trap like some wild animal?*

He shook his head, as if he was replying to
someone else. How could he request Commodore
Popham to detach some of his ships, when they
might be needed to evacuate the soldiers and
marines if the worst happened? And Warren; could
he be trusted any more than the arrogant Captain
Varian?

He found Allday waiting near the weather
shrouds and said, 'I have been thinking...'

Allday faced him. 'You saw th' size o' that ball,
Sir Richard? It's a fortress. We'd need more ships,
an' even then we'd be hard put to close with the
buggers.' Then he gave a great sigh and rubbed his
chest, where the pain of a Spanish sword-thrust
lurked as a constant reminder. 'But I sees it's no use
me arguing—is it, Sir Richard?'

Bolitho eyed him fondly. 'I don't want to see men
butchered to no good purpose, old friend.'

'Nor I, but...'

'And I want to go home. The two enjoined make
only one course to take. And if we delay I fear that
we shall lose the both.'

From the opposite side Tyacke watched them
thoughtfully.

Simcox joined him and mopped his face with his
red handkerchief. 'A close thing, James.'

Tyacke saw Bolitho clap his hand on Allday's
thick arm, the same impetuous gesture he had used
to himself. The youthful vice-admiral with the wild
black hair blowing in the wind, in his soiled shirt
and tar-smeared breeches, was actually laughing,
until his coxswain responded with a reluctant grin.

Almost to himself Tyacke replied, 'We are not

95

out of the woods yet, Ben.' He tried to hide his relief from his friend as the haze-shrouded headland began to swing away across the quarter. 'But they'll cheer as loud as all the rest when the call comes. They've never seen a real battle, that's why.' But Simcox had gone to supervise his men again, and did not hear.

CHAPTER FIVE

'MUST THEY DIE FOR NOTHING?'

'If you would care to follow me, Sir Richard?' The young army captain stared at Bolitho as he strode up the sloping beach, as if he had just dropped from the moon.

Bolitho paused and glanced at the closely anchored vessels in the bay. Between them and the land every sort of boat was pulling back and forth, some disgorging red-coated soldiers into the shallows to wade ashore, others making heavy weather of it. They seemed loaded down with weapons and stores so that one or two looked in some danger of capsizing.

Bolitho saw *Miranda*'s longboat threading her way back to the schooner to await his next instructions. Tyacke would be only too glad to be out of this place, he thought.

If it was hot aboard ship it was doubly so ashore. The heat seemed to rise from the ground like a separate force, so that within minutes Bolitho's clothing was clinging to him. For the army's sake he was fully dressed in the frock coat and gold-laced

96

hat he had collected from *Themis* during their brief pause to inform Warren what was happening, and to pass his orders to the other captains.

He walked behind the young officer, watching for signs of success or delays in the army's progress so far. There were plenty of soldiers in evidence, working to haul powder and shot from the beach while others marched steadfastly in squads and platoons towards the hills. A few glanced at him as they passed, but he meant nothing to them. Some of them were very bronzed, as if they had come from garrisons in the Indies; others looked like raw recruits. Weighed down as they were with packs and weapons, their coats were already darkly patched with sweat.

Allday tilted his hat over his eyes and commented, 'Bloody shambles, if you asks me, Sir Richard.'

Bolitho heard the far-off bang of light artillery—English or Dutch it was impossible to tell. It seemed impartial and without menace, but the canvas-covered corpses awaiting burial along the rough coastal track told a different story.

The captain paused and pointed at some neat ranks of tents. 'My company lines are here, Sir Richard, but the General is not present.' When Bolitho said nothing he added, 'I am sure he will be back shortly.'

Somewhere a man screamed out in agony, and Bolitho guessed there was a field hospital here, too, with the headquarters company. Progress *was* slow. Otherwise the army surgeons would be beyond that forbidding-looking ridge, he decided.

The captain opened a tent flap and Bolitho ducked to enter. The contrast was unnerving. The

97

ground was covered by rugs and Bolitho imagined the challenge it must have been for the orderlies to find somewhere flat enough to lay them, and pitch this large tent so securely.

A grave-faced colonel, who had been seated in a folding campaign chair, rose to his feet and bowed his head.

'I command the Sixty-First, Sir Richard.' He took Bolitho's proffered hand and smiled. 'We knew of your presence here, but not *amongst* us of course!' He looked tired and strained. 'There was no time to receive you with due honours.'

Bolitho looked up and saw a singed hole in the top of the tent.

The colonel followed his glance. 'Last evening, Sir Richard. One of their marksmen got right through our pickets. Hoping for an important victim, no doubt.' He nodded to the orderly who had appeared with a tray of glasses. 'This may quench your thirst while you are waiting for the General.'

'Are the enemy well-prepared?'

'They are, Sir Richard, and they have all the advantages.' He frowned and added disdainfully, 'But they use methods I find unsoldierly. That marksman, for instance, was not in uniform, but dressed in rags which matched his surroundings. He shot two of my men before we ran him to earth. Not the kind of ethics I care for.'

Allday remarked, 'I think I sees him just now, Sir Richard, hanging from a tree.'

The colonel stared at him as if seeing him for the first time.

'What...?'

Bolitho said, 'Mr Allday is with *me*, Colonel.'

98

He watched as Allday took a tall glass of wine from the orderly and winked at him. 'Don't you stray too far, matey.' In his fist, the glass looked like a thimble.

Bolitho sipped the wine. It, like the General, travelled well.

The colonel walked to a folding table where several maps were laid out.

'The enemy falls back when pressed, Sir Richard—there seems no eagerness to stand and fight. It is a slow business all the same.' He shot Bolitho a direct glance. 'And if, as you say, we can expect no further support in men and supplies, I fear it will be months rather than weeks before we take Cape Town.'

Bolitho heard horses clattering amongst loose stones, the bark of commands and the slap of muskets from the sentries outside the tent. The horses would be glad to be on dry land again, Bolitho thought, even if nobody else was enjoying it.

The General entered and threw his hat and gloves on to a chair. He was a neat man with piercing blue eyes. A no-nonsense soldier who claimed that he asked nothing from his men that he could or would not do himself.

There were instructions; then the General suggested that the others should leave. Allday, with three glasses of wine under his belt, murmured, 'I'll be in earshot if you needs me, Sir Richard.'

As the flap fell across the entrance the General commented, 'Extraordinary fellow.'

'He's saved my life a few times, Sir David; my sanity a few times more.'

Surprisingly, some of the sternness left the

99

General's sun-reddened face.

'Then I could use a few thousand more like him, I can tell you!' The smile faded just as quickly. 'The landings went well. Commodore Popham worked miracles, and apart from the inevitable casualties it was very satisfactory.' He looked at Bolitho severely. 'And now I am told that I shall receive no reinforcements, that you even intend to strip the squadron of some of the frigates.'

Bolitho was reminded vividly of his friend Thomas Herrick. His eyes were that blue. Stubborn, loyal, hurt even. Was Herrick still his friend? Would he never accept his love for Catherine?

He said shortly, 'It is not merely *my* intention, Sir David!' Thinking of Herrick and the gulf which had come between them had put an edge to his voice. 'It is the King's own signature on those orders, not mine.'

'I wonder who guided his hand for him?'

Bolitho replied quietly, 'I did not hear that, Sir David.'

The General gave him a wry smile. 'Hear what, Sir Richard?'

Like two duellists who had changed their minds, they moved to the maps on the table.

Once, the General looked up and listened as distant gunfire echoed sullenly around the tent. It reminded Bolitho of surf on a reef.

Bolitho laid his own chart on top of the others and said, 'You are a soldier, I am not; but I know the importance, the vital necessity of supplies to an army in combat. I believe that the enemy expect to be reinforced. If that happens before you can take Cape Town, Sir David, what chances have you of

100

succeeding?'

The General did not answer for a full minute while he studied Bolitho's chart, and the notes which he had clipped to it.

Then he said heavily, 'Very little.' Some of his earlier sharpness returned. 'But the navy's task is to prevent it! Blockade the port, and fight off any would-be attempt to support the garrison.' It sounded like an accusation.

Bolitho stared at the chart, but saw only Warren's handful of ships. Each captain had his orders now. The three frigates would watch and patrol the Cape and the approaches, while the remaining two schooners maintained contact between them and the commodore. They might be lucky, but under cover of darkness it would not be too difficult for other vessels to slip past them and under the protection of the shore batteries.

And then the choice would remain as before. Attack into the bay and risk the combined fire of the batteries and the carefully moored ships—at best it would end in stalemate. The worst did not bear contemplating. If the army was forced to withdraw in defeat because of lack of supplies and the enemy's continued stubborn resistance, the effect would resound right across Europe. The crushing victory over the Combined Fleet at Trafalgar might even be cancelled out by the inability of the army to occupy Cape Town. France's unwilling allies would take fresh heart from it, and the morale in England would crumble with equal speed.

Bolitho said, 'I suspect that neither of us welcomed this mission, Sir David.'

The General turned as the young captain Bolitho

101

had seen before appeared at the entrance. '*Yes?*'

The captain said, 'A message from Major Browning, Sir David. He wishes to re-site his artillery.'

'Send word, will you? Do nothing until I reach there. Then tell an orderly to fetch my horse.'

He turned and said, 'The news you have brought me is no small setback, Sir Richard.' He gave him a level stare. 'I am relying on you, not because I doubt the ability of my officers and men, but because I have no damned alternative! I know the importance of this campaign—all eyes will be watching it as a foretaste of what lies ahead. For make no mistake, despite all the triumphs at sea, they will be as nought until the English foot-soldier plants his boots on the enemy's own shores.'

There were hushed voices outside the tent, the dragging steps of a horse being led reluctantly back to duty.

The General tossed back the glass of brandy someone had brought for him and picked up his hat and gloves. They were probably still warm from his last ride.

He gave a wry smile. 'A bit like Nelson yourself, y'know. He used to think he was just as able a brigadier ashore as he was a good sailor afloat!'

Bolitho said coldly, 'I do recall that he captured Bastia and Calvi with his sailors, and not the army.'

'*Touché!*' The General led the way from the tent and Bolitho saw more soldiers marching past, their boots churning up clouds of red dust.

The General said, 'Look at 'em. Must they die for nothing?'

Bolitho saw Allday hurrying down the beach to signal for the boat. He answered, 'If you knew me,

102

Sir David, you would not ask that.'

The blue eyes flashed like ice as the General lifted one foot to the stirrup. 'It is because I know *of* you, Sir Richard; and I am not asking. For the first time in my career, I am *begging*!'

The colonel joined Bolitho near the water's edge, and together they watched the boat pulling strongly around an anchored storeship.

He said, 'I have never seen him like that before, Sir Richard.'

Allday was pointing to where he wanted the boat to come in, but his mind was still with Bolitho. What he had not heard, he could guess. Whoever knew the rights and wrongs of all this must have realised the hopeless task they had given him.

He heard the colonel snap his boots together as he said, 'I hope we shall meet again, Sir Richard.'

Bolitho turned and looked up the shelving beach. 'Be certain of it, Colonel. In Cape Town or in hell, only greater powers will decide which!'

The boat had almost reached the anchored schooner when Bolitho turned and spoke to Allday again.

'You remember *Achates*, Allday?'

The big coxswain grimaced and touched his chest. 'Not likely to forget that little lot, Sir Richard!' He tried to grin, to shrug it off. 'But that were four years past.'

Bolitho touched his arm. 'I did not mean to bring it back, old friend, but I had an idea concerning it. There was a time when I thought we had lost "Old Katie" just as surely as *Hyperion*.'

Allday stared at his grave features, his spine suddenly like ice despite the strong sunlight. 'A *fireship*, d'you mean, sir?' He spoke almost in a

103

croak, then glanced at the stroke oarsman to make certain he was not listening as he threw himself back on his loom.

Bolitho seemed to be thinking aloud. 'It might prove useless. I realise what I am asking others to do.' He stared abeam as a fish leaped from the water. 'But set against the cost in lives and ships...'

Allday twisted round and looked at the boat's coxswain. But the man's eyes were fixed on the final approach, his knuckles whitening on the tiller bar. It was unlikely that *Miranda* would carry a flag-officer again. He would be fully aware of the consequences if he ruined it.

Not one of them in the boat would realise what agony Bolitho was going through, nor understand if they did.

Bolitho said, 'I recall what Mr Simcox said about the wind. Little use to us maybe, but it might entice the enemy to cut and run for it.'

He turned as the schooner's masts swept above them. 'They will have to be volunteers.'

Allday bit his lip. These were not Bolitho's men, but strangers. They had not followed his flag when they had broken the enemy's line with all hell coming adrift around them. He could remember that other time at San Felipe as clearly as yesterday. *Achates* at her moorings, and then suddenly the approaching ship bursting into flames, bearing down on them while they stared with horror at the inferno. There was only one thing worse than being snared by a fireship, Allday thought grimly, and that was being the crew of one. *Volunteers?* They were as likely as a virgin on Portsmouth Hard.

Bolitho reached up for the side as the boat

104

lurched against the hull and the seamen tossed their oars, like white bones in the sunshine.

He looked down at Allday's troubled face and said calmly, 'It is not a question of choice this time. For there is none.' Then he was up and over the bulwark. Allday followed and saw him already talking with Tyacke, who mercifully had his terrible scars turned away.

After what he had suffered, it was unlikely that Tyacke would offer much support.

★   ★   ★

Commodore Arthur Warren watched with open astonishment, while Bolitho tossed his crumpled shirt to Ozzard before slipping into a clean one. The little servant was fussing round him and almost got knocked over as Bolitho hurried between the table and the stern windows of *Themis*'s great cabin.

Before *Themis* began to swing again to her cable, Bolitho had seen the busy activity aboard the nearest transport. The captured slaver was hidden on her seaward side, and he wondered how long it would take to complete the arrangements he had ordered.

Bolitho had never understood his own instincts; how he could *sense* that time was in short supply. He felt it now, and it was vital that Warren knew what was happening.

He said, 'You will have the schooner *Dove* to repeat your signals to the offshore patrol.' In his mind he could see the thirty-six gun frigate *Searcher* tacking back and forth somewhere beyond the horizon, Warren's first line of defence should an enemy approach from the west. The second schooner was retained to keep the same contact with the main squadron at Saldanha Bay. It was up to each captain, from the senior, Varian, to the lieutenants who commanded the schooners, to use their own initiative if the wind changed against them, or they sighted any vessel which was obviously hostile. In his written orders Bolitho had stressed his requirements precisely and finally. There would be no heroics, no ship-to-ship actions without informing the commodore.

The anchorage looked strangely deserted and even more vulnerable, and he wondered if Warren were regretting the removal of his aftermost cannon to replace them with useless 'quakers'. It was too late for regrets now.

Warren said, 'I don't like it, Sir Richard. If you fall in this venture, or are taken prisoner, how will I explain?'

Bolitho looked at him impassively. *Is that all it means?* Perhaps Varian was right after all.

He answered, 'I have left some letters.' He saw Jenour turn from an open port. 'But have no fear.' He failed to conceal his bitterness. 'There are some who would not grieve too much!'

Allday entered through a screen door and handed Bolitho his old sword. He ran his eyes critically over Bolitho's appearance and nodded.

Bolitho smiled. 'Satisfied?'

'Aye. But it don't signify that I've changed my mind!'

Allday too had changed into his fine blue jacket and nankeen breeches. He glanced at Bolitho's other sword on the rack and remarked to Ozzard, 'Take good care o' that, matey.' He patted the little man's bony shoulder. 'Like the last time,

106

remember?'

Bolitho walked to the table again and stared at the chart. Captain Poland's *Truculent* should be on her station to the west of Table Bay, ready to rendezvous with *Miranda* and her dangerous consort. Varian's *Zest*, the most powerful of the frigates, would be standing to the south-west. If the attack was successful, it would be Varian's task to chase and take any vessels which tried to put to sea to escape the fireship.

Whether the enemy recognised the *Albacora* or not made little difference to the attack. Only to those who remained with the fireship until the last moment would it be important.

The marine sentry called from the door, 'Surgeon, *sir*!'

The man who entered was a thin, unsmiling individual whose skin was as pale as Warren's.

He said abruptly, 'I am sorry to intrude, sir, but *Miranda*'s midshipman wishes to return to his ship immediately.'

Warren frowned, irritated by the interruption. 'Well, that is for you to say, surely. I am too busy for—'

Bolitho asked, 'Is he recovered enough?'

Confused by the presence of the admiral dressed as he was now in his proper uniform, instead of the casual open shirt, the surgeon stammered, 'It was a severe wound, sir, but he is young and very determined.' His mouth closed in a thin line, as if he had just decided not to say what he had been about to add. It was not his affair.

'Then he can come over to *Miranda* with us. See to it, Stephen.' Bolitho saw the undisguised relief on the flag-lieutenant's features and added, 'Did you think I would leave you yet again?' He tried to smile. 'If Allday is my right arm, you surely must be my left!'

He thought of Jenour's face when he had boarded the flagship only hours ago. A courier brigantine had paused at the anchorage and had sent over a despatch bag without even stopping long enough to anchor. She had been so fast that it was little wonder *Miranda* had not seen any sign of her.

Jenour had dropped his voice as they had walked aft to the cabin. 'Inside your official envelope there is ... a letter ... for you, Sir Richard.'

Bolitho had turned on him. 'Tell me, Stephen—I beg of you!'

Warren had been coming towards them, dragging his feet, trying to control his painful breathing, and Jenour had answered quickly, 'It is from your lady, Sir Richard.' He had recognised Bolitho's remaining uncertainty and clarified, 'From Falmouth.'

'Thank God.' At long last. The first letter. He had half expected it might be from Belinda. With distance to give her confidence she might have been demanding more money, or suggesting another reconciliation for the sake of appearances.

The letter was in his pocket now. Somehow, even in *Miranda*'s crowded world, he would find a private place where he could read it, feel her presence, hear her voice. When this was over he would write to her again, tell her all the longings he had built up since their wretched parting.

He looked towards the glittering water beyond the stern windows. *If I should fall* ... Then there would be the other letter which was locked in his strongbox.

Bolitho raised his arm to allow Allday to clip the old family sword to his belt. So many times; and too many had seemed like the last.

Bolitho left the cabin and paused where Ozzard was waiting with his hat. 'When we are finished with this matter we shall return to Falmouth.' He saw the anxiety in Ozzard's eyes and added gently, 'You are better off here.' He looked across his rounded shoulders. 'Commodore Warren will see that you are taken care of.'

He hurried to the entry port and glanced at the silent figures who had paused in their work to watch him leave. How different from England, he thought. These men were probably glad to see him go, as if by remaining their own lives would be more at risk.

The sun was dipping very slowly, like a gigantic red ball which quivered above its own reflection and made the horizon glisten like a heated wire.

Commodore Warren doffed his hat and the calls trilled, while the flagship's reduced section of Royal Marines slapped their muskets in salute.

Then he lowered himself to the longboat and got a brief glimpse of the midshipman, who was sitting crammed beside Jenour and Allday.

'Good day—Mr Segrave, is it not?' The youth stammered something, but at that moment the boat was cast off with oars pulling and backing, steered away from the side.

Jenour peered astern, glad he was not remaining in *Themis* with Yovell and Ozzard. He touched the lanyard on his fine sword and lifted his chin as if in defiance.

Allday was watching the fiery sunset. It had taken on a new meaning, a threatening aspect, with

Death the winner one way or the other.

To break the silence Bolitho asked, 'What else do you have in your important-looking bag, Stephen?'

Jenour tore his mind from the letter he was writing in his mind to his parents in Southampton.

'For *Miranda*, Sir Richard.' He could guess what Bolitho was thinking and recalled the letter he had given to him. Bolitho had taken it as if it were life itself. It should have surprised him that his admiral could be two such different men: the one who inspired and commanded, and the other who needed that lady's love so much, but could not hide it as he did his other fears and hopes.

Lieutenant Tyacke waited by the ladder and touched his hat as Bolitho climbed aboard. He even managed an ironic smile as he looked at Jenour and Midshipman Segrave. 'Two bad pennies together, eh, Sir Richard?' He took the package from Jenour and said, 'The *Albacora* is all but ready, sir.' They stared across the darkening water to the other, untidy schooner. In the sunset's glow she looked as if she were already burning from within.

'We did our best, sir. But not being pierced for gunports to draw the flames, we had to cut makeshift ones to the main hold an' the like.' He nodded grimly. 'She'll burn like a torch when need be.'

He turned away; his men were waiting for his attention. Both schooners would sail at nightfall, slink away from the other ships like assassins. Thinking aloud, Tyacke said, 'With God's help we should rendezvous with *Truculent* at dawn. Then you'll have a mite more comfort in *her* than I can offer you, sir!'

Bolitho looked at him and saw the red glow on

110

the ruined face. Like melted wax. As if it had just happened.

He said simply, 'It is not comfort I need. Your ship has offered me what I want most.'

Tyacke asked with a touch of wariness, 'And what may that be, sir?'

'An *example*, Mr Tyacke. How all ships could be, large or small, offered the right trust and leadership.'

'If you will excuse me, sir.' He turned awkwardly. 'There is much to do.'

Bolitho gazed at the sun sliding into the horizon and the sea. There should be steam or an explosion, so powerful was its majesty, and menace.

Midshipman Segrave was groping beneath the companion hatch when Simcox found him and said, 'You'll have to sleep rough tonight, my lad. We're somewhat overfull till I can discover *Truculent*'s whereabouts.' The lighter mood eluded him and he said, 'Bob Jay told me about your other injuries.' He saw the youth staring at him in the gloom. ''E 'ad to. It was 'is duty to me.'

Segrave looked down at his clenched fists. 'You had no right...'

'Don't you lecture me about rights, *Mister* Segrave! I've had a bloody gutful o' them since I first donned the King's coat, so let's 'ave no more of 'em, see?' His face was only inches from Segrave's as he added vehemently, 'You was whipped like a dog to have scars like that, Bob Jay said. *Bully you*, did they? Some poxy scum who thought you was lettin' them down, was that it?' He saw the youth bow his head and nod. Afterwards Simcox thought he had never witnessed such despair. He said, 'Well, it's in the past now. Bob Jay'll never forget

111

you saved 'is skin.' He touched his shoulder and added roughly, 'I 'ad to tell the Cap'n.'

Segrave shivered, wiping his face with his forearm.

'That was your *duty* too.' But there was no sarcasm or resentment. There was simply nothing at all.

Simcox watched him with concern. 'All right then, son?'

Segrave looked at him, his eyes very bright in the lantern's glow from the cabin.

'You don't understand. I was told aboard *Themis*. I am to return to my old ship as soon as we leave the Cape.' He got to his feet and made for the companion ladder. 'So you see, it was a lie, like everything else!'

★   ★   ★

Later, as darkness folded over the anchorage and the stars were still too feeble to separate sea from sky, Bolitho sat at the cabin table, half listening to the muffled commands from the deck, the creak of the windlass as the cable was hove short. Jay, the master's mate, was across in *Albacora* with a small prize crew, so all hands would be working doubly hard and standing watch-and-watch until the rendezvous was made.

Tyacke peered through the door. 'Ready to proceed, Sir Richard.' He waited questioningly. 'Any further orders?'

Something about him was different.

Bolitho asked, 'What is troubling you?'

Tyacke said steadily, 'I received orders in the despatch bag, sir. Both Mr Simcox and Segrave are

112

leaving my command after this is over and done with.' He tried to smile, but it made him look desperate. 'Ben Simcox is a good friend, and I've come to feel differently about the midshipman since ...' He did not go on.

'I understand.' Bolitho saw the surprise on Tyacke's maimed face.

'Because I am what I am, is that it?' He shook his head and Tyacke caught a quick glimpse of the terrible scar which was only partly hidden by the lock of hair. 'I had another flag-lieutenant once. He used to call me and my captains, *We Happy Few*. By God, Mr Tyacke, there are precious few of us now! Oh yes, I know what it is to find a friend, then lose him in the twinkling of an eye. Sometimes I think it is best to know nobody, and to care for nothing.'

Somebody called from the deck, 'Th' slaver's under way, sir!'

'I—I am sorry, sir.' Tyacke had to leave, but wanted to remain.

'There is no need.' Bolitho met his gaze and smiled. 'And know this. I *do* care. And when I call for volunteers tomorrow—'

Tyacke turned to the ladder. 'You'll not lack them, Sir Richard. Not in this ship.' Then he was gone, and moments later came the cry, *'Anchor's aweigh!'*

Bolitho sat for several minutes, his ears deaf to the din of rudder and canvas as the schooner curtsied round, free of the land once more.

Why had he spoken to Tyacke like that? He smiled at his own answer. Because he needed him and his men more than they would ever know, or understand.

With great care he opened the letter, then stared with surprise as a dried ivy leaf fell to the table.

Her writing seemed to blur as he held the letter closer to the swaying lantern.

My darling Richard,

This leaf is from your house and my home—

It was enough. The remainder he would read later when he was quite alone.

CHAPTER SIX

WHILE OTHERS DARE...

Lieutenant James Tyacke clung to the weather rail and squinted through the spray as Bolitho appeared by the companionway.

'Sail in sight, sir!'

Bolitho clutched a backstay and nodded. 'I heard the call, Mr Tyacke. You've a good man aloft!'

It had been dark to all intents when he had caught the lookout's cry. Even in so small a vessel it had been difficult, and to anyone less experienced the overnight change in wind and weather would have appeared astonishing. The wind had veered several points and now came from the north, or near enough. With her bowsprit pointing due east, *Miranda* appeared to be lying hard over, the sea occasionally licking above the lee bulwark; when it touched your skin it felt like ice.

Bolitho peered to where the horizon should be, but could see nothing. Only the creaming wave-crests and the blacker depths of fast-moving troughs. It would make the two schooners' approach doubly challenging. A lantern was shuttered across the tumbling water, and Bolitho guessed that the captured slaver was less than half a cable away. It was a mark of Tyacke's and Jay's experience that they had managed to keep in close company all through the night. When dawn finally broke the seamen would be at their worst, he thought. Worn out by trimming sails, reefing and changing tack over and over again.

Tyacke shouted, 'Time to close with *Albacora*, sir.' He was watching him in the darkness, his eyes well accustomed to the night while Bolitho was still trying to adjust to it.

It was strange to realise that the lookout could not only see the rising dawn but the sails of another vessel. It had to be *Truculent*. If it was not, it could only be the enemy.

'Deck there! She's a frigate, sir. Hove-to.'

Bolitho heard Simcox release a sigh. So it was *Truculent*. Captain Poland could justly be proud of another successful rendezvous.

Someone called, 'Th' slaver's come about, sir. 'Er boat's in the water.'

Tyacke muttered, 'Lucky it's no further. It'll be a rough haul for the oarsmen.'

Bolitho touched Tyacke's arm and said, 'About the volunteers?'

Tyacke faced him. 'That deserter was sent over from the flagship with the prize crew. There was a Royal Marine too, for all the use *he'll* be.' He spoke with the unreasonable contempt of sailors for members of the Corps.

'Is that all?'

Tyacke shrugged. 'It's better this way, sir. My ship will provide the remainder.' His teeth showed

115

faintly through the shadows as the first hint of light fingered the horizon. 'I spoke to them myself, sir. Men I know and trust.' He added bluntly, 'More to the point, who trust *me*.'

'Mr Simcox knows what he must do?'

Tyacke did not answer directly. He was watching the approaching boat as it lifted and plunged like a winged fish while it fought around the stern to find shelter beneath *Miranda*'s lee. He said, 'Mr Simcox will remain in *Miranda*.' He paused as if expecting to be challenged.

Bolitho said, 'I placed you in charge. It must be your decision.'

Simcox suddenly lurched towards them. '*I must protest!* I know these waters, and in any case—' Tyacke seized his arm and spun him round. 'Do as you're bloody told, man! I command here! Now attend to that boat!'

Bolitho could barely see the acting-master in the gloom, but felt his disbelief and hurt as if Tyacke had struck him.

Tyacke said heavily, 'Ben is a fine sailor. If he survives this bloody war, begging your pardon, sir—and I said *if*—he'll have a career, something waiting for him even if they pitch him on the beach with all the others.' He gestured angrily towards the confusion in the waist of the schooner. 'God damn you, Morgan, catch a turn there, or you'll stove in the bloody boat!'

Bolitho had not heard him berate any of his seamen before. He was trying to get it out of himself, to forget what he had said and done to his only friend.

Figures lurched through the darkness and then Jay, the master's mate, appeared by the tiller.

116

'All prepared, sir! Ready to change crews!' He glanced quickly from Tyacke to Simcox, who was standing by the foremast, then asked, 'Ben not ready yet, sir?'

Tyacke said harshly, 'I am going in his place. So stay with him.' For a moment his voice softened. 'And the ship.'

Another figure appeared and Bolitho saw it was the midshipman, Segrave.

Tyacke murmured, 'He volunteered, sir, and I might need another officer, if things go badly.' He said more loudly, 'Are you still eager, Mr Segrave? You can still fall out—no one would blame you after what you did for Mr Jay.'

The youth's face seemed to grow out of the shadows as the first pale sunlight reflected from the dripping sails and rigging. He said firmly, 'I *want* to go, sir.'

The lookout's cry made them look up again. 'She's *Truculent* right enough, sir!' A further pause, then, 'She's shaken out some reefs an' she's comin' about.'

Tyacke said, 'She'll be sending a boat for you, sir.'

'Yes.' Bolitho saw Allday with the small bag of clothing which they had brought with them from *Themis*. So like those other occasions, when suddenly there is no more time left. Lastly came Jenour, yawning hugely. He had slept through everything. The other figures had disappeared into the pitching boat alongside; Tyacke was eager to leave. To get it over.

He said in a calm voice, 'I'll not let you down, sir.'

Bolitho took his hand. It was hard like Thomas

117

Herrick's. He replied quietly, 'You wouldn't know *how*, Mr Tyacke.'

Tyacke swung one leg over the bulwark, but paused as Simcox pulled himself along the side heedless of the sea sluicing along the scuppers, dragging at his legs.

'You want me, Ben?'

Simcox staggered and almost fell headlong, but Tyacke caught him with his arm. Watching from the mainmast bitts Bolitho saw and understood. It was like a last embrace.

Tyacke said roughly, 'You've too much to lose, Ben, and you know it. You'll make a fine master, with a proper captain to take care of, eh?'

Simcox said something but it was lost in the drumming rigging and the turmoil alongside.

When Bolitho looked again Tyacke had gone and the boat was surging away once more, spray flying from the oar blade like ragged silk.

Bolitho said, 'Get under way, Mr Simcox. The sooner we can meet with *Truculent*, the faster we can—' He left the rest unsaid.

Allday said gruffly, 'He's all aback, an' that's no error!'

Bolitho called, 'Mr Simcox, once I am in *Truculent* you will follow the fireship.' He had not used her name. By accident or design, he wondered? Perhaps to make Simcox accept her brutal role. What it might well mean for her crew.

Simcox stared at him. 'Pretend to give chase, Sir Richard?' He sounded vague.

'Yes. It is an old trick but it may well work, and give Mr Tyacke the opportunity to stand closer to the enemy.'

He glanced at his cuff and saw the gold lace

suddenly clear and bright; even felt the first warmth as the sunlight rolled down from the horizon.

Jenour asked, 'What *are* their chances, Sir Richard?'

Bolitho looked at him, steadily. 'Not good. With the wind against them they will have to lose valuable time tacking back and forth. After Mr Tyacke has fired the fuses he will have to pull away in the boat and head for the shore. They will fall into Dutch hands, but with our army so near I feel certain they will not be harmed.' He saw the doubt on Jenour's young face. 'If Mr Tyacke fails and is too late to get away, we will lose twelve good men. In a frontal attack we could lose every ship and every soul in the squadron.'

Allday gazed towards the land. 'Not a choice *I'd* care to make, Sir Richard.'

Bolitho pushed the lock of hair from his forehead. Allday understood. One man or a thousand; life or death; it was a decision which was damned either way.

Allday added, 'I'll lay odds at the Admiralty they never gives it a thought, nor lose a wink of sleep.'

Bolitho saw patches of cloud scudding out from the land and imagined he could feel dust between his teeth.

Allday was studying him grimly and said, 'I was a mite bothered back there, Sir Richard. Knowin' you, I did think once or twice that *you* might take charge o' the fireship.'

Bolitho looked at Simcox, who was still staring after *Albacora* as she laid herself over on her new course.

'Not this time, old friend.'

Allday watched *Truculent*'s pyramid of pale

119

canvas rising above the departing shadows while she bore down on the schooner.

His worry had been real enough, until he had remembered what Bolitho had said when they had been together. *I want to go home*. It was as if the words had been torn from his throat. Allday had shared most things with Bolitho but he had never heard him speak like that before. He released a huge sigh. But they were still a long way from England.

Even as the deck planking began to steam in the first morning warmth, *Truculent* went about and then lowered the gig smartly from her quarter.

Bolitho waited for Simcox to have his depleted company piped to halliards and braces to heave-to and await the boat, then said, 'I wish you well, Mr Simcox. I have written a report which will not come amiss at your final interview.'

Simcox nodded and replied, 'I am grateful, Sir Richard.' He struggled for the right words. 'Y'see, Sir Richard, we was friends, an' I know why he's doin' this for me.'

Bolitho said, 'If anyone can do it, *he* can.' He thought of that last handshake, firm and hard like Herrick's; and of Herrick's *Lady Luck* in whom he had always believed so fervently.

He saw the frigate's boat pulling strongly towards them, a lieutenant trying to stand upright in the sternsheets while the hull bucked beneath him. So like Poland, he thought, everything correct and beyond criticism.

To Simcox he said, 'I hope we meet again. You have a good company and a fine little ship.' Even as he spoke he knew what was wrong. It was better not to know them, see and recognise their faces,

120

before you made a decision which could kill them all. He had told himself often enough in the past, and after *Hyperion*'s end he had sworn it to himself again.

'Stand by, on deck!'

Bolitho nodded to those by the bulwark. Old Elias Archer the gunner, Jay the master's mate who would probably take Simcox's place when he quit the ship. Faces he had come to know in so short a while. He noticed that Sperry the boatswain was not here. It was good to know he would be with Tyacke. He wondered why the midshipman had insisted on going with the prize crew when he had just received orders to return to his old ship. Perhaps the one riddle answered the other? In Tyacke's hands they might manage to reach the shore. He shut it from his thoughts like slamming a door.

'And I shall not forget the beer, Mr Simcox!'

Then he was down and into the boat, gripping the lieutenant's shoulder and trying not to allow his legs to be caught by his sword.

Only Allday saw his face when he made that last carefree comment.

He was also the only one who knew what it had cost him.

*   *   *

'So this is where it happened?' Tyacke stooped to peer into the *Albacora*'s cabin. 'It's like a pig-sty!'

Midshipman Segrave darted a quick glance at the bunk as if he expected to see the naked slave-girl still chained there. Like the rest of the crew's quarters, the cabin was full of inflammable material

121

of every sort which had been piled or thrown on top of the original master's possessions. The whole schooner stank of it. Oil, old canvas and oakum soaked in grease, wood dipped in tar which had been gathered from Warren's two transports: anything which would transform *Albacora* into a raging torch. Segrave felt the air playing around his face from one of the jagged vent holes which had been cut in the deck to fan the flames. For the first time since he had pushed himself forward to volunteer he knew true fear.

Tyacke's voice helped to reassure him. He sounded completely absorbed in his own thoughts, almost matter-of-fact. As if he accepted the inevitability of his fate with the same coolness as he had changed roles with Simcox.

Segrave said, 'It seems easier, sir.'

'What?' Again, so distant. 'Yes, we're closer inshore. But the wind's as much an enemy as before.' He sat down unexpectedly on a cask and looked at the youth, his awful wound in shadow. 'Mr Simcox told me about your other injuries.' He eyed him calmly, as if there was nothing to do, with all the time in the world to do it. 'Beat you, did they? Because you were no use on board?'

Segrave clenched his fists. Remembering the first time, and all the others which were to follow. The captain had been uninterested in what went on in the midshipmen's berth, and as he had been heard to tell his first lieutenant on several occasions, he was only concerned with *results*. Another lieutenant had been chosen to divide the midshipmen into teams, and would set one against the other in all drills and exercises in seamanship, gunnery and boatwork. There were penalties for the laggards,

122

minor awards for the winners.

Tyacke was not far from the truth in his casual summing-up. Except that it was persecution of the worst kind. Segrave had been stripped naked and bent over a gun and flogged without mercy either by the lieutenant or some of the midshipmen. They had humiliated him in any way they could, had worked off a kind of madness in their cruelty. It was doubtful if he would ever lose the scars, any more than a sailor flogged at the gratings.

Segrave found that he was blurting it out in short, desperate sentences although he did not recall beginning to speak at all.

Tyacke said nothing until he had fallen silent. Then he said, 'In any ship where such brutality is tolerated it is the fault of her captain. It is the way of things. Disinterest in how his lieutenants administer discipline or enforce his orders must lie at his door. No lieutenant would dare to act in this fashion without the full knowledge of his captain.' His eyes gleamed in the shadows. 'The orders to return to your old ship in due course prompted you to volunteer, is that it?' When Segrave remained silent he said harshly, 'By God, boy, you would have done better to kill that lieutenant, for the end will likely be the same, without the satisfaction!' He reached across suddenly and gripped his shoulder. 'It was your choice.' He turned away and a shaft of sunlight filtered through the filthy skylight to lay bare his disfigurement. 'As it was mine.'

He twisted round as feet pattered along the deck overhead, and the boatswain's hoarse bellow chased some of the crew to their stations for altering course.

Segrave said simply, 'I'm glad I came, sir.'

123

He did not cringe as Tyacke pushed his face nearer and said, *'Well spoken!'*

They went on deck together, and after the foul stench below the air tasted like wine.

Tyacke glanced at the streaming masthead pendant, then at the compass. The wind was as before, but as the youth had noticed, it was less violent in the shelter of the land.

As he removed a telescope from a rack beside the compass box he glanced quickly at the men on deck. Including himself there were twelve of them aboard. He saw the seaman named Swayne, the deserter, hauling on a halliard to take out some slack. He moved quickly and easily, a proper Jack, Tyacke thought. Now that he had accepted what he had done by coming here with the others, he even looked cheerful. While there was life there was still hope. Aboard the flagship an award of two hundred lashes or more, with the only other alternative being an agonising dance at the yardarm, left no room for hope.

Tyacke stared at the other volunteer, a Royal Marine named Buller, under a similar sentence for striking a sergeant after getting fighting drunk on pilfered rum. When it came to such matters the 'Royals' could be merciless with one of their own.

The other faces he knew well. He saw the squat figure of George Sperry the *Miranda*'s boatswain, calling to two hands who were working with chain slings on the foreyard. Once the fire was started, the tarred rigging would ignite in seconds, the sails too if the deed were done too soon. Chain would keep their sails in place just that much longer. Tyacke's face twisted into a grimace. Or so he had been told. Like all sailors Tyacke hated the danger of fire more

124

than anything. He touched his burned face and wondered if he would break at the last moment; knowing in the same breath he would not.

He looked at Segrave, his hair ruffling in the wind, and thought of his faltering voice as he had stammered out his story. Tyacke had found his rage mounting to match the boy's shame. Those others should be the ones to feel shame, he thought. There would always be scum like that, but only where their cruelty was condoned.

Tyacke raised his glass and trained it past the midshipman's shoulder. The land was hard abeam, the very tip of the point which guarded the entrance to the bay reaching out rocky and green in the pale sunshine. He felt the deck planking growing warm again; very soon the whole schooner would be as dry as tinder. God help them if the enemy had sited some long-range guns as far out as the point. He doubted it; it was an impossible place for a landing party to scale or even disembark. But the doubt remained. No ship was a match for land artillery, especially those with heated shot. Tyacke forced his mind away from the picture of a red-hot ball slamming into the crammed hull beneath his shoes.

'Deck there!' The lookout was pointing astern. '*Miranda*'s tackin' to the point, sir!'

Tyacke turned his glass towards the open sea, where the water was a deeper blue as if unwilling to give up the night.

He felt a lump in his throat as he saw *Miranda*'s huge courses swinging above the waves, her single topsail flapping wildly as she began to change tack. To all appearances it might well look as if she was in pursuit of the shabby *Albacora*.

'Shake out all reefs, Mr Sperry! Lively there!' He

125

saw the boatswain give his broken-toothed grin as he added, 'We don't want a King's ship to catch us!' But he turned away in case Sperry saw, and understood, the lie.

He said to Segrave, 'Lend a hand at the helm. As far as I can calculate we shall have to make good some ten miles before we can attempt a final approach.'

Segrave watched him as he voiced his thoughts aloud. He found he could do it now without revulsion. There was something compelling about the tall lieutenant, and something frightening too.

Tyacke waved the telescope towards the full breadth of the bay as the point of land appeared to slide across the larboard quarter, like the opening of a giant gateway.

'We shall beat up to the nor'-east where the bottom shelves to a few fathoms. The sort of thing any ship's master might do if he was being chased by a man-o'-war. Then we'll come about and lay her on the starboard tack and run straight for 'em.' He glanced at Segrave's sensitive features. 'That's if they're still there, of course.'

Tyacke rubbed his chin and wished he had had a shave. The idea made him smile. As if it mattered now! He recalled the vice-admiral's coxswain, Allday, with the morning ritual. He thought also of his own private talks with Bolitho. Such an easy man to speak with, to share confidences. Like the time when Bolitho had asked him about his face and the Nile, when he had found himself answering without his usual defence and resentment.

And it was all true. There was no falseness in Bolitho, no using men as mere tools to complete some plan, or hiding indifference behind his rank.

126

'Stand by to alter course, Mr Segrave.' He saw him start with surprise. 'In a minute or so we shall steer nor'-east, so watch the mains'l no less than the compass!'

Segrave swallowed hard then joined the helmsman who acknowledged him almost shyly. Segrave saw that it was the young seaman named Dwyer, the one who had tried to tie up his wound in the cabin beneath them.

Dwyer said, 'We'll manage well enough, eh, Mr Segrave?'

Segrave nodded and discovered he could even offer a smile. 'We shall.'

Tyacke turned as a shot echoed across the water, and was in time to see a faint puff of smoke shred away from *Miranda*'s bows. Simcox had started to play his part. It was to be hoped he did not over-play it and outrun the *Albacora* as *Miranda* had done before.

Then he returned attention to the sailing of the fireship; but even as he signalled for Sperry to put two of his hard-pressed men on the foremast boom, he found himself thinking of the girl he had known in Portsmouth. *Marion.* He dashed the sweat from his eyes with his grubby shirt sleeve and believed for an instant that he had said her name aloud. *If only ...* Another shot echoed over the glittering water, and from a corner of his eye Tyacke saw the four-pound ball jag into the sea a good cable astern.

'Steady she goes, sir! Nor'-east it is!' It was strange to hear Segrave call out when he was usually so quiet and withdrawn.

Tyacke glanced at him sadly. *We are both scarred, inwardly or out.*

Spray dashed over the side and swept over the

127

patched and dirty deck like a tide. Tyacke saw the boatswain blink as another shot banged out astern, and the ball ploughed down a bit closer than the previous one. He glanced at the skylight and Tyacke knew he was thinking about the woman he had satisfied his lust with in the cabin. *We all have only memories now.*

Tyacke gazed along the busy deck as the schooner leaned over still further under her full press of sail.

Perhaps Marion would read about it someday. He gave a bitter smile. *My last command.*

★   ★   ★

Captain Daniel Poland remained a little apart from Bolitho as he stood by the cabin table, and used some dividers to measure off the calculations on his chart.

Bolitho said, half to himself, 'As far as we know, there have been no new arrivals in the bay. If there had been, either you or Captain Varian in *Zest* would likely have sighted them. Likewise, the big ships and frigate must still be at anchor.' He looked up in time to see Poland's doubtful expression. 'Don't you agree?'

Poland responded, 'It is a big area, Sir Richard. Four times the size of Table Bay.' He faltered under the grey stare. 'But as you say, it is perhaps unlikely.'

Bolitho watched the sunlight fanning through *Truculent*'s stern windows, swinging across the cabin like fiery bars as the frigate changed tack yet again.

Poland bit his lip with annoyance as someone or

something fell heavily on the deck above. *'Clumsy oafs!'*

Bolitho half-smiled. Maybe it was better to be like Poland. Caring only for the immediate and the things he knew best.

He tugged out his watch and studied it. Tyacke should be standing into his proper position by now, *Miranda* too. It was still stark in his mind, the way Tyacke had changed places with his friend. But it was more than a gesture to save his friend, to cast himself away. It was the act of a leader; what he had seen others do without a thought for the cost of it.

It did not occur to Bolitho that it was exactly what he would have done in Tyacke's position.

Jenour, who had been moving restlessly by the stern windows, straightened up and exclaimed, 'Gunfire, Sir Richard!'

Bolitho gave a last lingering glance over the chart. 'So it was, Stephen.' He looked around the cabin which had been his hiding-place on the passage from England. From Catherine. After *Miranda* it was like a ship-of-the-line. He faced Poland as feet clattered along the passageway towards the screen door.

'While others dare, we must wait, Captain.' His own words depressed him, and he added shortly, 'You may beat to quarters when convenient.' He touched his hip as if to find his sword. 'Tell Allday—'

Allday padded across the cabin. 'I'm here, Sir Richard.' He grinned as Bolitho raised his arm for him to fix the scabbard in place. 'Like always!'

Another far-off shot brought Allday's words into sharp focus and Bolitho said quietly, 'I am depending on it.'

Lieutenant Tyacke reluctantly lowered his glass. It would not be sensible to be seen watching the anchored ships rather than the pursuing *Miranda*. But in those last brief seconds he had seen the two large ships, and they certainly had all the appearances of Dutch Indiamen. The most important factor was that they were not moving with the wind and current. So Bolitho's first impression had been right. They were anchored fore-and-aft to provide two fixed batteries of guns against any attacker, which would be in trouble enough beating against the northerly wind.

Dwyer exclaimed admiringly, 'God, look at 'er *go*, Mr Segrave!' He was staring across the quarter at *Miranda*'s bulging sails as she came up into the wind yet again, cutting away the distance still further so that Segrave imagined he could see Simcox aft by the tiller, his unruly hair waving in the wind.

Another puff of smoke from her bow-chaser and this time the ball slammed down just a boat's length clear. Some of the spray pattered across the deck and Sperry cursed violently. 'God damn you, Elias Archer. If you lays another ball like that I'll not forgive 'ee.'

Segrave licked his dry lips. Like Dwyer, the boatswain seemed to have forgotten for the moment what they were attempting to do; that it was unlikely he would get a chance to argue with *Miranda*'s gunner ever again.

A lookout clinging in the foremast shrouds yelled, '*Guardboat, sir!*'

Tyacke was watching the sails and the masthead pendant. 'Stand by to wear ship, Mr Sperry!' He wiped his face again, gauging the distance and the power of the wind. It had taken over an hour to get this far and penetrate the bay without any apparent opposition, although there must be many glasses trained on the one ship fleeing from another. It seemed likely that the Dutch commander might already know the *Albacora*, while *Miranda*'s streaming ensign left little else to doubt.

Tyacke raised his glass again and peered at the boat just reported by the lookout. A small cutter, under a scrap of sail but with oars already angled from her rowlocks for extra power, was rounding the stern of the nearest merchantman. Metal gleamed in the sunshine, and he saw the gilt buttons of an officer in the sternsheets. The guardboat would challenge their presence. Tyacke frowned. There was only one chance.

He called, 'You! Private Buller!' The marine turned away from his place by the halliards as Tyacke added harshly, 'You're *supposed* to be a bit of a marksman, I'm told?'

Buller met his tone with equal insolence. 'Best shot in the company, *sir!*'

Tyacke grinned. 'Right. Fetch your piece and prepare to mark down the officer in charge of the guardboat. They've got a swivel mounted in the bows, so you must not miss!'

He turned away as Buller stooped down to where his weapons were rolled up inside his telltale scarlet coat.

'All ready, sir!'

Tyacke looked steadily at Segrave. 'Ready aft?'

Segrave nodded jerkily, his face pale despite the

131

sun's glare, but strangely determined.

Tyacke walked to the taffrail and made certain that the longboat was towing clumsily astern. Once again he stared hard at the land, then across the larboard quarter where the moored storeships appeared to be falling away into the distance. Even the guardboat seemed in no hurry to close with them, especially with *Miranda* charging in full pursuit.

'Ready about! Helm a-lee! Let go and haul, lads!' Tyacke's voice harried them until they were sweating and gasping to perform the work normally done by twice the number of hands.

Segrave's shoes slipped, then gripped on the tarred deck-seams while he threw his weight on the tiller, his eyes blind to everything but the great swinging sails and the shriek of blocks, while the schooner continued to tack into and then across the eye of the wind.

Dwyer gasped, 'Come round, you bloody bitch!' But he was grinning as the sails banged out on the opposite tack to thrust the deck over even more steeply. Where there had been empty land there suddenly lay the anchorage, the ships clear and real in the sunlight, even their Dutch ensigns visible against the land mass beyond.

Tyacke was holding on for support but even he gave a quick smile. This was no *Miranda*, but she had been used to fast handling in her rotten trade. He studied the guardboat: her sails were flapping and losing wind, and as he watched he saw the oars begin to move ahead and astern, pulling the hull around until the bow-gun was pointing, not at them but at *Miranda*.

Sperry gasped, '*Miranda*'ll blow 'er clean out of

132

the water. Wot's their game?'

The lookout shouted sharply, 'Deck there! Th' frigate's under way!'

Tyacke swung round, his heart sickened as he saw the frigate's topsails shaking out and hardening to the wind while she glided away from her inshore anchorage.

Sperry said hoarsely, 'We'll not stand a chance, sir.' He rubbed his eyes as if he could not believe what he saw. 'She's got th' wind, God damn her!'

Tyacke said, 'Let her fall off a point, Mr Segrave.' He raised his glass and felt a sudden pain, as if the breath had been knocked out of him. 'It's not us. It's *Miranda* she's going for!' Tyacke waved his arms and yelled at the top of his voice. 'Run for it, Ben! In the name of Christ—come about!' Their very helplessness, and the fact that nobody aboard *Miranda* could possibly hear him, made his voice crack with emotion.

'Get out of it, Ben!'

Segrave asked in a whisper, 'What's happening?'

Dwyer flung at him, 'Th' frigate's runnin' for open sea, that's what!'

Segrave watched. *Miranda*'s length began to shorten as she saw her danger and started to come about.

Tyacke trained his glass on the frigate. She was smaller than *Truculent*, but showed all the grace of her class as she changed tack, and her huge fore and main courses filled to the wind, pushing her over until he could plainly see the French Tricolour rippling from her peak. Getting away from the bay before she might be caught defending her ally's supply ships, and be held as much a prisoner as they were.

133

Sickened, Tyacke saw the frigate's ports open, could almost imagine the orders to aim their broadside. It was over a mile's range, but with a controlled assault it was impossible to miss.

He saw the smoke belch along the frigate's low hull, and even before he could swing his glass across the glistening water he heard the staccato crash of gunfire. The sea around and beyond the little *Miranda* seemed to boil, while spray burst skyward, standing in the sunlight like waterspouts—as if they were suddenly frozen and might never fall.

For one more second Tyacke clung to a spark of hope. At that range *Miranda* had somehow managed to escape the enemy's iron.

He heard some of his men groan as, with the suddenness of a great seabird settling to fold its wings, both of *Miranda*'s masts collapsed, burying the deck under a mass of writhing canvas and splintered spars.

The frigate did not fire again. She was already setting her royals, her yards alive with tiny figures as she pointed her jib boom towards the south-east, the wind carrying her speedily to open sea and freedom.

Tyacke wanted to look away but could not even lower his telescope. No wonder the French frigate had not fired a second broadside. *Miranda*'s hull had been blasted open in several places, and he saw smoke escaping from the fallen canvas to add to the horror of the men pinned beneath.

Then just as suddenly the fire was quenched, as quickly as it had begun.

Tyacke lowered the glass and stared into the sun until he could see nothing. The schooner, his *Miranda*, had gone. In trying to help him she had herself become a victim.

He realised that Segrave and some of the others were watching him. When he spoke again he was stunned by the calmness of his own voice.

'Shorten sail, Mr Sperry. The chase is over.' He pointed at the guardboat, where some of the oarsmen were waving and cheering towards the shabby schooner. 'See? They bid us welcome!'

Slowly, like drunken men, the hands turned to, to give the appearance of reducing sail.

Tyacke stood beside Segrave and rested his hand on the boy's until the tiller brought the bowsprit in line with the space between the two anchored ships.

'Hold her steady.' He looked at those nearest him and added, 'Then you take to the boat.' He studied their faces, but was seeing others in their place. Ben Simcox, who would have been leaving the ship to obtain his position as master. Bob Jay, and old Archer the gunner. So many faces. Gone in a moment. Those who had not died in the broadside would not escape the sharks.

He said, 'Be ready, lads.' He cocked his head as a trumpet echoed across the water. 'The alarm.' He glanced at the sudden activity in the guardboat as the oar blades churned up the water, and the boat began to swing round towards them.

Tyacke snapped, 'Stand by, Private Buller!' He knew the marine was crouching by the bulwark, his long musket resting beside him. Tyacke said, 'Think of what you just saw, Buller, and of the flogging you deserve but will never receive!

'*Ready, Buller!*'

He watched the officer in the guardboat as he got to his feet, his arm beating out the time to his confused oarsmen.

135

'*Now!*'

The musket bucked against Buller's powerful shoulder, and Tyacke saw the Dutch officer's arm halt in mid-air before he pitched over the side and floundered away from the hull.

The boat turned, out of command, while some of the crew attempted to reach their officer with an oar.

Segrave heard the sharp bang of the guardboat's swivel and Dwyer cry out before he slithered to the deck, blood pouring down his neck and side. Buller's musket cracked again and another man vanished inside the boat, its oars now in complete disarray.

Segrave saw Sperry the boatswain down on his knees, his teeth bared like fangs as he clutched his bulging stomach. He must have taken some of the guardboat's deadly canister shot even while he was helping to trim the sails.

Tyacke's eyes narrowed as he stared hard at the two big ships which seemed to lie across the bows barely yards away. In fact they were over half a cable distant—but nothing could save them now.

Segrave tore his eyes away as Sperry rolled kicking on to his back, his blood filling the scuppers while he choked out his life.

The Dutch sailors were probably wondering what the *Albacora* was doing, the boy thought wildly. As if reading his thoughts Tyacke shouted, 'Let's not leave them in suspense, eh?' He took the tiller and drew a pistol from his belt. 'Get below, Mr Segrave and take the slow-match to the fuses!'

Even Segrave could sense the fear which had so suddenly replaced the wildness, the urge to kill. Men Tyacke knew and trusted could soon change

136

once the fuses were lit, and they were standing on their own funeral pyre. Segrave ran past the dying boatswain, realising that his eyes were fixed on his as he hurried by, as if they alone were clinging to life.

In his dazed mind he seemed to hear more trumpets, the far-off squeal of gun-trucks as some of the Indiamen's officers understood at last what they were witnessing.

He was sobbing and could not stop himself as he stumbled down in the stinking hull, still shocked by *Miranda*'s unexpected end, and Tyacke's terrible grief and anger.

The man who had been his only friend and whom he had tried to save was dead, and the little schooner, which had been Tyacke's very life, his one escape, had been sent to the bottom.

Segrave fell back with a gasp as the first fuse hissed into life like a malevolent serpent. He had not even seen himself lighting it. He reached the second one and stared at the slow-match in his fingers. His grip was so firm it did not even quiver when he ignited the fuse.

As he scurried back towards the sunlight at the foot of the ladder, he thought of his mother. Perhaps *the admiral* would be satisfied now. But neither bitterness nor tears would come, and when he reached the tiller he saw Tyacke exactly as he had left him, propped against the tiller as if he were part of the ship.

Tyacke nodded. 'Look at 'em now!'

The Indiamen's decks were swarming with sailors. Some were clambering aloft to the yards, others were in the bows, probably attempting to cut their cables.

There was a dull thud below their feet, and seconds later black greasy smoke surged up through the vents, followed by the first vicious tongues of flame.

Tyacke said, 'Heave the boat alongside, *handsomely* now. I'll shoot the first man who tries a run for it!'

Segrave watched flames darting through the deck-seams, his eyes glazed as he felt the whole hull heating up like a furnace.

A man yelled, 'Ready in the boat, sir!' It was the one named Swayne, the deserter.

Segrave said in a strangely controlled voice, 'Don't stay with her, sir.' He waited for Tyacke to turn his terrible scars towards him. *'Please.'* He tried to shut out the growing roar beneath the deck and added, 'They all died back there, sir. Let it not be a waste, for their sakes!'

Surprisingly, Tyacke stood up and grasped his shoulders. 'I'll see you a lieutenant yet, my lad.'

They clambered down into the boat and cast off. They had barely pulled out of *Albacora*'s shadow when, with a savage hiss of flames, the deck appeared to burst open, fires starting everywhere, as if lit by one man's hand.

Tyacke rested his arm on the tiller bar. *'Pull*, lads. If we reach the headland, we may be able to get ashore and hide until we know what's happening.'

One of the oarsmen exclaimed, *'She's struck*, by Jesus!' His own eyes and face were shining in the reflected glare as the schooner, her rigging and sails already blowing away in ashes, crashed alongside the first Indiaman.

Tyacke swung round as the flames leapt up the

moored ship's tarred shrouds and darted out along the yards. Some of the men who had been working feverishly to loose the topsails found themselves trapped by the mounting fires. Tyacke watched without expression as their tiny figures fell to the decks below, rather than face that slower, more horrific death. The second Indiaman had managed to cut her stern moorings but she had freed her cable too late. Fires were already blazing on her forecastle and flowing along her hammock nettings like spurting red liquid.

Nobody spoke in the boat, so that the sounds of creaking oars and the men's rasping breathing seemed to come from somewhere else.

So short a while ago, they had all expected to be dead. Now Fate had decided otherwise.

'Watch out for any place to beach when we get closer.'

Buller the Royal Marine paused, ramming home a ball into his musket, and swore with harsh disbelief. 'You won't need no beach, sir!'

Tyacke stared until his mind throbbed and his eyes were too blind to see; all that remained was the memory. *Miranda*'s sails folding like broken wings.

He gripped Segrave's wrist and said, '*Truculent!* She's coming for us!'

The oars seemed to bend as with sudden hope they threw themselves on the looms. The boat headed away towards the frigate's silhouette while she rounded the point, as they themselves had done just a few hours earlier.

Segrave turned to look astern, but there was only a towering wall of black smoke which appeared to be pursuing them, its heart still writhing with flames. He glanced at Tyacke. He knew the

139

lieutenant had intended to stay at the helm and die. The pistol had been ready to prevent anyone dragging him to the boat by force; and for no other reason.

Then Segrave looked away and watched the frigate standing-off to receive them. His pleas had somehow given Tyacke the will to reach out for another chance. And for that, Segrave was suddenly grateful.

For if Tyacke had changed, so had he.

CHAPTER SEVEN

A CHANCE TO LIVE

Bolitho walked to one of *Themis*'s open ports and rested his hand on the wooden muzzle of a quaker. In the afternoon sunlight it felt as hot as iron, as if it were a real gun which had just been fired.

The flagship seemed unusually quiet and motionless, and he could see *Truculent* anchored close by, making a perfect twin of her reflection on the calm water. At the cabin table, Yovell, his secretary, was writing busily, preparing more despatches which would in time reach all the senior officers of both squadrons, and others which might eventually end their journey on Sir Owen Godschale's desk at the Admiralty. As the *Themis* swung very slightly to her cable, Bolitho saw part of the land, the unmoving haze above it, much of it dust. Occasionally he heard the distant bark of artillery and pictured the foot-soldiers pressing on towards Cape Town. The Admiralty seemed a million miles away from this place, he thought.

He saw Jenour dabbing his face and neck with a handkerchief while he leaned over Yovell's plump shoulder to check something. He looked strained, as he had done since *Miranda*'s sudden and violent destruction. After picking up the crew of the fireship, *Truculent* had made off under full sail to seek out the French frigate, or at least to be in time to assist Captain Varian's *Zest* when he confronted her. Placed as he was, Varian should have been in a perfect position to capture or attack any vessel which tried to escape the fireship's terrible devastation.

But there had been no sign of the enemy, and not until three days later had they met up with *Zest*. Varian had explained that another vessel had been sighted approaching from seaward, and he had given chase, but without success. Bolitho had expected Poland to make some criticism once the frigates had separated again, as it was rumoured there was bad blood between the captains. He had said nothing. Nor, upon reflection, had he seemed surprised.

Bolitho tried not to dwell on *Miranda*'s loss. Nor on Tyacke's contained anguish as he had clambered up from the fireship's boat. The column of black smoke above the anchorage had been visible for many hours, long after *Truculent* had headed out to the open sea.

The General's soldiers would see it and take new heart, and the Dutch might realise that there was nothing but their own courage to sustain them. But although he tried, Bolitho could not put the memory from his mind. *He must tell himself*. It had been a remarkable feat, the success far outweighing

141

the cost. But he could not forget. He had once again allowed himself to get too close. To Simcox, and Jay, even to an unknown Cornish lookout who had come from Penzance.

There was a tap at the door and then Commander Maguire entered the cabin, his hat beneath his arm.

'You sent for me, Sir Richard?' His eyes moved to the open stern windows as more gunfire echoed across the flat blue water.

Bolitho nodded. 'Be seated.' He walked past him to the table, each step bringing his body out in a rash of sweat. *Just to be in a moving ship again, to feel the wind. Instead of* ... He turned over some papers. 'When this campaign comes to a close, Commander Maguire, you will be sailing for England. It is all in your orders. You will place yourself with certain other vessels under the charge of Commodore Popham until that time is suitable.' He saw little response on the man's lined features. Perhaps, like some others in the squadron, he might be thinking that the fireship and *Miranda*'s sacrifice would make no difference; that it would drag on into stalemate. There was a thud from the adjoining cabin, then the sounds of a heavy chest being manhandled across the deck. Only then did Bolitho see some expression on Maguire's face. He had served with Warren for a long time.

On *Truculent*'s return to the anchorage Bolitho had realised that he would never speak with Warren again. He had apparently died even as *Truculent*'s topsails had been sighted standing inshore.

Now Warren's clerk and servant were gathering the last of his belongings for stowage in one of the transports to await passage—*where*, he wondered? Warren had no home but this ship, no relatives

142

apart from a sister somewhere in England, whom he had rarely seen even on his visits to the country he had seemingly rejected for the West Indies.

Maguire frowned and asked, 'What will become of the ship, Sir Richard?'

Bolitho saw Jenour watching them, his eyes fall as their gaze met.

'She will doubtless receive a much needed overhaul and refit.'

'But she's too *old*, Sir Richard!'

Bolitho ignored the protest. 'Not as old as my flagship.' He did not mean to let it come out so sharply, and saw the other man start. 'The war continues, Commander Maguire, and we shall need every ship we can lay hands on. Ships which can stand and fight and still give of their best.' He walked to the stern, and leaned on the heated sill to look down into the clear water as it lifted and gurgled around the rudder. He could see the trailing weed, the copper, which was dull and pitted with constant service. As his *Hyperion* had once been when he had first taken command, in that other world. Over his shoulder he added bitterly, 'We need more than wooden guns in the Channel Fleet too!'

It was a dismissal, and he heard the door close behind him, the sentry's musket coming down to rest again with a sharp tap.

'I suppose you think that was wrong of me?'

Jenour straightened his back. 'There comes a time, sir—'

Bolitho smiled, although he felt drained as well as impatient. 'Well, now. What has my sage to tell me?'

Jenour's open face lit up with a broad grin.

Relief, surprise; it was both. 'I know I am inexperienced when compared with some, sir.'

Bolitho held up his hand. 'A damned sight *more* experienced than a few I can mention! I was sorry for Warren, but he did not belong here. Like the ship, he had become a relic. That did not count for much once. But this is no game, Stephen, nor was it even when I entered the King's navy.' He looked at him fondly. 'But it took the blade of the guillotine to make some of our *betters* take heed. This war *must be won*. We have to care about our people. But there is no longer any stowage-space for sentiment.'

Allday entered by the other door and said, 'Some casks of beer have just been brought over, Sir Richard. Seems it was for *Miranda*'s people.' He watched Bolitho, his eyes troubled. 'Otherwise, I wouldn't have said—'

Bolitho loosened his shirt for the thousandth time and shook his head. 'I have been bad company since that day, old friend.' He glanced from one to the other. 'I will try to make amends, for my own sake as well as yours.'

Allday was still watching him warily, like a rider with an unknown mount. What did he mean, he wondered? *Since that day. Miranda*, or was he still fretting over his old flagship?

He said, 'There's a pin o' brandy for yourself, Sir Richard. From th' General, no less.'

Bolitho looked towards the land, his fingers playing with the locket beneath his damp shirt. 'Sir David said as much in his letter to me.' He had a sudden picture of Baird somewhere over there: in his tent, on horseback, or studying the enemy's positions. Did *he* ever consider defeat or disgrace? He certainly did not show it.

144

Of the Dutch defenders he had written, *'They will fight on, or they will surrender very soon. There will be no half measures, on either side.'* Of the fireship he had said, *'Brave men are always missed and then too often forgotten. At least others will not die in vain.'* Bolitho could almost hear him saying it, as he had on the shore when he had begged for his assistance. Baird had finished his letter by describing his opponent, the Dutch general Jansens, as a good soldier, and one not given to senseless destruction. Did that mean that he would capitulate rather than see Cape Town brought down in ruins?

Bolitho clutched his arms across his chest as a cold shiver ran through him, despite the scorching air in the cabin.

Warren had gone, but it felt as if he was still here, watching him, hating him for what he was doing with his ship.

Allday asked, 'All right, Sir Richard?'

Bolitho crossed to the windows and stood in the sunshine until the heat burned the chill out of his body. For an instant he had imagined it was a warning of the old fever. The one which had all but killed him. He smiled sadly. When Catherine had climbed into his bed without him knowing or remembering a thing about it. Her care, and the warmth of her nakedness, had helped to save him.

Maybe Warren *was* watching? After all, they had buried him nearby, weighed with shot, down in the depths where even the sharks would not venture. Maguire had used one of the longboats, and the oarsmen had continued to pull until a leadsman had reported 'no bottom' on his line.

The marine sentry shouted from beyond the

screen, 'Officer-o'-the-Watch, *sir!*'

The lieutenant seemed to be walking on tiptoe as he entered the presence of the vice-admiral. Bolitho wondered how much more they knew about him now since his arrival among them.

The lieutenant said, '*Truculent*'s boat has just cast off, Sir Richard.'

'Very well, Mr Latham. Please offer Lieutenant Tyacke all respects when he is come aboard the flagship. He *was* in command, remember.'

The lieutenant almost bowed himself out, his face astonished more by Bolitho's remembering his name than at his instruction.

Ozzard appeared as if spirited by a genie's lamp.

'A fresh shirt, Sir Richard?'

Bolitho shaded his eyes to watch the boat pulling slowly towards *Themis*'s side, pinned down in the hazy glare as if it could scarcely make the crossing.

'I think not, Ozzard.' He thought of the schooner's tiny cabin, where a clean shirt and ample drinking water were both luxuries.

Tyacke would be feeling badly enough as it was. The interview he was about to have with the tall lieutenant was suddenly important. It was not merely something to replace his loss, or to offer him compensation for his terrible wound. It *mattered*; but until now Bolitho had not really known how much.

He said quietly, 'Will you leave me, please?' He watched Yovell gather up his papers, his round features completely absorbed with his inner thoughts. A direct contrast to Allday, and yet . . . Neither would change even at the gates of Heaven.

To Jenour he added, 'I would like to dine with Mr Tyacke this evening, and for you to join us.' He saw Jenour's obvious pleasure and said, 'But for this moment it is better without an audience.'

Jenour withdrew and saw a marine guard presenting arms to the man in question as he climbed aboard and raised his hat to the quarterdeck. *Half a man*, Jenour thought, and now with his dreadful scars turned away he could see what he had once been: perhaps what Bolitho was hoping to restore.

Allday stood his ground as Tyacke walked aft and ducked beneath the poop.

Tyacke halted and said coldly, 'All waiting, are they?' He was very much on the defensive. But Allday knew men better than most, sailors more than any. Tyacke was ashamed. Because of his disfigurement; and because he had lost his ship.

He replied, 'Be easy with him, sir.' He saw the sudden surprise in Tyacke's eyes and added, 'He still feels the loss of his old ship very badly. Like one o' the family, *personal*.'

Tyacke nodded, but said nothing. Allday's casual confidence had unnerved him, scattered all his carefully prepared thoughts, and what he had been about to say.

Allday walked away and stooped thoughtfully over the pin of brandy which had been sent over by the redcoats. It was strange when you thought about it. Bolitho and Tyacke were very much alike. Had things been different for them they might even have changed roles.

He heard Ozzard right behind him. 'You can keep your eyes off that little cask, *Mister Allday*!' He stood, arms folded, his watery eyes severe. 'I *know* you when you get your hooks on some brandy.'

The guns ashore fired a long, unbroken salvo, like thunder echoing around those sombre, alien hills.

Allday put his hand on the little man's shoulder. 'Listen to 'em, matey. Don't even know what they're fighting about!'

Ozzard smiled wryly. 'Not like us, eh? *Heart of Oak!*'

He began to roll the brandy towards the poop's deeper shadow and Allday gave a sigh. A nice 'wet' of brandy would have made a change.

They both made a point of not looking towards the great cabin where Warren had died, and another was about to be given a chance to live.

*   *   *

Tyacke waited while the sentry called out his name, his eyes averted from the lieutenant's face.

He pushed open the door and saw Bolitho by the open stern windows. The cabin was otherwise empty. His eyes moved quickly around it, recalling the few times he had been there. As before, he noticed its total lack of personality. Impossible to judge its previous occupant, although he had lived here for such a long time. Perhaps Warren had had nothing to offer it? He tried not to think of all the clutter, the sense of *belonging* in *Miranda*'s tiny, cramped quarters. It was gone. He had to remember that.

'Please sit down.' Bolitho gestured to a small table with some wine and two glasses. 'It is good of you to come.'

Tyacke straightened his borrowed coat, giving himself time to gather his wits.

148

'I must apologise for my rig, Sir Richard. *Truculent*'s wardroom had a collection for me, you see?'

Bolitho nodded. 'I do see. All your things rest on the seabed. Like many of my most valued possessions.' He moved to the table and poured two glasses of the hock Ozzard had discovered somewhere. 'I am unused to this vessel, Mr Tyacke.' He paused with the bottle in mid-air, his eyes towards the windows as the air quivered to the distant cannon fire. 'I suppose that is the span between us and the military. Sailors are like turtles, in a way. We carry our homes around with us. They become personal to us; in some ways too much so. Whereas the poor soldier sees only the land in front of him.' He smiled suddenly over the rim of his glass. 'And to think I was lecturing my flag-lieutenant on the folly of sentiment!'

He sat down opposite Tyacke and stretched out his legs. 'Now tell me about the men who were with you. That marine, for instance—has he repented of being a volunteer?'

Tyacke found himself describing the long and difficult process of beating back and forth against the wind to get closer to the merchantmen. Of Buller's insolence, and his superb marksmanship. Of the deserter Swayne, and the midshipman who had somehow found courage when he needed it most. Shadowy figures became real as he told of their courage and their fear.

Bolitho refilled the glasses and doubted if either of them had noticed what they were drinking.

He said, 'You *gave* that boy courage—you know that, don't you?'

Tyacke answered simply, 'But for him I wouldn't

149

be here.'

Bolitho eyed him gravely. 'That was then. This is now. I would wish you to sup with me this evening. No talk of war—we shall let it take us where it fancies. I have enough burdens of my own. It would ease the load if I knew I was to achieve something personal before I leave this place.'

Tyacke thought he had misheard. Sup with the vice-admiral? This was not a lowly schooner, and Sir Richard Bolitho was no longer a tolerant passenger.

He heard himself ask, 'What is it, Sir Richard? If there is something I can do, you have but to ask. I may have been changed by events; my respect and loyalty to you have not. And I am not a man to offer false praise to gain favour, sir.'

'Believe me, I do know what you went through; what you are enduring now. We are both sea-officers. Rank divides us, but we still curse and rave at the incompetence of others, those who care nothing for Poor Jack, until *they* are in risk and danger themselves.' He leaned forward, his voice so quiet that it was almost lost in the gentle ship noises around them. 'My late father once said something to me, when I was younger than you are now, at a time when all things seemed set against us. He said, "England needs all her sons now."'

Tyacke listened, all resentment and despair held at bay, almost fearful of missing something of this reserved, compelling man who could have been his brother, and not an envied flag-officer.

Bolitho's eyes were far away. 'Trafalgar has not changed that. We *need* fine ships to replace our losses and old veterans like this one. But most of all we need officers and seamen of courage and experience. Like yourself.'

'You want me to forget *Miranda*, Sir Richard. To become a serving lieutenant again.' Tyacke's expression had changed. He looked trapped, even afraid. 'For if so—'

Bolitho said, 'Do you know the brig *Larne*, Mr Tyacke?' He watched the man's quiet desperation, his obvious inner struggle. 'She is with Commodore Popham's squadron at present.'

Tyacke said, 'Commander Blackmore. I have seen her on occasion.' He sounded mystified.

Bolitho reached over and picked up a piece of Yovell's hard work. 'Blackmore is fortunate. He is promoted to command a sixth-rate. I want *you* to take her.'

Tyacke stared at him. 'But I cannot—I do not have—'

Bolitho handed him the envelope. 'Here is the commission to take her in your charge. It will be confirmed at Their Lordships' leisure, but you are herewith promoted to the rank of commander.' He forced a smile to cover Tyacke's confusion and undisguised emotion. 'I will see what my aide can do about obtaining some more suitable uniform for you without delay!'

He waited, pouring more wine, then asked, 'Will you do this—for me, if for no other reason?'

Tyacke got to his feet without knowing it. 'I will, Sir Richard, and I'd ask no better reason than that!'

Bolitho stood up, very alert. '*Listen.*'

'What is it, Sir Richard?'

Before he turned away Tyacke saw the emotion clearly in Bolitho's eyes, as clearly as he himself had betrayed his own seconds earlier.

Bolitho said softly, 'The guns. They're silent

151

now.' He faced him and added, 'It means, *Commander* Tyacke, that it's over. The enemy have struck to us.'

There was a brief knock at the door, and Jenour almost burst into the cabin. 'I have just heard, Sir Richard!'

His admiral smiled at him. It was a moment Jenour was to remember for a long while afterwards.

Then Bolitho said, 'Now we can go home.'

★   ★   ★

Captain Daniel Poland stood, arms folded, and watched the throng of bare-backed seamen hurrying to their stations. From the capstan came the scrape of a fiddle accompanied by *Truculent*'s shantyman, an old sailor with a surprisingly carrying voice.

'When we did bang the damned mounseer,
You gave us beef an' beer,
Now we 'ave naught to eat an' drink,
For you 'ave naught to fear!'

A boatswain's mate bellowed in each interval, '*Heave! Heave!* Put yer bloody backs into it if you wants to see old England again!'

The first lieutenant gave a discreet cough. 'The admiral, sir.'

Poland glanced away from the busy figures on deck and aloft on the yards.

'Thank you, Mr Williams, but we have nothing to hide.'

He touched his hat as Bolitho walked beneath the driverboom, his face and chest like beaten copper in

152

the dying sunlight.

'We are ready to proceed, Sir Richard.'

Bolitho was listening to the fiddle and the sing-song voice of the shantyman. *For you have naught to fear.* A song which went back a long, long way with slight variations to suit the campaign or the war. Bolitho recalled his own father talking about it when he had described the battle of Quiberon Bay. The sailor's despair of those he fought and died for only too often.

It was an inspiring sunset, he thought; few painters could do it credit. The sea, the distant ridge of Table Mountain and all the anchored ships were glowing like molten metal. Only the offshore wind gave life to the picture, the low rollers cruising towards the shadows to awaken the hill and gurgle around the stem. Bolitho could feel the last heat of the day, like a hot breath, and wondered why Poland could not reveal any excitement at this departure.

He heard the sharp clank of the first capstan pawl, the boatswain's harsh encouragement for the seamen to thrust at the bars with all their might.

Bolitho watched the other ships, their open gunports gleaming like lines of watchful eyes. Their part was over, and as dusk had descended on Table Bay he had taken a telescope to look at the Union Flag which now flew above the main battery. It would remain there.

Some of the squadron had already weighed and headed out of the bay to begin the long passage back to England. Two ships-of-the-line, five frigates including Varian's *Zest*, and a flotilla of smaller, unrated vessels. While England waited for her old enemy's next move, these reinforcements would be more than welcome. Others, including *Themis*, would follow as soon as the army had fully established its control of Cape Town and the anchorages which would sustain them against all comers. The blackened bones of the two Dutch Indiamen would be grim reminders of the price of complacency, he thought.

He remembered Tyacke's face when they had shared a last handshake, his voice when he had said, 'I thank you for giving me another chance to live, Sir Richard.'

Bolitho had said, 'Later you may curse me too.'

'I doubt that. *Larne* is a fine vessel. She'll be a challenge after *Miranda*.' He had spoken her name as a man might dwell on a dead friend. 'But she and I will come to respect one another!'

Larne was already hidden in shadow, but Bolitho could see her riding light, and somehow knew that Tyacke would be over there now, on deck to watch *Truculent*'s anchor break out of the ground.

Shadows ebbed and flowed across the quarterdeck, and Bolitho moved clear to give the captain the freedom he needed to get under way. He saw Jenour by the nettings, a slight figure standing near him. The latter made to leave but Bolitho said, 'How does it feel, Mr Segrave? So short a stay, so much experience?'

The youth stared at him in the strong copper glow. 'I—I am glad I was here, Sir Richard.' He turned, his hair flapping in the hot breeze as the capstan began to clatter more eagerly, the pawls falling while the long cable continued to come inboard.

Bolitho watched him, seeing Tyacke, remembering his own early days at sea, when he

154

had shared the danger and the mirth with other midshipmen like Segrave.

'But you also regret leaving?'

Segrave nodded slowly, and momentarily forgot he was speaking with a vice-admiral, the hero whom others had described in so many different guises. 'I only hope that when I return to my old ship . . .' He did not have to finish it.

Bolitho watched as the guardboat drifted abeam, oars tossed in salute, a lieutenant standing to doff his hat to his flag at the fore. Perhaps to the man as well.

'You can be neither too young nor too old to have your heart broken.' Bolitho sensed Jenour turn to listen. 'Courage is something else. I think you will have little to worry you when you rejoin your ship.'

Jenour wanted to smile but Bolitho's voice was too intense. He knew that Yovell had already copied a letter for Segrave's captain. It would be enough. If it was not, the captain would soon learn that Bolitho could be ruthless where brutality was concerned.

'Thank you, sir.'

Bolitho leaned on the hammock nettings and thought of all the miles which lay ahead. It would be a far cry from the swift passage which had brought him here. What might he discover? Would Catherine still feel the same for him after their separation?

When he looked again, the midshipman had gone.

Jenour said, 'He'll do well enough, Sir Richard.'

'You knew then, Stephen?'

'I guessed. Allday put the rest together. His life must have been hell. He should never have been

155

put to sea.'

Bolitho smiled. 'It changes all of us. Even you.'

Then he felt his heart leap as the cry came from forward.

'Anchor's hove short, sir!'

Calls trilled, and a man grunted as a rope's end hurried him after the others to halliards and braces.

Lieutenant Williams reported, 'Standing by, sir!'

'Loose heads'ls.' Poland sounded calm, remote. Bolitho wondered what did move him, why he disliked Varian, what he hoped for beyond promotion?

He looked up at the yards where the strung-out, foreshortened bodies of the topmen tensed to release their charges to the wind. On deck, others stood by the braces, ready to transform their anchored ship into a flying thoroughbred. What awaited most of them when *Truculent* reached England? Would they be cooped up aboard while they awaited new orders, or sent to other ships to strengthen the ranks of landmen and newly-pressed hands ignorant of the sea and of the navy? The fiddle was scraping out a livelier tune and the capstan was turning even more quickly, as if to hasten their departure.

Bolitho said, 'It will be summer in England, Stephen. How quickly the months go past.'

Jenour turned, his profile in dark shadow, as if, like Tyacke, he had only half a face. 'A year for victory, Sir Richard.'

Bolitho touched his arm. *The hopes of youth knew no bounds.* 'I am past believing in miracles!'

'*Anchor's aweigh*, sir!'

Bolitho gripped the nettings. The ship seemed to rear away as the anchor was hauled up and secured

156

at the cathead. Even that seemed to symbolise the difference he had felt here. When they anchored once more in England, in another hemisphere, they would drop the one on the opposite side.

Truculent came about, canvas banging in confusion, shadowy figures dashing everywhere to bring her under control. Hull, the sailing-master, shouted, 'Steady there! *Hold her!*'

Bolitho watched him and his helmsmen as they clung on the double spokes, their eyes gleaming in the disappearing sun. He thought of Simcox, who would have been like Hull one day. He had wanted it more than anything. But not enough to leave his friend when his life was threatened.

He said, 'Fate is fate.'

Jenour looked at him. 'Sir?'

'Thoughts, Stephen. Just thoughts.'

The topsails hardened to the wind and the deck seemed to hold steady as *Truculent* pointed her bows towards the headland and the empty, coppery wastes beyond.

'West-sou'-west, sir! Full an' bye!'

Poland's mouth was set in a tight line. 'Bring her up a point. As close as she'll bear.' He waited for the first lieutenant to come aft again. 'Get the courses and royals on her as soon as we are clear, Mr Williams.' He glanced quickly at Bolitho's figure by the nettings. 'No mistakes.'

Bolitho remained on deck until the land and the sheltering ships were lost in the swift darkness. He waited until the world had shrunk to the leaping spray and trailing phosphorescence, when the sky was so dark there was no margin between it and the ocean. Only then did he go below, where Ozzard was bustling about, preparing a late meal.

157

Bolitho walked to the stern windows, which were smeared with salt and dappled in spray, and thought of his years as a frigate captain. Leaving port had always been exciting, a kind of rare freedom. It was a pity that Poland did not see it like that. Or perhaps he was merely counting the days until he could rid himself of his responsibility—looking after a vice-admiral.

He glanced up as feet thudded across the deck, and voices echoed through the wind and the din of sails and rigging. It never changed, he thought, even after all the years. He still felt he should be up there, making decisions, taking charge of the ship and using her skills to the full. He gave a grim smile. No, he would never get used to it.

In the adjoining sleeping-cabin, he sat down by his open chest and stared at himself in the attached looking-glass.

Everyone imagined him to be younger than he really was. But what would *she* think as the years passed? He thought suddenly of the young officers who were probably sitting down to enjoy their first meal out of harbour, sharing their table with Jenour and probably trying to pry out the truth of the man he served. It might make a change from all the plentiful rumours, he thought. He stared at his reflection, his eyes pitiless, as if he were inspecting one of his own subordinates.

He was forty-nine years old. The rest was flattery. This was the bitter truth. Catherine was a lovely, passionate woman, one whom any man would fight and die for, if indeed he was a man. She would turn every head, be it at Court or in a street. There were some who might chance their hand now that they knew something of their love, their *affair* as many

158

would term it.

Bolitho pushed the white lock of hair from his forehead, hating it; knowing he was being stupid, with no more sense than a heartsick midshipman.

I am jealous, and I do not want to lose her love. Because it is my life. Without her, I am nothing.

He saw Allday looking in from the door. He said, 'Shall Ozzard pour the wine, Sir Richard?' He saw the expression on Bolitho's face and thought he knew why he was troubled. Leaving her had been bad. Returning might be harder for him, with all his doubts.

'I am not hungry.' He heard the sea roar alongside the hull like something wilful, and knew that the ship was ploughing into the ocean, away from the land's last protection.

If only they could move faster, and cut away the leagues.

Allday said, 'You've done a lot, Sir Richard. Not spared yourself a moment since we made our landfall. You'll feel your old self tomorrow, you'll see.'

Bolitho watched his face in the glass. *I never give him any peace.*

Allday tried again. 'It's a nice plate o' pork in proper breadcrumbs, just as you like it. Not get anything as good after a few weeks of this lot!'

Bolitho turned on the chair and said, 'I want you to cut my hair tomorrow.' When Allday said nothing, he added angrily, 'I suppose you think that's idiotic!'

Allday replied diplomatically, 'Well, Sir Richard, I sees that most o' the wardroom bloods affects the newer fashion these days.' He shook his pigtail and added reproachfully, 'Don't see it signifies meself.'

'Can you do it?'

A slow grin spread across Allday's weathered face. 'Course I will, Sir Richard.'

Then the true importance of the request hit him like a block. 'Can I say me piece, Sir Richard?'

'Have I ever prevented you?'

Allday shrugged. 'Well, not hardly ever. That is, not *often*.'

'Go on, you damned rascal!'

Allday let out his breath. That was more like it. The old gleam in those sea-grey eyes. The friend, not just the admiral.

'I saw what you done for Mr Tyacke—'

Bolitho snapped, 'What *anyone* would have done!'

Allday stood firm. '*No*, they wouldn't lift a finger, an' *you knows it*, beggin' your pardon.'

They glared at each other like antagonists until Bolitho said, 'Well, spit it out.'

Allday continued, 'I just think it's right an' proper that you gets some o' the cream for yourself, an' that's no error neither!' He grimaced and put his hand to his chest and saw Bolitho's instant concern. 'See, Sir Richard, you're doing it this minute! Thinking o' me, of anyone but yourself.'

Ozzard made a polite clatter with some crockery in the great cabin and Allday concluded firmly, 'That lady would worship you even if you looked like poor Mr Tyacke.'

Bolitho stood up and brushed past him. 'Perhaps I shall eat after all.' He looked from him to Ozzard. 'It seems I shall get no rest otherwise.' As Ozzard bent to pour some wine Bolitho added, 'Open the General's brandy directly.' To Allday he said, 'Baird was right about you. We could indeed use a

160

few thousand more like you!'

Ozzard laid the wine in a cooler and thought sadly of the splendid cabinet *she* had given him, which lay somewhere on the sea-bed in the shattered wreck of the *Hyperion*. He had seen the glance which passed between Bolitho and his rugged coxswain. A bond. Unbreakable to the end.

Bolitho said, 'Take some brandy, Allday, and be off with you.'

Allday turned by the screen door and peered aft as Bolitho seated himself at the table. So many, many times he had stood behind him in countless different gigs and barges. Always the black hair tied at the nape of his neck above his collar. With death and danger all around, and in times of rejoicing it had always been there.

He closed the door behind and gave the motionless sentry a wink. Whatever the rights and wrongs of it, no matter how they sorted it out with so many set against them, Bolitho and his lady would come through it. He smiled to himself, remembering when she had taken the time to speak with him. *A real sailor's woman.*

And God help anyone who tried to come between them.

*   *   *

In the days and the weeks which followed, while *Truculent* battled her way north-west towards the Cape Verde Islands, against perverse changes of wind which seemed intent only on delaying her passage, Bolitho withdrew into himself, even more than when outward bound.

Allday knew it was because he had nothing to

161

plan or prepare this time, not even the affairs of the ship to divert his attention. Jenour too had seen the change in him when he had taken his daily walks on deck; surrounded by *Truculent*'s people and the busy routine found in any man-of-war, and yet so completely alone.

Each time he came on deck he examined the chart or watched the master instructing the midshipmen with the noon sights. Poland probably resented it, and took Bolitho's regular examinations of the calculations and knots made good as unspoken criticism.

Bolitho had even turned on Jenour over some trivial matter, and just as quickly had apologised. Had stared at the empty sea and said, 'This waiting is destroying me, Stephen!'

Now he was fast asleep in his cot after being awake half the night, tormented by dreams which had left him shaking uncontrollably.

Catherine watching him with her lovely eyes, then laughing while another took her away without even a struggle. Catherine, soft and pliable in his hands, then far beyond his reach as he awoke calling her name.

Seven weeks and two days exactly since Bolitho had seen Table Mountain swallowed up in darkness. He rolled over gasping, his mouth dry as he tried to remember his last dream.

With a start he realised that Allday was crouching by his cot, his figure in shadow as he held out a steaming mug. Bolitho's mind reeled, and all his old senses and reactions put an edge to his voice. 'What is it, man?' With something like terror he clapped his hand to his face, but Allday murmured, 'Tis all right, Sir Richard, your eye ain't playin'

162

tricks.' He stumbled from the cot and followed Allday into the stern cabin, the mug of coffee untouched.

If the ship seemed to be in darkness, beyond the stern windows the sea's face was already pale and hard, like polished pewter.

Allday guided him to the quarter window and said, 'I know it's a mite early, Sir Richard. The morning watch is only lately on deck.'

Bolitho stared until his eyes stung. He heard Allday say harshly, 'I thought you'd want to be called, no matter the hour.'

There was no burning sunshine or brilliant dawn here. He wiped the thick, salt-stained glass with his sleeve and saw the first spur of land as it crept through the misty greyness. Leaping waves like wild spectres, their roar lost in far distance.

'You recognise it, old friend?' He sensed that Allday had nodded but he said nothing. Maybe he could not.

Bolitho exclaimed, '*The Lizard*. A landfall—and surely there could be none better!'

He rose from the bench seat and stared around the shadows. 'Though we shall stand too far out to see it, we will be abeam of Falmouth at eight bells.'

Allday watched him as he strode about the cabin, the coffee spilling unheeded on the chequered deck covering. He was glad now that he had awakened to hear the lookout calling to the quarterdeck, '*Land on the lee bow!*'

The Lizard. Not just any landfall but the rocky coast of Cornwall.

Bolitho did not see the relief and the pleasure in Allday's eyes. It was like a cloud being driven away. The threat of a storm giving way to hope. She

163

would be in their room at this very moment, and would not know how close he was.

Allday picked up the mug and grinned. 'I'll fetch some fresh.'

He might as well have said nothing. Bolitho had taken out the locket she had given him, and was staring at it intently as the grey light penetrated the cabin.

Allday opened the door of the little storeroom. Ozzard was curled up asleep in one corner. With elaborate care he lifted one of Ozzard's outflung arms off the brandy cask and gently turned the tap over the mug.

Home again. He held the mug to his lips even as the calls trilled to rouse the hands for the new, but different, day.

And not a moment too soon, matey!

CHAPTER EIGHT

FULL MOON

Bryan Ferguson dabbed his face with his handkerchief while he leaned against the stile to regain his breath. The wind off the sea was no match for the sun which burned down directly across the grey bulk of Pendennis Castle, and threw back such a glare from the water it was not possible to look at it for long.

It was a view he never got tired of. He smiled to himself. He had been steward of Bolitho's estate for over twenty years now. Sometimes it did not seem possible. The Bolitho house was behind him, down

164

the sloping hillside where the fields were banked with wild flowers, while the long grass waved in the breeze like waves on water.

He squinted into the sunlight and stared towards the narrow winding path which led up and around the cliff. He saw her standing where the path turned and was lost around the bend—a treacherous place in the dark, or at any time if you did not take heed. If you fell to the rocks below there was no second chance.

She had told him to remain by the stile, to recover his breath or because she needed to be alone, he did not know. He watched her with silent admiration. Her hair, loosely tied, was whipping in the wind, her gown pressed to her body, making her look like some enchantress in an old poem or folk-tale, he thought.

The household had accepted her warily, unwilling to discuss her presence here with the local people, but, like Ferguson, prepared to defend her right as Bolitho had instructed.

Ferguson and his wife, who was the housekeeper, had expected Bolitho's lady to remain detached from the estate and its affairs. He shook his head as he saw her turn and begin to descend the pathway towards him. How wrong they had been. Almost from the moment she had returned from Portsmouth after saying farewell to Bolitho, she had displayed an interest in everything. But she had always *asked*, not ordered. Ferguson tried not to think of Lady Belinda who had been rather the opposite. It made him feel uneasy and vaguely disloyal.

She had ridden with him to visit the surrounding cottages which were part of the Bolitho heritage;

165

she had even managed to get him to reveal how much larger the estate had originally been in the days of Bolitho's father, Captain James. Much of it had been sold to clear the debts amassed by his other son Hugh, who had deserted the navy and joined the Americans in their fight against the Crown.

Ferguson glanced down at his empty sleeve. Like John Allday he had been pressed not far from here and taken to the frigate *Phalarope*, Bolitho's own command. Ferguson's arm had been taken off at the Saintes. He gave a wry smile. And yet they were still together.

At other times, like today, she had walked with him, asking about crops, the price of seed, ploughing, and the areas where grain and vegetables from the estate were sold. No, she was like nobody Ferguson had ever met.

He had come to understand her during her first days here, when he had been taking her around the old house, showing and naming the grave-faced portraits of Bolitho's ancestors. From old Captain Julius who had died right in Falmouth trying to break the Roundhead blockade of Pendennis Castle, to the recent past. In a small bedroom, covered by a sheet, she had discovered the portrait of Cheney. She had asked him to put it by the window so that she could see it. In that silent room Ferguson had heard her breathing, watched the quick movement of her breasts while she had studied it before asking, 'Why here?' He had tried to explain but she had interrupted him with quiet emphasis. 'Her Ladyship *insisted*, no doubt.' It had not been a question.

Then, after considering, it, 'We will have it

cleaned. All of them.' He had seen a rare excitement in her dark eyes and had known a sort of pride at sharing it. A woman who could make a man's head swim; but he could just as easily picture her with a Brown Bess to her shoulder, the way Allday had described.

She had stepped back to look at Cheney's portrait again. It had been Cheney's gift, as a surprise for Bolitho when he had returned from the war. Instead he found only the portrait waiting. Cheney and their unborn child had been killed in a coaching accident.

Catherine had faced Ferguson when he had tried to tell her about it, had gripped his arm with compassion. '*You* were the one who carried her.' Her eyes had moved to his empty sleeve. 'You did all you could.'

Then she had remarked, 'So when I came here you all decided to conceal it further. What did you expect of me, envy?' She had shaken her head, her eyes misty. 'Like the ocean, *his* ocean, some things are permanent.'

And so the portrait was returned to its original place, facing the window and the sea beyond, the colour of Cheney's eyes.

He straightened his back as she strode down to the stile and held out his hand to steady her while she climbed over. Even now, with her hair breaking away from the ribbon which she had used to control it, with wet sand and dust on her gown, she seemed to give off some inner force. She was taller than Ferguson; there could not be much difference between her and Bolitho, he thought. She squeezed his hand. A casual thing, but again he could feel it; strength, tenderness, defiance, it was all there.

167

'That land yonder. What has been done with it?'

Ferguson replied, 'Too many rocks washed down from the hill. No place for a plough. There's that old copse too.' He watched her lip curve, and imagined her and Bolitho together. When he spoke again his voice was hoarse, so that she looked directly at him, her eyes like dark pools; as if she saw right through him and into his passing thought.

Then she smiled broadly and said, 'I can see I shall have to watch *you*, Mr Ferguson, one arm or no!'

Ferguson flushed, which after serving at sea and then running the estate for so long, was almost unique.

He stammered, 'I beg your pardon, m'lady.' He looked away. 'We've not the men, you see. All taken by the press, or gone for a soldier. Old men and cripples, that's all we've got.'

When he looked at her again he was surprised by the emotion in her eyes.

She said, 'You're no cripple. Together we'll make something of that land.' She was thinking aloud, her voice suddenly fierce. 'I'll not stand by and see him milked by everyone who seems to have lived well off his courage! I don't believe the squire—' her mouth puckered '—*the King of Cornwall* as he is called, I believe? *He* seems to have no difficulty managing his land!'

'French prisoners, m'lady. He is a magistrate, too.' He was glad to change the subject. Again he felt the guilt, when he had known she was referring to Belinda in her great house in London.

She said, 'He is a fair man nevertheless. In any case I like his wife—Sir Richard's favourite sister, is she not?'

168

Ferguson fell into step beside her, but had to walk fast to keep up. 'Aye, m'lady. Miss Nancy, as she once was, was in love with Sir Richard's best friend.'

She stopped and gazed at him searchingly. 'What a lot you know! I envy you the smallest detail, every hour when you have known him and I have not.' She walked on, more slowly now, plucking a flower from a stone wall as she passed. 'You are very fond of him also?'

Ferguson waved to some workers in the field. 'I'd serve none other.'

She looked at the figures, who were pulling a large cart. Most of them were women, but she caught her breath as she recognised the old sailor, the one-legged man named Vanzell. Even he was adding his strength to the load.

Ferguson saw her face and knew she was remembering how Bolitho had taken her from the filth and horror of the Waites jail in London.

Her husband had connived and lied to have her transported. From what Allday had told him it seemed likely she would have died first. Allday had said that Bolitho had been beside himself, had half-carried her from the jail, bringing old Vanzell who had been a guard there out with him. There were several such on the estate. Men like Vanzell who had once served with Bolitho, or women who had lost husbands or sons under his command.

She said, 'He's done so much. We shall repay some of it by making the land come alive again. There's Scotland—they always need grain, surely?'

Ferguson grinned. 'Ships are expensive, m'lady!'

She looked at him thoughtfully, then gave the bubbling laugh he had heard when Bolitho had

169

been with her. 'There are always—' She broke off as they reached the gate to the stable-yard.

Her skin was still sun-burned despite the winter here, but Ferguson later swore to his wife that she had gone as white as death.

'What is it, m'lady? Is something wrong?'

Her hand went to her breast. 'It's the post-boy!'

The youth in his smart cocked hat and breeches was gossiping with Matthew, the head coachman.

Ferguson said, 'He'll be from the town, m'lady. Unusual time of day though.' He beckoned the youth urgently. 'Here, lad, lively now!'

The post-boy touched his hat and showed a gap-toothed smile. 'Fer 'ee, ma'am.'

Ferguson muttered, 'Show respect, or I'll—'

She said, 'Thank you,' then turned away from the sunlight and stared at the letter. 'It bears no mark!'

Ferguson stood by her elbow and nodded. 'A clerk's hand, I'll wager.'

She gazed at him but he knew she could not see him. *Something has happened to him.* In God's name, I cannot—'

The youth, who was willing but not very bright, said helpfully, ''Tes off the mail coach, y'see.' He grinned again. 'They 'ad to sign for that 'un.' He looked at their faces and added importantly, ''Tes from Lunnon!'

'Easy, m'lady,' Ferguson took her arm. 'Come into the house.'

But she was tearing open the cover which revealed another sealed letter inside.

Ferguson sensed his wife come down the stone steps to join them and was almost afraid to breathe. This was how it would happen. Those family

170

portraits told the same story. There was not a single male Bolitho buried in Falmouth. All had been lost at sea. Even Captain Julius had never been found when his ship had exploded down there in Carrick Road in 1646.

She looked at him and said, 'He is in London.' She looked at the letter as if she were dreaming. 'The fight is over at Good Hope. Cape Town has fallen.' She began to shake but no tears came.

Grace Ferguson put a plump arm round her waist and whispered, 'Thank God! 'Tis only right!'

Ferguson asked, 'What is the date, m'lady?'

She appeared to bring herself under control with a physical effort. 'It does not say.' She stared at his handwriting. So few lines, as if to reveal his haste, his need for her.

She exclaimed, 'I felt it. A few nights ago. I got out of bed and looked out to sea.' When she turned, her eyes were shining with happiness. 'He was there, on passage for Portsmouth. *I knew.*'

Ferguson thrust a coin into the post-boy's grubby hand. It had been a nasty moment. Now he guessed that the outer envelope had been to disguise its true contents from prying eyes. That was what he was returning to this time. What they would have to face together.

The post-boy had not gone, and seemed determined to discover what he had stumbled upon.

He said, 'Th' coachman was a-tellin' Oi, zur, why the mail is late, y'see? One o' they coaches cast a wheel along the way—proper excitin' it were!'

Ferguson glared at him. So the letter was late. He looked at her profile, the joy she had always tried to control while he was away. In case...

He said, 'He might be here in a day or so,

171

m'lady.' He ticked off the points in his mind. 'He would have to see them at the Admiralty. There would be a report.' He smiled, remembering Bolitho's constant frustration at the delays which had always followed the heat of action. 'Then, of course ...' He glanced round at the sound of hooves on the track which led down towards the town square and the church where the Bolithos were remembered.

Matthew said doubtfully, ''Tis not one o' *my* horses, m'lady.'

But she was already running, her arms outstretched, heedless of the staring eyes and gaping faces.

It was impossible; it could not be him so soon. Almost blinded, she ran through the gates as the horse and rider clattered over the cobbles towards the yard.

As Bolitho slipped from the saddle and caught her in his arms she pressed her face to his and gasped, 'Oh, dearest of men, what can you think? How must I look—when I wanted to be ready for you!'

He put his hand under her chin and gazed at her for several seconds, perhaps to reassure them both that it was no mistake, nor was it the dream which maybe they had shared.

He said, 'There were delays. I could not wait. I was afraid you might not—'

She put her fingers on his mouth. 'Well, I have, and I want you to know ...'

The rest was lost as their mouths came together.

★   ★   ★

'There. I was not too long, was I?'

Bolitho turned from a window and watched her come from the foot of the stairs. Her dark hair was still loose but brushed back across her shoulders, and she had changed into a simple dark green gown.

He walked to meet her and held her at arm's length. 'You would be beautiful if you wore a seaman's smock!'

She turned in his arms. 'When you look at me like that I feel I am about to blush like a silly young girl.' She searched his face. 'How *are* you? Your eye...'

He kissed her cheek, his whole being aware of her closeness, the pressure of her body against his. All the doubts, all the misgivings were as if they had never been. Like shadows which die in the dawn. It was as if he had never been away. Holding her, talking with her, seemed so natural that it excluded every other sound and feeling.

'It has improved, I think. Even in the African sun, I was rarely troubled.'

She tried to conceal her relief, so that he should not know how her mind had ached for him while he had been away.

Bolitho asked, 'And you? Has it been too bad?'

She laughed and tossed her hair on her shoulders. 'They do not think I am an ogre—in fact I believe they quite like me.'

She became serious again, putting her arm through his and guiding him through to the adjoining room.

'There was some bad news.' She met his gaze as he stopped and faced her. 'Your sister Nancy brought it a week ago. Your other sister has returned from India.'

Bolitho held her gently. 'Felicity?' He saw her nod and tried to picture his sister. She was two years his senior, and he had not laid eyes on her since he had been a lieutenant. She was married to an officer in the Eighty-First Foot, who had later been seconded to the service of the Hon. East India Company. It was strange, but he could remember her husband better than he could Felicity. A pleasant, unassuming officer who had met her when his company had been stationed in Truro.

'Her husband is dead, Richard. So she is come to live in Cornwall again.'

Bolitho waited, knowing there was more. 'She has two sons. One in the regiment, the other a sea-officer in John Company's fleet, as I recall. How did he die?'

Catherine replied, 'His horse threw him.'

'Have you met Felicity yet?'

He saw her chin lift, then she said, 'She would not come with Nancy.' She added defiantly, 'Because of me.'

He put his arm about her, hating how it must have been, how unfair. He said, 'I would to God I had been here!'

She touched his face and smiled gently. 'I had to tell you. But I did not want to spoil anything. Not now. Not with you here again . . .'

'Nothing will. Nothing can.' He felt her tremble and held her more tightly. 'It is so good to be home again.'

'How was it out there, Richard?'

He tried to think clearly. All the faces. Commodore Warren, Captains Poland and Varian, Tyacke and all the others. In the halls of Admiralty it was as if nothing had really happened; or so it had felt.

He said slowly, 'We lost some men, but it could have been worse. I saw Admiral Godschale in London.' He smiled, remembering his new pomposity. '*Lord* Godschale as he now is.'

She nodded. 'I know. It seems to pay to remain at home while others fight and dare.'

He gripped her hands in his. 'Nelson once wrote as much to me. I see that my tiger is still ready to leap out and protect me!'

She smiled despite her sudden bitterness. '*Always.*'

Bolitho looked out at the flowers and rustling trees. 'I wanted to get away, to be here with you.' He felt her watching him but hurried on as if to rid himself of a burden. 'I left poor Allday to follow with our baggage. He complained, but I think he understands.'

'It was strange to see you without him, your shadow.'

Bolitho said, 'Homeward bound we laid off Madeira to take on fresh water and supplies. I bought you some lace there. When Allday arrives you will see for yourself if it is any use, or that I am less of a shopper than I am a sailor!' He released her and picked up his coat from a chair where he had thrown it. 'I thought you might like this.' He took out a Portuguese fan of silver filigree and held it out to her. 'To replace the one you gave me and which I always have nearby.' He watched her pleasure, the expert way she flicked open its blades and held it to the sunlight.

'How beautiful!' When she faced him again her expression had changed, her dark eyes very steady.

175

'Is it so wrong of me, Richard?' She went to him and placed her head on his shoulder as if to hide her feelings. 'I cannot wait. I want you now. It is like a hunger, and I should be ashamed.' She looked at him, her face inches from his. 'But I am not.'

Then she pirouetted round and walked away from him. 'The sun shines on lovers too, my darling Richard!' He heard her laugh as she ran up the stairway and knew she had understood his uncertainty, his awkwardness when he had returned to her.

He found her by the window which faced the headland, her hands parting the curtains, so that she appeared to be held in the sunlight as if she were floating. She wore a long white robe with a plain gold cord around her throat, her hair hanging down her back. She neither moved nor turned as he came up behind her and after the briefest hesitation put his arms around her, pulling her against him. He stared at the same view and felt her gasp as his hands moved over her body, touching the nakedness of her limbs beneath the thin gown.

She whispered, 'Don't stop, for God's sake. Never cease to love me like this!' She arched her back as he ran his hands up and over her breasts, then she turned and waited for him to find and release the gold cord so that the gown fell about her ankles.

He barely remembered the next frantic moments as his shirt and breeches went unseen to the floor.

She was on the bed, her lips moist while she watched him.

'I am so cruel, Richard! You must ache from a dozen horses, and yearn for a good meal and some of your own wine.'

176

Then he was beside her, his hand exploring her while she returned his kisses, her fingers around his neck, caressing the short hair where his queue had been.

She wanted to ask him why he had done away with it; to learn how long they might be together, so many, many things, but neither her will nor her body could prolong the moment another second.

It was brief; the wild need of each other driving away patience and bringing instead a culmination which made Catherine cry out as if she had no care for those who might hear and wonder.

Later, Bolitho opened his eyes and found himself still in her arms, their bodies entwined as if they had never moved. The room was full of silver light, brighter even than the sun; or so it seemed.

'How long . . . ?'

She kissed him. 'Not long enough. I have been with you all the while. Did you know there is a pale patch on your neck where the skin was shaded by your hair?'

'Don't you like it, Kate?'

She pulled his head down to her breast. 'I will grow used to it. The man I love is unchanged!'

She stroked his hair. 'I must bring you something to eat. The whole house is abed. What must they think of us—of me?'

Bolitho propped himself on one elbow, watching the moonlight, knowing she was staring up at him, knowing that he wanted her again, and again.

'It is so warm.' As if to a secret signal they both left the bed and stood side by side at the window, feeling the soft warm air about their nakedness, the sense of peace as the sea boomed faraway on those hidden rocks which guarded the approaches like black sentinels.

He put his arm around her waist and felt her body respond to his touch. Then he looked up at the moon. It was full, like a great silver dish.

'I need you, Kate.' He was almost afraid to say it. He was unused to speaking out about something so secret and yet so powerful.

'And I you.'

Bolitho hugged her. 'But I will close the windows. There will be no food tonight, dearest Kate, and with that halo around the moon I think it may come on to blow before dawn.'

She drew him down again and without effort roused him to match her own excitement, until they were once again joined, and he lay across her, breathing hard, his heart beating against her body like a hammer.

Only when his breathing became regular and he lay close by her side did she allow the tears to come; she even spoke his name aloud, but he was in a deep sleep once more.

She turned her head to look at the window and felt the wetness of her tears on the pillow. The moon was as bright as before. She felt him stir and held him more tightly as if to protect him even in sleep. *But there was no halo*, and the sky was clear but for its stars.

So it was not over. In spite of his high hopes, the damaged eye was waiting; like a thief in the night.

CHAPTER NINE

SUMMER WINE

Bolitho reined his horse to a halt beside a low mossy wall and stared across the fields to a cluster of tiny cottages beside the Penryn road. It had been three days since his unexpected arrival in Falmouth and he had never felt so well nor known such happiness. Every hour seemed to be filled with exciting discoveries, although he knew it was only that he was sharing them with Catherine. He had been born here, had grown up amongst these same villages and farms until, like all the Bolitho ancestors, he had gone off to join his first ship, the old *Manxman* of eighty guns which had been lying at Plymouth.

For England it had then been a rare moment of peace, but to the twelve-year-old Midshipman Bolitho it had been the most awesome experience of his life. The very size of the ship, or so she had appeared at the time, had taken his breath away, the towering masts and spread yards, the hundreds of busy seamen and marines and the terrible thought that he would never be able to find his way about, were unnerving enough.

He was quick to learn and had managed to laugh off, outwardly at least, the usual taunts and the brutal humour which he came to recognise as part of any ship, as much as the tar and cordage which held them together. He had never even laid eyes on an admiral until he had joined his second ship, and at no time had he believed he would reach the lordly heights of lieutenant, let alone live to see his own flag leading the line of battle.

Catherine edged her horse closer to him and asked, 'What are you thinking?' She leaned over to put her gloved hand on his. 'You were so far away from me.'

He looked at her and smiled. She wore a dark green riding habit, and her hair was plaited above her ears, shining in the bright sunshine.

'Memories. All kinds of things.' He squeezed her hand. 'Of the past three days. Of our love.' Their eyes seemed to lock. Bolitho thought of the time they had found a quiet cove and left the horses to graze while they had explored it. By the tiny beach he had uncovered an old rusting and weed-covered ringbolt hammered into the stone. It was where, as a boy, he had come in his little dory, and had once been cut off by the tide and unable to pull the boat clear. They had found him clinging halfway up the cliff, the waves spitting at his ankles as if to pluck him down. His father had been away at sea, otherwise Richard doubted if he would have been able to sit down for a week.

She had listened to him and said, 'We shall make it *our* cove.'

It still made him feel dazed to think about it. How they had made love on that tiny crescent of sand, as if the world were abandoned but for themselves.

She said quietly, 'Then I was sharing your thoughts.'

They sat in silence for a long time while the countryside left them untroubled. The horses nuzzled one another, insects kept up a steady chorus and invisible birds joined in. A church clock seemed to rouse them, and Catherine took her hand away. 'I like your sister Nancy very much. She has been most kind. I suspect she has never met anyone like me before.' She looked up directly at the sprawling house which lay beyond a pair of open gates as if it were waiting for them. 'Her husband, too, has offered his services and advice without my asking.'

Bolitho followed her glance. It was huge, this place which Nancy and Lewis Roxby called their home; it had been in the Roxby family for generations, and yet Bolitho knew that for years Lewis, 'the King of Cornwall', had had his eye on the grey house below Pendennis Castle. His ancestors had perhaps been content to be the landowners and magistrates their position dictated. Not so Nancy's husband. Farming, tin mining, even a local packet company were all a part of his empire. He was a hard-drinking, hunting squire when he was not dealing in business or hanging local felons for their crimes. He had little in common with Bolitho, but he had treated Nancy well and was obviously devoted to her. For that, Bolitho would have forgiven him almost anything.

Bolitho urged his mount forward once more, wondering what awaited them. He had sent a note to Felicity to tell her that they were coming. The horses rather than a carriage had been his idea, to give the impression of a casual visit rather than any sort of formality.

As they clattered into the courtyard two servants ran to take their bridles while another brought a dismounting stool, only to stare with astonishment as Catherine slid easily to the ground.

She saw Bolitho's smile and put her head on one

181

side, the unspoken question in her eyes.

Bolitho put his arm round her shoulders and said, 'I am so proud of you, Kate!'

She stared at him. 'Why?'

'Oh, so many reasons.' He hugged her. 'The things you do, the way you look.'

'And there is someone peeping at us from an upstairs window.' For a brief instant her confidence seemed to falter. 'I am not sure I should have come.'

He looked at her and replied, 'Then here is something more to peep at!' He kissed her hard on the cheek. 'See?'

She seemed to shake it off; and when a footman opened the tall doors and Lewis Roxby, red-faced and rotund, bustled to greet them, she returned his welcome with a warm smile and offered her hand to him.

Roxby turned to Bolitho. 'Dammee, Richard, you're a sly old dog! I'd been hopin' you'd stay away a bit longer so that your lady and I could get the better acquainted, what!'

He put his arms round them and guided them to the great room which overlooked his rose gardens. The doors were open and the room was filled with their scent.

She exclaimed, 'What *perfume*!' She clapped her hands together and Bolitho saw the young girl she had once been in London. Not Belinda's town, but the other London of rough streets and markets, pleasure gardens and bawdy theatres, watermen and beggars. He still knew so little about her, but all he could feel was admiration for her, and a love he had never known before.

Bolitho turned to another glass door and through

182

it watched two women walking up towards the house.

Nancy never seemed to change, except that she was plumper each time he saw her. But with the kind of life she shared with Roxby it would have been surprising otherwise. She was the only one of his family who had their mother's fair looks and complexion; her children were the same. But Bolitho could only stare at her companion with a kind of disbelief. He knew it was Felicity, who would be about fifty-one; she had the same Bolitho eyes and profile, but the dark hair was gone, replaced entirely by grey, while her face and cheeks were ashen as if she had only recently recovered from a fever.

Even when she entered the room and nodded her head to him, very slowly, he could sense no contact. She was a complete stranger.

Nancy ran forward and threw her arms around him, kissing him. She smelt fresh and sweet—like the garden, he thought.

'After all these years, here is our Felicity back home again!' Her voice was too bright, and Bolitho thought he saw a warning glance from her husband.

Bolitho said, 'I should like to introduce you to Catherine.'

Felicity studied her coldly, then gave a brief curtsy. 'My lady. I cannot bid you welcome here, as this is not my house ... nor do I have one at present.'

Roxby said, 'We'll soon take care of that, what?'

Bolitho said, 'I was sorry to learn of Raymond's death. It must have been a terrible shock.'

She did not appear to hear. 'I have sent word to Edmund by way of the regimental agents, Cox and

Greenwood. My other son Miles has returned to England with me.' Her deepset eyes turned to Catherine again and seemed to strip her naked, as she added, 'It was not an easy life. I had a little girl, you know, but she died out there. Her father always wanted a girl, you see.'

Catherine looked at her gravely. 'I am sorry to hear that. I grew up in a demanding climate and I can sympathise.'

Felicity nodded. 'Of course. I had forgotten. You were married to a Spaniard before you met your present husband, the viscount.'

Roxby said thickly, 'Some wine, Richard?'

Bolitho shook his head. What had happened to Felicity? Or had she always been like this?

He said, 'Catherine sent word that you were always welcome at our house while you are deciding where to settle. While I was away at sea—and Catherine had no idea when I was returning home—she acted as she knew I would wish.'

Felicity sat down in a high-backed gilt chair. 'It has not been my home since I met and married Raymond. There is certainly no place there for me now.' She turned her gaze on Bolitho. 'But you always were a thoughtless fellow, even as a child.'

Catherine said, 'I find that hard to believe, Mrs Vincent. I know of no one more thoughtful when it comes to others.' Her eyes flashed but her voice remained calm. 'Even when that compassion is not returned.'

'Of course.' Felicity dusted a speck of dust from her sleeve. 'You would be in a better position than anyone to know his qualities, or otherwise.'

Catherine turned away and Bolitho saw her fingers digging into the fold of her riding skirt. It had been a mistake. He would make his excuses to Nancy and leave.

Felicity said, 'However, there is a favour I *will* ask of you, Richard.' She looked at him, her face quite composed. 'My son Miles has quit the East India Company. Perhaps you could arrange for him to be accepted for the King's service? I have but few funds, and he would be quick to gain promotion.'

Bolitho walked across the room and took Catherine's arm. 'I will do what I can for him. Perhaps I could meet him at some time.'

Then he said, 'I can accept the hurt which Raymond's loss has done you. But I cannot, will not, tolerate your rudeness to Catherine. This house is not mine either, otherwise I might forget myself further!'

In those few seconds he saw it all. Catherine, very still, Nancy, fingers to her mouth and near to tears, and Roxby puffing out his cheeks, doubtless wishing he was anywhere else but here. Only Felicity seemed cool and unmoved. She needed a favour of him, but her dislike for Catherine had almost ruined even that.

Outside the tall doors Roxby muttered, 'Sorry about that, Richard. Damn bad business all round.' To Catherine he added, 'She'll come round, m'dear, you'll see. Women are a funny lot, y'know!' He took her proffered hand and touched it with his lips.

She smiled at him. 'Aren't we, though?' Then she turned as the two horses were led around the house from the stable-yard. 'I never knew her poor husband, of course.' When she looked at Roxby again the smile was gone. 'But it sounds as if he is

185

well out of it. And as far as I am concerned I don't care if she *comes round* or not!'

Once outside the gates again Bolitho reached over and took her hand. Her whole body was shaking.

He said, 'I am so sorry, Kate.'

'It wasn't that, Richard. I am used to bitches, but I'll not have her talking to you like that!' The horses waited as if they sensed her anger. Then she looked at him and said, 'She is your sister but I would never have guessed it. After all you have done, for me and everyone else, and how you have paid dearly for it—' She shook her head as if to drive it all away. 'Well, she can just go to hell!'

He squeezed her arm and asked quietly, 'Tiger?'

She nodded and wiped her eyes with the back of her glove.

'Never doubt it!' Then she laughed, 'I'll race you back to the house.' Then she was gone, the horse kicking up dirt from the road before Bolitho could move.

Roxby watched from the steps of his great house until they had both vanished into the fields.

Beside him his groom, who had worked for him for many years, remarked, 'A lively mare an' no mistake, sir.'

Roxby stared at him but the man's eyes were devoid of amusement. 'Er, yes, quite so, Tom.' Then he ambled into the house, adjusting his face for whatever was waiting.

What a woman, he thought. No wonder Bolitho looked so well, so young. He caught sight of himself in a tall mirror as he passed through the hallway. Bolitho was about his own age, and looked years younger. With a woman like that . . . He closed his mind and strode into the room they had just left, and felt a sudden relief at finding his wife alone.

'She's gone to lie down, Lewis.'

Roxby gave a noncommittal grunt. But he was angry at seeing the tearstains on her cheeks.

'I'll see what I can manage about finding her a suitable house, m'dear.' He walked round the chair and patted her hair fondly, his mind busy with how soon he could rid the place of her sister.

Then he said abruptly, 'I wonder how she knows so much about Catherine's past? I certainly didn't tell her anything. Don't *know* anythin' neither, dammit!'

Nancy took his hand and kissed it. 'I wondered about that too.' She stood up, the mood passing. 'I'll go and arrange supper for this evening, Lewis.' Then she added, 'Richard looks so much better than when he lost his ship last October. They must be good for one another.'

Roxby made certain there were no servants nearby and patted her buttock as she passed.

'You're not so bad yourself, m'dear!' He saw the flush mount to her cheeks, and the way she tidied her hair. Perhaps she was remembering how they had been before the children, and all the work to increase their wealth and living standards. Maybe like the two people he had seen galloping down the lane as if they hadn't a care in the world.

It did not occur to him that his homely wife might have been thinking back down the years about the young midshipman she had fallen in love with; and had been seeing herself with him.

★　　　★　　　★

For two whole weeks life continued for Bolitho and

his Catherine in the same unplanned, idyllic fashion. Rides down forgotten lanes, or long walks above the sea, never at a loss for words, each ready to contribute towards their new-found isolation.

It was as if the other world of war and threats of invasion lay out of reach, and only once when they had been standing on the headland above the Helford River had Catherine mentioned it. A frigate had been tacking away from the land, her sails very pale in the bright sunshine, her hull low and sleek like the one which had done for Tyacke's *Miranda*.

'When will you be told?' He had put his arm around her shoulders, his eyes distant as he watched the frigate. Was all this just make-believe after all? At any day he might receive new instructions, perhaps a summons to the Admiralty. He was determined that they would spend every possible minute together until...

He had replied, 'There was a hint from Their Lordships about a new squadron. It seems the most likely. Provided enough ships can be found.'

The frigate had been setting her topgallants, shaking them out to the offshore wind like a creature awakening from a brief rest.

He thought suddenly of his nephew, Adam. That was one piece of good news he had come by at the Admiralty. He had commissioned his new command, a fifth-rate of thirty-eight guns named *Anemone*. What a proud moment it must have been for him. Captain of a frigate, his dream, at the age of twenty-six. *Anemone*, Daughter of the Wind. It seemed very suitable. He had Allday's son with him as coxswain exactly as he had promised, and the ship had been ordered to the North Sea to carry out patrols off the Dutch coast.

188

He had hoped that the news might pull Allday out of his present gloom. When he had reached Falmouth with Ozzard and Yovell with all the baggage which Bolitho had left in London, he had gone straight to the inn to see the landlord's only daughter.

Yovell had mentioned it to Bolitho in confidence. Not only had the inn passed into new ownership, but the young woman in question had gone away and married a farmer in Redruth.

At the end of the second week Bolitho was reading a copy of the *Gazette* where the recapture of Cape Town was mentioned for the first time. Time and distance had sharpened the memory for him, but the *Gazette* seemed to take it as a matter of course. There was no mention of the fireship at all.

Allday entered the room and said, 'There's a young gentleman who wishes to see you, Sir Richard. He is Mr Miles Vincent.'

'Very well. I will receive him now.' Catherine was down at the estate office with Ferguson. Bolitho was still amazed by the way she had sorted out facts and figures, and with Ferguson's ready help had prepared her own ploughing and planting suggestions for the coming year. She had even been making comparisons with local grain sales set against those in the North and as far as Scotland. He had expected that Ferguson might have resented her vigorous ideas for the estate, but like the property itself she seemed to have given him new heart for the future.

He crossed to a window and looked towards the road, now hidden by thick bushes. Eventually they would leave here and face up to the world outside Falmouth. To London, to places where people

189

would turn and stare. Where others might hide their envy behind false smiles.

The door opened and closed and he turned to see Felicity's younger son standing in the dusty sunshine. His dress was simple, a plain blue coat and a frilled white shirt, but he gave the immediate impression of incredible neatness. Except for a certain solemnity for one so young, he might have been like Adam when he had been his age.

'Please sit down.' Bolitho took his hand. 'We were sorry to learn of your father's untimely death. It must have been hard on the family.'

'Indeed yes, Sir Richard.' He arranged himself in the chair, his hands folded in his lap.

Bolitho thought, like a youth about to ask his father for his daughter's hand. Shy, but determined nonetheless. You would have known him for a Bolitho anywhere. He was nineteen years old, and had the same grey eyes, and hair almost as dark as his own. Behind this outer shyness was the barely concealed confidence which must be inevitable in any sea officer, no matter how junior.

'I understand that you intend to seek a King's commission. That being so I can foresee no difficulty. Volunteers for the berth of midshipman, even those forced by proud parents, are plentiful enough. Others with experience such as your own are very thin on the ground.' It was meant to relax him, to draw him out. It could not be easy to sit down with a vice-admiral whose exploits at sea and ashore were food for gossip on all levels. Bolitho had no way of knowing what Felicity might have said, so he had expected Miles Vincent to be on edge.

He had not anticipated the youth's reaction. He

exclaimed, 'I am most confused, Sir Richard! I was acting-lieutenant in the H.E.I.C., fully qualified in matters of seamanship and standing a watch. It was only a matter of time before I was advanced. Did you mean that I would be reduced to holding a warrant as a mere midshipman?'

The shyness was gone; instead, he looked closer to righteous indignation.

Bolitho replied, 'Be easy now. You will know, as well if not better than I, that holding a rank in one of John Company's ships is a far cry from the King's service. The pay and conditions are far superior, the ships are not manned by the sweepings of the jails or the press gangs, and they are only called on to fight to defend their own cargoes ... when I was a captain there was many a time I would have seized a few of their prime seamen for my own.' He paused. 'In the King's ships we are expected to do battle with the enemy, no matter what guise or force he comes in. My people do not serve for the money or the profit which any experienced man can make in the Company's vessels, nor do they for the most part fight for their King and country!' He saw Vincent's eyes widen and continued, 'That surprises you? Then let me explain. They fight for each other, for their ship, which must be their home until they are released from a harsh and demanding service.'

The youth stammered, 'You—make it very clear, Sir Richard.'

Bolitho smiled to himself. The nervous suitor was back again.

He said, 'So if you are still of the same mind I will certainly sponsor your request to a captain who requires young gentlemen. I feel certain that one

191

like yourself, with the qualities you have mentioned, will be promoted to lieutenant in a matter of months, perhaps less. The Fleet *needs* officers as never before. But if they cannot lead or encourage the people they are intended to command, I for one have no time for them.'

'If I may say, Sir Richard, your own gallant examples are much talked of.'

He sprang to his feet as Catherine walked through a garden door.

She stared from Bolitho to the stiff-backed figure in blue and commented, 'You must be Miles.' She tossed a wide-brimmed straw hat onto a chest and kissed Bolitho lightly on the cheek. 'It is such a lovely day, Richard, we must walk along the cliff this evening.' She shot him a questioning glance as the youth sprang forward to hold a chair for her. 'Thank you, young sir.'

Vincent was gazing at the portraits, which marked each section of the staircase like silent onlookers.

'All great sailors, Sir Richard. I would wish nothing more than to be like them.' He glanced at Catherine, his features expressionless. 'To add honour to the name of Bolitho!'

With the same precise care he made his excuses and left the house and Bolitho remarked, 'A pretty speech anyway.' He looked at her and then knelt beside her chair.

'What is it, dearest Kate? Tell me.'

She touched his face with sudden tenderness. 'That young man. His face, those eyes . . . he is so much a part of your family background. Like all the other mysteries I cannot share.'

Bolitho took her hand and tried to make light of

it. 'His manners are faultless, but they train them well in the H.E.I.C., so that their young officers may flirt with the ladies of quality and lovesick maidens who take passage to distant parts!' It was not working. 'I want to share everything with you, dearest Kate, and share *you* with nobody.'

Catherine placed her palm on his face and smiled. 'You always *know*, Richard. It is like a bond stronger even than marriage, because it is of our making and choice.' Her dark eyes searched his face feature by feature. 'I will be all that you want me to be. Lover, companion, friend—' She laughed and threw back her head. 'Or the lady for whom young officers carry chairs. What did you make of him?'

'What has Felicity made of him, would be a fairer question!' He took her arm. 'Come—the cliff walk. I never tire of it. You can tell me about your plans for the estate as we go.'

Allday closed the door as they walked out into the garden and down towards the small gate.

He tried not to think about the girl at the inn. What had he expected? How could he have hoped to marry her and still serve Bolitho at sea? The questions were still unanswered when he found Ozzard making his way to the kitchen, where he sometimes helped Mrs Ferguson with her duties.

'Did you see the lad who came about joining the service?'

Ozzard frowned. 'He's a dark one, I shouldn't wonder. Why did he quit the East India Company—that's what I'd like to know before *I* gave him any authority!'

Allday sighed. It had been good to see Bolitho and his lady walking together, but it only added to his own sense of being unwanted, with nothing useful to do until the next orders came. Even that prospect gave him no satisfaction.

He said half to himself, 'If only she'd waited.'

Ozzard turned on him with unexpected fury. '*Wait?* They never bloody well wait, any of 'em, and the sooner you get that through your skull the better—*matey*!'

Allday stared after him with astonishment. Usually there was none milder. So he wasn't the only one with troubles after all.

*   *   *

It was, many proclaimed, one of the best summers anyone could remember. The crops, like the lambing, had done well, and even the coastal fishermen were not heard to complain. But for the absence of young men around the farms and in the streets of Falmouth, they might have been at peace.

The news of the war was sparse and, apart from some reports of French men-of-war being sighted near Biscay, and then only in small numbers, it was as if the whole enemy fleet had been swallowed up. Bolitho sometimes thought of the French frigate which had been sheltering at Good Hope, or the coded letters they had found aboard the slaver *Albacora*. Was it part of an overall plan, or were these ship movements and occasional attempts to breach the tightly-stretched English blockade merely at the whim of their local commanders?

He had spoken infrequently of his thoughts to Catherine because she was preparing herself in her own way for the inevitable. When it came on the last day of August she said quietly, 'It is a part of your life which I cannot share; no woman can. But whatever it is, Richard, wherever duty takes you, *I shall be with you.*'

They had been riding along the cliffs and unlike other times they had said very little, had been content with each other's nearness. They had found the little cove again, where they had made love so passionately and had cast all inhibitions to the sea-breezes. This time they had dismounted but remained on the cliff, holding the horses' heads, then touching hands in silence. It was as if they had both known. As Catherine had sensed the nearness of his ship when it had sailed on to Portsmouth.

When they had entered the stable-yard Bolitho had seen Allday waiting by the door.

Allday looked first at Catherine, then at him. 'Th' courier's been an' gone, Sir Richard.'

Perhaps he too had been expecting it. He might even have been willing it to come. To be at sea again, serving the one who meant more to him than any other living soul. Doing what he had given his life to.

Now, with the late afternoon sunshine casting almost horizontal beams across the big room, the house seemed strangely silent as Bolitho slit open the heavy, red-sealed envelope with the Admiralty fouled anchor in its corner.

She stood with her back to him, her straw hat dangling from her hand, watching the garden, trying to remain calm perhaps, with the taste of the salt air on her lips. Like dried tears.

He laid down the letter and said, 'Apparently I am being given a squadron.' He watched her turn towards him as he added, '*Eventually*. Also a new flagship.'

She crossed the room in quick strides, her hat

195

falling unheeded to the floor. 'Does that mean we are not to be parted yet?' She waited for him to hold her. 'Just tell me that is so!'

Bolitho smiled. 'I must go to London.' He tightened his hold, feeling the warmth of her body against his own. 'We shall go together, if that is what you want.'

She nodded. 'I understand what you mean. What to expect from some quarters.' She saw the pain in his grey eyes and touched his face. 'I knew your thoughts just now about your next flagship. She will not be your old *Hyperion*. But *she* is safe from those who would dishonour her by turning her into a hulk after all her years of service.'

He stroked her hair. 'You read me like a book, Kate. I was thinking that. The new ship is named *Black Prince* and is completing fitting-out at the Royal Dockyard, Chatham. I will take you there, too ... I don't want to lose you for a moment!'

She seated herself near the great fireplace, now empty, but with the dark stains of countless winter evenings on the stonework. While Bolitho moved about the room she watched him, saying nothing which might distract him or interrupt his thoughts. This was the other man whom she cherished so dearly, so possessively. Once he paused in his restless pacing and looked at her, but she knew he had not seen her.

He said suddenly, 'I shall ask for a good flag-captain. I will insist.'

She smiled sadly. 'You are thinking of Valentine Keen?'

He walked over to her and took her hands. 'Once more, you are right. He is not yet called into service again; and it is not like Val not to have announced the day chosen for their marriage. Strange, too, that Zenoria has not written to you.' He shook his head, his mind made up. 'No, I would not request that he continues as my flag-captain. Neither of them would thank me for *that*!' He squeezed her hands. 'Like me, Val was late in finding the right woman with whom to share his life.'

She looked up at him, seeing the light in his eyes. 'When we are in London will you promise to see that surgeon? For me, if for no other reason.'

He smiled. It was what he had asked of Tyacke. 'If time allows.' He let out a sigh. 'We have to leave for London in two days. How I loathe that journey ... the only one in the world which gets longer every time!'

She stood up and looked around the quiet room. 'Such memories. Without these past weeks I do not think I could have faced this news. But now it is home to me. It will always be waiting.' She faced him and added, 'And do not fret over Val and his Zenoria. It is not long since they came together. They will want time to arrange matters, and then they will tell us.'

She dragged him to the window and exclaimed, 'And *if time allows*—' She saw him grin as she attempted to mimic his words, 'I shall show you some different sights in London so that you will not feel so gloomy each time you visit the Lords of Admiralty.'

They walked out into the garden and to the wall where the small gate opened on the path to the stile and the cliff. Where she had come to meet him on that first night.

She said eventually, 'And you must not worry about me while you are gone. I would never stand

197

between you and your ships. You are mine, so I am part of them too.'

Ozzard watched them from an upstairs window where he had been polishing some pewter dishes for Mrs Ferguson. He did not turn as Allday entered the room but remarked, 'We're off again then?'

Allday nodded and massaged his chest as the old ache returned. 'Aye. 'Tis London first though.' He chuckled. 'Just happened to hear it.'

Ozzard began to polish a dish he had already shone to perfection. He looked troubled, but Allday knew better than to disturb his thoughts. Instead he said, 'She's the *Black Prince*, brand-new second-rate of ninety-four guns. Bit larger than we've got used to, eh? Like a palace, an' that's no error!'

But Ozzard was far away. In that street along the old Wapping Wall where he had blundered from his little house on that hideous day.

He could hear her pleading and screams; and afterwards, when he had hacked his young wife and her lover to death until he had lost all strength in his arm, the terrible silence.

It had been haunting him ever since, revived by a casual comment made by the senior surgeon who had been in *Hyperion* during her last fight. When the old ship had started to go down, Ozzard had wanted to go with her, to stay with Bolitho's things in the hold, where he always went when the ship, any of their ships, had been in action.

But it was not to be. He let out a long sigh.

All he said was, 'It's London, then.'

198

CHAPTER TEN

THE WAY OF THE WORLD

Admiral the Lord Godschale was doing his best to show cordiality, to forget the coolness between himself and Bolitho when they had last met.

'It is time we had a good talk, Sir Richard. We in admiralty can too often become dry old sticks, missing out on greater deeds which officers like you seem to attract.'

Bolitho stood beside one of the tall windows and looked down at the sunlit roadway and the park beyond. Did London never rest, he wondered? Carriages and smart phaetons bustled hither and thither, wheels seemingly inches apart as their coachmen tried to outdo one another's skill. Horsemen and a few mounted ladies made splashes of colour against the humbler vehicles, carriers' carts and small waggons drawn by donkeys.

Jostling people, some pausing to gossip in the warm September sunshine, and a few officers from the nearby barracks, cutting a dash as they strolled through the park and trying to catch the eye of any likely young lady.

Bolitho said, 'We are only as good as our men.' Godschale meant nothing of the sort. He was well pleased with his appointment and the power it gave him, and very likely believed that no ship or her captain would amount to anything without his guiding hand from afar.

Bolitho studied him as he poured two tall glasses of madeira. It was strange to realise that they once served together, when they had both been frigate captains during the American Revolution. They had even been posted on the same day. There was not much to show of that dashing young captain now, he thought. Tall, powerfully built and still handsome, despite a certain florid complexion which had not been gained on an open deck in the face of a gale. But behind the well-groomed sleekness there was steel too, and Bolitho could still recall how they had parted the previous year when Godschale had attempted to manoeuvre him away from Catherine and back to Lady Belinda.

Bolitho did not believe that Godschale had had any hand in the terrible plan to falsify evidence which had put Catherine in the filthy Waites prison. Sometimes she had awakened at his side, even after all the months which had passed since he had rescued her, and had cried out as if she had been trying to fight off her jailers.

No, Godschale was a lot of things but he would have no stomach for a plan which might cast him down from his throne. If he had a weakness it was conceit, an actual belief in his own shrewdness. He had probably been used by Catherine's husband, convinced, as Belinda had been, that it was the only solution.

Bolitho gritted his teeth. He had no idea where Viscount Somervell was now, although he had heard rumours that he was on another mission for His Majesty in North America. He tried not to think about it, knowing that if ever they came face-to-face again he would call him out. Somervell was a duellist of repute, but usually with a pistol. Bolitho touched the old sword at his side. Perhaps someone else would cheat him of the chance.

Godschale handed him a glass and raised his eyebrows, 'Remembering, eh?' He sipped at his madeira. 'To great days, Sir Richard!' He eyed him curiously. 'To happier ones also.'

Bolitho sat down, his sword resting across one leg. 'The French squadrons which slipped through the blockade—you recall, m'lord? Before I sailed for Good Hope. Were they taken?'

Godschale smiled grimly. He saw the sudden interest, the keenness in Bolitho's eyes, and felt in safer waters. He was well aware that Viscount Somervell's wife was here in London, flaunting her relationship as if to provoke more hostility and rouse criticism. With Nelson it had been embarrassing enough; at least that affair had been allowed to rest. Nobody seemed to know where Emma Hamilton was now, or what had happened since his death at Trafalgar.

Godschale did not care much for Somervell's character and reputation. But he still had friends, some very powerful, at Court, and had been rescued from scandal and far worse by no less than His Majesty himself. But even the King, or more likely his close advisers, had conveniently removed Somervell from London's melting-pot until the problem of Bolitho's involvement was solved, or destroyed.

The admiral was sensible enough to accept that no matter how he felt about it, Bolitho was probably as popular in the country as Nelson had once been. His courage was beyond doubt, and in spite of some unorthodox methods and tactics, he *did* win battles.

In peacetime his affair with Lady Somervell would not be tolerated for an instant: they would both be shunned and barred from society, while Bolitho's own career would fly to the winds.

But it was not peacetime; and Godschale knew the value of leaders who won, and the inspiration they offered their men and the nation.

He said, 'The larger of the two enemy squadrons was under the flag of our old opponent Vice-Admiral Leissègues. He managed to slip through all our patrols—nevertheless Sir John Duckworth, who was cruising off Cadiz, gained some intelligence that a French squadron was at St Domingo. Duckworth had already been chasing Leissègues, but had been about to give up when he had the news. He eventually ran them to ground, and even though the French cut their cables when Duckworth's squadron was sighted, he brought them to close-action. All the enemy were taken, but the hundred and twenty gun *Impérial* went aground and was burned. She would have made a formidable addition to our fleet.' He sighed grandly. 'But one cannot do everything!'

Bolitho hid a smile. It sounded as if the admiral had won the victory from this very room.

Godschale was saying, 'The other French force was brought to battle and lost several ships singly before fleeing back to harbour.'

Bolitho put down his glass and stared at it bitterly. 'How I envy Duckworth. A decisive action, well thought out and executed. Napoleon must be feeling savage about it.'

'Your work at Cape Town was no less important, Sir Richard.' Godschale refilled the glasses to give himself time to think. 'Valuable ships were released for the fleet by your prompt intervention. It was why I proposed you for the task.' He gave a sly wink. 'Although I know you suspected my motives at the time, what?'

Bolitho shrugged. 'A post-captain could have done it.'

Godschale wagged an admonitory finger. 'Quite the reverse. They needed inspiration by example. Believe me, I *know*!' He decided to change the subject. 'I have further news for you.' He walked to his table and Bolitho noticed for the first time that he was limping. A problem he shared with Lord St Vincent, he thought. Gout—too much port and rich living.

Godschale picked up some papers. 'I told you about your new flagship, the *Black Prince*. A fine vessel to the highest requirements, I understand.'

Bolitho was glad he was looking at his papers and did not see his own rebellious smile. *I understand*. How like Captain Poland. Just to be on the safe side, in case something was proved to be amiss.

Godschale looked up. 'Chosen your flag-captain yet, or need I ask?'

Bolitho replied, 'Under different circumstances I would have picked Valentine Keen without hesitation. In view of his coming marriage, and the fact that he has been continuously employed under demanding circumstances, I am loath to ask this of him.'

Godschale said, 'My subordinate *did* receive a letter from your last captain, offering his services. I thought it odd. I might have expected him to approach you first.' His eyebrows lifted again. 'A good man, is he not?'

'A fine captain, and a firm friend.' It was hard to think clearly with Godschale talking about the new ship. What had happened to Keen? It made no sense.

Godschale was saying, 'Of course, in these hard times, the lieutenants may be quite junior, and the more seasoned professionals that much older. But then none of us loses any years, what?' He frowned suddenly. 'So I would appreciate a quick decision. There are many captains who would give their lives for the chance to sail *Black Prince* with your flag at the fore.'

'It would be a great favour to me, m'lord, if you would allow me the time to enquire into this matter.' It sounded as if he were pleading. He intended it to.

Godschale beamed at him. 'Of *course*. What are friends for, eh?'

Bolitho saw his quick glance at the ornate clock on the wall, an elaborate affair with gilded cherubs supporting it, their cheeks puffed out to represent the four winds.

He said, 'I shall be in London for the present, m'lord, at the address I have given to your secretary.'

Godschale's humour seemed to have faded; his smile was fixed to his mouth. 'Er, yes, quite so. Lord Browne's town house. Used to be your flag-lieutenant before he quit the navy?'

'Yes. A good friend.'

'Hmm, you don't seem to be lacking in those!'

Bolitho waited. Godschale was picturing it all in his mind. Himself and Catherine together, caring nothing for what people thought. He stood up and readjusted the sword at his hip.

Godschale said heavily, 'I don't wish to fan old flames, but is there any chance of your returning ... er ... Dammit, man, you know what I mean!'

204

Bolitho shook his head. 'None, my lord. It is better you know now—I am aware that your lady is a friend of my wife. It would be wrong to promote feelings which are not to be returned.'

Godschale stared at him as if trying to think of some crushing retort. When it failed him he said, 'We shall meet again soon. When that happens I hope I will have fresh information for you. But until that moment, let me remind you of something. A French ball can maim or kill a man, but ashore, his person can be equally hurt, his reputation punctured in a hundred ways!'

Bolitho walked to the door. 'I still believe the former to be the more dangerous, m'lord.'

As the door closed Admiral the Lord Godschale smashed one fist down on his papers. *'God damn his insolence!'*

Another door opened cautiously and the admiral's secretary peered around it.

'My lord?'

Godschale glared. *'Not a damn thing!'*

The man winced. 'Your next appointment will be here very shortly, m'lord.'

Godschale sat down carefully and poured himself another glass of madeira. 'I shall receive him in half an hour.'

The secretary persisted, 'But there *is* no one else, m'lord, not until . . .'

The admiral exclaimed harshly, 'Does *nobody* in the Admiralty listen to what I say? I *know* all about it! But with luck, Sir Richard Bolitho will renew his acquaintance with Rear-Admiral Herrick in the waiting-room. I wish to give them the opportunity to share *old times*. Do you see?'

The secretary did not see but knew better than to

wait for another tirade.

Godschale sighed at the empty room. 'One cannot do everything!'

*   *   *

There were two captains sitting in the outer waiting-room, each avoiding the other's eyes and trying to remain as separate as possible. Bolitho knew they were here to see some senior officer or Admiralty official; he had shared their apprehension and discomfort on more occasions than he could remember. Advancement or a reprimand? A new command, or the first step to oblivion? It was all in a day's work at the Admiralty.

Both captains sprang to their feet as Bolitho walked through the long room. He nodded to them, accepting their recognition and curiosity. Wondering why he was here and what it might indirectly imply for them. More likely they were curious about the man and not the vice-admiral; his reputation, if it were true or false.

Bolitho was more concerned with Godschale's announcement about his flag-captain. He could still scarcely believe it. He had known how worried Keen had been about the age difference between himself and the lovely Zenoria. The girl he had rescued from a transport on her way to Botany Bay. Keen was forty-one years old, and she would be nearly twenty-two. But their love for one another had bloomed so suddenly out of suffering and been visible to everyone who knew them. He must discover what had happened. If Keen had signified his readiness to be his flag-captain merely out of friendship or loyalty, Bolitho would have to

206

dissuade him.

He had almost reached the tall double doors at the far end when they swung open, and he saw Thomas Herrick standing stock-still and staring at him as if he had just fallen from the sky.

Herrick was stocky and slightly stooped, as if the weight of his rear-admiral's responsibilities had made themselves felt. His brown hair was more heavily touched with grey, but he had not changed since he had sailed to support *Hyperion* in that last terrible battle.

His palm was as hard as at their first meeting, when he had been one of Bolitho's lieutenants in *Phalarope*; and the blue eyes were clear and as vulnerable as that very day.

'What are you ...' They both began at once.

Then Bolitho said warmly, 'It is so good to see you, Thomas!'

Herrick glanced warily at the two captains as if to ensure they were well out of earshot. 'You too, Sir Richard.' He smiled awkwardly. *'Richard.'*

'That is better.' Bolitho watched his old friend's uncertainty. So it was still as before. Because of Catherine. He had refused to come to terms with it, could not bring himself to understand how it had happened between them. Bolitho said, 'I have been given *Black Prince*. I shall hoist my flag as soon as she is fitted-out, whenever that might be. You know the dockyards and their strange customs!'

Herrick was not to be drawn. He studied Bolitho's face and asked quietly, 'Your eye—how is it?' He shook his head and Bolitho saw something of the man he had always known and trusted. 'No, I have told no one. But I still think—'

Bolitho said, 'What are *you* doing?'

Herrick's chin was sunk in his neckcloth, something which had become a habit when he was grappling with a problem.

'I still have *Benbow*.' He forced a smile. 'New flag-lieutenant though. Got rid of that fellow with the Frenchie name, De Broux ... too soft for my taste!'

Bolitho felt strangely sad. Just a few years since *Benbow* had flown his flag and Herrick had been the captain. Ships, if they could think, must wonder sometimes about the men and the fates which controlled them.

Herrick pulled out his watch. 'I must present myself to Lord Godschale.' He spoke the name with dislike. Bolitho could well imagine how Herrick felt about the admiral.

As an afterthought Herrick said, 'I am to command a squadron in the North Sea patrols.' He gave a genuine smile. 'Adam's new command *Anemone* is my only frigate! Some things never change, but I am well pleased to have him with me.'

Somewhere a clock chimed and Herrick said quickly, 'You know me—I hate not to be punctual.'

Bolitho watched his struggle, but when it burst out it was not what he had been expecting.

'Your new flagship. She is completing at Chatham?' He hurried on as if the thing which troubled him could not be contained. 'When you visit the ship, and I have been your subordinate too many times in the past not to know your habits, would you find time to call upon my Dulcie?'

Bolitho asked gently, 'What is it, Thomas?'

'I am not sure and that is the God's truth. But she has been so tired of late. She works too hard with her charities and the like, and will not rest when I am away at sea. I keep telling her, but you know how they are. I suppose she's lonely. If we had been blessed with children, even the one like you and Lady Belinda—' He broke off, confused by his own revelation. 'It is the way of the world, I suppose.'

Bolitho touched his sleeve. 'I shall call on her. Catherine keeps trying to drag me to a surgeon, so we may discover someone who might help Dulcie.'

Herrick's blue eyes seemed to harden. 'I am sorry. I was not thinking. Perhaps I was too fouled by my own worries and forgot for a moment.' He looked along the room. 'Maybe it would be better if you did not pay Dulcie a visit.'

Bolitho stared at him. 'Is this barrier still between us, Thomas?'

Herrick regarded him wretchedly. 'It is not of my making.' He was going. 'I wish you well, Richard. Nothing can take my admiration away. Not ever.'

'*Admiration?*' Bolitho looked after him and then called, 'Is that all it has become, Thomas? God damn it, man, are we so *ordinary?*'

The two captains were on their feet as Herrick strode past them, their eyes darting between the flag-officers as if they could scarcely believe what they were witnessing.

Then Bolitho found himself outside the Admiralty's imposing façade, shivering in spite of the sunshine and strolling people.

'Be off with you, you wretch!'

Bolitho glanced up, still breathing hard, and saw a young man, accompanied by two girls, shaking his fist at a crouching figure by the roadside. The contrast was so vivid it made his head swim . . . the elegantly dressed young blade with his giggling

209

friends, and the stooping figure in a tattered red coat who was holding out a tin cup.

'*Belay that!*' Bolitho saw them turn with surprise while several passers-by paused to see what would happen. Ignoring them all, Bolitho strode to the man in the shabby red coat.

The beggar said brokenly, 'I wasn't doin' no 'arm, sir!'

Someone shouted, 'Shouldn't be allowed to hang about here!'

Bolitho asked quietly, 'What was your regiment?'

The man peered up at him as if he had misheard. He had only one arm, and his body was badly twisted. He looked ancient, but Bolitho guessed he was younger than himself.

'Thirty-First Foot, sir.' He stared defiantly at the onlookers. 'The old Huntingdonshire Regiment. We was doin' service as marines.' His sudden pride seemed to fade as he added, 'I was with Lord Howe when I got this lot.'

Bolitho turned on his heel and looked at the young man for several seconds.

'I will not ask the same of you, sir, for I can see plainly enough what *you* are!'

The youth had gone pale. 'You have no right—'

'Oh, but I do. There is at this very moment a lieutenant of the Tower Hill press gang approaching. A word, *just one word* from me, and you will learn for yourself what it is like to fight for your King and country!'

He was angry with himself for using such a cheap lie. No press gang ever ventured into an area of quality and wealth. But the young man vanished, leaving even his companions to stare after him with surprise and humiliation at being abandoned.

Bolitho thrust a handful of coins into the cup. 'God be with you. *Never think that what you did was in vain.*' He saw the man staring at the golden guineas with astonishment, and knew what he was saying was really for his own benefit. 'Your courage, like your memories, must sustain you.'

He swung away, his eyes smarting, and then saw the carriage pulling towards him. She pushed open the door before the coachman could jump down and said, 'I saw what you did.' She touched his mouth with her fingers. 'You looked so troubled . . . did something happen in there to harm you?'

He patted her arm as the carriage clattered back into the aimless traffic. 'It harms us all, it would appear. I thought I understood people. Now I am not so sure.' He looked at her and smiled. 'I am only certain of you!'

Catherine slid her arm through his and looked out of the carriage window. She had seen Herrick stride up the Admiralty steps. The rest, and Bolitho's angry confrontation with the young dandy, needed no explanation.

She answered softly, 'Then let us make the most of it.'

*　　　*　　　*

Tom Ozzard paused to lean against a stone balustrade to find his bearings, and was surprised he was not out of breath. The little man had been walking for hours, sometimes barely conscious of his whereabouts but at the back of his mind very aware of his eventual destination.

Along the Thames embankment, then crisscrossing through dingy side-streets where the shabby eaves almost touched overhead as if to shut out the daylight. Around him at every turn was the London he remembered as if it were yesterday. Teeming with life and street cries, the air rank with horse dung and sewers. On one corner was a man bawling out his wares, fresh oysters in a barrel, where several seamen were trying their taste and washing them down with rough ale. Ozzard had seen the river several times on his walk. From London Bridge to the Isle of Dogs it was crammed with merchantmen, their masts and yards swaying together on the tide like a leafless forest.

In the noisy inns along the river sailors jostled the painted whores and flung away their pay on beer and geneva, not knowing when or if they might ever return once their ships had weighed. None of them seemed at all perturbed by the grisly, rotting remains of some pirates which dangled in chains at Execution Dock.

Ozzard caught his breath; his feet had brought him to the very street as if he had had no part in it.

He found that his breathing was sharper as he hesitated before forcing his legs to carry him along the cobbled roadway. It was like a part of his many nightmares. Even the light, dusky orange as evening closed in on the wharves and warehouses of London's dockland; it was said that there were more thieves and cutthroats in this part of London than in all the rest of the country. This was or had been a respectable street on Wapping Wall. Small, neat houses owned or rented by shopkeepers and clerks, agents from the victualling yards and honest chandlers.

A shaft of low sunshine reflected from the top window of his old house. He caught his breath. As

212

if it was filled with blood.

Ozzard stared around wildly, his heart thumping as if to tear itself free from his slight body. It was madness; *he was mad*. He should never have come, there might still be folk here who remembered him. But when Bolitho had come to London he had accompanied him in another carriage. Allday, Yovell and himself. Each so different, and yet each one a part of the other.

Hardly daring to move, he turned his head to look at the shop directly opposite the row of neat houses.

On that horrific day when he had run from his home, heedless of the blood on his hands, he had paused only to stare at this same shop. Then it had been titled, *Tom Ozzard, Scrivener*. Now he had enlarged the premises and had added *& Son* to his name.

He thought of the time when the surgeon Sir Piers Blachford had spoken out about this same scrivener, and had remarked that it was the only time he had heard the name Ozzard. He had nearly collapsed.

Why did I come?

'You lookin' fer somethin', matey?'

Ozzard shook his head. 'No. Thank you.' He turned away to conceal his face.

'Suit yerself.' The unknown man lurched away towards a tavern which Ozzard knew lay behind the shops. Knew, because he had paused there for a glass of ginger beer on his way home. The lawyer who had employed him as his senior clerk had sent him off early to show his appreciation for all the extra work he had done. *If only he had not stopped for a drink*. Even as the hazy idea formed in his mind he knew he was deluding himself. She must have been laughing at him for months. Waiting for him to go to his office near Billingsgate, then for her lover to come to her. Surely others in the street must have known or guessed what was happening? Why hadn't someone told him?

He leaned against a wall and felt the vomit rising in his throat.

So young and beautiful. She had been lying in her lover's arms when he had walked in unsuspectingly from the street. It had been a sunny day, full of promise, just as today had started out.

The screams began again, rising to a piercing screech as the axe had smashed down on their nakedness. Again, again, and again, until the room had been like some of the sights he had seen since he had met with Richard Bolitho.

He did not hear the heavy tramp of feet and the clink of weapons until a voice shouted, 'You there! Stand and be examined!'

He could barely stop himself shaking as he turned and saw the press gang poised on the corner he had just come around. Not like the ones you saw in fishing villages or naval seaports. These men were armed to the teeth as they hunted for likely recruits in an area which was crammed with sailors, nearly all of whom would have the right papers, the 'Protection' to keep them free of the navy.

A massive gunner's mate, a cudgel hanging from his wrist, a cutlass thrust carelessly through his belt, said, 'Wot's this then?' He peered at Ozzard's blue coat with the bright gilt buttons, the buckled shoes beloved by sailors whenever they had funds enough to buy them. 'You're no sailor, I'll be damn sure o' that!' He put a hand on Ozzard's shoulder
214

and swung him round to face his grinning party of seamen. 'What say you, lads?'

Ozzard said shakily, 'I—I *do* serve—'

'Stand aside!' A lieutenant pushed through his men and regarded Ozzard curiously. 'Speak up, fellow! The Fleet needs more hands.' He ran his eye over Ozzard's frail person. 'What ship, if serve you do?'

'I—I am servant to Sir Richard Bolitho.' He found he was able to look up at the lieutenant without flinching. 'Vice-Admiral of the Red. He is presently in London.'

The lieutenant asked, '*Hyperion*—was she your last ship?' All his impatience had gone. As Ozzard nodded he said, 'Be off with you, man. This is no place for honest people after dark.'

The gunner's mate glanced at his lieutenant as if for consent, then pressed some coins into Ozzard's fist.

''Ere, go an' get a good wet. Reckon you've bloody earned it after wot you must 'er seen an' done!'

Ozzard blinked and nearly broke down. A *wet*. What Allday would have said. His whole being wanted to scream at them. Didn't they see the name on the shop front? What would they have said had he told them how he had run most of the way to Tower Hill to seek out a recruiting party? In those days there was always one hanging around near the taverns and the theatre. Ready to ply some drunken fool with rum before they signed him on in a daze of patriotic fervour. How would they have behaved if he'd described what he had left behind in that quiet little house? He made himself look at it. The window was no longer in the sun.

When he turned the press gang had vanished, and for a second longer he imagined it was another part of the torment, the stab of guilt which left him no peace. Then he looked down at his hand and opened the fingers while his body began to shake uncontrollably. There were the coins the gunner's mate had given him. *'I don't want your pity.'* The coins jangled across the cobbles as he flung them into the lengthening shadows. *'Leave me alone!'*

He heard someone call out, saw a curtain move in the house next to the one which had once been his. But nobody came.

He sighed and turned his back on the place, and the shop with his stolen name on the front.

Somewhere in the warren of alleys he heard a sudden scuffle, someone bellow with pain, then silence. The press gang had found at least one victim who would awake with a bloody head aboard the Thames guardship.

Ozzard thrust his hands into his coat pockets and began the long walk back to that other part of London.

His small figure was soon lost in the shadows, while behind him, the house was as before. Waiting.

★   ★   ★

Just a few miles upstream from Wapping where Ozzard had made his despairing pilgrimage, Bolitho bent over to offer his hand to Catherine, and assist her from the wherry in which they had crossed the Thames. It was early darkness, the cloudless sky pinpointed with countless stars: a perfect evening to begin what Catherine had promised to be 'a night of

216

enchantment'.

Bolitho put some money into the wherryman's hand, with a little extra so that he would be here to carry them back across the swirling black river. The man had a cheeky grin, and had not taken his eyes off Catherine while he had pulled his smart little craft lustily over the choppy water.

Bolitho did not blame him. She had been standing in Lord Browne's hallway beneath a glittering chandelier when he had come down the staircase. In a gown of shot silk, very like the one she had worn that night in Antigua when he had met her again for the first time after so long. Catherine loved green, and her gown seemed to change from it to black as she had turned towards him. It was low-cut to reveal her throat and the full promise of her breasts. Her hair was piled high, and he had seen that she was wearing the same filigree earrings which had been his first-ever gift to her. The ones she had somehow managed to sew into her clothing when she had been forced into the Waites prison.

The wherryman flashed him a broad grin. 'I'll be 'ere, Admiral—nah you go off an' enjoy yerselves!'

Bolitho watched the little boat speed back across the river to seek out another fare.

'I don't understand.' He looked down at his plain blue coat, bought in Falmouth from old Joshua Miller. He and his father had been making uniforms for the Bolitho family and other Falmouth sea-officers longer than anyone could recall. 'How did he know?'

She flicked open her new fan and watched him above it, her eyes shining in the glow of many lanterns. 'More people know about us than I

217

thought!' She tossed her head. 'What do you think, Richard? My little surprise—to take your mind off weightier matters?'

Bolitho had heard of the London pleasure gardens, but had never visited any. This one at Vauxhall was the most famous of all. It certainly looked enchanted. Lantern-lit groves, wild rose hedges, and the sound of birds who enjoyed the merriment and music as much as the visitors.

Bolitho paid the entrance fee of half a crown each and allowed Catherine to guide him into the Grand Walk, a place for promenade, lined with exactly matching elms, and past little gravel walks with secret grottoes and quiet cascades and fountains.

She tightened her grip on his arm and said, 'I knew you'd like it. *My* London.' She gestured with the fan towards the many supper booths where splendidly dressed women and their escorts listened to the various orchestras, sipping champagne, cider or claret as the fancy took them.

She said, 'Many of the musicians are from the finest orchestras. They work here to keep their pockets filled, their bellies too, until the season returns.'

Bolitho removed his hat and carried it. The place was packed with people, the air heavy with perfume to mingle with the flowers and the distant smell of the river.

Catherine had been wearing a broad Spanish-style shawl, for it was known to be cold along the river at night. Now she let it drop to her arms, her throat and breasts shining in lanternlight or changing into provocative depths and shadows as they walked along a path.

It was like an endless panorama, where comic

songs and bawdy ballads shared the same status as the work of great composers and lively dancing. There were plenty of uniforms too. Mostly red with the blue facings of the Royal regiments, and some sea-captains from the many ships moored below London Bridge, and the twisting route which would carry them back to the sea once more.

They paused where two paths crossed, so that it was possible to hear the music of Handel from one angle, while from the opposite direction they could listen to someone singing 'Lass of Richmond Hill'. And neither seemed to detract from the other, Bolitho thought. Or perhaps it really was enchanted...

On the extreme of the brightly lit gardens was 'The Dark Walk'. Catherine led him into the deep shadows where other couples stood and embraced, or merely held one another in silence.

Then she turned and lifted her face to him, pale in the darkness. 'And *no*, dearest of men, I never walked here with another.'

'I would not have blamed you, Kate. Or the man who would lose his heart to you as I did.'

She said, 'Kiss me. Hold me.'

Bolitho felt her arch towards him; sensed the power of their love which hurled all caution and reserve aside.

He heard her gasp as he kissed her neck and then her shoulder, and pulled her closer without even a glance as a pair of strolling lovers passed by.

He said into her skin, 'I *want* you, Kate.'

She pretended to push him away, but he knew her excitement matched his own.

She touched his mouth with the fan as he released her and said, 'But first we eat. I have arranged for a booth. It will be a private place.' She gave her infectious laugh, something which at times in the past Bolitho had thought never to hear again. 'As private as anything *can* be in Vauxhall Pleasure Gardens!'

The time passed with an impossible speed while they sat in their little flower-bedecked booth, toying with their salads and roasted chicken, enjoying the wine and the music, but most of all each other.

She said, 'You are staring at me.' She dropped her eyes and took his hand in hers across the table. 'You make me feel so wanton—I should be ashamed.'

'You have a beautiful neck. It seems wrong to hide it, and yet...'

She watched him wondering.

'I will buy something for it. Just to adorn what is already so lovely.'

She smiled. 'Only in your eyes.' Then she squeezed his hand until it hurt. 'I am so in love with you, Richard. You just don't know.' She touched her eyes with a handkerchief. 'There, see what you've done!' When she looked at him again they were very bright. 'Let us go and find our lecherous wherryman. I have such need of you I can scarcely wait!'

They walked back along the path towards the gates. Catherine pulled her long shawl over her bare shoulders and shivered. 'I never want the summer to end.'

Bolitho smiled, passion and excitement making him light-headed, as if he had had too much wine.

'Wait here in the shelter. I will make certain that the waterman you described so well is alongside.'

She called after him as he turned by the gates.

'Richard, I *do* like your hair like that. You look so
... *dashing*.'

She watched him pass into the shadows and drew
the shawl more tightly around her; then she turned
as a voice said, 'All alone, my dear? That's very
remiss of somebody!'

She observed him calmly. An army captain; not
very old, with a lopsided grin which told of some
heavy drinking.

She said, 'Be off with you. I am not alone, and
even if I were—'

'Now let's not be hasty, m'dear.' He stepped
closer and she saw him stagger. Then he reached
out and seized the shawl. 'Such beauty should never
be hidden!'

'Take your hand off my lady.' Bolitho had not
even raised his voice.

Catherine said shortly, 'He is full to the gills!'

The captain stared at Bolitho and gave a mock
bow. 'I did not realise; and in any case she looked
like the sort of woman who might favour a poor
soldier.'

Bolitho was still very calm. 'I would call you out,
sir—'

The captain grinned stupidly. 'And then I would
willingly accept your seconds!'

Bolitho opened his plain blue coat. 'You did not
let me finish. I would call you out *if* you were a
gentleman and not a drunken lout. So we will settle
it here.' The old sword simply seemed to
materialise in his hand. 'And now!'

Another soldier lurched through some bushes
and gaped at the small, tense scene. He was tipsy,
but not too drunk to recognise the danger.

'Come away, you damned fool!' To Bolitho he

exclaimed, 'On his behalf, Sir Richard, I crave your pardon. He is not normally like this.'

Bolitho looked at the captain, his eyes hard. 'So I would hope, if only for the sake of England's safety!'

He slid the sword into its scabbard and deliberately turned his back on the pair of them. 'The boat is ready and waiting, my lady.'

She took his proffered arm and felt it shaking. 'I have never seen you like that before.'

'I am sorry to behave like some hot-headed midshipman.'

She protested, 'You were wonderful.' She held up the small reticule which hung from her wrist, and added, 'But if he *had* tried to hurt you he would have got a ball in the buttocks to quieten him down. My little carriage pistol is quite big enough for that.'

Bolitho shook his head. 'You are full of surprises!'

By the time the wherry was halfway across the river, weaving expertly through packs of similar craft, he was calm again.

Then he said, 'It really was a night of enchantment, Kate. I shall *never* forget it.'

Catherine glanced at the staring waterman and then allowed the shawl to drop from her shoulders as she leaned against Bolitho and whispered, 'It is not yet over, as you will soon discover.'

The waterman left his wherry to assist them out on to the pier. In his trade he carried them all. Men with other men's wives, sailors and their doxies, young bucks on the hunt for excitement or a brawl which would end blade to blade. But his two fares this evening were like none he had ever carried, and for some strange reason he knew he would always remember them. He thought of the way she had teased him with her shawl and gave a rueful grin. It had been well worth it.

He called after them, 'Any time, Sir Richard! Just ask for Bobby—they all knows me on the London River.'

The carriage which had been put at their disposal was standing in line with many others, the coachmen nodding while they waited for their masters who were still over at Vauxhall.

Bolitho saw Ozzard's gilt buttons glinting in the carriage lamps. It was like a silent warning, and he felt Catherine's grip tighten on his wrist.

'Is something wrong, Ozzard? There was no need for you to wait with the carriage.'

Ozzard said, 'There was a messenger from the Admiralty, Sir Richard. I told him I didn't know where you were.' His tone suggested he would not have told him anyway. 'He left word for you to present yourself to Lord Godschale at your earliest convenience tomorrow.'

Somewhere in another world a church clock began to chime.

Catherine said in a small voice, '*Today*.'

When they reached the house in Arlington Street, Bolitho said, 'It cannot be so urgent. I have no flagship as yet, and in any case—'

She turned on the stairway and tossed her shawl impetuously over the curving banister rail.

'And *in any case*, my gallant admiral, there is still the night!'

He found her waiting for him beside one of the windows from which, in daylight, you could see the park. She looked at him, her face almost impassive

223

as she said, 'Take me, use me any way you will, but always love me.'

✶   ✶   ✶

Down in the deserted kitchen Allday sat at the scrubbed table and carefully filled a new clay pipe. It had cost him a fortune in London but he doubted if it would last any longer.

He had heard the carriage return and had seen Ozzard going quietly to his bed. Something was troubling him sorely; pulling him apart. He would try and find out what it was.

He lit the pipe and watched the smoke rising in the still air. Then he pulled a tankard of rum towards him and tried not to think of them upstairs.

All the same, he thought, it would make everything just perfect. To feel her defences giving way.

Allday snatched the tankard and took a great swallow.

Aloud he said thickly, 'Just watch out for squalls, that's all I asks of 'em!'

But as he thought of them up there together, he knew that nothing would make any difference.

CHAPTER ELEVEN

THE MISSION

Bolitho pushed open the tall doors of the drawing room and stood for a few moments in silence.

Catherine was by one of the windows, looking

224

down at the street, waiting as he was for the inevitable departure.

Then he crossed the room and put his hands on her shoulders, and touched her hair with his mouth. 'It is nearly time.'

She nodded and seemed to lean back against him. 'I will not let you down, Richard. We have been free to love these past weeks, free from everything. For that I can only be grateful.' She twisted round in his arms and searched his face despairingly. 'But perhaps I am greedy, and want so much more.'

Bolitho heard someone bumping his chest down the stairs and stared past her at the empty street. The shadows were lengthening already, each evening drawing in—an early autumn then.

He said, 'At least there is no danger. I am to go on a mission—' He hesitated, hating the secrecy. 'Should anything go amiss, I have taken care of—'

She pressed her hand over his lips. 'Say no more. I *do* understand. If secrecy is necessary, then I'll not plead to share it. But come back to me.'

Bolitho embraced her. Just a few days since his summons to the Admiralty. Maybe the secrecy was necessary; or was it merely another ruse to keep him out of the country? The latter was hard to believe. It all took organisation and trust. He was to go to Dover, not Portsmouth or Chatham as might be expected, and from there take passage to Copenhagen. He would be met at Dover and the rest of his mission explained.

As if to dispel his own doubts he said, 'It will not take long. Perhaps two weeks, certainly no longer. And then—'

She looked at him and asked, 'What would you have me do?'

'Oliver Browne has said that this house is ours for as long as we require it. His lordship is visiting his family estate in Jamaica.' He smiled. 'It is hard not to think of him still as my flag-lieutenant!'

'What of Lieutenant Jenour?' She too smiled, remembering. 'A fellow conspirator and a good friend.'

'He will already be at Dover waiting for me.'

'Then he is luckier than I!'

He felt her tense as iron-shod wheels rolled along the street and halted outside the house.

Bolitho spoke hurriedly. 'Ozzard will tend to your needs, Kate, and Yovell will apprise you of everything you wish to know. I am leaving you in their care. I would offer Allday's services but—'

She smiled. 'No. He would never allow it, and besides I need your "oak" to protect you!'

The doors opened a few inches and one of the servants said, 'The carriage is here, Sir Richard. Your chest is inside.' The doors closed silently. It was as if the house, even the street, was holding its breath for these last, fleeting moments.

'Come.' Bolitho put his arm around her shoulders and together they descended to the hallway. 'I have so much to say, and it will all come flooding out once we are parted.'

She looked back up the staircase, thinking perhaps of the night she had been carried here in her filthy clothing, her feet bare from her experiences in the Waites prison. Recalling their love and moments of tender passion. Now she would be looking at her other man, the King's officer; the service which would always be a rival if given the chance.

The front doors were wide open and there was a

chill in the evening air. She clutched his arm and said, 'I cause such trouble for you, when I would do anything but harm you. I have even come between you and your friends, and all because of our love!'

Bolitho held her. Somehow he had known that she had guessed or understood what had happened with Herrick that day at the Admiralty.

He replied, 'Nothing separates us.' He looked into the street, the house lights already reflecting on the side of the carriage. 'Except what I must do.' He had noticed that the carriage was unmarked by any crest or recognition. A secret indeed.

One of the horses stamped its feet, and the coachman murmured something to soothe its impatience. Behind the rear wheels Bolitho could see Allday's thick shadow waiting, as he had so many times.

Bolitho said, 'I wrote to Val Keen. It is all I *can* do. If you are staying here until I return it is possible he might come to see you.'

'It still troubles you?'

'Yes.' He smiled distantly. 'A war raging all about us while we stumble in personal crossfire. I suspect that has always been my real weakness.'

She shook her head. '*Strength.* I hear people talking of you as a man of war, and yet with you I have never before known such peace.'

He wrapped his boat-cloak around her shoulders as they walked down the steps together, then she stooped to pick up a dead leaf which had blown against her shoe.

When she faced him again her eyes were dark and shining. 'Remember when I sent you the ivy leaf from *our* house?'

'I still have it.'

'And now here is a messenger of another coming winter. Please God we may not be parted for too long.' She was speaking quickly as if fearful he would interrupt. 'I know I promised—I vowed to you I should be brave, but I have only just found you again.'

He said quietly, 'There is none braver than you, Kate.' He *had* to leave; it was best to do it quickly, for both their sakes. 'Kiss me.'

He felt her mouth mould into his body as if to hold them together for ever. Then they were just as suddenly apart. Allday held open the carriage door and raised his hat.

She handed him Bolitho's cloak and stood very upright on the bottom step, her body framed against the chandelier-lit hallway.

She said, 'I ask of you again, Mr Allday. Take the best care of him!'

Allday grinned, but felt the sadness like his own. 'We'll be back afore you knows it, m'lady.' He went around the carriage so that Bolitho could watch her from the window.

Bolitho said, 'You hold my heart, dear Kate!' He might have said something more, but freed from the brake and with the sharp crack of the coachman's whip, the words were lost in the din of wheels and the jangle of harness.

The carriage had been out of sight for some time before she eventually turned, oblivious to the cool air, and entered the house. How empty and alien it seemed without him.

She had considered returning to Falmouth, but something, a hint in his tone had made her believe that her place was here. Was it only a short distance he was going this time? She thought of his

228

sea-chest, the fine new shirts she had forced him to buy in London. She smiled, remembering again. *Her* London. He certainly was not carrying enough baggage for a lengthy mission.

She found Yovell waiting for her, to discover her requirements.

'Why *him*, Mr Yovell? Can you tell me that? Is there no limit to what they can demand?'

Yovell removed his small gold-rimmed spectacles and polished them vigorously with his handkerchief.

'Because he is usually the only one for the task, m'lady.' He smiled as he replaced his glasses. 'Even I do not know what he is about this time!'

She looked at him proudly. 'Will you sup with me tonight, Mr Yovell? I would take it as a favour.'

He stared at her, trying not to let his eyes stray over her hair, the way she lifted her chin, the very presence of her.

'It would be a privilege indeed, m'lady!'

She made for the staircase. 'There is a *price*, Mr Yovell. I will wish to hear everything you know about the man I love, more than life itself.'

Yovell was glad she did not press him further. Her frankness, the light of defiance which seemed to shine from her eyes, was like nothing he had ever experienced.

He took off his glasses and polished them again without even realising what he was doing.

And she trusted him. The woman who had created the gossip and lies but had just spoken so fervently of her love, could have done the round-shouldered secretary Daniel Yovell no greater honour.

It was four o'clock in the morning when, stiff and painfully aware of the fast drive from London, Bolitho finally stepped down from the unmarked carriage and tasted the salt air in his mouth.

It was pitch dark as, followed by Allday and two seamen who were waiting to carry his chest, he walked towards the gates of the guardhouse. When he looked up at the low clouds he saw just a hint of the castle's solid silhouette. It could easily have been a ridge of rock, a miniature Table Mountain.

He heard Allday cough, then stifle it with his hand. His coxswain was probably as glad as he was to have arrived in one piece. Thank God the Dover Road had been deserted, because the coachman had driven like a soul possessed. Bolitho had the feeling he was well used to this kind of work.

'*Halt!* Who goes there?'

Bolitho tossed his boat-cloak back from one epaulette and walked into a circle of lantern-light.

He heard Jenour's familiar voice, saw his pale breeches as he hurried out to greet him.

'Bravo, Sir Richard! You must have been blessed with wings!'

Bolitho shook his hand. It was cold, like his own, and he was reminded of Catherine's words about the coming winter.

Allday muttered, 'That bugger nearly did what the Dons an' the Frogs has failed to do many times!'

The Officer-of-the-Guard joined them and doffed his hat. 'Welcome to Dover, Sir Richard.'

Bolitho could feel the lieutenant's scrutiny even in the dark. Recognition again, curiosity too.

Bolitho had never really liked Dover. He found it difficult to forget the months before the outbreak of war—what was it? Thirteen years ago? It did not seem possible. He had been unemployed, still weakened by the fever which had struck him down so cruelly in the Great South Sea, and which had all but killed him. Too many captains, too few ships. In peacetime the fleet had been cut to the bone, sound vessels laid up to neglect and rot, sailors thrown on the beach unwanted with no jobs to go to.

Bolitho was still very bitter about it. Like the shantyman's song which had ended on that same note, *Now we have naught to eat and drink, For you have naught to fear* ... Would it be the same when this war was finally won, and a part of history?

More than anything he had wanted a ship then. To forget his experiences in the Great South Sea, to begin all over again with another fine frigate like his *Tempest* had been. Instead he had been offered the thankless task of recruiting men at the Nore and the Medway towns, and at the same time seeking out deserters who had fled the navy for the more lucrative and brutal trade of smuggling.

His work had sometimes brought him to Dover. To see a smuggler kick out his life on the gallows, or to pit his wits against the authorities, the men of power who were hand-in-glove with the Brotherhood, as it was called. But the guillotine's blade which had fallen on the neck of France's king had changed all that overnight. Not a frigate; they had given him the old *Hyperion*. It was as if she had been destined for him. Now like so many faces, she too had gone to the bottom.

He realised that the others were waiting and he

231

said, 'What ship?'

The lieutenant swallowed apologetically. 'My orders are—'

Bolitho snapped, 'Don't waste my time, man!'

'She lies out at anchor, Sir Richard. The *Truculent*, Captain Poland.' He sounded crushed.

Bolitho sighed. Like a family. You either lost touch completely, or faces and ships reappeared again and again. He knew that both *Zest* and *Truculent* had joined the North Sea squadron and would eventually serve under his flag once *Black Prince* was in full commission. He forced himself from going over the mystery of Keen's silence again and asked, 'Is there a boat waiting?'

'Er, yes, Sir Richard.'

Jenour hid a smile as the lieutenant led the way with a lantern, half-shuttered as if the dock area was filled with spies and French agents. He watched Bolitho's quick stride and was glad to be with him again. Jenour had enjoyed his freedom, which he had spent with his parents in Southampton, and yet when the messenger had brought his orders he had felt something like elation, without even the hesitation which might have been expected after his recent experiences.

Feet shuffled on cobbles, and as they turned a corner around some victualling sheds the sea-breeze swept amongst them like a boisterous greeting.

Bolitho stood on the edge of the jetty and stared past the other moored vessels, the gaunt shadows of rigging and furled sails, to the riding-lights of ships at anchor. He rarely thought about it at sea, but now, standing here on the wet cobbles which would soon reveal themselves in a grey dawn, it was a strange, unnerving feeling. Out there in the darkness, no more than twenty sea-miles away, was the enemy coast. In a man-of-war you could fight or run as your wisdom dictated. Along these shores, thinly protected by gunboats, the sea fencibles or some local militia, the ordinary people had no such choice. They more than any others probably thanked God for the weather-beaten ships of the blockade which day and night rode out storms and calms alike to keep the enemy bottled up in his harbours.

'Boat's ready, Sir Richard.'

Bolitho nodded to the Officer-of-the Guard. 'How sets the tide?'

The man's face looked paler in the gloom, or was it imagination? He replied, 'It'll be on the ebb in two hours, Sir Richard.'

'Good.' It would mean a quick start. But who was the one chosen to give him the information he needed? He relented slightly. 'You keep a good watch, Lieutenant. It is just as well in this port!'

Then he was down into the boat with unexpected familiarity; even the lieutenant who had been sent in charge of the gig he recognised instantly.

'I'll wager you never expected to see *me* again so soon, Mr Munro?'

Jenour watched it all; as he had tried to describe it to his parents. The way *Truculent*'s young second lieutenant responded with such obvious pleasure. Had it been daylight Jenour was certain he would have been blushing. Just small points, but Bolitho never seemed to forget, nor did he overlook the importance which these brief contacts he had with his men might carry for them when they most needed them later on.

Jenour shivered despite his warm cloak. It was

exactly like one of his old storybooks. A secret mission. Jenour was not so naive that he did not see past the excitement to the danger and death which might lie in store. He had witnessed plenty of it since he had joined Bolitho; was still surprised that he had not cracked because of it. Perhaps later? He pushed it aside and said, 'I see her, Sir Richard!'

Bolitho swung round and turned up the collar of his cloak as the spray from the oars spat over the gunwale and stung the tiredness from his mind.

He could guess what Jenour was thinking. But the mission, whatever it was, could already be common gossip on messdecks and in wardrooms alike.

He saw the frigate's spiralling masts cut across the clouds to tower over them, heard the ship's own noises moving out to receive them. Shouted commands carried away by the breeze which might soon be a strong south-westerly wind, the creak of tackles and the urgent shrill of calls. Men feeling their way about the decks or high above them on the treacherous yards and ratlines, slippery with spray; no place for the unskilled. But there were some of the latter, Bolitho thought. A man was calling out in fear, his pleas cut short by a blow. Captain Poland must have put a press gang ashore somewhere away from the port, or else the local flag-officer had sent him a few landsmen from the guardship. For them the long, hard lesson was about to begin.

He thought again of Catherine, all that they had done together, all that they had given each other, and still there had not been enough time. He had not found the necklace he wanted for her lovely throat, nor had they been to visit the surgeon, Sir

Piers Blachford. He had thought several times of his daughter Elizabeth, who would be four years old. The last occasion when he had seen her was when he had had his first confrontation with Belinda—she had passed him by with barely a glance. Not like a child at all. A doll in silks, a possession. But it would all have to wait.

'*Boat ahoy?*' Figures jostled around the light at the frigate's entry port.

Before the gig's coxswain could reply to the age-old challenge, Allday cupped his big hands and yelled, '*Flag! Truculent!*'

Bolitho pictured the tension on board. They might have been waiting and wondering for hours. Nobody could have known when his carriage would arrive or even when he had left London. But he had no doubts at all that Captain Poland would have kept every man alert and ready to receive him, if it had taken him another full day!

The gig's bowman managed to hook on to the main chains, while others did their best to control the boat's pitching and swaying as it felt the surge of the current alongside.

Bolitho reached the entry port and saw Poland and his officers waiting to be presented, even at this unearthly hour. As he had expected, they were all smartly dressed for his arrival.

He took Poland's hand and said, 'I see that I must congratulate you, Captain.'

Poland smiled modestly as the swaying lantern threw a glow across his matching pair of epaulettes.

He said, 'And I must *thank* you, Sir Richard. I cannot say how grateful I was to be told that my posting had been confirmed as a result of your report.'

Bolitho paused to watch the gig being hoisted up and over the nettings, then manhandled down on to the boat-tier with the others. A sense of urgency and mystery he had known often enough as a young frigate captain.

He said, 'It will be a mite different from the shores of Africa.'

Poland hesitated, sifting it through as if to seek out any possible traps. Then he admitted, 'I know our eventual landfall, Sir Richard, but in God's name I know nought else.'

Bolitho touched his arm and felt it stiffen. Poor Poland; like so many before him he had imagined that to gain the coveted rank of post-captain was to be beyond the reach of uncertainty, a summit from which nobody could topple you. Bolitho smiled to himself. He was learning otherwise. Like the epaulettes, the responsibility was also doubled. *As I discovered for myself many times.*

Poland glanced quickly at his hovering first lieutenant. 'Have the capstan fully manned, Mr Williams. We shall sail on the tide, or I shall need to know about it!'

To Bolitho he added, 'If you will come aft, Sir Richard, there is a gentleman who is taking passage with us.'

While the ship came alive with the noise of getting under way, Bolitho entered the stern cabin, which he had come to know so well in his solitude. The first thing he saw was a curly wig which stood on its rest by an open chest; the second was the man who walked unsteadily from the shadows by the stern window, his legs as yet unused to the uncomfortable motion of a ship eager to tear free from the ground.

236

He was older, or appeared so, perhaps more stooped in the light of the spiralling lanterns. Sixty at a guess, his head almost bald so that his old-fashioned queue hung down over his collar like a rope's end.

He put his head on one side and regarded Bolitho like a quizzical bird. 'It's a long while, Sir Richard, and many miles since we last met.'

Bolitho clasped both his hands in his own.

'Of course I remember. Charles Inskip! You guided me when I strained our country's diplomacy—that was in Copenhagen too!' They studied one another, their hands still gripped together as the memories flooded back. Bolitho had been sent to Denmark to help parley with the Danes after Napoleon had demanded that they hand over their fleet to his French admirals. The failure then to reach an agreement had led to the Battle of Copenhagen, when Nelson had defied his admiral's order to discontinue the action, and had forced the attack alone. The memories were flooding back. Keen had been there in his own command. Herrick had been Bolitho's flag-captain in *Benbow*, which was now his own flagship. Such was fate and the ways of the navy.

It had been a bloody battle between nations who had nothing against one another but for their fear of the French obtaining the upper hand over them both.

Inskip gave a small smile. 'Like you, Sir Richard, I, too, am honoured. *Sir* Charles, by His Majesty's gracious consent.'

They both laughed and Bolitho said, 'An unnerving experience!' He did not add that the King had forgotten his name at the moment of knighting him.

More cries echoed from the deck above, and then the thrashing thunder of freed canvas. They could not hear the cry of 'Anchor's aweigh!' but Bolitho braced his legs and felt *Truculent* respond like a released stallion, free of the halter, and responsible only to her captain's skills.

Inskip was watching him thoughtfully. 'You still miss it, don't you? Being up there with the people, pitting your wits against the sea? I saw it in your eyes, as I did those six years back in Copenhagen.'

He moved carefully to a chair as a servant entered with some glasses on a tray.

'Well, we are returning there, Sir Richard.' He sighed and patted his side pockets. 'In one I carry a promise, in t'other a threat. But sit you down and I'll tell you what we are about—' He broke off and covered his mouth as the deck reeled over to the thrust of the helm. 'I fear I have been too long in the comforts of London. My damned stomach defies me yet!'

Bolitho watched the servant's expressionless face—one of Inskip's men—as he poured the wine with some difficulty.

But he was thinking of Catherine and the London she had given him. *Enchantment.* Not at all like the one Inskip was already regretting leaving astern.

He leaned forward and felt her fan press against his thigh. 'I am all attention, Sir Charles, though what part I can play is still beyond me.'

Inskip held his glass up to the light and gave a nod of satisfaction. He was probably one of the most senior government officials employed on Scandinavian affairs, but at this moment he looked more like a village schoolmaster.

He said, 'Nelson is gone, alas, but the Danes know you. It is little enough, but when I explain further you will see we have no room for choices. There are sensible men in Copenhagen, but there are many who will see the value of *compromise*, another word for surrender, with Napoleon's army at the frontier.'

Bolitho glanced down at the gold lace on his sleeve. He was back.

★   ★   ★

Bolitho stood on the weather side of *Truculent*'s quarterdeck and strained his eyes through the first grey light of morning. Around him the ship reeled and plunged to a lively quarter-sea, spray and sometimes great surges of water dashing over the decks or breaking through the rigging where spluttering, cursing seamen fought to keep everything taut and free.

Captain Poland lurched up the slippery planking towards him, a tarpaulin coat flapping about him and running with water.

He shouted above the din, 'We should sight the narrows when daylight finds us, Sir Richard!' His eyes were red-rimmed with strain and lack of sleep, and his normally cool composure was less evident.

It had been a long, hard passage from Dover for him, Bolitho thought. No empty expanse of ocean with kind skies and prevailing winds, and Table Mountain as a mark of achievement at the end of it. *Truculent* had thrashed through the Channel and then north-east across the North Sea towards the coast of Denmark. They had sighted very little except for an English schooner and a small frigate which exchanged recognition signals before vanishing into a violent rain squall. It needed constant care with the navigation, especially when they altered course through the Skagerrak, then finally south, so close-hauled that the lee gunports had been awash for most of the time. It was not merely cold; it was bitter, and Bolitho was constantly reminded of the last great battle against the Danes at Copenhagen, with Nelson's flag shifted to the *Elephant*, a smaller seventy-four than his proper flagship, so that he could pass through the narrows close inshore and so avoid the enemy batteries until the final embrace.

Bolitho thought too of Browne's apt quotation for his own captains: *We Happy Few*. To think of it now only saddened him. So many had gone, returning only in memory at times like this while *Truculent* completed that very same passage. Captain Keverne of *Indomitable*, Rowley Peel and his fine frigate *Relentless*, Veitch in the little *Lookout*, and so many others. More were to fall from Browne's 'Few' in the following months and years. Firm friends like dear Francis Inch, and the courageous John Neale who had once been a midshipman in Bolitho's *Phalarope*, only to die a captain when they had been taken prisoner by the French after the loss of his frigate *Styx*. Bolitho and Allday had done all they could to save him and ease his agony; but he had joined all the others where nothing further could hurt him.

Bolitho shivered inside his boat-cloak and said, 'A difficult passage, Captain.' He saw the red-rimmed eyes watching him guardedly, probably seeking out some sort of criticism in his remark. Then he pictured Catherine as he had last seen her.

She would be wondering while she waited. It might be longer than he had promised. By the time *Truculent*'s anchor splashed down it would have taken them a full week to reach their goal. He added, 'I'm going below. Call me if you sight anything useful.'

Poland let out a sigh as Bolitho disappeared down the companion hatch. He called sharply, 'Mr Williams! Change the lookouts, if you please. When they sight land I want to know about it!'

The first lieutenant touched his dripping hat. No matter how worried the captain was he usually managed to find time for a little stab of sharp encouragement.

Below the quarterdeck it seemed suddenly quiet after the beat and bluster of the biting wind and spray. Bolitho made his way aft, past the sentry and into the cabin. Everything was damp and cold, and the bench seats below the stern windows were bloomed with moisture as if they had been left out on deck.

Sir Charles Inskip was sitting at the table, his head resting on one hand while his secretary, a Mr Patrick Agnew, turned over papers for him to examine by the light of a lantern which he held above them.

Inskip looked up as Bolitho seated himself, and waited for Allday to appear with his razor and hot water from the galley.

'Will this ship *never* be still?'

Bolitho stretched his arms to relieve the ache of clinging to one handhold or another, while trying to keep away from the watchkeepers bustling around him.

He said, 'Look at the chart. We are entering the

241

narrows where I made my mark yesterday. We should sight Helsingør presently—'

'Hmmm. We are being met by a Danish escort at that point.' Inskip did not sound too certain. 'After that, we are in their hands.' He glanced at his reedy secretary. 'Not for too *long* I trust, Mr Agnew?'

They both looked up as a shout probed thinly through the sealed skylight before being lost in the wind.

'What was that?' Inskip turned as usual to Bolitho. 'Did you hear?'

Bolitho smiled. 'Land.'

Allday padded through the door of the sleeping cabin and wedged his steaming bowl on a chair before stropping his deadly-looking razor.

Inskip was calling for his servant and searching for a heavy coat. 'We had better go on deck.'

Allday tucked a cloth around Bolitho's neck and could almost have winked. Poland would make damn certain that it was the right landfall before he reported as much to his admiral.

Bolitho closed his eyes while Allday prepared to shave him. Like the first strong coffee of each new day, it was a moment to think and contemplate.

Allday poised the razor and waited for the deck to steady again. He was still unused to seeing Bolitho's hair cut in the modern fashion. What her ladyship apparently admired. He smiled to himself as he remembered her pleasure when he had fumbled with the package he had brought home to Falmouth. He heard himself muttering, 'Sorry about the smell of baccy, m'lady. 'Twas all I had fit to carry it in without him seeing it, so to speak!'

He had been astonished by her reaction, the poignant pleasure in those dark eyes, which Allday

242

knew had said it all.

He had saved most of Bolitho's queue after his sudden insistence on having it cut off. After seeing her face he was glad.

Captain Poland entered the cabin just as Allday stood back and folded his razor.

'We are in sight of Helsingør, Sir Richard.' He waited, a puddle forming around his boots.

'I shall come up directly, Captain.' He smiled at him. 'Well done.'

The door closed and Bolitho allowed Allday to help him into his coat. Simple words of praise, yet Poland still frowned. When invited through the gates of Heaven he would likely seek out a reason before entering, he thought. Another hail floated down.

Bolitho looked up at the salt-stained skylight. 'That poor wretch must be frozen to the masthead!'

'Shouldn't wonder.' Allday grimaced. Not many captains would care about a lowly seaman, never mind a vice-admiral.

The door banged open and Inskip and his secretary rushed into the cabin. It was all confusion as they tore open their chests and called for the servant, while trying to find what they needed to wear.

Inskip gasped, '*A ship*, Sir Richard! It will be the Danish escort.'

Bolitho heard the sullen rumble of gun trucks as some of the main armament was freed from the breechings and loaded. Poland again. *Just in case*.

'Then we had best attend to our business.' He gave a wry smile. '*Whatever* it proves to be!'

'A moment, Sir Richard.' Allday plucked a shred of spunyarn from Bolitho's fine coat. What little

243

Ozzard would have seen to. Then he stood back and nodded with approval. The bright gold lace, the Nile medal which he always wore with such pride, and the old sword. Like one of the portraits, he thought. No wonder she loved him like she did. How could you not?

He said roughly, 'None better, Sir Richard, an' that's no error!'

Bolitho eyed him gravely. 'Then we are well matched, old friend.' He stepped aside as Inskip's servant dashed past with a crumpled shirt.

'So let us be about it, eh?'

CHAPTER TWELVE

STORM WARNING

Sir Charles Inskip peered gloomily from a narrow window and shivered as a sudden squall rattled the thick glass.

'This is hardly the treatment I had been expecting!'

Bolitho put down his empty coffee cup and joined him to look across the harbour at some of the vessels which lay at anchor. He had not failed to notice the thick bars across the window, nor the way they had been kept in semi-isolation since they had stepped ashore. Their quarters in what appeared to be a part of a fortress were comfortable enough, but the door was locked at night all the same. He saw *Truculent* tugging at her cable, her furled canvas quivering as the wind ruffled up the surface of the anchorage and pounded against her

244

hull and rigging. She, too, appeared isolated and vulnerable. The big Danish frigate *Dryaden*, which had met and then escorted them into Copenhagen, lay some two cables clear. Bolitho gave a grim smile. That was not a sign of trust, but to make sure she would suffer no damage if Captain Poland tried to cut and run. *Truculent* was lying directly beneath the guns of one of the main batteries. It would be an unhealthy place to be if it was forced to open fire.

Seven days. Bolitho tried not to let his mind linger on it. Inskip had told him repeatedly that they were here at the suggestion of a senior Danish minister named Christian Haarder. A man dedicated to keeping Denmark out of the war and safe from attack either by France *or* England.

Bolitho looked towards the array of anchored men-of-war, their scarlet flags with the distinctive white crosses taut and bright in the stiff wind. It amounted to quite a fleet despite the savage losses in this very harbour some five years back. The Danes had probably mustered all their available warships from the mainland to place them under a single command. It made good sense, no matter what happened.

Inskip said irritably, 'I have sent two messages with no effect. Out of courtesy the palace was informed, and my own letters should have made further delays totally unnecessary.'

'People must be wondering about the presence of one of His Majesty's frigates in the harbour.' Bolitho watched a long-oared galley pulling slowly past the *Truculent*, the red blades rising and falling gracefully like a relic of ancient Greece. But Bolitho knew from hard experience that they were not

245

simply for decoration. They could outmanoeuvre almost any ship under sail, and for armament they carried a solitary, heavy cannon with which they could maul a vessel's stern and pound her into submission while her prey was unable to bring a single gun to bear. To be attacked by several at once, as the flagship had been, was like being a beast torn apart by fleet-footed wolves.

Inskip said, 'They'll soon find out if they keep us waiting much longer.'

Bolitho saw Allday gathering up the cups although Inskip's own servant was in an adjoining room. He glanced at his watch. Jenour should have returned long ago. Inskip had sent him with another letter which he had written himself. Bolitho bit his lip. Too many secrets. Like trying to carry sand in a fishing-net.

He asked, 'Do you think the French may be involved at this stage?'

Inskip wrenched his thoughts into perspective. 'The *French*? Dammit, Bolitho, you see the Frenchman's fingers in everything! But I believe—' He broke off as Agnew, his long nose red from the cold, peered around the door and whispered, 'The lieutenant has returned, Sir Charles.'

Inskip adjusted his wig and glared at the main doorway. 'Not alone by the sound of it, by God!'

The door swung inwards and Bolitho saw Jenour, accompanied by the *Dryaden*'s captain and a tall man in a dark velvet coat whom he guessed was the minister named Haarder.

Bows were exchanged and to Inskip Haarder offered his hand. Like old antagonists, Bolitho thought, rather than friends. A sort of familiar wariness which he guessed was as much a part of

246

them as their political evasiveness.

Haarder looked steadily at Bolitho and said, 'You I know from your last visit to my country.'

Bolitho searched for hostility but found none. 'I was treated with great courtesy.' He did not add, *unlike this time*. He did not need to.

Haarder shrugged. 'We are under no illusions here, Admiral. The Danish fleet is once again a rich prize to those who would seize it for their own cause.' His eyes flickered in amusement. 'Or those who might wish to destroy it for another reason, yes?' He glanced at their faces and said, 'My associates are hard to convince. Either way they lose—' He raised one hand as Inskip seemed about to argue. 'If, as your government is suggesting, the French intend to demand authority over our fleet, what will we do? Deny them, face them in battle? How could we survive when your own powerful nation has been at war with the same enemy for over twelve years? Think what you are asking before you condemn our uncertainty. We want only peace, even with our old foes in Sweden. Trade, not war—is that so alien that you cannot envisage it?'

Inskip sat back wearily and Bolitho knew he had given up before he had had a chance to negotiate.

Inskip said, 'Then you cannot, or *will* not help us in this matter? I had hoped—'

Haarder eyed him sadly. 'Your hope was mine also. But my voice is only one against many.'

Bolitho said, 'On my last visit I saw the Crown Prince, although his identity was kept secret from me until later.'

Haarder smiled. 'It is often better for royalty to stay removed from affairs of state, Admiral. I think I will have your agreement on *that* at least.'

247

Bolitho knew that Inskip was watching him anxiously, as if he expected him to rise to the bait.

Bolitho replied, 'I am a sea-officer, sir, not a politician. I came here to advise, if required, on the balance of naval power in a very small area. But in all honesty I would not wish to see Denmark suffer the same terrible losses as before. I believe I have *your* agreement on that!'

Haarder stood up and said heavily, 'I will keep trying. In the meantime I am instructed to end this attempted interference in Danish neutrality. Captain Pedersen of the *Dryaden* will escort you to open waters.' He held out a sealed envelope and handed it to Inskip. 'For your Prime Minister, from someone far more senior than I.'

Inskip stared at the envelope. 'Lord Grenville dislikes being threatened no less than Mr Pitt did.' He straightened his back and smiled, the old antagonist once again. 'But it is not over.'

Haarder shook his hand gravely. 'Nor is it yet begun, my old friend.'

To Bolitho he said simply, 'I have long admired your achievements.' Again the twinkle of a smile. 'Ashore as well as afloat. Be assured that my King would have wished to receive you but—' He shrugged. 'We are in a vice. To show favour to one is to open the gates to another, yes?'

More bows and solemn handshakes and then Haarder took his leave.

The Danish captain said politely, 'If you will permit?' Some armed seamen entered the outer room and waited to collect their belongings. 'I will have a boat waiting to take you to your ship. After which,' he spoke haltingly but clearly, 'you will please obey my directions.'

The captain walked from the room and Inskip said, 'I wonder why they kept Haarder waiting so long. Just to tell me that he could do nothing?' It was the first time Bolitho had heard him sound puzzled.

Bolitho turned as if to watch Allday directing the Danish seamen into the other room for his sea-chest.

But he did not want Inskip to see his face, as his simple remark seemed to explode in his thoughts like a mortar shell.

Was it just imagination, a twist of words? Or had the tall Dane been trying to warn him, knowing at the same time that Inskip would not recognise it, or might challenge even a hint of suggestion?

Lieutenant Jenour remarked quietly, 'At least we shall be back in England before the winter gales return to the North Sea, Sir Richard.'

Bolitho took his arm and felt him tense as he said, 'I think *we* were delayed deliberately, Stephen, not the other way round.' He saw the understanding in Jenour's eyes. 'And it is a long way yet to England, remember?' He heard Inskip calling to his secretary and added sharply, 'Not a word. Just hurry our departure as much as you can without causing a stir.' He shook his arm lightly. 'Something else to tell your parents about, eh?'

Allday watched their exchange. Bolitho's alertness, like a reawakening, and the young lieutenant's sudden excitement. Jenour had never been able to hide his feelings anyway.

He walked across and clipped the old sword to Bolitho's belt. Like the moment when they had prepared to leave *Truculent* and transfer to the Danish frigate for the final approach to

Copenhagen. Something unspoken seemed to pass between them.

Bolitho looked at him searchingly until Allday murmured, 'Seems we might soon be needing this old blade again, Sir Richard?'

Inskip bustled into the room. 'A good hot tub and a fine English serving of roast beef, that's what I—' His eyes flashed between them and he asked suspiciously, 'I suppose you think it was all a waste of time, what?'

Bolitho faced him grimly, the first elation of danger already contained. 'Indeed, Sir Charles, I hope that *is* all it was!'

The same short journey in a sealed carriage as when they had arrived, and then on to the wet, windswept jetty, where a boat was hooked on waiting for them. Inskip pulled his heavy coat around his body and gave the Danish captain a curt nod before he clambered down into the boat.

His face was a mask, his mind already grappling with what he had heard and probably with what had remained unsaid.

Bolitho waited for the others to fit themselves amongst the baggage in the sternsheets and turned to look across at the city, now blurred with rain like a painting left out in bad weather. He was moved by what he saw. The familiar green spires and handsome buildings, none of which he had been allowed to revisit. Catherine would love it.

He realised that the Danish captain was waiting. To make certain that he shared no contact with anyone; or was he merely curious to discover more about the man whose cannon had once pounded their ships into submission? Richard Bolitho, next to Nelson the youngest vice-admiral on the Navy

List. Now, with Nelson gone—Bolitho shook it from his thoughts. Perhaps this very captain was a part of some scheme to delay them.

The captain said, 'I wish you God's speed, Sir Richard. Perhaps we shall meet again?'

No, he was not part of some sinister plot. Bolitho smiled, remembering his own remark to Haarder. *I am a sea-officer, sir.*

He replied, 'In fairer times, Captain Pedersen, when you and I are no longer needed.'

He climbed down into the boat, one hand gripping Allday's shoulder as the hull lurched against the piles.

Apart from an occasional command from the boat's coxswain, nothing was said by the passengers huddled in the sternsheets. Bolitho glanced at a passing guardboat, the lieutenant rising to doff his hat as he passed. All the correct courtesies, he thought, and was suddenly saddened by it. Like *in fairer times*. It was more than likely that the next time he met with that captain or any other, it would be across the muzzles of a full broadside.

Captain Poland was waiting with his side-party to greet them as they climbed aboard and the Danish longboat backed away from the chains in a welter of icy spray.

Poland began, 'I hope all is well, Sir Richard?' He stared after Inskip as he pushed past the reception and hurried aft to the poop.

Bolitho said, 'Prepare to get under way immediately, Captain Poland. We are to be escorted by *Dryaden* as before, but yours is the faster ship. Once clear of the narrows I want you to sail *Truculent* like you did to Good Hope!' He wished that Poland would stop staring at him. 'I shall

251

explain why, directly, but I believe we may have to fight before we are much older.'

Poland was at last coming out of his daze. 'Er, *yes*, Sir Richard. I shall attend to it—' He peered round for his first lieutenant. 'If fight we must then my ship will give good account—' But when he looked again, Bolitho had vanished. He cupped his hands, his voice shattering the stillness of the side-party while they shivered in the intermittent rain.

'Mr Williams! Prepare to get the ship under way! Have the master lay aft!' He swung round, rain water running from his hat. 'Mr Munro, be so good as to pipe all hands, unless of course you are too engrossed in staring at the city yonder. I daresay you'll see more than *that* before long!' He watched the lieutenant as he fled from the quarterdeck. Then he snapped, 'Once clear of land we shall exercise gun crews, Mr Williams.' He derived some pleasure from the lieutenant's surprise. 'It seems we are a passenger-vessel no longer!'

Lieutenant Williams watched him stride away, his hat and coat shining in the downpour like wet coal. Poland never explained anything until he was himself absolutely certain. Williams gave a wry grin, then picked up his speaking-trumpet as the midshipman of the watch reported that the Danish frigate was already shortening her cable.

Why should he anyway? He was, after all, the captain!

As the calls shrilled and echoed between decks and the seamen came pouring from every hatch and along each gangway, *Truculent*'s first lieutenant felt the excitement run through him like heady wine. Then he took a deep breath and raised his

252

speaking-trumpet.

'*Man the capstan!*' He squinted through the rain. '*Hands aloft, loose tops'ls!*'

He saw his friend gazing at him, grinning despite the captain's sarcasm. 'Remember, lads, they're all watching us over yonder. Let's show 'em that nobody can weigh faster than *Truculent!*'

In the stern cabin Bolitho paused over the chart, the rain still dropping from his coat and hair on to his calculations.

The clank of the capstan, the surge of water alongside which drowned the sounds of shantyman or violin, and the feeling of life running through the hull like no other sensation.

He knew Poland would be down shortly to report that the anchor was hove short. That part of it was no longer his concern. Bolitho sighed and leaned over the chart again. *Then so be it.*

*　　*　　*

Bolitho felt Jenour's hand on his shoulder and was instantly awake. A second earlier and he had been trudging up the hill towards the house, his eyes searching for her, his legs refusing to carry him any closer. Now as his eyes took in the faint grey light from the stern windows he saw Jenour holding on to the swaying cot, his face wet as if he had been in the rain.

Jenour gasped, 'First light, Sir Richard!' He swallowed and clenched his jaws. 'I—I've been sick, sir!'

Bolitho listened to the roar of water against the side, the heave and groan of timbers as the frigate fought her way through the gale. He could also hear someone vomiting and guessed it was Inskip. Seasoned traveller in his country's service he might be; frigate sailor he was not.

Bolitho saw Allday's dark shadow edging down the cabin towards him, his body leaning over like a tree in the wind.

Allday showed his teeth in the gloom and held out a mug of steaming coffee. He said above the chorus of sea and wind, 'Last coffee for a bit, Sir Richard. Th' galley's flooded!' He looked unsympathetically at the flag-lieutenant. 'Nice bit o' salt pork is what you needs, sir.'

Jenour ran down the sloping deck and disappeared.

Bolitho sipped the coffee and felt it restoring him, driving sleep and dreams into memory.

'What's happening?'

Allday reached up and steadied himself by gripping the edge of a deckhead beam. 'We're still under reefed tops'ls an' jib, 'though the Cap'n was fair reluctant to shorten anything 'til the main t'gallant blew to ribbons! I heard the master say that the Danish ship is preparing to go about.'

Bolitho slid carefully to the deck as he had done ten thousand times, in so many vessels from topsail-cutter to a lordly first-rate. Allday unshuttered a lantern and held it over the table while he peered at his chart. Poland was doing well in spite of the savage weather which had plagued them since they had left the sheltered narrows. *Truculent* would now be at the northern limits of the Kattegat and would soon be changing tack to head south-west through the Skagerrak—more sea room, less chance of running afoul of any fishermen who were mad enough to be out in weather like this.

Allday said helpfully, 'Wind's shifted since the first watch, Sir Richard. A real nor'-easter, blowin' fit to bust every spar. Straight down from the Arctic if you asks me.'

He produced a heavy tarpaulin coat, knowing Bolitho would want to see for himself. As the deck rose and plunged down again, Allday held on to one of the tethered nine-pounders to meet the violent motion. He felt the old wound in his chest come to life, sear his insides until he could scarcely stop himself from calling out.

Bolitho watched him and held out his hand. 'Here, hold on!'

Allday felt the pain recede as if it was reluctant to offer him peace. He shook himself like a great dog and forced a grin. 'Not too bad, sir. Comes at you when you're least ready, the bugger!'

Bolitho said, 'You know what I told you before. I meant it then, I mean it still.' He saw Allday stiffen, ready to argue. 'You deserve it anyway, after what you've done for your country.' He dropped his voice. 'For me.'

Allday waited for the deck to sway upright again and replied, 'An' what'd I do then, Sir Richard? Stand around the inn tellin' lies like all the other old tars? Be a sheep-watcher again? Or marry some rich widow-woman, an' God knows there are enough of *them* around with this war goin' on an' on!'

Bolitho lurched towards the screen door and saw the marine sentry clinging to a stanchion, his face no better than Jenour's. It was useless to try and convince Allday, he thought.

Water tumbled over the companion-way coaming and down to the deck below, and when Bolitho managed to reach the top of the ladder the wind nearly took his breath away.

Both watches were on deck, the air filled with shredded shouts and the slither of feet in water as it surged over the lee side.

Poland saw him and pulled himself along the quarterdeck rail to join him.

'I am sorry you were disturbed, Sir Richard!'

Bolitho smiled at him, his hair already thick with salt spray. 'You cannot be blamed for the weather!' He was not sure if Poland heard him. 'What is our position?'

Poland pointed across the lee bow. 'The last point of land, Skagen's Horn. We will change tack in about half an hour.' His voice was hoarse from shouting into the gale and the cold spray. 'I have barely lost an hour, Sir Richard!'

Bolitho nodded. 'I know. You are doing well.' Always the uncertainty, the search for criticism. It was a pity he did not remember that when he was berating his lieutenants.

Poland added, '*Dryaden* split a tops'l yard and most of her driver during the night.' He sounded pleased. 'We'll be leaving her soon.'

Bolitho shivered and was glad that he had had the last coffee as Allday had put it.

Poland had done what he had asked of him. Had kept *Truculent* in the lead all the way. *Dryaden* was not even in sight now except possibly from the masthead. He stared up through the shining black web of rigging and felt his head swim. Who would be a lookout in this gale?

Poland muttered something as several men ran to secure one of the boats on the tier; they were wading waist deep in water one moment, then seeming to rise higher than the quarterdeck the next.

Poland shouted, 'I've three men below with injuries. I ordered the surgeon to make certain they were real and proper—no malingerers, I told him!'

Bolitho looked away. *I'm sure of that*, he thought.

Aloud he said, 'Once clear of the Skaggerak we can use this nor'-easterly to good advantage.' He saw Poland nod, not yet committed. 'We will have a companion for the final passage across the North Sea. You can reduce sail then if need be to carry out repairs and relight the galley fire.'

Poland showed no surprise that Bolitho should know about the galley. Instead he said bluntly, 'You ordered *Zest* to make the rendezvous, Sir Richard? I make no secret of it—Captain Varian and I do not see eye to eye.'

'I am aware of it. I am also conscious that even with our reinforcements from Cape Town and the Caribbean we are pitifully short of frigates.' He did not add *as usual* although it had always been so; he had heard his father complaining about it often enough. 'So you had best forget your private differences and concentrate on the task in hand.'

In the bitter wind, with sea and spindrift reaching further out on either beam as the grey light continued to expand, it was hard to think of plots and schemers in high places. This was the place which truly counted. If England lost command of the seas she would surely lose everything else, with freedom at the top of the tally.

He was glad all the same that he had taken every precaution he could think of. If he was to be proved mistaken he would have lost nothing. But if not—He turned as the lookout yelled, 'Deck there! Th' Dane's gone about!'

257

Poland staggered as another sea lifted and burst over the beakhead, his hands gripped behind him, his body responding to the deck's movements with the ease of a rider on a well-trained stallion.

Bolitho moved away, his eyes slitted against the weather as he watched a faint blur of land seemingly far away to larboard. In fact he knew it was probably less than two miles distant. Poland was staying as close-hauled as he dared, using the north-east wind to weather the headland, The Skaw as it was respectfully called. He thought suddenly of his own elation when he had been roused by Allday on that other occasion when they had sighted The Lizard; what Catherine had later told him about her certainty that he had been near, although she could not possibly have known.

'All hands! All hands! Stand by to wear ship!'

Red-eyed and sagging with fatigue, their bodies bruised and bloodied by their fight with wind and sea, *Truculent's* seamen and marines staggered to their stations at halliards and braces like old men or drunkards.

Poland called sharply, 'Get your best topmen aloft, Mr Williams—I want the t'gan's'ls on her as soon as we are on the new course.' He glared at Hull, the sailing-master. 'This must be smartly done, sir!' It sounded like a threat.

Williams raised his speaking-trumpet. How his arm must ache, Bolitho thought. 'Stand by on the quarterdeck!' He waited, judging the moment. 'Alter course three points to larboard!' He gestured angrily with the speaking-trumpet as a wave swept over the nettings and hurled several men from their positions, while others stood firm, crouching and spitting out mouthfuls of water.

'Mr Lancer! More hands on the lee braces there!'

Poland nodded, his chin close to his chest. 'Put up your helm!'

With a thunder of canvas and the squeal of blocks *Truculent* began to pay off to the wind, so that the sails refilled and held the ship almost upright instead of lying over to the mercy of the gale. Poland consulted the compass and said, 'Hold her *steady*, Mr Hull.'

Bolitho saw the master glare at his back as he replied smartly, 'Steady she goes, sir! West-by-north.'

'Deck there!'

Poland peered up at the scudding, full-bellied clouds, his features raw from endless hours on deck. 'What does that fool want?'

The lookout called again, 'Sail on the starboard quarter!'

Poland looked along the length of his ship where men bustled about amidst the confusion of water and broken rigging, while they carried out repairs as they would perform under fire. Duty, discipline and tradition. It was all they knew.

He said, 'Get somebody aloft with a glass, Mr Williams.' Poland darted a quick glance at Bolitho by the weather rail. How could he have known?

Bolitho saw the glance. It was as if Poland had shouted the question out loud. He felt the tension draining out of him, the uncertainty replaced by a cold, bitter logic.

A master's mate, Hull's best, had been sent to the masthead, and soon he bellowed down in a voice which had become as hardened to a sailor's life as a cannon which has seen a world of battles.

'Deck thar! Man-o'-war, zur!' A long pause while

Truculent surged and dipped her jib-boom into a mountainous wave. It felt like striking a sandbar. Then he yelled, 'Small 'un, zur! Corvette, aye, 'tis a corvette!'

Hull muttered, 'If 'e says she's a corvette, then *that she be!*'

Poland walked unsteadily towards Bolitho and touched his hat with stiff formality. 'Frenchman, Sir Richard.' He hesitated before adding, 'Too small to hamper us.'

'Big enough to seek us out, Captain Poland, to hang to our coat-tails until—' He shrugged and said, 'Whatever it is we shall soon know.'

Poland digested it and asked, 'Orders, Sir Richard?'

Bolitho looked past him at the listless exhausted seamen. Poland was right. No corvette would dare to challenge a thirty-six gun frigate. So her captain must know that he would not be alone for much longer; and then . . .

He heard himself reply, 'Have the boatswain's party clear out the galley and relight the fires immediately.' He ignored Poland's expression. His face was full of questions; the galley had obviously not been high on his list. 'Your people are in no state to fight—they are worn out. A good hot meal, and a double ration of rum, and you will have men who will follow your orders and not give in at the first whiff of grape.' He saw Poland nod and said, 'I must see Sir Charles Inskip. I fear he is in for another unpleasant surprise.'

Allday was standing close by and saw one of the seamen nudge his companion with a grin. 'See, Bill? Our Dick's not bothered, so why should we be, eh?'

Allday sighed. *Our Dick*. Now they were his men too.

Then he thought about the rum and licked his lips in anticipation. A good 'wet' was always welcome. Especially when it might be your last.

*　　　*　　　*

Catherine paused at the foot of the steps and glanced along the street with its tall elegant houses and leafless trees. It was late afternoon and already dark enough for the carriages to show their lamps. She had been shopping in some of the adjoining streets with Yovell as her companion, and sometimes adviser, especially on matters concerning the man he served so loyally.

She waved to the coachman, still called Young Matthew even though his grandfather Old Matthew, who had been the Bolitho coachman for many years, was long dead. It was good to have the light, elegant carriage here, she thought. A part of home. It seemed strange that she could think of Falmouth and the old grey house as *home*.

'You can go to the mews, Young Matthew, I'll not need you again today.' He grinned down at her and touched his hat with his whip. 'Very well, m'lady.' One of Lord Browne's servants had come down the steps and she curtsied, her apron ribbons whipping out in the cold wind, before going to help Yovell with their many parcels.

'Oh, m'lady!' The girl called after her but Catherine was already in the hall. She stood stock-still with surprise, even shock, as she saw a uniformed figure standing inside the book-lined library, his hands held out to the fire.

261

She waited a few seconds, her hand to her breast, until her breathing became steady again. It was foolish, but just for a moment she had believed—But the tall captain had fair hair and blue eyes: a friend for so many reasons. Captain Valentine Keen took her hand and kissed it. 'I beg your pardon, m'lady, for coming unannounced. I was at the Admiralty, too near to miss the chance of seeing you.'

She slipped her hand through his arm and together they walked towards the fire.

'You are always welcome, Val.' She studied him thoughtfully. He too had known Richard a long time and had served him as midshipman and lieutenant, until he had eventually become his flag-captain. She said quietly, 'Please call me Catherine. We are friends, remember?' She seated herself opposite and waited for him to follow suit. 'What ails you, Val? We have been worried. About you and Zenoria. Is there something I can do?'

He did not reply directly. 'I heard about Sir Richard at the Admiralty.' He glanced around as if expecting to see him. 'He is not returned yet?'

She shook her head. 'It is far longer than we supposed. Four weeks today.'

Keen watched her as she turned to stare into the fire. A beautiful, sensuous woman. One whom men would fight over, one who could excite the one she loved to do almost anything. But she was deeply troubled, and was not trying to hide it.

He said, 'I was told by one of Lord Godschale's aides that he had been on a mission of some importance. But the weather is foul, especially in our waters. I daresay they are riding it out.' He felt her gaze settle on him and he said, 'Zenoria was staying with my sisters. Perhaps they smothered her with too much kindness ... maybe she felt she no longer cared about me—'

Catherine said, 'The marriage—is it not agreed upon?'

'She left to return to the West Country. There is an uncle, apparently, in whom she used to confide when she was a child, before he went to the Indies. Now he is back in Cornwall—I know not where. She is with him.'

Catherine watched his despair. She knew it, remembered it.

'But you *love* her?' She saw him nod. It made him look like a young boy. 'And I do know she loves you, for many, many reasons. You saved her life, you cared for her when others would have turned their backs. Believe me, Val, I know about such matters at first hand!'

'That is partly why I came. I received a letter from Sir Richard. Did you know ... Catherine?'

She smiled despite her anxiety. 'That is better. Yes, I knew. About his new flagship, the *Black Prince*. He wants you as his captain, but I will lay odds that he spoke only of your hoped-for marriage?'

'You know him well.' He smiled ruefully. 'It is why I went to see Lord Godschale. He was becoming impatient.'

She touched her throat and remembered what Bolitho had said about it.

'That is not so unusual, I believe.'

Keen faced her resolutely. 'I have made it clear I *will* serve as his flag-captain.' He was surprised at her reaction, as if some sort of threat had been removed. 'Are you pleased?'

'Of course I am. Who better to stand by my man's side in times of peril? He loves you in the same way he cares for young Adam. I was afraid he would have some stupid captain like—' She dropped her eyes. 'That is another matter.' When she looked up again her dark eyes were flashing. 'And have no fear about your Zenoria. I will find her, although I suspect she will find me first once I am returned to Falmouth. We understand one another. She *shall* be your bride, Val, but you must be gentle with her. I know from what Richard tells me that you are a decent man, and have only loved one other in your life.' She watched the memories clouding his eyes. 'This will be different, more wonderful than you can conceive. But as *she* will learn to accept your calling as a sailor, so must you be patient with her.' She let each word sink in. 'Remember what happened to her. A young girl. Taken and used, with no hope, and nothing to live for.'

He nodded, seeing her naked back as the whip had laid it open from shoulder to hip. The way she had withdrawn when he had spoken of marriage and how it would be for them.

'I never thought. Or perhaps I did not want to think about it. How she would feel, or if she was tormented that she might never be able to accept—' He could not continue.

She stood up and walked to his chair, and laid her hand on his shoulder, touching his epaulette. Each time she saw a sea-officer she thought of him. What he might be doing; whether or not he was in any danger.

'There, Val. You feel better now? And so do I.' She made light of it. 'After all, I cannot rely on Mr
264

Allday for everything!'

The door opened and she felt a chill draught from the hallway, although she had heard no bell or knock at the street entrance.

'Who is it, Maisie?'

The girl stared at her, then at Keen.

'Beg pardon, m'lady, but 'tis a gentleman for the captain.'

Keen stood up. 'I mentioned I would be here a while. I hope that was acceptable?'

Catherine watched him, her gaze very level. 'What is it? Something has happened.'

He said only, 'Please wait here, Catherine.'

The servant girl gaped at her. 'Would you like some tea, m'lady?'

She realised only vaguely what she had asked. 'No, but thank you.'

The door closed, reluctantly or so it seemed, as if the servant had wanted to share what was happening.

Keen came back, his handsome features grave as he shut the door behind him. He strode across the carpet and took her hands in his. They were like ice. 'It was a messenger from the Admiralty.' He gripped her hands more tightly as she pulled away. 'No, hear me. He will want you to know.' He saw a pulse beating in her throat, saw the way she lifted her chin. Dread, defiance; it was all there.

'There has been a sea-fight. Richard's ship was involved but they know little more as yet. He must have been returning to England from his mission. A schooner brought the news to Portsmouth, and the telegraph sent word from there to the Admiralty.'

She stared round the room like a trapped animal. 'Is he hurt? What must I do? I must be there if—'

He guided her to a chair, knowing it was not strength or courage she was lacking, but a direction to point herself.

'You must wait here, Catherine.' He saw the anxiety change to resistance and refusal, and persisted, 'He will *expect* you to be here.' He dropped on one knee beside her chair. 'You have helped me so much. Let me at least try to do the same for you. I will remain at your service until we learn what is happening.'

'*When?*' One word, which sounded as if it was torn from her.

'It must be soon. Tomorrow, the next day. I felt something was wrong, and yet—' He looked past her into the fire. 'I was too beset with my own troubles.'

Catherine looked at the gold lace on his sleeve. Was this how it was? How it would be? After all their hopes. Their love. So many women must have known it.

She thought suddenly of Nelson, of Bolitho's bitterness at those who had hated him the most but who had mourned his death the loudest. Nobody spoke of Emma Hamilton any more. It was as if she had never been, even though she had given him the things he had lacked and had needed more than anything. Love and admiration. It was rare to have one without the other.

She said quietly but firmly, 'I will never give him up.'

Keen was not certain how it was meant, but he was deeply moved.

She stood up and walked towards the door where she turned, the lights reflecting from her dark hair.

'Please stay, Val.' She seemed to hesitate. 'But I am going to our room for a while. So that we may be together.'

CHAPTER THIRTEEN

NO ESCAPE

Bolitho gripped the quarterdeck rail and watched the sky brighten to a harsh intensity. Beneath his fingers the rail was so caked with salt that it felt like rough stone. But the motion was easier as *Truculent*, now with her topgallants filled hard to the wind, plunged over a wild succession of curling wavecrests.

He stared at the sun as it tried to break through the morning haze. It was like a bright silver platter, he thought, while the aimless bunches of cloud reminded him of fog above the Helford River at home in Cornwall. The air was still tinged with the smell of grease from the galley, and he had seen the seamen at work about the upper deck showing less strain than before he had suggested to Poland that a good hot meal was a priority.

He tried to picture the ship as she headed south-west, the wind following her from dead astern so that she seemed to bound over the water. Somewhere, about forty miles across the starboard quarter, were the bleak shores and fjords of Norway, beyond which lay only the Arctic. Part of the Danish coast was still abeam, and according to the sailing-master's rough calculations some thirty miles distant. Far enough to be out of sight but still within the range of *Zest*'s patrol area. He thought of Poland's dislike for *Zest*'s captain. If he had had more time in London he might have discovered some reason for it. But he doubted it. It was like some secret held closely by each captain as if for protection, or threat.

He shaded his eyes to stare astern but their pursuer was not in sight from the deck. A lance of silver sunlight touched his eye, and he winced before pressing his hand over it while he took another look.

Inskip had appeared at his side. 'Your eye bothering you?'

Bolitho snatched his hand away. '*No*.' He added in a calmer voice, 'You are feeling more the thing now that we are in open water again?' He must try not to be taken by surprise by such an innocent comment. Inskip had no way of knowing. And besides, there was every hope that his eye would recover completely. Grasping at straws? Perhaps, but it barely troubled him.

Inskip smiled. 'I suspect your man Allday can take more credit than the damned sea.'

Bolitho noticed for the first time that there was an unusually strong smell of rum, and that Inskip's normally pallid features were glowing.

Inskip cleared his throat noisily. 'Damme if he didn't produce a potion he had concocted himself. Hot gruel, rum and brandy seem to be the main ingredients!'

Bolitho glanced at Poland who was deep in conversation with his first lieutenant. They both looked to the mastheads, and after a further discussion a warrant officer was sent aloft to join the lookout, a heavy telescope bouncing from one hip.

Inskip asked worriedly, 'What does it mean?' He gestured vaguely towards the taffrail. 'That Frenchman can't do us any harm, surely?'

Bolitho saw Poland gazing at him across the deck. It was almost like defiance.

'I'd tell the captain to come about and go for that corvette, if I didn't think it would waste valuable time.' He rubbed his chin while he pictured his chart again. 'He's hanging on to the scent. A scavenger—like a wild dog on a battlefield, waiting to pick off the bones.' He heard Poland call, 'Prepare to set the maincourse, Mr Williams! I'll not lose this soldier's wind!'

The deck shuddered and the taut rigging seemed to whine as the ship plunged forward under a growing pyramid of canvas.

Bolitho saw Jenour by the compass, and wondered if he had guessed why Poland was piling on more sail.

Inskip said vaguely, 'Funny thing about eyes, though.' He did not see Bolitho glance at him warily. 'When I was honoured by the King, for instance—' His words were becoming slurred; Allday's cure must be working well—'His Majesty wore a green eye shield all the while, and they say he cannot recognise a single soul without a strong glass.'

Bolitho recalled the general's dry comment about guiding the King's hand. Truer than he had realised perhaps.

Inskip said abruptly, 'You think we're running into a trap, don't you?' The combined power of rum and brandy had put an aggressive edge to his tone. 'How could that possibly be—and where would be the point?'

269

Bolitho replied quietly, 'We were delayed a full week. Where would be the point of *that*?'

Inskip brooded on it. 'It was all a secret, and anyway, what could the enemy hope to achieve in a week?'

Bolitho said, 'When the schooner *Pickle* arrived at Falmouth on November fourth last year, her commanding officer, a Lieutenant Lapenotière, was the first man to bring the news of Trafalgar and Nelson's death to England.' He let each word sink in; it was important that Inskip should understand. 'Lapenotière posted all the way from Falmouth to London to carry the word to the Admiralty.'

'*And?*' Inskip was sweating despite the bitter air.

'He reached London on the morning of the sixth. All that way, *in just two days*. Imagine what French intelligence could make of a full week!'

He looked at the sky, a thinning here and there in the clouds revealing slivers of glacier blue.

The senior helmsman called, 'Steady she be, zur! Sou'-west!'

Bolitho added, 'South-west, Sir Charles, but over four hundred miles to make good, unless—' He saw Poland moving towards him. 'What is it?'

Poland turned as if to keep his comments from Inskip's ears. 'May I suggest we alter course and run further to the south'rd, Sir Richard?' He looked towards the misty horizon, the drifting spray like steam over the beakhead. 'It would add to the distance, but—'

Bolitho faced him impassively. 'We should also lose any chance of a rendezvous on *Zest*'s station. But you already knew that?'

It was rare for Poland to offer such a definite suggestion, one which might later lay him open to

270

criticism or worse.

Bolitho persisted. 'Do you have any cause to doubt Captain Varian's intentions?' He watched the emotions, the anxieties troubling Poland's features. 'It is your *duty* to tell me. The responsibility of command which you have earned, and which you obviously cherish, makes that duty unavoidable!'

Poland looked trapped. Alone with his command he was second only to God. Faced by a vice-admiral whose name was known throughout most of the country, he was suddenly stripped of power, endangered by his one, unexpected outburst.

He answered wretchedly, 'I served with Varian some years ago. I was his first lieutenant, and I must admit that out there in the Indies I saw small chance of promotion, let alone a ship to command. We were ordered to Jamaica at the urgent request of the Governor ... there was a slave uprising with some danger to the residents and the plantations.'

Bolitho could see it. That would have been during the uneasy Peace of Amiens when many had thought the war had ended, that France and her allies, like England, had exhausted themselves in constant battle at sea and on land. As first lieutenant, Poland would have grasped at the chance of action like a drowning man clutching a piece of cork.

'I recall it. There were a lot of killings and some savage reprisals, to all accounts.'

Poland did not seem to have heard him. 'We had word from a trader that a plantation was under siege by a mob of slaves. It was too far inland to quell it with gunfire, so Captain Varian ordered me to take an armed party to rout the slaves.' He wiped his mouth with the back of his hand, oblivious to

271

Jenour and the watchful eyes of Lieutenant Williams by the quarterdeck rail. '*Mob?* By God, when we reached the place it was more like a blood-crazed army!' He shuddered. 'The owners and their people had been hacked to death like ribbons, their wives—well, they must have welcomed death when it came!'

'And Varian weighed anchor, am I right?'

Poland gaped at him. '*Aye*, Sir Richard. He thought we would share the same fate as those poor butchered creatures. Varian could not stand the prospect of failure, or being associated with one. He sailed away and reported to the admiral that he had lost contact with us and had been unable to help.' He added with sudden anger, 'But for the arrival of some local militia, he would have been right too!'

'Deck there! Corvette's makin' more sail!'

Bolitho saw the emptiness in Poland's stare and thought he may not even have heard.

Poland continued in the same flat voice. 'Varian's never been in a big action. Hunting smugglers and chasing privateers were more to his taste.' He seemed to draw himself up as he faced Bolitho with some of his old stiffness. 'I should have denounced him. I am not proud of what I did. He recommended me for command.' He looked along his ship. 'I got *Truculent*, so I said naught.'

Bolitho tugged his hat more firmly over his forehead to give himself time to think. If half of it was true then Varian was a menace to everyone who depended on him. He thought of *Zest's* being off-station at Good Hope; the terrible end of the little schooner *Miranda* while her executioner sped to safety.

A coward then?

'Deck there!' Bolitho saw Jenour shading his eyes to peer up at the foremast crosstrees. 'Sail on the weather bow!'

Poland stared from the masthead to Bolitho. 'I am sorry, Sir Richard. I spoke too soon!' He was probably seeing his only command already slipping away from his grasp.

Inskip swallowed hard. 'You're *both* wrong, dammit!' He wiped his eyes with his handkerchief. 'I'll wager *Zest* makes that damned Frenchie show a clean pair of heels!'

'Deck there!' The foremast lookout's voice was suddenly loud as wind spilled from the topsails. *'She's a French frigate, sir!'*

Bolitho saw faces turn to look towards him, not at their captain this time. So *Zest* was not waiting for them. Instead, the trap was about to be sprung. Bolitho looked at Inskip's flushed face and kept his voice calm. 'No, Sir Charles, *I fear we were both right.*' He swung on Poland. 'Clear for action, if you please!'

'Deck there!' Someone by the wheel gave a groan as the lookout yelled, '*Second* sail astern of t'other, sir!'

'The corvette has run up her colours, sir!'

Poland licked his lips. Two ships closing on a converging tack, another still hounding them from astern. To starboard was the full power of the wind, on the opposite beam and still out of sight was the Danish coast. In those fleeting seconds he could see it all. Jaws closing around his ship. Be run ashore in a hopeless stern-chase, or stand and be destroyed by overwhelming odds. He looked at his first lieutenant, his eyes dull. 'Beat to quarters, Mr Williams, and clear for action at your convenience.'

The marine fifers ran to the stations, adjusting their drums until they received a curt nod from the Royal Marines sergeant.

Bolitho saw Allday striding across the deck, his cutlass wedged carelessly through his belt. Jenour too, fingering his beautiful sword, his face suddenly determined as the drums commenced their urgent rattle to arms.

Inskip gasped, 'Maybe *Zest* will be here yet?' Nobody spoke, and his voice was almost drowned by the rush of bare feet, the stamp of marines across the poop and the thud and clatter of screens being torn down to clear the ship of obstructions. 'Why such a show of force?' He was almost pleading.

Bolitho watched *Truculent*'s big ensigns mounting to gaff and masthead. A challenge accepted.

He said, 'They *knew*, Sir Charles. One of His Majesty's most important emissaries and a senior officer for good measure! Exactly the excuse the French have been looking for. If we are taken, Napoleon will have all he needs to discredit the Danes for their secret discussions with us, and so weaken Sweden's and Russia's resolution to stand against him! Good God, man, even a child should see that!'

Inskip did not rise to Bolitho's angry contempt. He stared around at the gun-crews, the bustle with tackles and hand-spikes as each weapon was prepared to fight.

Then he peered overhead at the nets which were being rigged across the decks from gangway to gangway to protect these same crews from falling spars and debris. Even the boats were being swayed out and made ready to lower and cast adrift for the victors to recover.

Boats represented survival to most sailors, and Bolitho saw some of them turn from their work to watch, and the grim response from the scarlet squads of marines who fingered their Brown Bess muskets and fixed bayonets. If so ordered, they would shoot down anyone who created a panic or provoked any sort of disorder.

It was always a bad moment, Bolitho thought. Survival perhaps; but the peril of razor-sharp splinters hurled from tiered boats once battle was joined was far more dangerous.

Williams touched his hat, his eyes wild. 'Cleared for action, sir!'

Poland looked at him coldly and then said, 'That was smartly done, Mr Williams.' He looked past him and at the lines of watching gun-crews, men who moments before had been thinking only of getting another tot to reward them for their efforts. 'Do not load or run out as yet.' He turned and faced Bolitho. 'We are ready, Sir Richard.' His pale eyes were opaque, like a man already dead.

Inskip touched Bolitho's sleeve. 'Shall you *fight* them?' He sounded incredulous.

Bolitho did not answer. 'You may hoist my flag at the fore, Captain Poland. I think there are no more secrets left to keep.'

Inskip's shoulders seemed to droop. It was perhaps the clearest reply of all.

*   *   *

As the next hour dragged remorselessly past, the sky grew clearer, the clouds breaking up as if to give every light to the scene. But the sun held no warmth, and spray when it flew over the tightly-packed hammock nettings felt like fragments of ice.

Bolitho took the big telescope from the senior midshipman and walked to the mizzen shrouds. Without haste he climbed into the ratlines and steadied himself while he waited for his mind to clear. He could see the leading French frigate quite easily, still holding on to her original converging tack, every sail spread and bulging from the wind. She was big, forty guns or more at a guess, with her Tricolour standing out like bright metal. The other vessel was slightly smaller, but well equal to *Truculent*. Very deliberately he raised the heavy glass and watched the picture sharpen. How near she looked now; he could imagine the sounds of voices and the creak of gun-tackles as the crews waited impatiently for the order to run out. Around and behind his back he could sense a silence, and knew that all eyes were on him as he studied the enemy. Measuring their chances against his confidence. Seeing death in any uncertainty. The French were taking their time despite the great press of canvas. If there was to be any chance ... he slammed the glass shut with sudden anger. *I must never think like that, or we are already lost.*

He returned to the deck and handed the telescope to the midshipman.

'Thank you, Mr Fellowes.' He did not see the pleased surprise in the youth's eyes at the easy familiarity of his name. He crossed to Poland's side where Inskip and his secretary, the lugubrious Agnew, waited anxiously for his assessment.

Bolitho avoided the others and said, 'Captain Poland, make more sail if you please.' He glanced up at the braced yards and lofty sails framed by the

276

washed-out blue sky. 'The wind has eased somewhat—you will not tear the sticks out of her, I think.'

He expected a protest, even an argument, but before Poland turned away to pass his orders to the first lieutenant, Bolitho thought he saw something like relief on his set features. Calls trilled and once again hands clambered aloft with the agility of monkeys. From the quarterdeck Bolitho saw the great mainyard bending like a bow to the following wind, heard the crack and rattle of canvas as the remaining royals were freed to lend their thrust to the ship.

Poland came back breathing hard. 'Sir?'

Bolitho looked at him searchingly. Not a man who would crack, no matter what he might think of the coming fight and its likely conclusion. 'The French will adopt their usual tactics today. The leading ship will continue to close until she can reach us with her fire.' He saw Poland's bleak eyes following his arm as he pointed over towards the enemy, as if he could already see the lurid flash of cannon fire. 'It is my belief that their senior officer will be confident, perhaps too much so.'

Inskip muttered, 'So would *I* be, in his shoes!'

Bolitho ignored him. 'He will try to cripple *Truculent*, doubtless with chain-shot or langridge, while his consort attempts to rake our stern. A divided attack is commonly used in this way.' He watched his words hitting home. 'It must not happen.' He saw Poland flinch as a line snapped somewhere high above the deck. Like a pistol shot. 'If they are allowed to board us we'll be done for.' He nodded beyond the stern. 'And there is always our little scavenger waiting to lend her weight to the fight.'

Poland licked his lips. 'What must we do, Sir Richard?'

Inskip snapped, 'It's hopeless, if you ask me!'

Bolitho turned on him. 'Well, I do *not*, Sir Charles! So if you have nothing sensible to offer I suggest you go below to the orlop and do something useful to help the surgeon!' He saw Inskip flush with anger, and added bitterly, 'And *if* you ever reach London again, may I suggest that you explain to your masters, and mine, what they are asking people to do!' He waved his hand briefly over the crouching gun-crews. 'What *they* face each time a King's ship is called to arms!'

When he turned again Inskip and his secretary had disappeared. He smiled at Poland's surprise and said, 'It were better left to us, I think, eh, Captain?' He felt suddenly calm again, so much so that there was no sensation left in his limbs. 'I ordered more sail so that the French will think we are trying to run for it. They are already following suit, I see, every stitch they can muster, for this is a rich prize indeed. English *plotters* and a fine frigate to boot—no, the Frenchman will not wish to lose out on this!'

Poland nodded with slow understanding. 'You intend to luff and come about, Sir Richard?'

'Aye.' He touched his arm. 'Come walk awhile. The enemy will not be in useful range for half an hour at a guess. I have always found it helps to loosen the muscles, relax the mind.' He smiled at him, knowing how important it was for *Truculent*'s company to see their captain at ease.

Bolitho added, 'It will have to be smartly done, sails reduced instantly as the helm goes over. Then we can tack between them and rake them both.'

Poland nodded jerkily. 'I have always trained them well, Sir Richard!'

Bolitho clasped his hands behind him. That was more like it. Poland rising to any sort of criticism. *He had to believe.* He must think only of the first move.

Bolitho said, 'May I suggest you place your first lieutenant by the foremast so that he can control, even point each gun himself. There will be no time for a second chance.' He saw him nod. 'It is no place for a junior lieutenant.'

Poland called to Williams and while they were in deep discussion, with several meaning glances towards the nearest pyramid of sails, Bolitho said to Jenour, 'Keep on the move, Stephen.' He saw the flag-lieutenant's eyes blink. 'It will be warm work today, I fear.'

Allday massaged his chest with his hand and watched the too familiar preparations, and the way the third lieutenant stared at Williams as he passed him on his way aft. He probably saw his own removal from the forward guns as a lack of confidence in his ability. He would soon know why, Allday decided. He thought suddenly of Bolitho's offer.

Perhaps a little alehouse near Falmouth, with a rosy-cheeked widow-woman to take care of. No more danger, the scream of shot and dying men, the awful crash of falling spars. And pain, always the pain.

'Leadin' ship's runnin' out, sir!'

Poland glanced at Bolitho and then snapped, 'Very well, open the ports. Load and run out the *starboard* battery!'

Bolitho clenched his fist. Poland had remembered. Had he run out the guns on either side it would have shown the enemy what he intended as plainly as if he had spelled out a signal.

'Ready, sir!' That was Williams, somehow out of place up forward instead of on the quarterdeck.

'*Run out!*'

Squealing like disgruntled hogs, the maindeck eighteen-pounders trundled up to their ports, each crew watching the other so that the broadside was presented as one.

There was a dull bang and seconds later a thin waterspout leapt from the sea some fifty yards from the starboard bow. A sighting shot.

Poland wiped his face with his fingers. 'Stand by to come about! *Be ready*, Mr Hull!'

Bolitho saw Munro, the second lieutenant, stride to the chart-table near the companion hatch and pull aside its canvas cover.

Bolitho walked slowly past the tense group around the wheel, the marines waiting at braces and halliards, knowing that with so much canvas above them one error could crush them under an avalanche of broken masts and rigging.

The young lieutenant stiffened as Bolitho's shadow fell across the open log book, in which he had just noted the time of the first shot.

'Is there something I can do, Sir Richard?'

'I was just looking at the date. But no, it's not important.'

He moved away again and knew that Allday had drawn nearer to him.

It was his birthday. Bolitho touched the shape of the locket through his shirt. *May love always protect you.*

It was like hearing her speak those same words aloud.

Poland slammed down his hand. *'Now!'*

In seconds, or so it seemed, the great courses were brailed and fisted to their yards, opening up to the sea around them like curtains on a stage.

'Helm-a-lee! Hard over, damn your eyes!'

Voices and calls echoed over the deck as men threw themselves on the braces to haul the yards round while the deck swayed over to the violent change of course. Gun-crews abandoned their charges and ran to the opposite side to supplement the depleted numbers there, and as the ports squeaked open they ran out their eighteen-pounders, aided this time by the steep tilt of the deck. Spray lanced through the ports and over the nettings, and some of the crew gaped in astonishment as the leading French frigate seemed to materialise right before their eyes, when moments earlier she had been on the opposite beam.

'As you bear!' Lieutenant Williams held up his sword as he lurched along the deck by the larboard carronade. 'A guinea for the first strike!'

A midshipman named Brown shouted, 'I'll double that, sir!'

They grinned at one another like urchins.

'Fire!'

The battery fired as one, the deafening roar of the long eighteen-pounders completely blocking out the sounds of the enemy's response. The French captain had been taken by surprise, and only half of his guns had been brought to bear on the wildly tacking *Truculent*. The enemy's sails were in total chaos as her topmen tried to take the way off her and follow *Truculent*'s example.

Aft by the compass box, Bolitho felt the deck shudder as some of the enemy's iron crashed into the hull. The sea's face was feathered with flying chain-shot which had been intended for *Truculent*'s mast and rigging.

Poland yelled, 'Stand by to starboard, Mr Williams!'

Men scampered back to their stations at the other battery, as they had drilled so many times. The range was much greater, and the second French ship lay bows on, her topsails rippling and spilling wind while her captain tried to change tack.

'As you bear, lads!' Williams crouched by the first division of guns, then sliced the air with his sword. *'Fire!'*

Bolitho held his breath as gun by gun along *Truculent*'s side the long orange tongues spat out from this carefully timed broadside. But the enemy was still almost end-on, a difficult target at a range of some two cables. He hid his disbelief as like a great tree the frigate's foremast seemed to bow forward under the pressure of the wind. But it did not stop; and with it went the trailing mass of broken shrouds and running rigging, and then the whole topmast, until the forward part of the vessel was completely hidden by fallen debris. It must have been almost the last shot of the battery. But just one eighteen-pound ball was enough.

Bolitho looked at Poland's smoke-stained features. 'Better odds, Captain?'

The seamen, who were already training the quarterdeck nine-pounders with their handspikes, looked at him and gave a hoarse cheer.

Allday slitted his eyes against the funnelling

smoke and watched the leading frigate as she eventually came under command. She lay down to larboard now, her maincourse brailed up, but several others punctured by *Truculent*'s cannon fire. Bolitho had stolen the wind-gage from the Frenchie, but it was all they had. One thing was certain: Poland could never have done it, would never have *tried* to attempt it. He saw Bolitho glance up at the sails and then towards the enemy. As in memory. Like at The Saintes in their first ship together, the *Phalarope*. Bolitho was still that captain, no matter what his rank and title said. He glared at the cheering, capering seamen. *Fools.* They would change their tune damn soon. He gripped his cutlass more tightly. *And here it comes.*

Williams raised his sword and looked aft at the captain. 'Ready to larboard, sir!'

'Fire!'

The ship staggered to the thunder and recoil of the guns, while the pale smoke billowed downwind towards the enemy.

It was like grinding over a reef or running into a sandbar, so that for a long moment men seemed to stare at one another as the enemy's broadside crashed into the hull or screamed through the canvas and rigging overhead. The spread nets jumped with fallen cordage and blocks, and a scarlet-coated marine dropped from the maintop before lying spreadeagled above one of the gun-crews.

Bolitho coughed out smoke and thought briefly of Inskip down in the reeling gloom of the orlop. The first wounded would already be on their way there. He looked at the marine's corpse on the nets. It was a marvel nothing vital had been shot away.

He saw Jenour wiping his eyes with his forearm, dazed by the onslaught.

'Captain Poland, prepare to alter course, if you please. We will steer due west!' But when he looked through the thinning smoke he saw that Poland was down, one leg doubled under him, his fingers clutching his throat as if to stem the blood which flooded over his coat like paint. Bolitho dropped on his knee beside him. 'Take him to the surgeon!' But Poland shook his head so violently that Bolitho saw the gaping hole in his neck where a fragment of iron had cut him down. He was dying, choking on his own blood as he tried to speak.

Lieutenant Munro joined him, his tanned face as pale as death.

Very slowly, Bolitho stood up and looked towards the enemy. 'Your captain is dead, Mr Munro. Pass the word to the others.' He glanced down at Poland's contorted features. Even in death his eyes were somehow angry and disapproving. It was terrible to see him die with a curse on his lips, although he guessed that he had been the only one close enough to hear it.

His last words on earth had been, *'God's damnation on Varian, the cowardly bastard!'*

Bolitho saw Williams staring aft towards him, his hat gone but the sword still gripped in his hand.

Bolitho watched a seaman cover Poland's body with some canvas, then he walked up to the quarterdeck rail as he had done so many times in the past.

He thought of Poland's despairing curse and said aloud, 'And *my* damnation too!' Then he dropped his hand and felt the ship's anger erupt in another savage broadside.

Jenour called huskily, 'The corvette's closing, sir!'

'I see her. Warn the starboard battery, then pass the word to the marines in the tops. *Nobody will board this ship!*' He stared at Jenour and knew he was speaking wildly. *'Nobody!'*

Jenour tore his eyes away and called to a boatswain's mate. But just for a few seconds he had seen a Bolitho he had not known before. Like a man who faced destiny and accepted it. A man without fear; without hate and maybe without hope either. He saw Bolitho turn away from the drifting smoke and look towards his coxswain. The glance excluded everyone, so that the death and danger seemed almost incidental for that one precious moment. They smiled at each other, and before the guns opened fire once again Jenour tried to recall what he had seen in Bolitho's expression as he had glanced at his friend. If it was anything, it was like an apology, he decided.

Bolitho had seen Jenour's desperate gaze but forgot him as the guns thundered again and recoiled on their tackles. Like demons the crews flung themselves to their tasks of sponging out the smoking muzzles, before ramming home fresh charges and finally the black, evil-looking shot. Their naked backs were begrimed from powder smoke, sweat cutting pale lines through it in spite of the bitter wind and floating droplets of spray.

There was blood on the deck too, while here and there great blackened scores cut across the usually immaculate planking, where French balls had come smashing inboard. One of the larboard eighteen-pounders had been upended and a man lay dying beneath its massive weight, his skin burning

285

under the overheated barrel. Others had been pulled aside to keep the deck clear for the small powder monkeys who scurried from gun to gun, not daring to look up as they dropped their charges and ran back for more.

Two corpses, so mutilated by flying metal that they were barely recognisable, were lifted momentarily above the nettings before being cast into the sea. Burial when it came was as ruthless as the death which had marked them down.

Bolitho took a telescope from its rack and stared at the other frigate until his eye throbbed. Like *Truculent*, she had been hit many times and her sails were shot through, some ripping apart to the pressure of the wind. Rigging, severed and untended, swayed from the yards like creeper, but her guns were still firing from every port, and Bolitho could feel some of the iron hitting the lower hull. In the rare pauses, while men fell about their work like demented souls in hell, he could hear the tell-tale sound of pumps, and almost expected to hear Poland's incisive tones urging one of his lieutenants to bid them work all the harder.

The glass settled on the other frigate's poop and he saw her captain staring back at him through his own telescope. He shifted it slightly and saw dead and dying men around the wheel, and knew that some of Williams' double-shotted guns had reaped a terrible harvest.

But they must hurt her, slow her down before her guns could find some weakness in *Truculent's* defences.

He lowered the glass and yelled to Williams, 'Point your guns abaft her mainmast and fire on the uproll!'

His words were lost in another ragged barrage, but a petty officer heard them, and knuckled his forehead as he dashed through the smoke to tell the first lieutenant.

He saw Williams peer aft and nod, his teeth very white in his bronzed face. Did he see his real chance of promotion now Poland was dead, as his captain had once done? Or did he only see the nearness of death?

Pieces of gangway burst from the side and scattered ripped and singed hammocks across the deck like faceless puppets. Metal clanged from one of the guns and men fell kicking and writhing as its splinters pitched them down in their own blood. One, the young midshipman named Brown whom Bolitho had seen joking with the first lieutenant, was hurled almost to the opposite side, most of his face shot away.

Bolitho thought wildly of Falmouth. He had seen enough stones there. This young fourteen-year-old midshipman would probably have one too when the news reached England. *Who died for the Honour of his King and Country*. What would his loved ones think if they had seen the 'honour' of his death?

'*Again, on the uproll!*' Bolitho reeled back from the rail while the guns roared out. Some spars fell from the Frenchman's mizzen, and one of her topsails was reduced to floating ribbons. But the flag still flew, and the guns had not lost their fury.

Lieutenant Munro shouted, 'She's closing the range, Sir Richard!'

Bolitho nodded, and winced as a ball slammed through an open port and cut a marine in half while he stood guarding the mainhatch. He saw Midshipman Fellowes stuffing his fist into his mouth to prevent himself from retching or screaming at the sight—he could be blamed for neither.

Munro lowered his glass. 'T'other frigate is still adrift, Sir Richard, but they're cutting the wreckage clear.'

'Yes. If she rejoins the fight before we can cripple the—'

There was a loud crack behind him and he heard more splinters whine through the air and thud into woodwork. He felt something strike his left epaulette, and rip it away to toss it to the deck like a contemptuous challenge. A foot lower, and the iron splinter would have cut through his heart. He reached out as Munro reeled against the side, his hand under his coat. He was gasping as if he had been punched in the stomach, and when Bolitho tore his hand away he saw the bright red blood running from his white waistcoat and breeches, even as Allday caught him and lowered him to the deck.

Bolitho said, 'Easy, I'll have the surgeon attend you.'

The lieutenant stared up at the empty blue sky, his eyes very wide as if he could not believe what had happened.

He gasped, 'No, sir! *Please, no*—' He gasped again as the pain increased and blood ran from one corner of his mouth. 'I—I want to stay where I can see . . .'

Allday stood up and said gruffly, 'Done for, Sir Richard. He's shot through.'

Someone was calling for assistance, another screaming with pain as more shot hammered into the side and through the rigging. But Bolitho felt

unable to move. *It was all happening again.*
Hyperion and her last battle, even to holding the
hand of a dying seaman who had asked '*Why me?*' as
death had claimed him. Almost defiantly he stooped
down and took Munro's bloodied hand, and
squeezed it until his eyes turned up to his. 'Very
well, Mr Munro. You stay with me.'

Allday sighed deeply. Munro's eyes, which
watched Bolitho so intently, were still and without
understanding. *Always the pain.*

Hull, the sailing-master who had fought his own
battle with wind and rudder throughout the fight,
yelled hoarsely, 'Corvette's takin' t'other frigate in
tow, sir!'

Bolitho swung round and noticed that Jenour was
still staring down at the dead lieutenant. Seeing
himself perhaps? *Or all of us?*

'Why so?' He trained the glass, and wanted to cry
out aloud as the roar of another disjointed broadside
probed his brain like hot irons.

He found the two ships through the pall of
drifting smoke and saw the boats in the water as a
towline was passed across. There were flags on the
corvette's yards, and when Bolitho turned the glass
towards the attacking ship he saw a signal still flying
above the flash of her armament. She showed no
sign of disengaging, so why was the other ship
under tow? His reeling mind would make no sense
of it. It refused to answer, even to function.

He heard Williams' voice. 'Ready to larboard!
Easy, my lads!' It reminded him of Keen with his
men in *Hyperion*, quietening them as will a rider
with a nervous horse.

Bolitho saw the Frenchman's yards begin to
move, while more sails appeared above and below

289

the punctured rags as if by magic.

Jenour cried with disbelief, 'He's going about!'

Bolitho cupped his hands. 'Mr Williams! Rake his stern as he tacks!'

Allday sounded dazed. 'He's breaking off the fight. But why? He's only got to hang on!'

There was a sudden stillness, broken only by the hoarse orders of the gun-captains and the thud of the pumps. From somewhere aloft, from lookout or marine in the fighting tops, nobody knew.

'Deck below! Sail on th' weather bow!'

The Frenchman was gathering way as she continued to turn until the pale sunlight lit up her shattered stern windows, where Williams' carronade had scored the first strike for the price of a midshipman's two guineas; and beneath, across her scarlet counter her name, *L'Intrépide*, was clear to see for the first time.

Bolitho said, 'Aloft, Mr Lancer, as fast as you can. I want to know more of this newcomer!'

The lieutenant bobbed his head and dashed wild-eyed for the shrouds. He faltered only when Williams' guns fired again and then he was up and climbing through the smoke as if the devil was at his heels.

Allday exclaimed, 'By God, the bugger's still making more sail!'

Men stood back from their smoking guns, too stunned or crazed to know what was happening. Some of the wounded crawled about the torn decks, their cracked voices demanding answers when there were none to offer.

Bolitho shouted, '*Stand to!* She's run out her stern chasers!' As he had watched his powerful enemy standing away, he had seen two ports in her mauled stern open to reveal the unfired muzzles pointing straight at *Truculent* even as the range began to open.

Williams yelled, 'Ready on deck!'

As if he was totally unaware of the danger and the battle beneath him, Lieutenant Lancer shouted down in the sudden silence, 'She's making her number, sir!'

Allday whispered harshly, '*Zest*, by God—but too bloody late.'

But he was wrong. Even Lancer, struggling with his telescope and signal book from his precarious perch aloft, sounded confused.

'She's *Anemone*, thirty-eight.' His voice seemed to shake. '*Captain Bolitho.*'

At that very moment *L'Intrépide* fired first one stern chaser then the other. A ball crashed into the quarterdeck and cut down two of the helmsmen, covering Hull with their blood before scything through the taffrail. The last ball struck the mizzen top and brought down a mass of broken woodwork and several blocks. It was a miracle that Lancer had not been hurled down to the deck.

Bolitho was more aware of falling than of feeling any pain. His mind was still grappling with Lancer's report, hanging on although it was getting harder every second.

Hands were holding him with both anxiety and tenderness. He heard Allday rasp, 'Easy, Cap'n!' What he had called him in the past. 'A block struck you—'

Another voice and misty face now, the surgeon. *Have I been lying here that long?*

More probing fingers at the back of his skull; sounds of relief as he said, 'No real damage, Sir

291

Richard. Near thing though. A block like that could crack your head like a nut!'

Men were cheering; some seemed to be sobbing. Bolitho allowed Jenour and Allday to get him to his feet amidst the fallen debris from the last parting shot.

The pain was coming now, and Bolitho felt sick. He touched his hair and felt where he had taken a glancing blow. He rubbed his eyes and saw the dead Munro watching him with an intense stare.

Williams was yelling, 'She's an English frigate, lads! The day is won!'

Allday asked in a whisper, 'Is something wrong, Sir Richard?'

Bolitho covered his left eye and waited for the fog of battle to leave his brain. Adam had come looking for him, and had saved them all.

He turned to Allday as his question seemed to penetrate. 'There was a flash.'

'*Flash*, Sir Richard? I'm not sure I understands.'

'In my eye.' He removed his hand and made himself look towards the distant French ships as they withdrew from their near-victory. 'I can't see them properly.' He turned and stared at him. 'My eye! That blow ... it must have done something.'

Allday watched him wretchedly. Bolitho wanted him to tell him it would go away, that it would pass.

He said, 'I'll get a wet for you, sir. For me too, I reckon.' He reached out and almost gripped Bolitho's arm as he would a messmate, an equal, but he did not. Instead he said heavily, 'You stay put till I gets back, Sir Richard. There's help a'comin'. Captain Adam'll see us right, an' that's no error.' He looked at Jenour. 'Keep by his side. For all our sakes, see?' Then he groped his way past the dead and dying, the upended guns and bloodstained planking.

It was their world and there *was* no escape. All the rest was a dream.

He heard a man cry out in private torment.

Always the pain.

CHAPTER FOURTEEN

HONOUR BOUND

'Well now, that wasn't too demanding, was it?' Sir Piers Blachford turned up his sleeves and rinsed his long, bony fingers in a basin of warm water which a servant had brought to the spacious, elegant room. He gave a dry smile. 'Not for a seasoned warrior like you, eh?'

Bolitho leaned back in the tall chair and tried to relax his whole body, muscle by muscle. Outside the window the sky was already tinged with the gloom of evening, although it was only three in the afternoon. Rain pattered occasionally against the glass, and he could hear the splash of horses and carriage wheels in the street below.

He moved to touch his eye. It felt raw and inflamed after all the poking Blachford had given it. He had used some liquid too, which stung without mercy, so that he wanted to rub his eye until it bled.

Blachford glared at him severely. 'Don't touch it! Not yet anyway.' He wiped his hands on a towel and nodded to the servant. 'Some coffee, I think.'

Bolitho declined. Catherine was downstairs

somewhere in this high, silent house, waiting, worrying, hoping for news.

'I have to go. But first, can you tell me . . .'

Blachford regarded him curiously, but not without affection. 'Still impatient? Remember what I told you aboard your *Hyperion*? How there might have been hope for the eye?'

Bolitho met his gaze. Remember? How could he forget? And this tall, stick-like man with the spiky grey hair and the most pointed nose he had ever seen had been there with him, in the thick of it, until he had been forced to give the order to abandon ship.

Sir Piers Blachford was a senior and most respected member of the College of Surgeons. Despite the privations of a man-of-war, he and some of his colleagues had volunteered to spread themselves throughout the squadrons of the fleet to try and discover measures to ease the suffering of those wounded in combat or cruelly injured in the demanding life of the common seaman. Resented at first as an intruder by some of *Hyperion*'s people, he had won the hearts of nearly all of them before he had left.

A man of boundless energy, he, although being some twenty years Bolitho's senior, had explored the ship from forecastle to hold, and spoken with most of her company, and had, in the ship's final battle, saved the lives of many.

Then, as now, he reminded Bolitho of a heron in the reeds near the house at Falmouth. Waiting patiently to strike.

Bolitho said abruptly, 'I could not be spared then.'

He thought suddenly of the homecoming just two

days ago after leaving the battered *Truculent* in the hands of the dockyard. Sir Charles Inskip had left for London with barely another word. Shocked by the grim events, or still smarting from Bolitho's bitter words before the battle, he neither knew nor cared.

For long, long minutes he had held Catherine while she had allowed him to find his composure again in his own time. She had knelt at his feet, the firelight shining in her eyes while he had eventually described the short, savage engagement, of *Anemone*'s arrival when all time had run out. Of Poland's despair and death, of those who had fallen because of the folly and treachery of others.

Only once had she touched on Captain Varian and the *Zest*. She had tightened her grip on his hands as he had answered quietly, 'I want him dead.'

Eventually she had dragged out of him an admission about the falling block which had struck him a glancing blow on the head.

Even now, in this quiet, remote room above Albemarle Street, he could feel her compassion, her anxiety. While he had been at the Admiralty to complete his report to Admiral the Lord Godschale she had come here to see Blachford, to plead for his help in spite of his constantly full programme of interviews and operations.

Blachford had been joined in his probing examinations by a short, intense doctor by the name of Rudolf Braks. The latter had barely said a word but had assisted in the examination with an almost fanatical dedication. He had a thick guttural voice when he did eventually speak with Blachford, and Bolitho thought he might be German, or more

295

likely a renegade Dutchman.

One thing was evident; they both knew a great deal about Nelson's eye injury, and Bolitho imagined that, too, was included in the lengthy volumes of their report to the College of Surgeons.

Blachford sat down and thrust out his long, thin legs.

'I will discuss it further with my eminent colleague. It is more in his field than mine. But I shall need to make further tests. You will be in London for a while?'

Bolitho thought suddenly of Falmouth, with winter closing in from the grey waters below the headland. It was like a desperate need. He had expected to be killed, and had accepted it. Perhaps that was why he had managed to hold *Truculent*'s people together when they had nothing left to give.

'I was hoping to go home, Sir Piers.'

Blachford gave a brief smile. 'A few more days, then. I understand that you have a new flagship to commission?' He did not elaborate on how he knew or why he was interested. But then he never did.

Bolitho thought of Admiral Godschale's sympathy; his anger at what had happened. *One cannot do everything oneself.*

The admiral had probably already selected a flag-officer to replace him if the French plan to take *Truculent* had succeeded, or Bolitho had fallen in battle.

Bolitho replied, 'A few more. Thank you for your help, and especially your courtesy to Lady Catherine.'

Blachford stood up, the heron again. 'Had I been made of stone, and some insist that I am, I would have done what I could. I have never met another

296

like her. I had thought that some of the tales of envy might be overplayed, but now I know differently!' He held out his bony hand. 'I will send word.'

Bolitho left the room and hurried down the gilded circular staircase. A grand house and yet somehow spartan, like the man.

She stood up as a servant opened the doors for him, her dark eyes filled with questions. He pulled her against him and kissed her hair.

'He said nothing bad, dear Kate.'

She leaned back in his arms and searched his face. 'I nearly lost you. Now I know it. It is all there in your eyes.'

Bolitho stared past her at a window. 'We are together. The rain has stopped. Shall we send Young Matthew away and walk back? It is not far, and I need to walk with you. It is not the lanes and cliffs of Cornwall, but with you it is always a kind of miracle.'

Later, as they lingered together on the wet pavements while the carriages and carts clattered past, she told him of a report she had seen in the *Gazette*. 'There was nothing written about you or Sir Charles Inskip.' It sounded like an accusation.

He held his cloak across her as a troop of soldiers trotted past, their hooves throwing up muddy water from the many puddles.

He smiled at her. 'My tiger again?' He shook his head. 'No, it was a pretence that neither of us was aboard at the time. No longer a secret from our enemies, but it will throw some doubts amongst them. They will not be able to use it against the Danes, to bring more threats against them.'

She said softly, 'It tells of Poland fighting his ship

297

against all odds until your nephew's arrival.' She halted and faced him, her chin lifted. 'It was you, wasn't it, Richard? *You* beat them off, not the captain.'

Bolitho shrugged. 'Poland was a brave man. He had it in his eyes. I think he knew he was going to die ... he probably blamed me for it.'

They reached the house just as the rain began again. Bolitho remarked, 'Two carriages. I'd hoped we might be alone tonight.'

The door was opened even as their feet touched the first step. Bolitho was surprised to see the red-faced housekeeper Mrs Robbins peering down at them. She had been away at Browne's big estate in Sussex, but had been here when Bolitho had rescued Catherine from the Waites prison. A formidable Londoner born and bred, who had had some definite ideas about keeping them both apart during their stay in his lordship's house.

Catherine threw the hood back from her head. 'It is good to see you again, Mrs Robbins!'

But the housekeeper peered at Bolitho and exclaimed, 'I didn't know where you was, sir. Your man Allday was out, yer lieutenant gone 'ome to South'ampton to all accounts—'

It was the first time Bolitho had seen her distressed or so anxious. He took her arm. 'Tell me. What has happened?'

She raised her apron and held it to her face. 'It's 'is lordship. He's been callin' for you, sir.' She looked up the stairs as if to see him. 'The doctor's with 'im, so please be quick.'

Catherine made to move to the staircase but Bolitho saw the housekeeper shake her head with quiet desperation.

298

Bolitho said, 'No, Kate. It were better you stay and look after Mrs Robbins. Send for a hot drink.' He held her gaze with his own. 'I'll be down directly.'

He found an elderly servant sitting outside the double doors of Browne's rooms. He looked too shocked to move, and for some reason Bolitho thought of Allday.

It was dark in the big room except around the bed. There were three men sitting by it; one, apparently the doctor, was holding Browne's hand, perhaps feeling his pulse.

One of the others exclaimed, 'He's here, Oliver!' And to Bolitho, 'Oh, thank God, Sir Richard!'

They made way for him and he sat down on the edge of the bed, and looked at the man who had once been his flag-lieutenant until he had succeeded to his father's role and title.

He was still dressed in his shirt, and his skin was wet with sweat. His eyes as they settled on Bolitho seemed to widen with effort, and he gasped, 'I—I heard you were safe! A while I—I thought—'

'Easy, Oliver, it will be all right.' He shot a glance at the doctor. 'What is it?'

Without a word the doctor raised a dressing from Browne's chest. The shirt had been cut open and there was blood everywhere.

Bolitho asked quietly, 'Who did it?' He had seen enough wounds left by pistol or musket to recognise this one.

Browne said in a fierce whisper, *'No time—no time left.'* His eyes fluttered. *'Closer, please closer!'*

Bolitho lowered his face to his. The young flag-lieutenant who had walked the deck with him, as Jenour had done, with all hell around them. A fine, decent young man who was dying even as he watched him fighting a hopeless battle.

Browne said, 'Somervell. A duel.' Each word was a separate agony but he persisted, 'Your lady—your lady is a widow now.' He clenched his jaw so that his teeth brought blood to his lips. 'But he's done for me all the same!'

Bolitho looked desperately at the doctor. 'Can't you *do* something?'

He shook his head. 'It is a marvel he has lived this long, Sir Richard.'

Browne gripped Bolitho's cuff and whispered, 'That damned rogue killed my brother—like this. I have settled the score. Please explain to—' His head lolled on the pillow and he was still.

Bolitho reached out and closed his eyes. He said, 'I shall tell Catherine. Rest now, Oliver.' He looked away, his eyes smarting worse than before. *Browne with an 'e'*. He walked to the doors and said, 'Tell me when—' But nobody answered him.

In the room where he had told Catherine about the battle, she was waiting for him. She held out a goblet of brandy and said, 'I know. Allday heard it in the kitchen. My husband is dead.' She put her hand up to the goblet to press it to his lips. 'I feel nothing, but for you ... and your dead friend.'

Bolitho felt the brandy sting his throat, remembering, putting each picture in place.

Then, while she refilled the goblet, he heard himself say, 'Oliver used the phrase, *We Happy Few*. The few are much fewer, and now poor Oliver has paid the price.'

In the kitchen Allday sat with a half-demolished mutton pie and paused to refill his pipe. He said, ''Nother stoup of ale wouldn't go amiss, Ma
300

Robbins.' He shook his head and was surprised how much it ached. 'Second thought, I'll take some more o' that rum yonder.'

The housekeeper watched him sadly, grieving over what had happened, but apprehensive about her own future. Young Oliver, as he had been known in the kitchen, was the last in direct line for the title. There was talk of some distant cousin, but who could tell what might become of her?

She said, 'I'm surprised 'ow you can carry on at a time like this, John!'

Allday focused his red-rimmed eyes with difficulty.

'Then I'll *tell* you, Ma Robbins. It's 'cause I survived!' He gestured vaguely to the room above them. '*We've* survived! I'll shed a tear with the next bugger, beggin' yer pardon, Ma, but it's *us* I cares about, see?'

She pushed the stone jug across to him. 'Just you mind your manners when the men come to take 'is lordship away. Quality or not, it's against the law, wot they done!'

She reached out to save the rum as Allday's head thudded down on the table. In this gracious house the war had always been at a distance. There had never been any shortages, and only when young Oliver had been away at sea had it meant much to those who served belowstairs.

But in Allday's last burst of despairing anger, the war had been right here on the doorstep.

She heard a door close and knew they were going upstairs, perhaps to sit with the body. Her red features softened. Young Oliver would rest easy with the man he had loved more than his own father so close at hand.

The doctor who had attended both participants in the duel scrutinised his watch repeatedly, and made no secret of his eagerness to leave.

Catherine sat by a low fire, one hand playing with her necklace, her high cheekbones adding to her beauty.

Bolitho said, 'So Oliver left a letter. Was he so certain that he was going to die?'

The doctor glanced unhappily at Catherine and murmured, 'Viscount Somervell was a renowned duellist, I understand. It would seem a likely conclusion.'

Bolitho heard whispers on the staircase, the sounds of doors opening and closing as they prepared Browne for his final journey to his Sussex home.

Catherine said sharply, 'This waiting! Is there no end to it?' She reached out and took his offered hand, and held it to her cheek as if they were alone in the room. 'Don't worry, Richard. I will not disappoint you.'

Bolitho looked at her and wondered at her strength. Together and with the doctor's aid they had discovered the whereabouts of Somervell's seconds, and his body. It had already been taken to his spacious house in Grosvenor Square. Was she thinking of that? That she would be required to go there and complete the process of her dead husband's burial? He tightened his hold on her fingers. He would be with her. There was already scandal enough; a little more could do no further harm.

When the news got out there were many who might think he had killed Somervell. He looked away, his eyes bitter. *I would that I had*.

Word had been sent to Browne's country estate at Horsham. They would be coming for him. *Today*.

Bolitho said, 'I gather that Oliver's older brother died in a similar affair with Somervell. It was in Jamaica.' Who could have guessed that someone like the outwardly carefree Browne would set out to find Somervell and settle the debt, in the only way he knew?

A red-eyed servant opened the door. 'Beg pardon, but the carriage is 'ere.'

More feet and murmured exchanges, and then a powerfully-built man in sombre country clothing entered to announce he was Hector Croker, the estate manager. Three days since they had sent a message by post-horse. In rain-washed lanes and pitch-dark roads, Croker must have driven without any rest at all.

The doctor handed him some papers, his relief even more obvious. Like a man ridding himself of something dangerous or evil.

He saw Mrs Robbins waiting with her bags and said kindly, 'You'll ride with us, Mrs Robbins. His lordship left word you were to stay in your employment.'

Catherine walked to the doorway and gave the housekeeper a hug. 'For caring for me as you did.'

Mrs Robbins gave an awkward curtsy and hurried down the steps, with barely a glance at the house where she had witnessed so much.

From the lower floor Allday peered up through the small window, and watched in silence as Browne's body was carried down the steps to the

303

carriage by several men in dark clothing. Aloud he said, 'An' there's an end to it.'

Bolitho followed the men to the carriage and gave some money to their leader. More quick glances, men who were used to this kind of work. Theirs was not to ask questions.

Bolitho felt her slip her hand through his arm and said, 'Goodbye, Oliver. Rest in peace.'

Rain pattered across their bared heads but they watched until the carriage had turned up towards Piccadilly. In his letter Browne had requested that if the worst should befall him, he was to be buried on the family estate.

Bolitho turned and saw her looking at him. *Now she is free to marry me, but I am not.* The thought seemed to torment him.

She said softly, 'It changes nothing, you know.' She smiled, but her dark eyes were sad.

Bolitho replied, 'I shall be with you until—'

She nodded. 'I know. That is my only concern. What it may do to your reputation.'

Bolitho saw Yovell waiting inside the door. 'What is it?'

'Shall I pack our things, Sir Richard?'

He saw her look up at the staircase. Remembering how this place had been their haven in London. Now they must leave it.

Then she said, 'I shall deal with it, Daniel. You assist Sir Richard.' Her eyes were quite calm. 'You will have letters, I expect. To Val, and perhaps Rear-Admiral Herrick?'

Bolitho thought he saw a message in her eyes but was not sure.

'Yes, Val would wish to know.' He thought how busy Keen would be, preparing to commission the newly completed *Black Prince*. It was a nightmare for any captain of a large man-of-war, let alone one which was to wear a vice-admiral's flag at the fore. Shortage of trained hands and seasoned warrant officers, obtaining raw recruits by any manner or means, always more difficult in a naval port like Chatham where the press gang would be betrayed by anyone from tailor to beggar. Arguing with the victualling yards and making sure that the ship's purser was not doing deals to procure rotten stores, so that purser and supplier could pocket the difference between them. Making a forest of oak into a fighting ship.

Bolitho smiled grimly. And yet Keen had found the opportunity to visit Catherine until he himself could reach London and report on the battle.

He would also send word to Adam, although his *Anemone* had barely had time to anchor after escorting the leaking *Truculent* to the security of the dockyard. Adam, too, had once been Bolitho's flag-lieutenant. More than most, he would appreciate how closely the appointment joined the man to his admiral.

He heard Allday's heavy tread on the kitchen stair. Except for him, of course.

Catherine said thoughtfully, 'He had no relatives to speak of, and most of them live abroad.'

Bolitho noticed that she never spoke of Somervell by name. 'He had friends at Court, I believe.'

She seemed to become aware of the concern in his voice and looked up. 'Yes, so he did. But even the King was angered by his behaviour—his quick temper and his craving for the tables. He took all that I owned.' She touched his face with sudden tenderness. 'Another of Fate's little whims, is it

305

not? For now, what there is left will come to me.'

That afternoon Jenour arrived quite breathless after changing six horses on the ride from Southampton. When asked why and how he had heard the news, Jenour explained, 'Southampton is a great seaport, Sir Richard. News flies on the wind there, although the circumstances were not known.' He added simply, 'My place is here with you. I know how you valued Lord Browne's friendship, and he yours.'

Catherine had gone to visit a lawyer with Yovell as her escort. She had declined Bolitho's offer to accompany her and had said, 'It is better I do it without you. You might be hurt ... I could not bear that, dearest of men.'

He said now, 'You are just in time, Stephen. We shall quit this place today.'

Jenour dropped his eyes. 'It will be painful, will it not, Sir Richard?'

Bolitho touched his sleeve. 'So old a head on so young a pair of shoulders!'

Somehow Jenour had guessed his innermost feeling, even though he was young and inexperienced. Catherine was free now, and soon, it seemed, she would be independent again. Might Falmouth and his constant absences at sea seem a poor replacement for the life she had once known, and might want again?

Life was like the ocean, he thought; sunshine one moment, a raging storm the next.

He found that he was touching his eye, and felt his heart sink lower. What might she think of him if the worst happened?

'Is there something you wish me to do, Sir Richard?'

Bolitho had forgotten Jenour was there. 'We shall be going to Kent shortly, to the new flagship.' He let his mind dwell on the prospect. He knew that once he would have been on board immediately, no matter what anybody said or thought. But to be so near to death, and to lose another friend, put caution where recklessness had once ruled.

'And there is something else,' he said.

Jenour said, 'I know, Sir Richard. The court-martial.'

'Aye, Stephen. War is no place for personal greed and selfish ambition, though God knows you might not be blamed for thinking otherwise. Captain Varian betrayed his trust, just as he did those who depended on him in their greatest need.'

Jenour watched his grave profile, the way he occasionally touched his eye. As if he had something in it.

The door opened and Bolitho swung round, ready to greet her. But it was a messenger boy, one of the servants watching him suspiciously from the hall.

'I have brought word from Doctor Rudolf Braks, Sir Richard.' He screwed up his face as if to help memorise his message. 'You may visit him on the morrow at ten o'clock.'

Jenour looked away but was very aware that Bolitho showed no resentment at the curt message. It sounded more like a summons. Jenour had thought Bolitho would be at the Admiralty at about that time. *Braks*. A foreign-sounding name, one he was almost certain he had heard his father mention; but why?

Bolitho gave the boy a coin and thanked him, his voice distant. Then he heard the carriage returning and said abruptly, 'No word of that to Lady Catherine, Stephen. She has enough to face up to as it is.'

'Yes, I see, Sir Richard.'

'Damn it, you don't, my lad!' Then he turned away and when she entered the room, he was smiling.

She gave her hand to Jenour and then embraced Bolitho.

He asked quietly, 'Was it bad?'

She shrugged, that one small gesture which always touched him like a sensitive nerve.

'Enough. But 'tis done for the present. A report will go to the magistrates.' She looked at him steadily. 'But both men are dead. No one can be charged for what happened.'

Jenour discreetly left them alone and she said, 'I know what you are thinking, Richard. You are so wrong. If I did not love you so much I would be angry that you could harbour such ideas. You took care of me when I had nothing ... now we shall take care of each other.' She gazed at the fire and said, 'We shall leave now. Quit this haven where we shared our love, and the world was a million miles away.'

They looked at the window and the rain which ran down the panes.

'Very apt.' She was speaking to the room. 'There is no more light here.'

*   *   *

The day ended more quickly than either of them had believed possible. There were many comings and goings, friends of the deceased and those who were merely curious, as their stares betrayed.

The same doctor was in attendance, and when he asked if Catherine wished to see where the body of her husband was laid out she shook her head.

'I have been wrong many times, but never, I hope, a hypocrite.'

There was only one really unpleasant incident.

The last visitor was introduced as a Colonel Collyear of the King's Household guard. A tall, arrogant soldier with a cruel mouth.

'We meet again, Lady Somervell. I find it grotesque to offer my condolences, but duty requires me to pay my respects to your late husband.'

He saw Bolitho for the first time and said in the same affected drawl, 'At first, I thought perhaps it might have been you, sir. Had it been—'

Bolitho said calmly, 'You will always find me ready enough, and that is a promise. So if you continue to demean an honourable uniform in the presence of a lady, I may forget the solemnity of the occasion.'

Catherine said, 'I would have put it less politely. Please go.'

The man backed away, his spurs and accoutrements jingling as he attempted a dignified retreat.

Bolitho thought suddenly of *Hyperion*'s first lieutenant, Parris, whose mangled body had gone down with the ship after he had shot himself, rather than face the surgeon's saw.

Catherine had recognised him for what he was; and yet Bolitho had not. Only while Parris lay pinned beneath an upended cannon, when he had confessed his passion for Somervell, had he understood. In this very room she had just recognised another in the arrogant colonel.

Jenour hovered by one of the beautiful pillared doorways. 'They are all gone, m'lady.'

Catherine looked at herself in a great gilded mirror. 'I see this woman, and yet I feel another.' She seemed to hear what Jenour had said. 'Then we shall make ourselves as comfortable as we can. Is his steward still in the house?'

'Yes, m'lady.' He glanced at Bolitho as if for assistance. 'I found him weeping in his room.'

She said coldly, 'Send him away. I will not have him here. He will be paid, but that is all.'

As Jenour left she said, 'This is my house now. It will *never* be my home.'

She crossed the room and put her arms around his shoulders, and kissed him very slowly and with great tenderness. Then she said, 'I want you so much that I should feel ashamed.' She shivered. 'But not here, not yet.'

Ozzard padded through yet another door with some fresh coffee. Bolitho noticed that the little man was carrying one of the old silver pots from Falmouth. Only he would have thought of that.

Allday glanced in and said, 'I think I'll pipe down early tonight if you don't need me, m'lady.'

Bolitho smiled. It was easy to forget tomorrow and what the doctor might tell him. He could even forget the corpse which lay upstairs, unloved, and soon forgotten.

She replied, 'Please do, Allday. Take something strong to soothe your aches and pains.'

Allday grinned at them. 'You always knows, m'lady.' He went off chuckling to himself.

Bolitho said, 'An oak indeed.'

'I was thinking.' She laid a hand on his arm. 'Your friend Oliver. He could have been speaking for us. *We Happy Few.*'

When the servants bolted the front doors and laid straw in the roadway to lessen the din of iron-shod wheels, they were still sitting there, close to a dying fire.

Ozzard crept quietly into the room and put some fresh logs on the fire before picking up the cold coffee pot and padding softly away again. Just once he glanced at the couple who slept together, half reclining on one of the great sofas. She was covered with his heavy dress coat, and her hair hung loose and free across his arm, which held her about her waist.

He knew again the sadness and loss that would always stay with him now. At least they had each other; only God knew how long they would be granted such happiness.

He found Allday outside the door and exclaimed, 'I thought you'd piped down with a bottle of rum!'

Allday did not rise to it this time. 'Don't feel much like sleep. Thought you might share a wet or two with me.'

Ozzard regarded him warily. 'Then what?'

'You're an educated fellow. You might read somethin' to me till we feels more like turnin' in.'

Ozzard hid his surprise. *He knows it too*. There was a storm brewing. But he remarked, 'I've found a book about a shepherd—you'd like that one.'

They made for the deserted kitchen, the burly coxswain and the tiny servant who carried his terrible secret like a disease which would eventually destroy him.

But storm or not, they were Bolitho's men, and

they would see it through as they always had. Together.

CHAPTER FIFTEEN

FULL CIRCLE

Captain Valentine Keen cast a searching glance along the full length of his new command before turning and striding aft where a group of senior officers, Admiralty officials and their ladies, waited beneath the shelter of the poop.

The *Black Prince*, a powerful second-rate of ninety-four guns, had been completed here in the Royal Dockyard, Chatham, several months ahead of schedule.

For the latter weeks, after his appointment had been confirmed, Keen had stayed aboard for most of the time. On this bitter November forenoon he was very aware of the long days, and the constant demands on his services. He could feel the wind off the River Medway cutting through his limbs and body as if he were naked. Now, all but the formalities were over, and this towering three-decker was to be his.

Lying nearby was an old seventy-four like *Hyperion*. It was hard to believe that she had been so much smaller than *Black Prince*, and he found himself wondering if this great ship would ever match her in performance and memory. He had been reminded too that it was in this same dock area that Nelson's last flagship *Victory* had had her keel laid, all of forty-seven years ago. And what

312

might the navy become in the same period which lay ahead?

He doffed his hat to the port admiral and then turned to the man he had come to admire and love.

'The ship is prepared, Sir Richard.' He waited, sensing the silence at his back where the ship's company had been piped to witness the official handing over of the new ship. On nearby walls and slipways the dockyard workers waited in the cold wind to watch. Pride of workmanship; and with the war showing little sign of ending it meant that another great keel would be laid down once *Black Prince* had been worked out to the Medway, and finally to the open sea.

Not so with most of the ship's company, he thought. Some had been transferred from other vessels now laid-up for repair or refit without ever being allowed ashore to see their homes or loved ones. The press gangs had gathered the sweepings of the dockside and local harbours. Scum to be made, by example or more brutal methods, into seamen who would, when required, fight this ship with the loyalty of seasoned tars.

The assizes had provided a good sprinkling of poachers and petty thieves, and one or two harder men who chose the King's service instead of the gallows.

Bolitho looked strained and tired, Keen thought. That last fight aboard the frigate *Truculent* must have demanded a lot from him. But it had not been difficult to picture Bolitho casting down his flag-officer's rank to replace Poland as captain when he had fallen. Keen had served with Bolitho in frigates as midshipman and lieutenant, and had seen him in action so many times that he often

313

wondered how they had survived this long.

Bolitho smiled at him. 'It is good to be here on this proud day, Captain Keen.'

There was warmth in his voice, and he was probably amused by the formality they must maintain in front of such important visitors.

Keen turned about and walked to the quarterdeck rail, his eyes taking in everything, and marvelling how well his lieutenants and warrant officers had managed to be ready for this day. There had been moments when Keen had believed it would never end. The work, the hull full of carpenters and joiners, sailmakers and painters, while the newly appointed midshipmen were driven from pillar to post by Cazalet, his first lieutenant. Keen knew little of him yet as a man. But as his second-in-command, appointed from another ship-of-the-line, he was beyond value. He never seemed to be without energy or an answer to somebody's problem. Day by day Keen had watched him striding through the piled confusion of rigging and spare cordage, anchors and stores which descended on the dockside like an endless invasion. He looked up at the crossed yards and neatly furled sails, that same tangled cordage now in position, and tarred-down like black glass. On the forecastle he saw the scarlet square of Royal Marines matching their smart lines across the poop behind him.

The lieutenants in blue and white and in strict order of seniority; beyond them the midshipmen and warrant officers. Some of the 'young gentlemen' would see this huge ship as the sure step to a lieutenant's exalted rank, while others, so small they looked as if they should be with their mothers,

314

stared around at the great masts and the double lines of the upper deck twelve-pounders. They would be reminded, no doubt, of the twelve miles of rigging they would have to know by name at first, then by touch if required when called on deck in a raging storm and in pitch darkness.

And there was the company of seamen. Old hands and new, pressed men and vagrants, watching him, knowing that of everyone aboard he could control their lives, while his skill as the captain might well decide if they lived at all.

His voice was clear and steady as he read from the scroll with its round copper-plate writing and the crest of Admiralty at the top. It was like hearing someone else reading it to him, he thought.

'... *and once satisfied you will go on board and take command of captain in her accordingly* ...'

He heard one of the women give a gentle cough behind him, and recalled how he had seen some of them peering around after Bolitho had stepped aboard. Looking for Catherine, preparing the gossip. But they had been disappointed, for she had remained ashore, although Keen had not yet had time to speak with Bolitho about it.

'... *all officers and company appointed to said ship shall obey, follow and serve you to this purpose, when His Britannic Majesty King George shall charge to accept the said ship* Black Prince *into his service* ...'

Keen glanced over the scroll and saw his coxswain Tojohns standing beside the powerful figure of Allday. Their familiar faces gave him strength, a sense of belonging in this teeming world of a ship-of-the-line where every man was a stranger until proved otherwise.

'... *hereof, not you nor any of you may fail as you*

315

*will answer the contrary at your peril and according to
the Articles of War ... God Save the KING!'*

It was done. Keen replaced his hat and tucked
the scroll inside his coat again while the first
lieutenant, Cazalet, stepped smartly from the group
of officers and shouted, 'Three cheers for His
Majesty, lads!' The response could have been
better, but when Keen glanced round he saw that
the port admiral was beaming, and there were a lot
of handshakes amongst the men who had planned
and supervised for this day, and those who would
profit by the end of it.

Keen said, 'Dismiss the hands, Mr Cazalet, then
come aft to my quarters.'

He thought he saw the other man raise an
eyebrow. It was now time to entertain the visitors.
By the look of some of them it was going to be
difficult to get rid of them. He called after the first
lieutenant, 'Tell Major Bourchier to double his
marine guard.' He had almost forgotten the major's
name. In a few weeks he would know them better
than they did each other.

Lieutenant Jenour touched his hat. 'I beg your
pardon, sir, but Sir Richard is leaving now.'

'Oh, I had hoped ...' He saw Bolitho standing
apart from the others, as they flowed aft on either
side of the great double-wheel which was yet to feel
the fury of wind and rudder in contest.

Bolitho said, 'Pay my respects, Val. But I have to
go. Lady Catherine ...' He looked away as some
visitors passed by, one of the women staring at him
quite unashamedly.

He added, 'She would not come aboard. She
thought it best. For me. Later perhaps.'

Keen had heard about Browne's death and the

duel which had preceded it. He said, 'She is a wonderful lady, Sir Richard.'

'I cannot thank you enough for standing by her in my absence. My God, Fate soon determines who your true friends are!'

He walked slowly to the quarterdeck to look down at the guns, the neatly-packed hammock nettings.

'You have a fine ship, Val. A floating fortress. There's no flag-captain I'd rather have, and you know it. And have faith, as I did, although to others the odds against my finding Catherine again were a million-fold. Zenoria needs time. But I am certain that she loves you.' He clapped his arm. 'So no more melancholy, eh?'

Keen glanced aft where the din of voices and laughter was already growing. 'I'll see you over the side, Sir Richard.'

They went down to the entry port together, and Keen noticed there were already more marines in evidence with their muskets and fixed bayonets and immaculate, pipeclayed, cross-belts. Their major had acted promptly; there were still those who might try to desert before the ship was at sea, and order and discipline took root. Keen was a fair and understanding captain, but he was mindful that he was still fifty men short of his full complement of eight hundred officers, marines and sailors. The sight of the armed sentries might make the foolhardy think twice.

'Man the side!' The gleaming new barge was rolling gently in the sluggish confinement of the dockyard, Allday in the sternsheets, the crew neatly turned out in checkered shirts and tarred hats.

Bolitho hesitated. A ship without history,

317

without memory. A new start. Even the idea seemed to mock him.

He said, 'You will receive further orders within the week. Use all the time you can to work the people into a team we can be proud of.'

Keen smiled, although he hated to see him leave after so brief a visit. 'I have had the best of teachers, sir!'

Bolitho turned, then felt himself falling. Keen seized his arm, and there was a clatter as one of the marines dropped his musket with surprise. The lieutenant in charge of the side-party snarled something at the luckless marine and gave Bolitho a few seconds to recover his wits.

'Is it the eye, Sir Richard?' Keen was shocked to see the expression of utter despair on Bolitho's features when he faced him again.

'I've not told Catherine yet. They can do naught to help me, it seems.'

Keen stood between him and the guard and boatswain's mates with their silver calls still poised and ready.

'I will lay odds she knows.' He wanted to offer some kind of help so badly that even his own worries seemed beyond reach.

'If that is the case . . .' Bolitho changed his mind and touched his hat to the guard before lowering himself down the stairs from the entry port, where Allday's hand was outstretched to guide him the last few steps into the barge.

Keen watched the boat until it was out of sight beyond a moored transport. He had commanded several ships during his service, and this should have been his greatest reward. Older captains than himself would give their blood for such a command.

A new ship, soon to fly a vice-admiral's flag, could only bring honour to the man who controlled her destiny. So why did he feel so little? Was he so affected by the *Hyperion*, or was it that he had been so near to death on too many occasions?

He frowned at the laughter from his quarters. They neither knew nor cared about the people who would serve this ship.

A lieutenant blocked his way and touched his hat. 'I beg pardon, sir, but another lighter is putting off from the victualling pier.'

'Are you the Officer-of-the-Watch, *Mister* Flemyng?' The young lieutenant seemed to shrink as Keen added sharply, 'Then do your work, sir, for if you cannot I will seek out another who can!'

Almost before the lieutenant had made to move away he regretted it.

'That was uncalled for, Mr Flemyng. A captain's rank has privileges, but abuse of them is beyond contempt.' He saw him staring in astonishment. 'Ask as much as you like. Otherwise we may all be the poorer when it concerns something vital. So send for the boatswain and the duty-watch to deal with these stores, eh?'

As the lieutenant almost ran across the quarterdeck, Keen gave a sad smile. How true had his words been just now to Bolitho.

I have had the best of teachers.

The thought seemed to rally him, and he looked along the deck again to the black, armoured shoulder of the proud figurehead. Then he stared aloft at the curling masthead pendant and some gulls which screamed through the rigging with an eye for scraps from the galley. Almost to himself he said, '*My ship.*' Then he spoke her name, '*Zenoria.*'

Afterwards he thought it had been like releasing a bird from captivity. Would she ever call him in return?

★   ★   ★

The light carriage, with mud splashed as high as its windows, reached the top of a rise and reined to a halt, the two horses steaming in the cold air.

Yovell groaned and released his grip on a tasselled handle and exclaimed, 'These roads are indeed a disgrace, m'lady.'

But she lowered a window and leaned out regardless of the fine, intermittent drizzle which had followed them all the way from Chatham.

'Where are we, Young Matthew?'

Matthew leaned over from his box and grinned down at her, his face like a polished red apple.

'The house is yonder, m'lady.' He pointed with his whip. ''Tis the only one hereabouts.' He puffed out his cheeks and his breath floated around him like steam. 'A lonely spot, in my opinion.'

'You know these parts, Young Matthew?'

He grinned again, but with a certain wistfulness as the memory clouded his eyes. 'Aye, m'lady. I was here 'bout fourteen years back—I were just a boy then, working for my grandfather who was head coachman for the Bolitho family.'

Yovell said, 'Before my time with Sir Richard, I think.'

'What were you doing in Kent?'

'The master was sent here to hunt down smugglers. I was with him an' helped a bit. Then he sent me back to Falmouth 'cause he said it were too dangerous, like.'

Catherine withdrew her head. 'Drive on, then.' She sat back in the seat as the carriage rolled forward through a succession of muddy ruts. Another part of Bolitho's life she could not share. Allday had made some mention of it. How Bolitho had still been recovering from the terrible fever he had caught in the Great South Sea, but had desperately tried to obtain a ship, *any* ship. War with France had still been just a threat, but England had allowed the fleet to rot, her sailors thrown on the beach. There were few ships, and only Bolitho's persistence, his daily visits to the Admiralty, had found him employment at the Nore. Recruiting, but also hunting smugglers, to stamp out their vicious trade, a far cry from the romantic tales which abounded about their exploits.

But when the blade fell on the King of France's neck everything had changed. Allday had put it in his simple way. 'So they gave us the old *Hyperion*. It were a bit of a shock for the Cap'n, as he was then, him being a frigate man. But that old ship changed our lives, m'lady. He found you, and I found out I had a grown-up son.' He had nodded, his clear eyes faraway. 'Aye, we sailed through some blood and tears together.'

She had pressed him to add, 'That was why he fought *Truculent* like he did. Cap'n Poland could never 'a' done it, not in a thousand years.' He had shaken his head like an old dog. 'There'll not be another like *Hyperion*, I'm thinkin'. Not for us anyways.'

She watched the River Medway in the distance. All the way from Chatham it had barely been out of sight, twisting and turning, a wide stretch of water, sometimes silver, sometimes the colour of lead, as

321

the sky and weather dictated. She had found herself
shivering when she had caught sight of some prison
hulks moored out in the stream. Mastless and
forlorn, and somehow frightening. Full of
prisoners-of-war. She had another stark memory of
the Waites prison, the degradation and filth. Surely
it would be better to die?

Bolitho would be on board his new flagship.
After that they would be together again—but for
how long? She swore that she would make every
moment a precious one.

For a few moments she forgot why she had made
this journey, and the fact that Rear-Admiral
Herrick's wife might not even allow her in the
house. She was back in the small chapel in South
Audley Street, then in the adjoining St George's
Burial Ground, at any other time just a short walk
from the Somervell house.

Nobody had spoken to her except the vicar, and
he had been a total stranger. A few faceless people
had been in the chapel, but by the graveside there
had been only her Richard. There had been several
carriages, but the occupants had not alighted,
content apparently to watch and pass judgment.
One figure had hurried away from a wall as she had
made to leave. His steward, no doubt, who for
whatever true reason had always been with him.

The carriage responded to Matthew's brake, and
slowed again while it turned off the road and along
a well-laid driveway.

Catherine could feel her heart pumping against
her ribs and was surprised at her sudden
nervousness. She had come uninvited and without
sending word of her intention. To do so would have
invited a snub. But she accepted that it was

important to Bolitho that she should try to get to know the wife of his old friend. She knew that Herrick would never change towards her and it saddened her, although she had managed to hide it from the one she loved more than life itself.

Yovell groaned; he had obviously suffered from the joltings of the journey. 'A goodly house.' He said it with approval. 'A big step.'

Catherine did not know what Yovell meant but guessed it might be because Herrick had come from humble, even poor beginnings locally, and his marriage to his beloved Dulcie had brought him the comfort and encouragement denied him in his struggle for eventual recognition in the navy. She felt a momentary bitterness as Yovell handed her down from the carriage. Bolitho had given his friend much more than encouragement. This should have been the time to repay him with the loyalty and friendship he needed. Instead ... She shook her head and said, 'Stay with Young Matthew, will you please, Daniel.' She bit her lip. 'I do not expect to be long.'

Matthew touched his hat. 'I'll take the horses to the yard for some water.' He and Yovell exchanged glances as she mounted the stone steps and lifted a large brass knocker in the shape of a dolphin. The door opened instantly, and she vanished into the interior.

When the carriage reached the stable-yard Yovell, who had climbed up beside the coachman, emitted a grunt of anxiety. Two stable hands were washing down another carriage.

'It's Lady Bolitho's.' Matthew gave it a professional scrutiny. 'No mistakin' that 'un!'

Yovell nodded. 'Too late now. I'd better go

round—Sir Richard'll never forgive me.'

Young Matthew climbed down and said, 'Leave 'er be. You can't 'andle two mares at once.' He gave his cheeky smile. 'My money's on our Lady Catherine!'

Yovell stared at him. 'You damned rogue!' But he stood fast all the same.

After the creak of wheels and leather and the occasional slashing rain across the windows, the house felt oppressively still. Like a tomb. Catherine looked at the small servant who had opened the door. 'Is your mistress at home?'

The girl stammered, 'She is, Ma'am. She be in bed.' She peered anxiously at some double doors which led off the hallway. 'They moved 'er downstairs. She got a visitor.'

Catherine smiled. The girl was too open to be a liar. 'Would you please announce me? Catherine Somervell—Lady Somervell.'

She walked into an anteroom and through its misted windows watched two men working in the gardens, in spite of the rain.

But it was getting heavier, and they paused beneath the windows to wait its passing. It was still a few moments longer before she realised they were speaking Spanish.

She heard the doors swing open across the hall and when she turned she saw Belinda, framed in the light from other windows on the far side of the room.

She had never laid eyes on her before, and yet she knew instantly who she was. She had something of the looks in the portrait Catherine had had restored to its place at Falmouth, the hair, the shape of the face—but nothing more.

324

'I did not know you were here, otherwise—'

Belinda replied sharply, '*Otherwise* you would have stayed in your proper place! I don't know how you have the brazen audacity to come.' Her eyes moved slowly over Catherine from head to toe, lingering on the dull black silk of her mourning gown.

'I am surprised you have the impudence to—'

Catherine heard someone call out in a small voice and said, 'Frankly, your reactions, disgust or otherwise, don't matter a jot to me.' She could feel the anger rising like fire. 'This is not your house, and I shall see whom I intended, if she will allow it!'

Belinda stared at her as if she had struck her. 'Don't you *dare* take that tone with me—'

'Dare? You talk of daring after what you tried to do to me when you connived with my husband? I wear these clothes because it shows respect, but it is for Richard's dead friend, not my damned husband!' She strode to the door. 'I notice that you have no difficulty in dressing in the latest, and finest fashion!'

Belinda fell back, her eyes never leaving Catherine's face. 'I shall never . . .'

'Give him up? Is that what you were about to say?' Catherine looked at her coldly. 'He is not yours to give. I suspect he never was.'

The voice called again and Catherine walked past her without another word. Belinda was exactly what she had expected. It made her angrier and sad at the same time. *A woman like that with*—She stopped short of a large bed, and gazed at the woman who was propped there on several pillows and cushions. Herrick's wife studied her much as Belinda had

325

done; but there was no hostility.

Belinda said, 'I shall be back shortly, Dulcie my dear. I need some air.'

Catherine heard the doors close. 'I beg forgiveness for this intrusion.' It no longer seemed to matter, and she could feel her body go cold despite the great fire in the room.

Dulcie placed one hand on the bed and said softly, 'Sit here where I can see you the better. Alas, my dear Thomas has sailed just recently to join his squadron. I miss him so much.' The hand moved towards Catherine and after the slightest hesitation took hers in it. It was hot and dry. She murmured, 'Yes. You *are* very beautiful, Lady Somervell . . . I can see why he loves you.'

Catherine squeezed her hand. 'That is a kind thing to say. Please call me Catherine.'

'I was sorry to hear about your late husband's death. Is it still raining?'

Catherine felt something like fear, usually a stranger to her. Dulcie was rambling, even as she clung to her hand.

She asked carefully, 'Have you seen a doctor recently?'

Dulcie said distantly, 'So much sadness. We couldn't have any children, you know.'

'Nor can I,' she said gently. She tried again. 'How long have you been unwell?'

Dulcie smiled for the first time. It made her look incredibly frail.

'You are like Thomas. Always fussing and asking questions. He thinks I work too hard—he does not understand how empty it can be when he is at sea. I could not be idle, you see.'

Catherine felt terribly alone with her secret.

'Those men working in the gardens. Who are they?'

For a moment she thought Dulcie had not heard, as she whispered, 'Belinda is such a *good* person. They have a little girl.'

Catherine glanced away. *They*. 'The men were speaking Spanish...'

She had not heard the door re-open, and Belinda's voice was like a knife. 'Of course, you were also married to a Spaniard at one time, were you not? So *many* husbands.'

Catherine ignored the sneer in her voice and turned back to the bed as Dulcie said wearily, 'They are prisoners. But they are allowed here on trust. They are very good gardeners.' Her eyes flickered. 'I am so tired.'

Catherine released her hand and stood up. 'I will take my leave.' She backed away from the bed, oblivious of Belinda's bitter stare, her hatred for her.

'I would like to talk again with you, dear Dulcie.' She turned away, unable to lie.

Outside the room she faced Belinda. 'She is very ill.'

'And you are concerned, is that it? You came prepared to *win her over*—to prove that you are the only one who really cares!'

'Don't be a fool! Has she seen a doctor?'

Belinda smiled. Arrogantly, she thought. 'But of course. A good local man who has known Dulcie and Rear-Admiral Herrick for years.'

Catherine heard the carriage moving to the front of the house again. Yovell was a good judge.

'I must leave. I will send for a competent doctor from London.'

Belinda said violently, 'How can you speak like

this? I can see for myself what you are, but don't you know what you are doing to my husband's career and reputation?' She was spitting out each word, unable to hide her spite. 'He has fought duels over you before, or didn't you know? One day he will pay for it!'

Catherine looked away, and did not see the flash of triumph in Belinda's eyes. She was remembering the Vauxhall Pleasure Gardens, where Bolitho had tossed a contemptuous challenge to the drunken soldier who had fondled her arm as if she was a common whore. And only days ago when he had sent the effeminate Colonel Collyear packing after a similar challenge.

But when she raised her eyes again she saw Belinda's features had gone pale, her sudden confidence evaporated.

Catherine said evenly, 'I know that you have no true pride in Richard. You are not fit to carry his name. And let me assure you that had we two been men I would willingly call you out. Your ignorance is far more offensive than your smugness!'

She walked towards the door. 'Dulcie has a fever. I heard the gardeners speaking of it before you found me.' Her eyes flashed dangerously. 'Yes, being married to a Spaniard does have its advantages!'

Belinda said, 'You are trying to frighten me.' But there was no defiance now.

'There is an outbreak on the hulks—it sounds like jail fever. You should have been told. How long has she been like that?'

Belinda's hands plucked at her rich gown, confused by the swift change of events.

'A few days. After her husband's ship sailed.'

Her voice faltered. 'What of it?'

Catherine did not answer immediately. 'Send for Mr Yovell. He must take a message for me. Do not make a stupid scene of it. All the servants will go if they understand. It would be better if they were kept away from this room.'

'Is it so terrible?'

Catherine regarded her thoughtfully; she would be useless. 'I shall stay with her.'

She remembered Belinda's frantic question. 'It is typhus.' She saw the word bring terror to her eyes. 'I fear she will not survive it.'

The door opened and Yovell tiptoed across the hallway, although he had not yet been summoned. He listened, his round face expressionless while Catherine explained what had happened.

'This is bad, m'lady.' He watched her gravely. 'We should send for expert help.'

She saw his anxiety, and laid her hand on his plump arm. 'Even then it will be too late. I have seen it before. Had she been treated earlier ...' She looked at the windows; a watery sunlight was breaking through. 'Even then I think it would have been hopeless. She is in pain, and there were traces of a rash when her shawl was moved. I must stay with her, Daniel. No one should die alone.'

Belinda crossed the hallway, her hands agitated. 'I will have to return to London. My daughter is there.'

Catherine said, 'Go then.' As Belinda hurried to the stairs she remarked, 'You see, Daniel? I have no choice now, even if I wanted one.'

'What do you wish, m'lady? Anything, and I shall do it.'

She smiled, but her thoughts were once more in

the past. When she had climbed naked into Bolitho's bed when he had been dying of fever, to bring warmth to his tormented body. And he had never remembered it.

'Go to Chatham. We have sworn to have no secrets, so I must let him know.'

She smiled again and thought sadly, *As he will eventually tell me about his eye.*

Yovell said, 'I shall do that, m'lady.' Then, with a glance at the closed doors, he hurried away.

Belinda came slowly down the staircase, her eyes all the while on the woman in the dull black gown.

By the door she turned and said, *'I hope you die!'*

Catherine looked after her impassively. 'Even then he would not come to you.' But Belinda had gone; and she heard her carriage moving rapidly over the cobbles towards the road.

The same servant was back, staring at Catherine as if she were some secret force which had suddenly come amongst them.

Catherine smiled at her. 'Fetch the housekeeper and the cook.' She saw her uncertainty, the beginning of fear perhaps. 'What is your name, girl?'

'Mary, m'lady.'

'Well, Mary, we are going to look after your mistress. Make things easier for her—do you understand?'

The girl bobbed and showed her teeth. 'Make 'er better, like?'

'That is so. Now off you go and fetch them, while I make a list of things we shall require.'

Alone once more, Catherine leaned her head in her hands and closed her eyes tightly to hold back the hot tears which were waiting to betray her. She had to be strong, as she had been in the past when her world had turned into a nightmare. Danger and death were not new to her, but the thought of losing him now was far more than she could bear. She heard Dulcie calling for someone; she thought she had spoken Herrick's name. She clenched her fists. *What else can I do?*

She seemed to hear Belinda's hatred hanging in the still air. *I hope you die!*

Curiously, it seemed to give her the strength she needed, and when the two women who controlled Dulcie's household entered she spoke to them calmly and without hesitation.

'Your mistress must be bathed. I shall attend to it. Prepare some nourishing soup, and I will need brandy.' The cook bustled away and the housekeeper said quietly, 'Don't 'ee fear, missus, I'll stay with 'ee till it's over.' She bowed her grey head. 'She's bin good to me since my man died.' She raised her head and looked at Catherine steadily. 'He went for a soldier, missus. Fever took 'im from me in the Indies.'

'So you knew?'

The old housekeeper shrugged. 'Guessed, more like. But 'er ladyship said I was bein' foolish.' She glanced around. 'I see *she's* gone all the same.' Then she looked at Catherine and nodded as if in recognition. 'Your man would know about it, I reckon. Rats leavin' the sinkin' ship.' She unbuttoned her sleeves. 'So let's make a start, shall we?'

'Send someone for the doctor. Good or bad, he *should* know.'

The housekeeper studied Catherine's gown. 'I got some servants' clothin' you could wear. It can be

331

burned afterwards.'

The word *afterwards* was still with Catherine when night, like mourning, eventually covered the house.

*   *   *

It was very late by the time Young Matthew turned the carriage through the familiar gates, the air from the sea cold enough for snow. As they had rattled through the town, Bolitho had stared out of the window as if expecting to see changes. He always felt like that when he returned to Falmouth, no matter how long or short his absence had been.

Lights still twinkled from some houses and shops, and when they climbed the hill to his home he saw the cottages, their windows lit by candles, with coloured paper and leaves as decoration. It even felt like Christmas. Catherine, muffled in her cloak and fur-lined hood, watched the passing scene with him; she had never expected to see this place again.

It made Bolitho feel sick just to imagine what could so easily have happened. When Yovell had brought word of Dulcie's terrible illness to the inn where they had been staying near the dockyard, he had been beside himself. More so because the carriage had lost a wheel in the darkness, adding an extra day to her lonely vigil.

Bolitho had not waited for the carriage but had taken a horse, and with Jenour keeping pace beside him had ridden hard all the way to Herrick's house. It had been over even before he reached her. Dulcie had died, mercifully after her heart had failed, so that she was spared the final degradation of the fever. Catherine had been lying on a bed, covered by a blanket but otherwise naked as the old housekeeper had burned her borrowed clothes. How easily she might have been infected; she had tended to Dulcie's most painful and intimate needs to the end, had heard her despairing delirium, when she had called out names Catherine had never heard before.

The doctor had eventually attended, a weak sort of man who had been overwhelmed by the manner of Dulcie's death.

The carriage had followed several hours after Bolitho, when Yovell had commented that Lady Belinda had left since his departure for Chatham. He glanced at Catherine's profile and held her arm even tighter. Not once had she mentioned that Belinda had abandoned her to cope with Dulcie on her own. Almost anyone in her position would have done so, if only to bring contempt and scorn on a rival. It was as if she no longer cared. Only that they were together. Six days on the awful roads, a long and tiring journey, but now they were here.

Ferguson and his wife, the housekeeper, were waiting for them, while other familiar faces floated into the carriage lamps, gathering luggage, calling greetings, glad to see them back.

Ferguson had had no idea of the exact date of their return but he had been well prepared. Great fires in every room, even in the stone hallway, so that the contrast with the cold outside was like an additional welcome. Alone at last in their room facing the headland and the sea beyond, Catherine said she would have a hot bath. She looked at him gravely. 'I want to wash it all away.' Then she held him tightly and kissed him.

She said just one word before she prized herself away. '*Home*.'

Ozzard came up to collect his uniform coat and left with it, humming softly to himself.

She called through the door, and Bolitho guessed it had been on her mind for much of the time.

'When will he be told?'

'Thomas?' He walked to the low window and peered out. No stars, so it was still overcast. He saw a tiny light far out to sea. Some small vessel trying to reach port for Christmas. He thought of Herrick coming to him and bringing the news of Cheney's death; it was something he could never forget. He answered quietly, 'Admiral Godschale will send word on the first vessel carrying despatches to the squadron. I sent a letter to go with it. From us both.' He thought he heard a catch in her voice and he said, 'You are not only lovely, you are also very brave. I would have died if anything had happened to you.'

She came out wearing a robe, her face glowing from the bath which was something else Ferguson had thought of.

'Dulcie said something of that to me.' Her lip trembled but she composed herself. 'I think she knew what was happening to her. She called for her husband several times.'

Bolitho held her against him so that she could not see his face. 'I will have to join the *Black Prince* quite shortly, Kate. A few weeks, perhaps less.'

She rested her head against his shoulder. 'I know ... I am prepared. Don't think of it—take care of yourself as much as you can. For me. For us.'

He stared desperately at the crackling log fire. 'There is something I did not tell you, Kate. There

334

was so much to do, after the duel and ... everything—then poor Dulcie.'

She leaned back in his arms as she so often did to study him, as if to read his innermost thoughts before he uttered a word.

She whispered, 'You look like a little boy, Richard. One with a secret.'

He said bluntly, 'They can't help me with my eye.' He gave a great sigh, relieved to have got it out at last, fearful what she might think. 'I wanted to tell you, but—'

She broke away from him and took his hand to lead him to the window. Then she thrust it wide open, oblivious to the bitter air. 'Listen, darling—church bells.'

They clung to each other as the joyous peal of bells echoed up the hill from the church of Charles the Martyr, where so many Bolitho memories were marked in stone.

She said, 'Kiss me. It's midnight, my love. Christmas morn.'

Then she closed the window very carefully and faced him.

'Look at me, Richard. What if it were me? Would you cast me aside? Do you think it makes any difference, *could* make any? I love you, so much you'll never know. And there is always hope. We shall keep trying. No doctor is God.'

There was a tap at the door and Ozzard stood there with his tray and some finely cut goblets. He blinked at them. 'Thought it might be proper, m'lady.'

It was champagne, misted over with ice from the stream.

Bolitho thanked the little man and opened the

335

bottle. 'The only thing of any value to come out of France!'

She threw back her head and gave her bubbling laugh, something Bolitho had not heard since the pleasure gardens.

Bolitho said, 'You know, I think this is the first Christmas I have been in Falmouth since I was a midshipman.'

She turned down the bed, the half-empty glass still in her other hand. Then she let her robe fall to the floor and faced him, with pride and love in her dark eyes.

'You are my man. I am your woman. Then let us celebrate.'

Bolitho bent over and kissed her breast, heard her gasp, all else forgotten. And so it would be, he thought. The new flagship, Herrick, a court-martial ... even the war could wait. He touched her breast with some champagne and kissed it again.

She pulled him down. 'Am I stone that I can wait so long?'

*   *   *

Ferguson and Allday were crossing the yard to share a last drink before the festivities in the house and on the estate commenced in earnest. Allday glanced up at a candlelit window. Ferguson, his friend since being pressed into Bolitho's *Phalarope*, heard him sigh, and guessed what he was thinking. He had known his wife Grace since childhood. Allday had nobody to call his own.

He said, 'Come and tell us all about it, John. We've heard a few rumours, but not much else.'

'I was thinking about Rear-Admiral Herrick.

336

Takes you back, don't it, Bryan? *Phalarope*, the Cap'n, us an' Mr Herrick. Come a long way. Now he's lost *his* wife. Full circle, that's what.'

Ferguson opened the door of his little house and glanced round to make sure Grace had retired at long last.

'Here, I'll fetch some grog from the pantry.'

Allday gave a sad grin. Like them up there in that great bedroom. *A sailor's woman.* 'I'd relish that, matey!' *All of us, holding things at bay, knowing it must end, but making the best of it.*

He coughed on the rum and spluttered, 'God, this is the stuff to fill the sails!'

Ferguson smiled. 'Got it off a trader from Port Royal.' He saw the shadow lifting from Allday's face, and held up his glass.

'Welcome home, old friend!'

Allday's eyes crinkled. What Bolitho called him. 'An' here's to those who won't never come home.' He laughed, and the cat sleeping by the fire opened one eye with irritation. 'Even the officers—well, some of 'em!'

As Ferguson went away to open another bottle, Allday added quietly, 'An' to you both over yonder. May God protect you!'

When he looked out, their window was in darkness and only the distant boom of the sea gave him an answer. Always waiting.

CHAPTER SIXTEEN

THE SQUADRON

His Britannic Majesty's ship *Black Prince* seemed to hesitate for a moment before plunging her massive one thousand eight hundred tons into the next procession of troughs.

Aft in his spacious day cabin, Bolitho looked up from his final cup of coffee before starting the new day, and was surprised how easily the big second-rate took even the heaviest sea.

It was eight o'clock in the morning, and he could vaguely hear the muffled movements of the forenoon watchkeepers as they relieved the men on deck. Unlike *Hyperion* or any other two-decker, there was a sense of protected remoteness in *Black Prince*. Bolitho's quarters with their own private sternwalk were sandwiched between the wardroom beneath his feet and Keen's own domain directly above.

He shivered and looked at the leaping patterns of salt spray on the stern windows, frozen there like the ramblings of some insane artist. The day cabin was finely painted and moulded with carved panels, the stern bench seat and chairs finished with dark green leather. Catherine could have chosen it herself, he thought. But now it was bloomed with damp, and he could picture without effort the discomfort and as yet unfamiliarity endured by the flagship's company of eight hundred souls, including one hundred Royal Marines. Bolitho had once been a flag-captain in a big first-rate, the

338

Euryalus, renamed after being taken as a prize from the French. *Twelve years ago*. At the worst time for England's embattled shores, when the fleet had mutinied at the Nore and Spithead. If ever Napoleon had missed his chance, it had been then. They could be thankful a hundred times over that he was a land-creature and not a sailor.

Allday entered the cabin and regarded Bolitho impassively. 'First day o' February, Sir Richard.' He did not sound very enthusiastic about it. 'Like ice on deck.'

'How are things, Allday?' *My eyes and ears*.

Allday shrugged his broad shoulders and winced. He felt his wound more in cold weather.

'*Things?* I think most o' the people are in irons about the new ship.' He glanced around the magnificent cabin with neither dislike nor contentment. 'You can't find nothing when you needs it. All different from *Hyperion*.' His eyes gleamed momentarily and he added, 'I'll say one thing, Sir Richard, she's a good sailer for a big 'un. A few months' drill and who knows what Cap'n Keen will make her do.'

Bolitho understood. It was often so in a brand new vessel. Everything to be learned from the beginning again. *Black Prince* was no frigate, and with her towering hull and three lines of ports for her total firepower of ninety-four guns and two carronades, she would need firm handling.

'I heard a pipe just now.' Bolitho saw Ozzard pause beside the beautiful wine cooler and cabinet which he had found waiting on board when he had hoisted his flag at the fore. Catherine had made no mention of it. A gift like the previous one which now lay on the bottom with his old flagship. She

339

had taken great care; the mahogany cabinet was perfectly matched, and on the top was an inlaid shield—the Bolitho coat of arms.

Ozzard wiped some of the damp bloom from it with his cloth and nodded approvingly. He had no need for words.

Allday watched him warily. 'It was a pipe to witness punishment in the forenoon watch, Sir Richard.'

Bolitho eyed him steadily. Keen would hate that, even when there was no other obvious solution. Bolitho had known too many captains who had flogged first and sought explanations only when it was too late.

There were voices at the outer screen door and Bolitho heard the marine sentry tap the deck with his musket. Keen, reporting at his usual time after he had checked the log, seen the new watch take over, and discussed the day's work with his first lieutenant.

He entered the cabin and said, 'Fresh nor'westerly, Sir Richard.' He nodded to Allday. 'But the decks are dry. She takes it well.' He looked strained, and there were shadows beneath his eyes. 'I am assured we will make contact with the squadron by noon if the weather holds.'

Bolitho noticed that Allday and Ozzard had quietly departed.

'Be seated, Val. Is something wrong?' He forced a smile. 'Is there ever a time in a sailor's life when there is not?'

Keen stared through the spray-dappled glass. 'There are several familiar faces in the company.' He shot him a quick glance. 'I thought you should know before you have cause to meet them.'

Bolitho watched the sea, silent beyond the thick windows, leaping and breaking, so dark it was almost black. There were always old faces. The navy was like that. A family, or a prison. With faces went memories. It could not be otherwise.

He answered, 'That was thoughtful of you, Val. I have deliberately kept out of your way since I stepped aboard.' He saw a big roller break astern and felt the responding shudder of the tiller-head one deck below. He had been at sea for four days. But for Catherine, it might have seemed that he had never left it.

He asked, 'How has my nephew settled down? With his H.E.I.C. experience he should soon prove ready for a lieutenant's examination, eh?'

Keen frowned. 'I have to speak my mind, Sir Richard. I think I know you too well to do otherwise.'

'I would expect nothing but honesty, Val. Despite demands on our authority, we are friends. *Nothing* can change that.' He paused, seeing the uncertainty on Keen's handsome features. 'Besides which, you command here, not I.'

Keen said, 'I am obliged to order another flogging. A seaman named Fittock, who was allegedly insolent to Mr Midshipman Vincent. The lieutenant of his division is young, perhaps too much so in experience if not in years, and maybe...'

'And *maybe*, Val, he thought better than to dispute Midshipman Vincent's testimony. *The vice-admiral's nephew* might do him harm.'

Keen shrugged. 'It is not easy. A new ship, a larger proportion of landsmen than I would wish, and a certain listlessness amongst the people—any

341

kind of weakness would be seen as something to exploit.'

'In other words, Vincent provoked the seaman?'

'I believe so. Fittock is a skilled hand. It's foolish to berate such a man in front of pressed landsmen.'

Bolitho thought of *Hyperion*'s captain before Keen had taken his place. He had been driven mad, and had tried to shoot his first lieutenant. He thought also of the sick and overworked commodore, Arthur Warren, at Good Hope, and of the wretched Varian, now awaiting a court-martial which might easily end with his own sword pointing towards him on the table, and death. Captains all; but all so different.

He suggested, 'It could be inexperience, or a need to impress.'

Keen said softly, 'But you don't think so.'

'It seems unlikely. Either way there is little we can do. If I admonish Vincent—' He saw the unspoken protest on Keen's face and added, 'You are his captain. But *if* I took a hand, they would see it as interference, a lack of trust, perhaps, in you. On the other hand if you quash the sentence the end result would be the same. The people might believe that *no* junior officer, Vincent or any other, is worth the cut of his coat.'

Keen sighed. 'Some would say it was a small thing, Sir Richard, but this ship is not yet of one company and does not have the loyalty which will unite the people, given time.'

Bolitho smiled grimly. 'Aye, that's so. Time is also in short supply.'

Keen prepared to leave. 'I have spoken with my first lieutenant about it. Mr Cazalet is already my right arm.' He gave a rueful grin. 'But doubtless he

342

will soon be promoted out of my ship for a command of his own.'

'A moment, Val. I merely wanted you to know that Catherine intends to call upon Zenoria. They were very close to one another and their suffering was much the same. So take heart—who would have believed that *I* might find Catherine again?'

Keen was silent, his eyes faraway. He was remembering how she had spoken to him, her sincerity about Zenoria matched only by the passion in her words.

Then he said, 'Shall you visit Rear-Admiral Herrick before *Benbow* quits the station?' When Bolitho did not answer immediately he added, 'I know there was bitterness between us ... but no man should learn of his wife's death in such fashion.' He hesitated. 'I beg your pardon, Sir Richard. That was a thoughtless and indiscreet thing to say.'

Bolitho touched his sleeve. 'Indiscretion is not unknown to me.' He became grave. 'But yes, I hope to see him when we meet with the squadron.'

There was a knock at the outer screen door and the marine sentry bawled, 'Midshipman-of-the-Watch, *sir*!'

Bolitho winced. 'God, you would think we were three fields away from the fellow!'

Ozzard had appeared in the other cabin, and opened the door to admit the midshipman.

Keen said quietly, 'Someone else whose life you changed, I think, Sir Richard?'

Bolitho looked at the pale-faced youth who was staring back at him, his eyes shining with a barely-contained recognition.

Bolitho said, 'I am glad you are in this ship, Mr
343

Segrave.' He seemed older than when he had helped the cruelly disfigured Lieutenant Tyacke to steer the blazing *Albacora* into the moored supply ships at Good Hope.

'I—I wrote to you, Sir Richard, to thank you for your sponsorship. My uncle the Admiral was full of admiration!' It sounded as if he was about to add *for once*.

Segrave turned to Keen. 'Mr Cazalet's respects, sir, and the masthead has just sighted a sail to the nor'-east.'

'My compliments to the first lieutenant. I shall come up presently.'

As the door closed Keen said, 'I heard all about that lad, and the bullying he received in his other ship. Your Mr Tyacke has become a bit of a hero in his eyes, I think.' He smiled, so that the strain seemed to fall away. 'Next to *you*, of course, Sir Richard!'

It was good to see him smile again. Perhaps his lovely Zenoria came to him in his dreams and tormented him, as Catherine had done and would do again if they were too long separated.

'Lieutenant Tyacke is a remarkable man. When you meet him there is only pity. Afterwards you can only find admiration, pride, even, at knowing him.'

They went on deck together and walked out on to the broad quarterdeck, where at their approach the watchkeepers and the hands who were working there adopted stances and attitudes as if they were mimers.

Bolitho looked up at the dull sky, the tall masts and rigging dark against it. Under topsails and courses the *Black Prince* was leaning only slightly to leeward, her sails quivering to the wind's wet
344

pressure.

'Deck there!' After *Truculent*, the lookout sounded a mile distant. 'Frigate, zur!'

Keen turned up his collar as the wind probed the rawness of his skin. 'Not a Frog, then. He'd be about and running by now if it was!'

Bolitho tried not to touch his left eye. Many were watching him, some seeing him for the first time. A new ship, a well-known flag-officer; it would be easy to lose their confidence before he had found it.

A tall, dark-haired midshipman whose generally aloof behaviour to the other 'young gentlemen' was obvious even on the busy quarterdeck snapped, 'Aloft, Mr Gough. Take a glass, lively now!' A minute midshipman scampered to the shrouds and was soon lost from view amongst the dark crisscross of rigging. Bolitho smiled to himself. The tall youth was named Bosanquet, the senior member of the gunroom, and next to go for promotion. It was not hard to see him as a lieutenant, or even a captain for that matter.

'*Deck there!*' Several of the seamen exchanged grins at the midshipman's squeaky cry from the crosstrees. '*She's made her number!*'

Cazalet, the first lieutenant, a tough-looking man with dark, bushy eyebrows, raised his speaking-trumpet. 'We are all in suspense, Mr Gough!'

The boy squeaked again, although even from that dizzy height he sounded crushed. '*Number Five-Four-Six*, sir!'

Bosanquet already had his book open. '*Zest* sir, forty-four, Captain Charles Varian!'

Jenour had appeared at his side like a shadow. 'You will need to change the captain's name.' He

345

darted a glance at Bolitho. 'He is no longer in command.'

Keen said, 'Make our reply, if you please.'

Bolitho turned away. Some of the watching faces probably saw him as Varian's executioner, and might judge him accordingly.

He saw the boatswain, whose name was already slotted into his mind as Ben Gilpin, with a small working party, supervising the rigging of a grating on the lee side of the deck. Ready for the ritual of punishment. It would seem so much worse for those who had never been to sea in a King's ship before. And for many of the others, it could only brutalise them further.

Bolitho stiffened as he saw Felicity's son standing nearby, watching with fixed attention. Bolitho touched his eye and did not see Jenour glance across at him. He saw only Vincent's face. For one so young he had an expression of cruel anticipation.

Keen called, 'Alter course two points, Mr Cazalet, we will wait for *Zest* to run down on us!'

Jenour stood apart from the bustling seamen as they manned the braces for retrimming the great yards to hold the wind, immersed in his private thoughts. All of his family were in or connected with the medical profession, and he had mentioned the foreign-sounding doctor Rudfolf Braks to his uncle just before leaving to join the flagship.

His uncle, a quiet and much respected physician, had responded instantly.

'Of course—the man who attended Lord Nelson and visits the King because of his failing sight. If he can do nothing to help your admiral, then there is nobody who can.'

The words still hung in his mind like part of a

guilty secret.

He heard the first lieutenant ask, 'Pipe the hands aft to witness punishment, sir?' Then Keen's equally taut reply. 'Attend to it, Mr Cazalet, but I want loyalty, not fear!'

Bolitho walked towards the poop and knew Allday was following him. He had sensed the unusual bitterness in Keen's words. Had he perhaps been remembering how he had saved Zenoria from a savage whipping aboard the convict transport, when he had rescued her and helped to confirm her innocence? But not before she had taken one stroke across her naked back from shoulder to hip, something which she would never lose. Was that, too, keeping them apart?

He entered the stern cabin and threw himself on to the bench seat.

A new ship. No experience, unblooded, a stranger to the line of battle. Bolitho clenched his fist as he heard the staccato roll of the Royal Marines' drums. He could barely hear the crack of the lash across the seaman's body, but he felt it as if it were happening to himself.

He thought of Herrick, how he would be; what he was going through. Bolitho had heard from Admiral Godschale that it had been *Anemone*, Adam's command, which had carried the news of Dulcie's death. A double twist, he thought. It would have been better if it had been a total stranger.

He tried to think about the squadron he was taking from Herrick. Five ships-of-the-line and only two frigates. There were never enough.

Allday walked across the cabin, his eyes watchful. 'Punishment's over, Sir Richard.'

Bolitho barely heard. He was thinking of Vincent again, of his sister's reproachful coldness towards Catherine.

He said distantly, 'Never hold out your hand too often, old friend.' Then he turned away and added, 'You can get badly bitten.'

*　　*　　*

'Watch your stroke!' Allday leaned forward, one hand on the tiller bar, as if he were riding across the choppy water instead of steering the *Black Prince*'s barge. Even with all his experience it was going to be a difficult crossing from one flagship to the other. He knew better than to use some of his stronger language in front of his admiral, but later he would have no such qualms. In their turn, the bargemen put all their weight on the painted looms, conscious more of Allday's threatening gaze, perhaps, than their passenger.

Bolitho turned and looked back at his new flagship. It was the first time he had seen her properly in her own element. The light was dull and grey, but even so the powerful three-decker seemed to shine like polished glass, her black and buff hull and the chequered pattern of gunports making a splash of welcome colour against the miserable North Sea afternoon. Beyond her, and turning away almost guiltily, the *Zest* was standing-off to resume her proper station.

Bolitho felt Jenour watching him as the green-painted barge lifted and plunged over the water in sickening swoops.

Keen had done well, he thought. He must have been pulled around the ship before and after he had first taken her to sea. He had checked the trim of the great hull, and had ordered some of the ballast to be moved, and many of the stores shifted to different holds to give the ship the right lift at the stem. He saw the figurehead reaching out with his sword from beneath the beakhead. It was one of the most lifelike he had yet seen, carved and painted more to impress than frighten. The son of Edward III, complete with chain mail, fleur-de-lis and English lions. From the black crowned helmet to the figure's unflinching stare, it could have been a living being. The carver had been one of the most famous of his breed, old Aaron Mallow of Sheerness. Sadly, *Black Prince*'s figurehead had been his last; he had died shortly after the ship had been launched for fitting-out.

Bolitho looked instead at *Benbow*, once his own flagship, when Herrick had been his captain. A seventy-four like *Hyperion* but much heavier, for she had been built much later when there were still the oak forests to provide for her. Now the forests of Kent and Sussex, Hampshire and the West Country were left bare, raped by the mounting demands of a war which never lessened in its ferocity.

He saw the scarlet of the marines, the dull glint of metal in the fading light, and felt a pang of anxiety. Herrick was his oldest friend. Had been until . . . He thought suddenly of what Keen had told him about the man who had been flogged. Stripped and seized up to the grating by wrists and knees, he had taken a dozen lashes without a protest, only the usual sound of the air being beaten from his lungs with each blow of the cat.

It was while he was being cut down that an

unknown voice had yelled out from the silent onlookers, 'We'll make it even for you, Jim!'

Needless to say, the ship's corporal and the master-at-arms had been unable to discover the culprit. In a way, Bolitho was glad, but he had shared Keen's uneasiness that anyone should show defiance in front of his captain and the armed marines.

And so the unknown seaman named Jim Fittock had become something of a martyr because of Felicity's son Miles Vincent. Bolitho tightened his jaw. It must not happen again.

The other flagship loomed over him, and he sensed Allday's seething exasperation as the bowman had to make several attempts to hook on to the main chains.

As he clambered up the salt-caked side he was thankful for the dull light. To trip and fall like the other time would not rouse any confidence either.

The quarterdeck seemed quiet and sheltered after the blustery crossing in an open boat, so that the sudden din of drums and fifes, a Royal Marines captain shouting orders to the guard plus the dwindling echo of the calls which had piped him aboard took him by surprise.

In those few moments he saw several familiar faces, suitably expressionless for the occasion, with the flag-captain Hector Gossage standing like a rock in front of his officers. He saw the new flag-lieutenant who had replaced De Broux, the one with the *damned Frenchie name* as Herrick had put it. The newcomer was plump, and his face was empty of animation or intelligence.

Then he saw Herrick and felt a cold hand around his heart.

Herrick's hair, once brown and only touched with grey like frost, was almost colourless, and his bronzed features seemed suddenly lined. He could recall their brief meeting in the Admiralty corridor, the two visiting captains gaping at them as Bolitho had called after Herrick, his voice shaking with anger and with hurt. It did not seem possible a man could change so much in so short a time.

Herrick said, 'You are welcome, Sir Richard.' He shook hands, his palm hard and firm as Bolitho had always remembered. 'You will remember Captain Gossage, of course?'

Bolitho nodded, but did not take his eyes from Herrick. 'My heart is full for you, Thomas.'

Herrick gave what might have been a shrug, perhaps to cover his innermost feelings. He said in a vague tone, 'Dismiss the hands, Captain Gossage. Keep station on *Black Prince*, but call me if the weather goes against us.' He gestured aft. 'Join me, Sir Richard. We can talk a while.' Bolitho ducked beneath the poop and studied his friend as Herrick led the way into the shadows between decks. Had he always been so stooped? He did not recall so. As if he were carrying the pain of his loss like a burden on his back.

In the great cabin where Bolitho had so often paced and fretted over the next action or the enemy's intentions, he looked around as if to see something of himself still lingering here. But there was nothing. It could have been the great cabin of almost any ship-of-the-line, he thought.

A servant he did not recognise brought a chair for him, and Herrick asked in an almost matter-of-fact voice, 'A drink perhaps?'

He did not wait for answer. 'Bring the brandy,

351

Murray.' Then he faced Bolitho and said, 'I received word you were coming. I am relieved so that *Benbow* can have some repairs carried out. We almost lost the rudder in a gale . . . but I expect you were in England at the time. It was bad—the sea took a master's mate and two seamen, poor devils. No chance of finding 'em.'

Bolitho tried not to interrupt. Herrick was coming around to what he wanted to say. He had always been like that. But brandy, that was something else. Wine, yes, ginger beer more likely; he must have been drinking heavily since Adam had brought him the news.

Herrick said, 'I got your letter. It was good of you.' He nodded to the servant and then snapped, 'Leave it, man, I can manage!' That, too, was not like the old Herrick, the champion of the common seaman more than anyone he had known. Bolitho watched the hand shaking as he slopped two huge measures of brandy into the goblets, some of it spilling unheeded on to the black and white chequered deck covering. 'Good stuff this. My patrols took it off a smuggler.' Then he turned and stared at him, his eyes still as clear and blue as Bolitho remembered. It was like seeing someone familiar peering out of another's body.

'God damn it, I wasn't with her when she needed me most!' The words were torn out of him. 'I'd warned her about working amongst those bloody prisoners—I'd hang the lot of them if I had my way!' He walked to a bulkhead where Bolitho had once hung his swords. Herrick's fighting hanger dangled from it, swaying unevenly to the pitch of the ship as she fought to keep station on *Black Prince*. But Herrick was touching the finely

352

finished, silver-mounted telescope, the one which Dulcie had bought for him from the best instrument maker in London's Strand; Bolitho doubted if he knew what he was doing. He probably touched it for comfort rather than to be reminded.

Bolitho said, 'I could not get to the house in time. Otherwise I would . . .'

Herrick tilted the goblet until it was empty. 'Lady Bolitho told me all about those damned Dons who worked around the house. She would have sent them packing!' He looked at Bolitho and asked abruptly, 'Was it all taken care of?'

'Yes. Your sister was there. A lot of Dulcie's friends too.'

Herrick said in a small voice, 'I wasn't even there to see her buried. *Alone* . . .' The one word echoed around the cabin until he said, 'Your lady tried her best . . .'

Bolitho said quietly, 'Dulcie was not alone. Catherine stayed with her, attended to her every need until she was mercifully released from her suffering. It took courage, for there was no little danger to her.'

Herrick walked to the table and lifted the brandy, then waved it vaguely towards the sea.

'Just her? With my Dulcie!'

'Aye. She'd not even allow your housekeeper in close contact.'

Herrick rubbed his eyes as if they were hurting him. 'I suppose you think that gives you the opportunity to redeem her in my opinion.'

Bolitho kept his voice level. 'I am not here to score points from your grief. I am well reminded when you came to me with terrible news. I grieve

353

for you, Thomas, for I know what it is to lose love—just as I understand how it feels to discover it.'

Herrick sat down heavily and refilled his goblet, his features set in tight concentration, as if every thought was an effort.

Then he said in a thick voice, 'So you've got your woman, and I've lost everything. Dulcie gave me strength, she made me feel somebody. A long, long step from the son of a poor clerk to rear-admiral, eh?' When Bolitho said nothing he leaned over the table and shouted, 'But *you* wouldn't understand! I saw it in young Adam when he came aboard—it's all there in him too, like they speak of it in the news-sheets. The Bolitho charm—isn't that so?'

'I shall leave now, Thomas.' His despair was so destructive it was too terrible to watch. Later Herrick would regret his outburst, his words so bitter that it had sounded like something he had been nursing all down the years. A warmth gone sour; envy where there had once been the strongest bond of true friendship. 'Use your time in England to think and relive the good things you found together—and when next we meet—'

Herrick lurched to his feet and almost fell. For an instant his eyes seemed to clear again and he blurted out, 'Your injury? Is it improved now?' Somehow through the mist of distress and loss he must have recalled when Bolitho had almost fallen on this same vessel.

Then he said, 'Lady Catherine's husband is dead, I hear?' It was a challenge, like an accusation. 'Convenient—'

'Not so, Thomas. One day you might understand.' Bolitho turned and recovered his hat and cloak as the door opened a few inches, and Captain Gossage peered in at them.

'I was about to inform the rear-admiral that the wind is rising, Sir Richard.' His glance moved quickly to Herrick who was slumped down again in his chair, his eyes trying to focus, but without success.

Gossage said swiftly, with what he thought was discretion, 'I will call the guard, Sir Richard, and have you seen over the side.'

Bolitho looked gravely at his friend and answered, 'No, call my barge.' He hesitated by the screen door and lowered his voice, so that the marine sentry should not hear.

'Then attend your admiral. There sits a brave man, but badly wounded now—no less than by the enemy's fire.' He nodded curtly. 'I bid you good-day, Captain Gossage.'

He found Jenour waiting for him on deck and saw a messenger running from Gossage to recall the barge to the chains.

Jenour had rarely seen him look so grim, so sad at the same time. But he was not so inexperienced in Bolitho's ways to ask what had occurred during his visit, or mention the glaring fact that Rear-Admiral Herrick was not on deck to show the proper respect at Bolitho's departure.

Instead he said brightly, 'I heard the sailing-master confide that yonder lies the Dutch coast—but we are losing it fast in another squall.' He fell silent as Bolitho looked at him for the first time.

Bolitho touched his eye with his fingers, and felt it sting like a cruel reminder. Then he asked, 'Is the barge alongside, Stephen?'

As Jenour left him he thought he heard him murmur, 'Dear God, I would that it were Cornwall.'

The captain of marines yelled, 'Guard of Honour, pre-sent *arms!*'

The rest was lost as Bolitho swung himself out and down to the pitching barge, as if the sea had reclaimed him.

★　　　★　　　★

Lieutenant Stephen Jenour tucked his hat beneath his arm and entered Bolitho's day cabin. Outside on the open deck the air was still very cold, but a lull in the blustery wind had smoothed out the North Sea's short, steep waves and remained with them. The presence of some watery sunlight gave an illusion of warmth in the crowded messes, and here in the great cabin.

Bolitho was leaning over a chart, his hands spread across it as if to encompass the squadron's limits. He looked tired, Jenour thought, but calmer than the moment he had left his friend aboard *Benbow*. He could only guess at what had come between them but knew it had affected Bolitho deeply.

Beyond the tall stern windows he could see two of the squadron's seventy-fours, the *Glorious* and the old *Sunderland*. The latter was so elderly that many aboard *Black Prince* had thought her either hulked or sunk in battle. There were few campaigns she had missed; she would be, Jenour thought, about the same age as *Hyperion*.

With *Benbow* returned to England there were five ships-of-the-line awaiting *Black Prince*'s signals, and two others, the *Tenacious* and the *Valkyrie*, were undergoing repairs in England. Jenour had thought it strange that Rear-Admiral Herrick had detached two of his depleted strength without waiting to hear Bolitho's views on the subject. But he had kept his thoughts to himself. He had learned to recognise most, if not all of Bolitho's moods and sensitivities, and knew that he was occasionally only partly in his flagship, while the rest of the time he was in spirit with Catherine in England.

He realised that Bolitho had raised his eyes from the chart, and was watching him patiently. Jenour flushed, something he still did far too often—much to his own annoyance.

'The captains are assembled on board, Sir Richard. Only *Zest*'s commander is absent and on his patrol area.'

Bolitho nodded. Two weeks since he had parted from Herrick, with too much time to think back over their exchange. Now, for the first time, because of the improved weather conditions, he had drawn the bulk of his squadron together in the hard glare which made the sea look like beaten silver. It was the first time, also, that his captains had managed to reach the flagship.

'What about our courier-brig?'

Jenour flushed still further. How could Bolitho have known that the brig had been reported by *Glorious*'s masthead lookout? He had been here in his quarters since a dawn stroll, not on his private sternwalk, but on the quarterdeck in full view of everyone.

Bolitho saw his confusion and smiled. 'I heard the signal being repeated on deck, Stephen. A sternwalk has its uses—the sound carries quite

357

well.' He added wryly, 'Even the things that people say, when they are being somewhat indiscreet!'

He tried not to hope that the little brig, named *Mistral*, was bringing a letter from Catherine. It was too soon, and anyway she would be very busy. He laid out each careful excuse to hold his disappointment at bay.

He said, 'Signal her commander to report on board when the time comes.'

He thought of the captains who were waiting to meet him. Not one of them a friend; but all were experienced. That would suffice. After Thomas Herrick ... his mind thrust it away, feeling the same hurt and sense of betrayal. There had been a time when, as a captain himself, he had fretted about meeting a new ship's company. Now he knew from experience that usually they were far more worried than he.

All through the past hour or so, calls had shrilled at the entry port as the various captains had been piped aboard. Each one of them might be thinking more about the rumours of scandal than what lay ahead.

He said, 'Please ask Captain Keen to bring them here.' He had not noticed the sudden edge to his voice. 'He was quite surprised to see his old *Nicator* as one of the squadron ... he commanded her six or seven years back. We were at Copenhagen together.' His grey eyes became distant. 'I lost some good friends that day.'

Jenour waited, and saw the sudden despair depart from his face like a cloud across the sea.

Bolitho smiled. 'He said to me once that *Nicator* was so rotten there were many times he believed only a thin sheet of copper stood between himself

358

and eternity. Heaven knows what the old ship is like now!'

Jenour paused by the door, hating to break into these confidences. 'Are we so short of ships, Sir Richard?'

Bolitho walked to the quarter galley and watched the uneasy water, the way some circling gulls appeared to change colour as they dipped and drifted through the sunlight.

'I fear so, Stephen. That is why those Danish ships are so important. It might all come to nothing, but I think not. I did not *imagine* Poland's death, nor did I invent the near destruction of *Truculent*. They *knew we were there*.' He remembered how Sir Charles Inskip had scoffed at him because of his suspicions about French intentions. But that had been before the desperate battle; he had not scoffed since.

He became impatient with his memories and said, 'Tell Ozzard to fetch some wine for our guests.'

Jenour closed the door, and saw Ozzard and another servant already preparing goblets and standing them inside the fiddles in case a sudden squall came down on the ship.

Bolitho walked to the wine-cooler and touched the inlay with his fingers. Herrick would be at his home. Remembering how it had been; expecting to see his Dulcie and feel the warmth of her obvious adoration for him. Herrick was probably blaming him too for *Benbow*'s being relieved; as if it had happened because Bolitho wanted the squadron for himself. How little he knew—but it was always easy to find a bitter reason if you wanted it enough.

The door opened and Keen ushered the others

inside so that they could introduce themselves to Bolitho on arrival.

He had a mixed impression of experience, competence and curiosity. All were post-captains except the last one to arrive. Ozzard bustled amongst them with his tray, but their eyes were on the captain of the frigate *Anemone* as he reported to their vice-admiral. More like a younger brother than a nephew.

Bolitho clasped Adam's hand but could no longer restrain himself, and put his arm around his shoulder and hugged him.

The dark hair which matched his own; even the restless energy of a young colt when he had first joined *Hyperion* as a skinny midshipman of fourteen years. It was all still there. Bolitho held him at arm's length and studied him feature by feature. But Adam was a man now, a captain of his own frigate; what he had always dreamed about. He was twenty-six years old. Another twist of Fate? Bolitho had been the same age when he had been given command of his first frigate.

Adam said quietly, 'It is *good* to see you, Uncle. We barely had an hour together after *Truculent*'s return to port.'

His words seemed to linger in the air like the memory of a threat. But for *Anemone*'s sudden appearance, the three French vessels would surely have overwhelmed Poland's ship by sheer weight of artillery.

Bolitho thought grimly, *And I would be dead*. He knew he would never allow himself to be taken prisoner again.

Keen had got the others seated and they were watching the reunion, each man fitting it into his

360

own image of the Bolitho they knew, or had only heard about. There was no sort of resentment on their faces; Bolitho guessed that Adam was far too junior to present any kind of threat to their own status in the squadron.

Bolitho said, 'We will talk far longer this time. I am proud to have you under my flag.'

All at once the midshipman with the cheeky grin was back again. Adam said, 'From what I hear and read, it is barely safe to leave you on your own, Uncle!'

Bolitho composed himself and faced Keen and the other captains. There was so much he wanted to tell Adam, *needed* to tell him, so that there would never be any doubts, no secrets to plague them when they were alone.

Adam looked so *right* in his dress coat; but more like a youth playing the part of a hero than the man who held the destiny of a thirty-eight gun frigate and some one hundred and eighty souls in his hands. He thought of Herrick's distress, his scathing comments about *the Bolitho charm*. Maybe he had been right? It was easy to picture Adam's face now in one of the portraits at the house in Falmouth.

'I wanted to meet you as soon as possible, for I have discovered in the past that circumstances often prevent us from taking our time over such matters.' There were several smiles. 'I am sorry that we are short of two in our numbers—' He hesitated as he realised what he had said. It was as if Herrick was right here, watching, resenting the implication; blaming him for sending the two ships into port without waiting. He said, 'This is not a time for loosening our grip on the reins. There are many

361

who saw Trafalgar as a victory which would end all danger at a single stroke. I have seen and heard it for myself, in the fleet and on the streets of London. I can assure you, gentlemen, it is a foolish and misinformed captain who believes this is a time for relaxation. We *need every ship we can get*, and the men who care enough to fight them when the time comes, as come it must. The French will exploit their gains on land and have proved that few troops can withstand them. And who knows what leaders they will put to sea once they have the ships again to use against us? The French navy was weakened by the very force which brought Napoleon to power. During the blood-letting of the Terror, loyal officers were beheaded in the same blind savagery as the so-called aristocrats! But new faces will appear, and when they do we must be ready.' He felt suddenly drained, and saw Adam watching him with concern.

He asked, 'Have you any questions?'

Captain John Crowfoot of the *Glorious*, a tall, stooping figure with the solemn looks of a village clergyman, asked, 'Will the Danes offer their fleet to the enemy, Sir Richard?'

Bolitho smiled. He even sounded like one. 'I think not. But under extreme pressure they might yield. No Dane wants the French army on his soil. Napoleon's armies have a habit of staying put after they have invaded, no matter on what pretext.'

Bolitho saw Keen lean forward to look at the next captain to speak. It was Captain George Huxley who commanded *Nicator*, Keen's old ship. He was probably wondering what kind of man could be expected to hold the rotting seventy-four together.

Huxley was stocky and level-eyed, giving an

immediate impression of unwavering self-confidence. A hard man, Bolitho thought.

Huxley insisted, 'We must have more frigates, Sir Richard. Without them we are blind and ignorant of affairs. A squadron, nay, a fleet could pass us in the night, to seaward or yonder along the Dutch coast, and we might never know.'

Bolitho saw one of them glance round as if he expected to see the Dutch coastline, even though it was more than thirty miles abeam.

He said, 'I share that sentiment, Captain Huxley. I have but two under my command. That of my nephew, and the *Zest*, whose captain I am yet to meet.'

He thought of Keen's remark: 'Captain Fordyce has the reputation of a martinet, sir. He is an admiral's son, as you will know, but his methods are hardly mine.' It was rare for Keen to speak out on the subject of a fellow captain. Their lordships probably thought that *Zest* needed a firmer hand after Varian's example.

There were more questions on repairs and supplies, on patrol areas and shortages. Some of the questions were directed at Bolitho's proposed signals and fighting instructions, because of their brevity rather than their context.

Bolitho looked at them thoughtfully. *They do not know me. Yet.*

He replied, 'Too much time is lost, wasted by unnecessary exchanges in the midst of a sea-fight. And time, as you know from experience, is a luxury we may not always have.' He let each word sink in before he added, 'I had correspondence with Lord Nelson, but like most of you, I never had the good fortune to meet him.' He let his gaze rest on Adam.

'My nephew is the exception. He met him more than once—a privilege we can never share. Gone for ever he may be, but his example is still ours to be seized and used.' He had all their attention, and he saw Adam touch his cheek surreptitiously with the back of his hand.

'Nelson once said that in his opinion no captain could do very wrong if he laid his ship alongside that of an enemy.' He saw Crowfoot of the *Glorious* nod vigorously, and knew that by the door Jenour was staring at him as if afraid he might miss something.

Bolitho ended simply, 'In answer to some of your questions—I don't think Our Nel's words can ever be improved on.'

It was another two hours before they all departed, feeling better for the plentiful supply of wine, and each man preparing his own version of the meeting for his wardroom and company.

As Ozzard remarked ruefully, 'They certainly made a hole in the cheese Lady Catherine sent aboard!'

Bolitho found some time to speak with the youngest captain in his squadron, *Mistral*'s Commander Philip Merrye, whom Allday later described contemptuously, ''Nother one of those twelve-year-old cap'ns!'

Then under a gentler north-westerly than they had known, the five sail-of-the-line took station on their flagship and brought in another reef for the coming night. Each captain and lieutenant was very aware of the man whose flag floated from *Black Prince*'s foremast, and the need not to lose contact with him in the gathering darkness.

Keen had been going to ask Bolitho to sup with

him, but when the brig's commander had produced a letter for him he had decided otherwise.

It was to be a private moment, shared by nobody but the ship around him, and with Catherine. This was a man none of his captains would recognise, as he bent over his table and carefully opened her letter. He knew he would read it many times; and he found he was touching the locket beneath his shirt as he straightened the letter under a deckhead lantern.

Darling Richard, dearest of men, so short a while since we were parted and yet already a lifetime . . .

Bolitho stared around the cabin and spoke her name aloud. 'Soon, my love, soon . . .' And in the sea's murmur, he thought he heard her laugh.

CHAPTER SEVENTEEN

'YOU HOLD THEIR HEARTS...'

If the officers and men of Bolitho's North Sea squadron had expected a quick relief from the dragging boredom of blockade duty, they were soon to be disappointed. Weeks overlapped into months. Spring drove away the icy winds and constant damp of winter, and still they endured the endless and seemingly pointless patrols. Northward from the Frisian Islands, with the Dutch coast sometimes in view, often as far as the Skagerrak where Poland had fought his last battle.

Better than most Bolitho knew he was driving them hard, more so than they had probably ever endured before. Sail and gun drills, in line ahead or abreast to a minimum of signals. Then he had divided his squadron into two divisions with the clergyman-like Crowfoot's *Glorious* as senior ship of the other line. Bolitho had now been reinforced by the two remaining seventy-fours, *Valkyrie* and *Tenacious*, and a small but welcome addition of the schooner *Radiant*, the latter commanded by an elderly lieutenant who had once been with the revenue service.

Small *Radiant* might be, but she was fast enough to dart close inshore and make off again before an enemy patrol vessel could be roused enough to weigh anchor and come out to discourage her impudence.

Allday was shaving Bolitho one morning and for the first time since they had come aboard, the stern windows were open, and there was real warmth in the air. Bolitho stared up at the deckhead while the razor rasped expertly under his chin.

The blade stilled as he said, 'I suppose they hate my insides for all the drills I am forcing on them?'

Allday waited and then continued with his razor. 'Better this way, Sir Richard. It's fair enough in small craft, but in big ships like this 'un it's wrong to draw officers and sailors too close together.'

Bolitho looked at him curiously. *More wisdom.* 'How so?'

'"Tween decks they *needs* someone to hate. Keeps them on edge, like a cutlass to a grindstone!'

Bolitho smiled and let his mind drift again. Cornwall would be fresh again after the drab weather. Bright yellow gorse, sheets of bluebells along the little paths to the headland. What would Catherine be doing? He had received several letters in the courier brig; once he had three altogether, as

366

often happened with the King's ships constantly at sea. Catherine always made her letters interesting. She had dispensed with Somervell's property in London, and after paying off what sounded like a mountain of debts she had purchased a small house near the Thames. It was as if she had felt his sudden anxiety all the miles across the North Sea and had explained, 'When you must be in London, we will have our own haven—we shall be beholden to nobody.' She spoke too of Falmouth, of ideas which she and Ferguson had put in motion to clear more land, to make a profit, and not merely sustain its existence. She never mentioned Belinda, nor did she speak of the enormous amount of money Belinda required to live in the only style she had come to accept.

There was a knock at the outer door and Keen entered and said apologetically, 'I thought you should know, Sir Richard. Our schooner is in sight to the east'rd and is desiring to close on us.'

Allday dabbed Bolitho's face and watched the light in his eyes. There was no sign of injury. No change, he thought. So perhaps after all...

Bolitho said, 'News, d'you think, Val?'

Keen said impassively, 'She comes from the right direction.'

In Catherine's last letter she had mentioned her meeting with Zenoria. 'Tell Val to take heart. The love is as strong as before. It needs a sign.' Keen had taken the news without comment. Resigned, hopeful or desperate; whatever his emotions were, he hid them well.

When Allday had left them alone Bolitho exclaimed, 'In God's name, Val, how much longer must we beat up and down this barren coast waiting for some word? Every morning the horizon is empty but for our own companions, each sunset brings more curses from the people because of all this futility!'

There were more delays, while the schooner tacked this way and that before she could lie under *Black Prince*'s lee and drop her boat in the water.

Lieutenant Evan Evans had served with the Revenue cutters before joining the King's navy, but he looked more like a pirate than a law-abiding sailor. A great block of a man with rough grey hair which looked as if he cut it himself with shears, a brick-red face so battered and so ruined by hard drinking that he was a formidable presence even in Bolitho's great cabin.

Ozzard brought some wine but Evans shook his shaggy head. 'None o' that, beggin' yer pardon, Sir Richard—it plays hell with my gut!'

But when Ozzard produced some rum Evans drained the tankard in one swallow. 'More like it, see?'

Bolitho said, 'Tell me what you found.'

Together they walked to the table where Bolitho's own chart was spread with his personal log open beside it.

Evans put a finger as thick and as hard as a marlin spike on the chart and said, 'Three days back, Sir Richard. Makin' for the Bay o' Heligoland, she was, leastways 'twas a fair guess at her direction.'

Bolitho contained his impatience. Evans was reliving it. It would destroy the picture in his mind if he was goaded. It was strange to hear the local landmarks described in his rich Welsh accent.

Keen prompted gently, 'She?'

Evans glared at him and continued, 'Big as a cathedral, she was. Ship-o'-th'-line.' He shrugged heavily. 'Then two frigates came from nowhere, out o' th' sun to all intents. One was a forty-four.' He frowned, so that his bright eyes seemed to vanish into thick folds of skin.

Bolitho straightened his back and clasped his fingers together behind him. 'Did you see her name, Mr Evans?'

'Well, we were proper busy when she let fly with a bow-chaser, but my little schooner can show a clean pair o' heels as anyone will tell you . . .'

Bolitho remarked, 'She was *L'Intrépide*, was she not?'

The others stared at him and Keen asked, 'But how could you know, sir?'

'A premonition.' He turned from the table to conceal his face from them. It was here; he could feel it. Not just yet, but soon, quite soon.

'The larger vessel—how big, d'you think?'

Evans nodded to Ozzard and took another tankard of rum. Then he wiped his lips with the back of his rough hand and frowned. It seemed habitual.

'Well, I'm no real judge, but she were a liner right enough.' He glanced professionally around the cabin. 'Bigger'n this 'un, see?'

'*What?*' Bolitho turned back at Keen's sudden surprise and doubt. 'Must be a mistake, sir. I have read every word of those reports from the Admiralty. No ship larger than a seventy-four survived Trafalgar. They were either taken or destroyed in the gale that followed the battle.' He looked almost accusingly towards the wild-haired lieutenant. 'No agent has reported the building of

369

any vessel such as the one you describe.'

The lieutenant grinned. The burden was no longer his, and the rum was very good.

'Well, that's what I saw, Sir Richard, an' I've been at sea for twenty-five year. I were nine when I ran out o' Cardiff. Never regretted it.' He shot Keen a pitying glance. 'Long enough to know which is the sharp end o' a pike!'

Keen laughed, the strain leaving his face as he retorted, 'You are an impudent fellow, but I think I asked for it!'

Bolitho watched him, the news momentarily at arm's length. Only Keen would be man enough to make such an admission to a subordinate. It would never have occurred to Bolitho that he might have learned it from his own example.

Bolitho said, 'I want you to carry a despatch to Portsmouth. It could be urgent.'

Keen said, 'The Nore would be a shorter passage, sir.'

Bolitho shook his head, thinking aloud. 'They have the telegraph at Portsmouth. It will be faster.' He eyed Evans meaningly as he swallowed some more rum. 'I take it you have a reliable *mate*?'

It was not lost on the shaggy Welshman. 'I won't let you down, Sir Richard. My little schooner will be there by Monday.'

'There will be a letter also.' He met Evans' searching stare. 'I would appreciate if you send it by post-horse yourself. I shall pay you directly.'

The man grinned. 'God love you, no, Sir Richard. I know them buggers at Portsmouth Point an' they *owe* me a favour or two!'

Keen seemed to come out of his thoughts. 'I have a letter as well which could perhaps go with it, Sir
370

Richard?'

Bolitho nodded, understanding. If the worst happened he might never know Zenoria's love. It did not bear even thinking about.

'You are doing the right thing, Val,' he said quietly. 'My lady will ensure she receives it.'

By noon the schooner was under way again, watched with envy by those who knew her destination, and wished that their next landfall would be England.

While Bolitho and Keen thought about their respective letters, carried in the schooner's safe with the despatches, other smaller dramas were being enacted deep in the hull, as is the way with all large men-of-war.

Two seamen who had been working under the direction of Holland, the purser's clerk, to hoist a fresh cask of salt pork from the store, were squatting in almost total darkness, a bottle of cognac wedged between them. One of the men was Fittock, who had been flogged for insubordination. The other was a Devonian named Duthy, a ropemaker and, like his friend, an experienced seaman.

They were speaking in quiet murmurs, knowing they should not still be here. But like most of the skilled hands they disliked being cooped up with untrained ignorant landsmen who were *always bleating about discipline*, as Duthy put it.

He said, 'I'll be glad to swallow the anchor when me time's up, Jim, but I'll miss some of it, all the same. I've learned a trade out of the navy, an' provided I can stay in one piece...'

Fittock swallowed hard and felt the heat of the spirit run through him. No wonder the wardroom

371

drank it.

He nodded. '*Provided*, yes, mate, there's always that.'

'Yew think we'm goin' to fight, Jim?'

Fittock rubbed his back against a cask. The scars of the lash were still sore, even now.

He showed his teeth. 'You knows the old proverb, mate? If death rakes the decks, may it be like prize money.'

His friend shook his head. 'Don't understand, Jim.'

Fittock laughed. 'So that the officers get the biggest share!'

'*Now here's a fine thing!*'

They both lurched to their feet as someone slid the shutter from a lantern, and they saw Midshipman Vincent staring at them, his mouth lifted in a faint smile. Behind him, his cross-belt white in the gloom, was the ship's corporal.

Vincent said coldly, 'Just as well I came to complete the rounds.' The officer-of-the-watch had sent him after seeing the purser's clerk appear on deck alone, but he made it sound as if it was his own idea. 'Scum like you, Fittock, never learn, do you?'

Duthy protested, 'We weren't doin' nothin', sir. We was standin' easy, so to speak!'

'Don't lie to me, you pig!' Vincent thrust out his hand. 'Give me that bottle! I'll see your backbones for this!'

Anger, resentment, the scars on his back, and of course the cognac were part and parcel of what happened next.

Fittock retorted angrily, 'Think you can't do no wrong 'cause yer uncle's the vice-admiral, is that it?

Why, you little shite, I've served with 'im afore, an' you're not fit to be in the same ship as 'im!'

Vincent stared at him glassily. It was all going wrong.

'Corporal, seize that man! Take him aft!' He almost screamed. *That's an order, man!'*

The ship's corporal licked his lips and made as if to unsling his musket. 'Come on, Jim Fittock, you knows the rules. Let's not 'ave any trouble, eh?'

Feet scraped on the gratings between the casks and some white breeches moved into the lantern's glow.

Midshipman Roger Segrave said calmly, 'There'll *be* no trouble, Corporal.'

Vincent hissed, 'What the hell are you saying? They were drinking unlawfully, and when I discovered them—'

'They were "insubordinate", I suppose?' Segrave was astonished by his own easy tones. Like a total stranger's.

He said, 'Cut along, you two.' He turned to the corporal, who was staring at him, his sweating face full of gratitude. 'And you. I'll not be needing you.'

Vincent shouted wildly, 'What about the cognac?' But of course, like magic, it had vanished.

Fittock paused and looked him in the eyes, and said softly, 'I'll not forget.' Then he was gone.

'One more thing, Corporal.' The leggings and polished boots froze on the ladder. 'Close the hatch when you leave.'

Vincent was staring at him with disbelief. *'Are you mad?'*

Segrave tossed his coat to the deck. 'I used to know someone very like you.' He began to roll up his sleeves. 'He was a bully too—a petty little tyrant who made my life a misery.'

Vincent forced a laugh. In the damp, cool hold it came back as a mocking echo.

'So it was *all too much for you*, was it?'

Surprisingly, Segrave found that he could answer without emotion.

'Yes. It was. Until one day I met your uncle and a man with only half a face. After that I accepted fear—I can do so again.'

He heard the hatch thud into position. 'All this time I've watched you using your uncle's name so that you can torment those who can't answer back. I'm not surprised you were thrown out of the H.E.I.C.' It was only a guess but he saw it hit home. 'So now you'll know what it feels like!'

Vincent exclaimed, *'I'll call you out—'*

The smash of Segrave's fist into his jaw flung him down onto the deck, blood spurting from a split lip.

Segrave winced from the pain of the blow; all those years of humiliation had been behind it.

'Call me out, *sonny*?' He punched him again in the face as he scrambled to his feet, and sent him sprawling. 'Duels are for *men*, not pigmies!'

Four decks above them Lieutenant Flemyng, who was the officer-of-the-watch, took a few paces this way and that before glancing again at the half-hour glass by the compass box.

He beckoned to a boatswain's mate and snapped, 'Go and find that damned snotty, will you, Gregg? Skylarking somewhere, I shouldn't wonder.'

The man knuckled his forehead and made to hurry away, but was stopped by the harsh voice of Cazalet, the first lieutenant.

'Not just yet, Mr Flemyng!' He came from Tynemouth and had a voice which carried above the strongest gale.

Flemyng, who was the ship's third lieutenant, stared at him questioningly.

Cazalet smiled to himself and trained his glass on the old *Sunderland*. 'I think he should have a *mite* longer, don't you?'

★   ★   ★

Admiral the Lord Godschale flapped a silk handkerchief before his hawk-like nose and commented, 'The damn river is a bit vile this evening.'

He looked powerfully magnificent in his heavy dress coat and shining epaulettes, and as he stood watching the colourful throng of guests which overflowed the broad terrace of his Greenwich house he found time to reflect on his good fortune.

But it was extremely hot, and would remain so until night touched the Thames and brought some cool relief to the officers in their coats of blue and scarlet. Godschale watched the river winding its endless journey up and around the curve into Blackwall Reach, the ant-like movement of wherries and local craft. It was an imposing house and he was constantly grateful that the previous owner had sold so eagerly and reasonably. At the outbreak of war with France, as all the hideous news of the Terror had insinuated its way across the Channel, the former owner had taken his possessions and investments and had fled to America.

Godschale smiled grimly. So much for his faith in his country's defences at the time.

He saw the slight figure of Sir Charles Inskip threading his way through the laughing, jostling

375

guests, bobbing here, smiling there—the true diplomat. Godschale felt the return of his uneasiness.

Inskip joined him and took a tall glass of wine from one of the many sweating servants.

'Quite a gathering, m'lord.'

Godschale frowned. He had planned the reception with great care. People who mattered in society, evenly mixed with the military and those of his own service. Even the Prime Minister was coming. Grenville had only held office for a year and after Pitt, whatever people had said about him, he had been a disaster. Now they had a Tory again, the Duke of Portland no less, who would probably be even more out of touch with the war than Grenville had been.

He saw his wife deeply engaged in conversation with two of her closest friends. The latest gossip no doubt. It was hard to picture her as the lively girl he had first met when he had been a dashing frigate captain. Plain, and rather dull. He shook his head. Where had that girl gone?

He glanced at the other women nearest to him. The hot weather was a blessing as far as they were concerned. Bare shoulders, plunging dampened gowns which would never have been tolerated a few years ago in the capital.

Inskip saw his hungry expression and asked, 'Is it true that you have recalled Sir Richard Bolitho? If so, I think *we* should have been informed.'

Godschale ignored the careful criticism. 'Had to. I sent *Tybalt* for him. He anchored at the Nore two days ago.'

Inskip was unimpressed. 'I don't see how it will help.'

Godschale tore his eyes from a young woman whose breasts would have been bare if her gown had been stitched half an inch lower.

He said in a deep whisper, 'You've heard the news? Napoleon has signed a treaty with Russia and has had the damned audacity to *order*, if you please, *order* Sweden and Denmark to close their ports against us and to sever all trade. In addition France has demanded their fleets to be put at *their* disposal! God damn it, man, that would be close on two hundred ships! Why did nobody see the nearness of this sorry affair? Your people are supposed to have eyes and ears in Denmark!'

Inskip shrugged. 'What shall we do next, I wonder?'

Godschale tugged at his neckcloth as if it was choking him. '*Do?* I'd have thought it was obvious!'

Inskip recalled Bolitho's bitterness and contempt when *Truculent* had sighted the three Frenchmen.

He said, 'So that is why Bolitho will be here?'

Godschale did not answer directly. 'Admiral Gambier is even now assembling a fleet and all the transports we will need to carry an army across to Denmark.'

'*Invade?* The Danes will never be willing to capitulate. I think we should wait—'

'Do you indeed?' Godschale studied him hotly. 'D'you believe Denmark's sensibilities are more important than England's survival? For that is what we are talking about, dammit!' He almost snatched a glass from a servant and drained it in two gulps.

The orchestra had struck up a lively gigue but many of the guests seemed unwilling to leave the great terrace, and Godschale guessed why.

At the Admiralty this morning he had told

Bolitho of this reception, how it would prove an ideal setting where deeper matters of state might be discussed without arousing attention. Bolitho had replied calmly enough but had left no doubt as to his conditions.

He had said, 'There will be many ladies there, my lord. You will have not had time to arrange an "official" invitation for me as I am *ordered* here.'

Godschale spoke aloud without realising it. 'He simply stood there and told me he would not come here unless he could bring that woman!'

Inskip let out a deep breath of relief. He had imagined that Bolitho might have brought even worse news with him.

'Are you surprised?' Inskip smiled at Godschale's discomfort; Godschale, whom he had heard had a mistress or two in London. 'I have seen what Lady Somervell has done for Bolitho. I hear it in his voice, in the fire of the man.'

Godschale saw his secretary making signals from beside a tall pillar and exclaimed, 'The Prime Minister!'

The Duke of Portland shook their hands and glanced around at the watching eyes. 'Handsome levee, Godschale. All this talk of gloom—rubbish, is what I say!'

Inskip thought of Bolitho's men, the ordinary sailors he had seen and heard cheering and dying in the blaze of battle. They hardly compared with these people, he thought. His men were real.

The Prime Minister beckoned to a severe-looking man dressed in pearl-grey silk.

'Sir Paul Sillitoe.' The man gave a brief smile. 'My trusted adviser in this unforeseen crisis.'

Inskip protested, 'Hardly unforeseen—'

Godschale interrupted. 'I have had the matter under constant surveillance. There is a new squadron in the North Sea with the sole duty of watching out for some move by the French, any show of force towards Scandinavia.'

Sillitoe's eyes gleamed. 'Sir Richard Bolitho, yes? I am all eagerness to meet him.'

The Prime Minister dabbed his mouth. 'Not *I*, sir!'

Sillitoe regarded him impassively; he had hooded eyes, and his features remained expressionless.

'Then I fear your stay in high office will be as short as Lord Grenville's.' He watched his superior's fury without emotion. 'The French Admiral Villeneuve said after he was captured that at Trafalgar every English captain was a Nelson.' He shrugged. 'I am no sailor, but I know how they are forced to live, in conditions no better than a jail, and I am quite certain that they were inspired more by Nelson—enough to perform miracles.' He looked at them almost indifferently. 'Bolitho may not be another Nelson, but he is the best we have.' He turned as a ripple of excitement ran through the guests. 'Forget that at your peril, my friends.'

Godschale followed his glance and saw Bolitho's familiar figure, the black hair marked now by grey streaks in the lock above that savage scar. Then, as he turned to offer her his arm, Godschale saw Lady Catherine Somervell beside him. The mourning was gone, and the hair which was piled above her ears shone in the sunshine like glass. Her gown was dark green, but the silk seemed to change colour and depth as she turned and took his arm, a fan hanging loosely from her wrist.

She looked neither right nor left, but as her

glance fell on Godschale he swore he could feel the force of her compelling eyes, and a defiance which seemed to silence even the whispers which surrounded her and the tall sea-officer by her side.

Godschale took her proffered hand and bowed over it. 'Why, m'lady, *indeed* a surprise!'

She glanced at the Prime Minister and made a slight curtsy. 'Are we to be introduced?'

He began to turn away but Bolitho said quietly, 'The Duke of Portland, Catherine.' He gave a small bow. 'We are honoured.' His grey eyes were cold, and said the opposite.

Sir Paul Sillitoe stepped forward and introduced himself in the same flat voice. Then he took her hand and held it for several seconds, his gaze locked against hers. 'They say you inspire him, m'lady.' He touched her glove with his lips. 'But I believe you inspire England, through your love of him.'

She withdrew her hand and watched him, her lips slightly curved, a pulse flickering at her throat in the strong light. But when she had searched his face and found no sarcasm, she answered, 'You do me a great kindness, sir.'

Sillitoe seemed able to ignore all those around them, even Bolitho, as he murmured, 'The clouds are darkening again, Lady Catherine, and I fear that Sir Richard will be required perhaps more than ever before.'

She said quietly, 'Must it always be him?' She felt Bolitho's warning hand on her arm but gripped it with her own. 'I have heard of Collingwood and Duncan.' Her voice shook slightly. 'There must be others.'

Godschale was poised to interrupt, his carefully prepared words flying to the wind at her sudden, unexpected insistence. But Sillitoe said, almost gently, 'Fine leaders—they have the confidence of the whole fleet.' Then, although he glanced at Bolitho, his voice was still directed to her. 'But Sir Richard Bolitho holds their hearts.'

Godschale cleared his throat, uncomfortable at the turn the conversation had taken and especially because of the watching faces around the terrace. Even the orchestra had fallen silent.

He said too heartily, 'A sailor's lot, Lady Catherine—it demands much of us all.'

She looked at him, in time to see his eyes lift quickly from her bosom. 'Some more than *others*, it would appear.'

Godschale beckoned to a footman to cover his embarrassment. 'Tell the orchestra to strike up, man!' He gave a fierce grin at the Prime Minister. 'Are you ready, Your Grace?'

Portland glared at Sillitoe. 'You attend to it. I have no stomach for this kind of diplomacy! I will discuss the situation tomorrow, Godschale. There is much I have to do.'

Again he turned to leave but Bolitho said, 'Then I may not see you again before I sail?' He waited for Portland's attention. 'There are some ideas I would like to offer—'

The Prime Minister eyed him suspiciously, as if seeking a double meaning. 'Perhaps another time.' He turned to Catherine. 'I bid you good evening.'

As Godschale hurried after his departing guest Bolitho said in a savage whisper, 'I should never have brought you, Kate! They sicken me with their hypocrisy and over-confidence!' Then he said with concern, 'What is wrong—have I done something?'

She smiled and touched his face. 'One day you

are across the sea, and now you are here.' She saw his anxiety and tried to soothe it. 'It is far more important than their false words and posturing. When we drove here today, did you not see the people turn and stare—how they cheered when they saw us together? Always remember, Richard, they *trust* you. They know you will not abandon them without lifting a hand to help.' She thought of the impassive Sillitoe, a strange creature who could be friend or enemy, but who had spoken like a truthful man. 'You hold their hearts, he said.'

There was a small stone-flagged passageway which led out on to a quiet garden, with a solitary fountain in its centre. It was deserted; the music, the dancing and the wine were on the far side of the house.

Bolitho took her arm and guided her around some bushes, then held her closely against him.

'I must speak with them, Kate.' He saw her nod, her eyes very bright. 'And then we shall leave.'

'And *then?*'

He lowered his head and kissed her shoulder until she stirred in his arms, and he felt her heart beating to match his own.

'To the house on the river. Our refuge.'

She whispered, 'I want you. I *need* you.'

When Sir Paul Sillitoe and Inskip returned to the terrace with Godschale they found Bolitho watching a small barge as it was manoeuvred downriver past the Isle of Dogs.

Godschale said brightly, 'You are alone?'

Bolitho smiled. 'My lady is walking in the garden ... she had no wish to go amongst strangers on her own.'

Sillitoe studied him and said without a trace of

humour, 'She found it a trifle *stuffy*, I suspect?'

Godschale turned, irritated, as his wife plucked insistently at his gold-laced coat, and drew him aside.

'What *is* it?'

'I saw them! Together, just now, in the pine garden. He was fondling her, kissing her naked shoulder!' She stared at him, outraged. 'It is all true, what they say, Owen—I was so shocked I could not look!'

Godschale patted her arm to reassure her. She had seen quite a lot for one who would not look, he thought.

'Not for long, my dear!' He beamed at her but could not drag his thoughts from Catherine's compelling eyes, and the body beneath her dark green gown.

He saw Sillitoe pause to look back for him and said abruptly, 'I have to go. Important, *vital* matters are awaiting my attention.'

She did not hear. 'I'll not have that woman in my house! If she so much as speaks a word to me—'

Godschale gripped her wrist and said harshly, 'You will return the smile, or I shall know the reason, *my love*! You may despise her, but by God's teeth, she is right for Bolitho—'

She said in a small voice, 'Owen, *you swore*!'

He replied heavily, 'Go amongst your friends now. Leave the war to us, eh?'

'If you're certain, dearest?'

'Society will decide; you cannot flout it as you will. But in time of war—' He turned on his heel and fell in step beside his secretary. 'Anything further I should know?'

The secretary was as aware of his good fortune as

his master, and wanted it to remain that way. He said softly, 'That young woman, the wife of *Alderney*'s captain.' He saw the memory clear away Godschale's frown. 'She was here again to crave a favour on his behalf.' He paused, counting the seconds. 'She is a most *attractive* lady, my lord.'

Godschale nodded. 'Arrange a meeting.' By the time he reached the private study where the others were waiting, he was almost his old self again.

'Now, gentlemen, about this campaign...'

★   ★   ★

Bolitho opened the glass doors and stepped out on to the small iron balcony, watching the lights glittering along the Thames like fireflies. It was so hot and airless that the curtains barely moved. He could still feel the heat of their love, the endless demands they had made on one another.

Her words at Godschale's great house still lingered in his mind, and he knew they would keep him company when they were parted again. *One day you are across the sea, and now you are here.* So simply said, and yet so right. Set against it, even the unavoidable separation seemed less cruel. He thought of the people in their fine clothes, pressing forward to see them, to stare at Catherine as she passed through them. Her composure and grace had made their flushed faces empty and meaningless. He watched a tiny lantern moving across the river and thought of their first visit to Vauxhall Gardens ... they would return when they had more freedom. The house was small but well-proportioned, one in a terrace with a tree-lined square between it and the Thames-side walk.

Tomorrow he would have to leave for the Nore where *Tybalt* would be waiting. It was merely coincidence that *Tybalt* should be the frigate ordered to collect him from the squadron, then take him back. She had been the same vessel which had brought him home, still shocked by the loss of his old *Hyperion*. All else was different, he thought. The rugged Scots captain had gone to a seventy-four, his officers allotted to other ships where their experience, even among the youngest, would be priceless.

Bolitho was glad. Memories could be destructive, when he might need all his resolution.

He thought too of the squadron, which was still out in the North Sea, beating up and down, back and forth, waiting to learn the enemy's intentions, sifting information as fishermen will search for a good catch.

Whatever lay ahead of them, his experience or intuition must decide how they would all face it. It was like being in the hub of a great wheel. At first he had taught himself to reach out around him from the *Black Prince*'s poop or quarterdeck, placing names and faces, duties and reactions of the men who control a ship in battle. They would all know him by reputation or hearsay, but he must understand those closest to him in case the worst should happen. The sailing-master, and Cazalet the first lieutenant; the other officers who stood their watches day and night in all conditions; the gun-captains and the Afterguard. Like spokes reaching out and away to every deck and cranny in the ship.

And far beyond, to his individual captains in the line of battle, the others like Adam who roamed

385

beyond the vision of the lookouts to find evidence, clues which their vice-admiral might fit into the pattern, if indeed there was one. One thing was quite evident. If Napoleon did succeed in seizing the fleets of Denmark and Sweden, and some said there were over a hundred and eighty ships between them, the English squadrons, still reeling from the damage and demands made upon them since Trafalgar, would be swamped by numbers alone.

He had asked Godschale about Herrick's part in the overall plan. The admiral had tried to shrug it off, but when he had persisted had said, 'He will be in command of the escorts for the supply ships. A vital task.'

Vital? An old passed-over commodore like Arthur Warren at Good Hope could have done it.

Godschale had tried to smooth things out. 'He is lucky—he still has *Benbow* and his flag.'

Bolitho had heard himself retort angrily, '*Luck?* Is that what they call it in Admiralty? He's been a fighter all his life, a brave and loyal officer.'

Godschale had watched him bleakly, 'Highly commendable to hear so. Under the present, um—circumstances—I think it surprising you should speak out in this fashion.'

Damn the man! He gave a bitter smile as he remembered Godschale's confusion when he had told him that Catherine would accompany him to the levee.

The moon slipped out of a long coamer of cloud and brought the river to life, like the shimmering silk of Catherine's gown. In the little square he saw the tops of the trees touched with moonlight as if they were crowned with powdered snow.

He gripped the iron rail with both hands and

stared at the moon, which appeared to be moving independently, leaving the clouds behind. He did not blink, but continued to stare until he saw the misty paleness begin to form around and beside it. He dropped his gaze, his mouth suddenly dry. It was surely no worse. Or was that another delusion?

He felt the curtains swirl against his legs like frail webs, and knew she was with him.

'What is it, Richard?' Her hand moved between his shoulders, persuasive and strong, easing away his tension if not the anxiety.

He half-turned and slipped his arm beneath the long shawl which she had had made from the lace he had brought from Madeira. She shivered as if from a chill breeze as his hand moved across her nakedness, exploring her again, arousing her when she had believed it impossible after the fierceness of their passion.

He said, 'Tomorrow, we are separated.' He faltered, already lost. 'There is something I must say.'

She pressed her face to his shoulder and moved so that his hand could complete its exploration.

'At the funeral.' He could feel her looking at him, her breath warm on his neck as she waited for him. 'Before the coffin was covered, I saw you toss your handkerchief into the grave...'

She said huskily, 'It was the ring. *His* ring. I wanted no part of it after what happened.'

Bolitho had thought as much, but had been afraid to mention it. Was it that he could still harbour doubts, or had he not believed it possible that she could love him as she did?

He heard himself ask, 'Will you face more scandal and wear *my* ring, if I can find one beautiful

387

enough?'

She caught her breath, surprised at his request, and deeply moved that the man she loved without reservation, and who would be called to battle and possibly death if it was so decided, could still find it so dear and important.

She allowed him to take her inside the windows and stood looking at him while he removed her shawl, her limbs glowing in the light of two bedside candles.

'I will.' She gasped as he touched her. 'For we are one, if only in each other's eyes.' It had always been rare for her to shed tears, but Bolitho saw the wetness beneath her closed lashes as she whispered, 'We will part tomorrow, but I am strong. Now take me as you will. For you, I am *not* strong.' She threw back her head and cried as he seized her, 'I am your slave!'

★　　　★　　　★

When dawn broke over London, Bolitho opened his eyes and looked at her head on his shoulder, her hair in disorder and strewn across the pillow beside him. There were red marks on her skin although he could not remember how they had been caused, and her face, when he combed some hair from it with his fingers, was that of a young girl, with no hint of the unspoken anxieties they must always share.

Somewhere a clock chimed, and he heard the grind of ironshod wheels in the street.

Parting.

CHAPTER EIGHTEEN

FIRE AND MIST

Bolitho stood by the *Black Prince*'s stern windows and half listened to all the familiar sounds as she made more sail again and got under way. In the quarter gallery he could see the ghost-like reflection of the frigate *Tybalt*, as she stood off from the flagship and prepared to return to the Nore for orders.

Her new captain was doubtless relieved to have delivered his passenger without mishap or risk of any blame for delays, and that he could now resume his own individual role.

Bolitho thought of that last farewell in the house on the river. Catherine had wanted to drive with him to Chatham, but she had not pleaded when he had said, 'Go to Falmouth, Kate. You will be amongst friends there.' They had parted as passionately as they had lived together. But he could still see her. Standing on the stone steps, her eyes filling her face, her high cheekbones holding shadows as the sun reflected from the river.

Bolitho heard Ozzard banging about in the sleeping compartment: he seemed to be the only one of his little band who was actually glad to be back with the squadron.

Even Allday was unusually depressed. He had confided that when he had seen his son aboard *Anemone*, the younger man had confessed that he wanted to quit the navy after all. It was like a slap in the face for Allday. To discover a son he had known nothing about, to learn of his courage when he had first suspected him a coward, and then to see him made coxswain to Captain Adam Bolitho—it had been more from life than he had ever hoped.

His son, also named John, had explained that he wanted an end to war. He loved the sea, but he had said that there were other ways of serving it.

Allday had demanded to know what they might be, and his son had replied without hesitation, 'I want to fish, and one day own my own boat. Settle down with a wife—not like so many.'

Bolitho knew that last remark was what had really hurt him. *Not like so many*. His father, perhaps?

Allday had described his son's enthusiasm as he had relived their too-brief encounter after the battle. He had ended by saying, 'When he told me that Cap'n Adam agreed with him, I knew I was beaten.'

Maybe Allday had been comparing his own life, and what might become of him one day.

There was a knock at the outer door, and Keen entered and gave his hat to Ozzard.

'Come in, Val.' He watched him curiously. Keen looked more relaxed than for a long time. Even his face was untroubled by the duties which lay heavily on any squadron's flag-captain. Bolitho had carried a letter for him which Catherine had been holding in her care.

Bolitho said, 'You can scan these papers at your leisure, Val. But to cut it short, it seems that Admiral Godschale's prophesies and plans have been put into motion.' They crossed to the table and looked at the chart. 'A large fleet, including some of the ships released from Good Hope, has

390

been gathered at North Yarmouth in Norfolk. It's about the nearest anchorage of any size to Denmark. Admiral Gambier has hoisted his flag in *Prince of Wales*, and he has some twenty-five sail-of-the-line under his command.'

He smiled at Keen's alert profile. 'I gather the admiral originally intended to take *Black Prince* as his flagship, but he feared she would not be completed in time.' He became serious, thinking suddenly of Herrick as he said, 'There will be many transports and troopships—some will carry all the flat-bottomed boats they will need for landing the army, as well as artillery for laying siege. It will be the biggest combined operation since Wolfe took Quebec in fifty-nine.' He thought of the General at Good Hope and added slowly, 'Lord Cathcart commands the army, and I'm told he has some ten major-generals in company, one of whom is Sir Arthur Wellesley. I believe that Cathcart and many others will see this attack as a preparation for the eventual assault on Europe.'

Keen said gravely, 'Then God help the Danes.'

Bolitho slipped out of his heavy coat and tossed it onto a chair.

'We will remain on station until Gambier's fleet is through the Skagerrak, in case the French attempt to pounce on the supply vessels—it would leave the army high and dry if they succeeded! Then we follow in support.'

'As ordered, sir, Captain Crowfoot's *Glorious* is still with our second division to the north'rd.'

'I know.' He rubbed his chin vigorously. 'Have a signal repeated to *Anemone*, Val. Recall her to the squadron and I will send Adam with my despatches for Crowfoot. I think it best if we stand together until we know what is happening.'

As Keen made for the screen Bolitho asked, 'What *other* news, Val?'

Keen looked at him searchingly and then gave a huge grin. 'I have heard from Zenoria, sir.'

Bolitho gave a wry smile. 'I rather gathered so!'

'The date is arranged.' The words seemed to flood out of him. 'Lady Catherine's hand was in it, it seems. They talked together, and she has asked her to visit her at Falmouth.'

Bolitho smiled. 'I am glad to know it.' He walked around the table and clasped Keen's hands. 'There is nobody who better deserves the love and happiness she will offer.'

When Keen had gone to have the signal made which would eventually be repeated to *Anemone* beyond the horizon, Bolitho wondered what the two women had spoken of. Catherine had said little about it, but had obviously been very pleased about their meeting. Something in her tone had suggested that Zenoria's uncle, newly returned from the Indies, might have tried to discourage the marriage. Had he wanted the lovely girl with the moonlit eyes for himself, perhaps?

He went back to the canvas-covered folder, which he had carried in *Tybalt* in its lead-weighted bag in case they had run into a stronger enemy force again, and turned over the pages. A door opened and closed and he heard Jenour whispering, Yovell's deeper response. They were gathering around the wheel's hub again, the spokes waiting to reach out to other ships and different minds from the man who led them.

But Bolitho was seeing reality in the beautiful writing. Twenty thousand soldiers, artillery and mortars, with all the small vessels like bombs and gun-brigs to support their landings.

They would batter their way ashore between Elsinore and Copenhagen itself. If the Danes persisted against a long siege, that lovely city of green spires would be laid in ruins. It did not seem right. The Danes were good people who wanted only to be left alone.

Bolitho slammed the cover shut. But there was no other way. *So be it then.*

Keen returned and said, 'Signal made, sir. The visibility is good, so *Anemone* should be here before dusk.'

They were still discussing tactics and the correct wording of his orders to the squadron's captains when the midshipman-of-the-watch entered to report that *Anemone*'s topgallants were in sight.

Bolitho realised it was his nephew, and asked, 'How are you settled, Mr Vincent?' Then he saw a dark bruise on his cheek, and several scars around his mouth.

Vincent answered sulkily, 'I am well enough, Sir Richard.'

As he left the cabin Bolitho suggested mildly, 'A little altercation, no doubt?'

Keen shrugged. 'It is difficult sometimes to watch over all the young gentlemen at once, sir.'

Bolitho observed his discomfort and said, 'That young fellow is a bully, with a conceit as wide as this cabin. Because he is related to *me*, it makes no difference in matters of discipline. And I will share something else with you. He will never make lieutenant unless you believe in miracles!'

Keen stared at him, astonished by such frankness, and that Bolitho could still surprise him.

'It was a fight, sir. A sort of gunroom court of law. The other one was Mr Midshipman Segrave.'

Bolitho nodded slowly. 'I should have guessed. No one would understand better how to deal with a petty tyrant!'

The mood left him and he touched Keen's arm and grinned. 'Just be thankful you do not have to be the one to tell my sister Felicity!'

Lanterns were being lit when *Anemone* finally hove-to under *Black Prince*'s lee and rounded-up into the wind.

Yovell was sealing the despatches for Captain Crowfoot when the calls trilled at the entry port, and Keen led Adam aft to the great cabin.

Bolitho related the bones of what he had already explained to Keen.

'If the French make any show of strength or attempt to interfere with the attack or our supply vessels, I must know without delay. I will send word to *Zest* and *Mistral* at first light, but our little schooner can do it.'

Adam asked, 'What do they say in London about the big liner *Radiant* sighted?'

Keen said sharply, 'They do not believe it.'

Adam murmured, 'I do, sir.'

Bolitho watched him. Adam must return to his ship before darkness closed in and they took up their stations for the night. But something was wrong. He could hear it in Adam's voice; he had always been very close to this other nephew. He allowed himself to think it. *His brother's son.* There had been many times when Bolitho had wished he had been his own.

He said, 'Perhaps Lieutenant Evans did make a mistake.' He recalled how the Welshman had

394

swallowed the tankards of rum. 'But I trust him.'

Adam stood up. 'I had better go, Uncle.' He faced him, with troubled, restless eyes. 'If we fight, Uncle—you will take good care? For all our sakes?'

Bolitho embraced him. 'Only if you do the same.' He saw Keen leave the cabin to order his men to call Adam's gig and said quietly, 'You are worried about something, Adam. You may command a King's ship, but to me you are still the midshipman, you know.'

Adam forced a smile but it only made him look more wistful. 'It is nothing, Uncle.'

Bolitho persisted, 'If there is anything, please tell me. I will try to help.'

Adam turned aside. 'I know that, Uncle. It has always been my sheet-anchor.'

Bolitho accompanied him to the companion ladder while shadows between decks watched them pass in silence, thinking themselves invisible, or beneath their admiral's notice. How wrong they were.

Bolitho listened to the sea's subdued murmur and was conscious that this might be the last time he saw Adam before the sea-fight which every one of his senses had now warned him was imminent. He felt a sudden chill. *Perhaps the last time ever.*

He said, 'Allday told me about his son.'

Adam seemed to rouse himself from his mood. 'I was sorry, but in truth, he has no place in the line of battle. I understand how Allday must feel, but I also know that his son will fall in battle if he remains. I see the signs.'

Bolitho watched him in silence. It was like hearing somebody much older speaking from past experience. As if his dead father was still a part of

395

him.

'You are his captain, Adam—I suspect you know him much better than his father. A coxswain must be close to his commander. The nearest of all men maybe.' He saw Allday with the side-party, his bronzed face standing out in the slow sunset. *The nearest of men.*

'Side-party, *stand by*!'

That was Cazalet, another link in the chain of command. Keen, Cazalet, and the embattled midshipmen, drawing together as one company; in spite of the ship, or perhaps because of her.

Adam held out his hand. 'My warm wishes to Lady Catherine when next you write to her, Uncle.'

'Of course. We often speak of you.' He wanted to press him further, to drag out of Adam what was weighing him down. But he knew Adam was too much like himself, and would tell him only when he was ready.

Adam touched his hat and said formally, 'Your permission to leave the ship, Sir Richard?'

'Aye, Captain. God's speed go with you.'

The calls shrilled, and the side-boys waited at the foot of the ladder to steady the gig for a departing captain.

'I wonder what ails him, Val?'

Keen walked with him towards the poop, where he knew Bolitho would fret out his worries in a measured walk.

He smiled. 'A lady, I shouldn't wonder, sir. None of us is a stranger to the havoc they can create!'

Bolitho watched *Anemone*'s lower yards change shape in the gold light as her fore and main courses filled to the wind.

He heard Keen add admiringly, 'By God, if he can handle a fifth-rate like that, he should be more than a match for a saucy glance!'

Again he saw Allday standing by a tethered twelve-pounder; alone, despite the bustling shadows around him.

Bolitho nodded to Keen and climbed down to the quarterdeck.

'Ah, there you are, Allday!' Once again he saw the watching eyes, figures still unknown to him. How would he convince them when the time came?

In a quieter voice he said, 'Come aft and share a glass with me. I want to ask you something.'

Somehow he knew Allday was going to refuse; his pride and his hurt would leave him no choice.

He added, 'Come, old friend.' He sensed his uncertainty, even though Allday's features were now lost in shadow. 'You are not the only one who is lonely.'

He turned away, and heard Allday say awkwardly, 'I was just thinkin', Sir Richard. You takes risks all your life at sea—you fight, an' if Lady Luck favours you, you lasts a bit longer.' He gave a great sigh. 'An' then you dies. Is that all there is to a man?'

Lady Luck ... it reminded him of Herrick, the man he had once known.

He turned and faced him. 'Let us wait and see, eh, old friend?'

Allday showed his teeth in the shadows and shook his head like some great dog.

'I *could* manage a wet, Sir Richard, an' that's no error!'

Lieutenant Cazalet, who was about to do his evening rounds of the ship, paused by Jenour and watched the vice-admiral and his coxswain disappear down the companion ladder. 'A most unusual pair, Mr Jenour.'

The flag-lieutenant studied him thoughtfully. Cazalet was a competent officer, just what any captain needed, in a new ship more than ever. Beyond that, he decided, there was not much else.

He replied, 'I cannot ever imagine the one without the other, sir.'

But Cazalet had gone and he was alone again, mentally composing his next letter home about what he had just seen.

* * *

Captain Hector Gossage of the seventy-four gun *Benbow* moved restlessly about the ship's broad quarterdeck, his eyes slitted against the hard sunlight. Eight bells had just chimed out from the forecastle and the forenoon watch had been mustered; and yet already the heat seemed intense. Gossage could feel his shoes sticking to the tarred seams and silently cursed their snail's progress.

He stared across the starboard bow and saw the uneven line of twenty store and supply ships reaching away towards the dazzling horizon. A pitifully slow passage—their destination Copenhagen, to join Admiral Gambier's fleet in support of the army.

Gossage was not a very imaginative man but prided himself on *Benbow*, a ship which had been in almost continuous service for several years. Many of the seasoned hands and warrant officers had been in the ship since he had assumed command; it had been, if there was such a creature in the King's

398

navy, a happy ship.

He glanced at the open skylight, and wondered what his rear-admiral's mood would be when he eventually came on deck. Ever since he had received news of his wife's death, Herrick had changed out of all recognition. Gossage was prudent enough not to mention certain things which his rear-admiral had overlooked, or more likely forgotten. As flag-captain he might easily have the blame laid at his own door, and this he intended to avoid at all costs. He was nearly forty, and he had his sights set on a commodore's broad-pendant before another year had passed—the obvious step to flag rank which he cherished more than anything. Rear-Admiral Herrick had always been a reasonable superior, ready to listen, or even to use an idea which Gossage had put forward. Some admirals would bite your head off for so doing, then present the idea as their own. But not Herrick.

Gossage bit his lip and remembered the terrible nights at sea when Herrick had been incapable of speaking with any coherence. A man who had always taken his drink in moderation, and who had been quick to come down hard on any officer who saw wine and spirits as a prop for his own weakness.

He took a glass from the rack and levelled it on the wavering column of ships. Deep-laden, they were barely making a few knots, and with the wind veering due north overnight it would be another day before they entered the Skagerrak. A rich convoy, he thought grimly. Two hundred troopers of the light brigade and their horses, foot guards and some Royal Marines with all the supplies, weapons and powder to sustain an army throughout

399

a long siege. He turned away and felt his shoe squeak free of the melting tar. At this rate, the war would be over before they even reached Copenhagen.

He moved the glass slightly before the sunlight blinded him and made him blink the tears from his eye. He had seen *Egret*, the other escort, an elderly sixty-gun two-decker which had been brought out of retirement after many years as a receiving vessel. Then the sea-mist blotted her out again.

Relics, he thought with bitterness. Anything which would stay afloat long enough for their lordships' purposes.

At first light, the masthead lookout of one of the supply ships had sighted land far off on the starboard bow, a vague purple shadow which was soon hidden by the haze as the August sunshine changed the North Sea to an endless procession of undulating glass humps.

Lieutenant Gilbert Bowater climbed through the companion hatch and touched his hat vaguely.

'Rear-Admiral Herrick is coming up, sir.'

Even the piggy flag-lieutenant had entered into a conspiracy with the other officers to keep out of Herrick's way, and avoid another blistering scene like the time recently when Herrick had berated a midshipman for laughing on watch.

The forenoon watchkeepers straightened their backs and a master's mate peered unnecessarily at the compass.

Gossage touched his hat. 'Wind's still steady from the north, sir. The convoy's closed-up since dawn.'

Herrick walked to the compass box and turned over the limp, damp pages of the log. His mouth and throat were raw, and when he turned towards the sun he felt his head throb without mercy.

Then he shaded his eyes and looked at the ships which they had escorted all the way from North Yarmouth. A meaningless task, a burden more than a duty.

Gossage watched him warily, as a post-boy will study a dangerous hound.

'I have put the boatswain's party to blacking-down, sir. She'll be smart enough when we enter harbour.'

Herrick saw his flag-lieutenant for the first time. 'Nothing to *do*, Bowater?' Then he said, 'Don't let these ships straggle like a flock of sheep, Captain Gossage. Signal *Egret* to come about and take charge of them.' Once again, his anger overflowed like water across a dam. 'You should not need to be *told*, man!'

Gossage flushed and saw some of the men by the wheel glance at one another. He replied, 'There is a thick sea-mist, sir. It is difficult to maintain contact with her.'

Herrick leaned against the nettings and said heavily, 'It will take a month to repeat a signal along this line of grocery captains!' He swung round, his eyes red in the glare. 'Fire a gun, sir! That will wake *Egret* from her dreams!'

Gossage flung over his shoulder, 'Mr Piper! Call the gunner. Then have the larboard bow-chaser cleared away!'

It all took time, and Herrick could feel the heat rising from the deck to match the raw thirst in his throat.

'Ready, sir!'

Herrick gave a sharp nod and winced as the pain

jabbed through his skull. The gun recoiled on its tackles, the smoke barely moving in the humid air. Herrick listened to the echo of the shot going on and on as it ricocheted across each line of rollers. The supply ships continued on their haphazard course as if nothing had happened.

Herrick snapped, 'A good man aloft, *if* you please. As soon as *Egret* is in sight I wish to know of it!'

Gossage said, 'If we had retained our frigate—'

Herrick looked at him wearily. 'But we did not. *I* did not. Admiral Gambier so ordered it once we had reached this far. The North Sea squadron is also with him by now.' He waved one hand around him. 'So there is only us, and this melancholy collection of patched-up hulks!'

A dull bang echoed over the ship and Gossage said, '*Egret*, sir. She'll soon harry them together!'

Herrick swallowed and tugged at his neckcloth. 'Signal to *Egret* immediately. *Close on the flag.*'

'But, sir—' Gossage glanced at the others as if for support. 'She will lose more time, and so shall we.'

Herrick rubbed his eyes with his hands. He had not slept for so long that he could scarcely remember what it was like. Always he awoke with the nightmare which instantly froze into reality and left him helpless. Dulcie was dead. She would never be there to greet him again.

He said sharply, '*Make the signal.*' He walked to the poop ladder and peered over the side. 'That shot came from yonder, not from *Egret*.' He was suddenly quite calm, as if he was somebody else. The air quivered again. 'Hear it, Captain Gossage? What say you now?'

Gossage gave a slow nod. 'My apologies, sir.'

402

Herrick eyed him impassively. 'You hear what you want to hear. It is nothing new.'

Lieutenant Bowater murmured nervously, 'The merchantmen are drawing into line, sir.'

Herrick smiled bleakly. 'Aye, they smell the danger.'

Gossage felt that he was going mad. 'But how can it *be*, sir?'

Herrick took Dulcie's telescope and levelled it carefully across the quarter as *Egret*'s topsails appeared to float, unattached, above a bank of white mist. He said, 'Perhaps Sir Richard was right after all. Maybe we were all too stupid, or too stricken to listen to him.' He sounded detached, indifferent even, as a midshipman yelled, '*Egret*'s acknowledged, sir!'

Then he said, 'The North Sea squadron is no longer on station.' He trained the splendid telescope on the nearest merchantman. 'But the convoy is still our responsibility.' He lowered it and added irritably, 'Signal *Egret* to make more sail, and take station ahead of the flag.' He watched as Bowater and the signals midshipman called their numbers and sent the bright bunting soaring up the yards.

One hour, then two dragged past in the melting heat. A faulty challenge? An exchange between privateer and smuggler? Each was a possibility.

Herrick did not glance up as the masthead shouted, 'Deck there! Land on the lee bow!'

Gossage remarked, 'Another hour or so and we shall be in sight of the Skagerrak, sir.' He was beginning to relax, but slowly. Herrick's unpredictable temper was having its effect.

'Deck there! Sail on the starboard quarter!'

Men ran across, and a dozen telescopes probed

the blinding mirrors of water and the gentle mist.

There was something like a gasp of relief as the lookout cried, 'Brig, sir! She wears our colours!'

Herrick contained his impatience while he watched the brig as she beat this way and that to close with the flagship.

The signals midshipman called, 'She's the *Larne*, sir. Commander Tyacke.'

Herrick screwed up his eyes to clear his aching brain. *Larne?* Tyacke? They triggered off a memory, but he could not quite grasp it.

Gossage exclaimed, 'God, *she*'s been mauled, sir!'

Herrick raised his telescope and saw the brig rise up as if from the sea itself. There were holes in her fore topsail, and several raw scars in the timbers near her forecastle.

'She's not dropping a boat, sir.' Gossage sounded tense again. 'She's going to close with us to speak.'

Herrick moved the glass still further and then felt the shock run through him. He could see the sunlight glinting on the commander's single epaulette, the way he was clinging to the shrouds, a speaking-trumpet already pointing towards the *Benbow*.

But his face ... even the distance could not hide its horror. It was like being drenched with icy water as the memory flooded back. Tyacke had been with Bolitho at Cape Town. The fireship, the escaping French frigate—his head reeled with each revelation.

'*Benbow* ahoy!' Herrick lowered the glass and thankfully allowed the man's identity to fall back into the distance. '*The French are out!* I have met with two sail-of-the-line and three others!'

Herrick snapped his fingers and took a

speaking-trumpet from the first lieutenant.

'This is Rear-Admiral Herrick! What ships did you see?' Each shouted word made his brain crack.

The man's powerful voice echoed across the water and Herrick thought it sounded as if he were laughing. A most unseemly sound.

'I didn't wait to discover, sir! They were eager to dampen my interest!' He turned away to call some commands as his brig slewed dangerously across *Benbow*'s quarter. Then he shouted, 'One is a second-rate, sir! No doubt of that!'

Herrick faced inboard and said, 'Tell him to carry word to Sir Richard Bolitho.' He stopped Gossage and revised it. 'No. To Admiral Gambier.'

He walked to the compass and back again, then glanced at the old *Egret*'s pyramid of tanned canvas which seemed to tower directly beyond *Benbow*'s jib-boom. He saw all and none of it. They were things and moments in his life too familiar to comment on. Even the old cry, *The French are out!* could not move him any more.

Gossage came back, breathing hard as if he had just been running.

'The brig's making more sail, sir.' He eyed him despairingly. 'Shall I order the convoy to scatter?'

'Have you forgotten *Zest*'s captain so soon, man? Waiting somewhere for his wretched court-martial? They once executed an admiral for failing to press home an attack—d'you imagine they would even hesitate over Captain Varian?' *Or us*, he thought, but did not say it.

He looked for the little brig but she was already tacking around the head of the column. The man with the horribly disfigured face might find Gambier or Bolitho by tomorrow. It was probably

405

already pointless.

But when he spoke again, his voice was steady and unruffled.

'Signal the convoy to make more sail and maintain course and distance. Spell it out *word by word* if you have to, but I want each master to know and understand the nearness of danger.'

'Very well, sir. And then . . . ?'

Herrick was suddenly tired, but knew there would be no respite.

'*Then*, Captain Gossage, you may beat to quarters and clear for action!'

Gossage hurried away, his mind groping for explanations and solutions. But one thing stood out above all else. It was the first time he had seen Herrick smile since his wife had died. As if he no longer had anything to lose.

★　　★　　★

Captain Valentine Keen held his watch against the compass light, then glanced around at the shadowy figures on the quarterdeck. It was strange and unnerving to hear and see the flash of cannon fire from the land while *Black Prince* lay at anchor, another cable run out from aft so that they could kedge her round to use at least one broadside against attack.

When there was a lull in the bombardment Keen felt blind, and could sense the tension around him. A boat was hooked on to either cable, with Royal Marines crouched over the bulwarks armed with muskets and fixed bayonets in case some mad volunteer attempted to swim out and cut them adrift. Other marines lined the gangways, while the

406

swivel guns were loaded and depressed towards the black, swirling current of Copenhagen's great harbour.

The first part of the attack had gone well. The fleet had anchored off Elsinore on the twelfth of August; there had been no opposition despite the presence of so many men-of-war. Three days later the army had begun to advance on the city. The closer they got the heavier became the Danish opposition, and in the last attack the navy had been savaged by a fleet of *praams*, each mounting some twenty powerful guns, and a flotilla of thirty gunboats. They were eventually driven off after a fierce engagement, and the military and naval batteries ashore were soon repaired.

Keen looked up as Bolitho crossed the quarterdeck, and guessed he had not slept.

'It is timed to begin soon, Val.'

'Aye, sir. The army have got their artillery in position. I heard they have seventy mortars and cannon laid on Copenhagen.'

Bolitho looked around in the darkness. *Black Prince* had followed Gambier's main fleet to Elsinore and had soon been engaged with the Danish guns of the Crown Battery. It was not that much different from their other attack on Copenhagen, except that here they were fighting small craft and shadows, while the army pressed forward against persistent and dogged resistance.

Two divisions of sail-of-the-line were anchored between the defenders and the Danish fleet, most of which appeared to be laid up in ordinary or in a state of repair, perhaps to appease the English and French predators.

In the midst of the bombardments and the far-off

407

forays of cavalry and infantry, Lord Cathcart, the commander-in-chief, had found time to grant passports to the Princess of Denmark and the King's nieces to travel safely through the English lines, '*So that they could be spared the horrors of a siege.*'

When Keen had remarked on the effect that might have on Danish morale, Bolitho had answered with sudden bitterness, 'King George the Second was the last British monarch to lead his army into battle—at Dettingen, I think it was. I doubt if we'll ever see such a thing again in our lifetimes!'

He winced as the whole sky burst into flame and the systematic bombardment started. To add to the horror, powerful Congreve rockets were soon falling on the city, disgorging their deadly loads of fire, so that within the hour many of the buildings nearest the waterfront were ablaze.

Keen said between his teeth, 'Why don't the Danes strike? They have no chance!'

Bolitho glanced at him and saw his face flickering in the red and orange reflections, while the hull, deep beneath them, shook to each fall of shot.

The Danes, he thought. No one ever referred to them as the enemy.

'*Boat ahoy! Stand off, I say!*'

Marines ran along the deck and Bolitho saw a boat pause abeam, rocking gently in the current and laid bare by the lurid flash of rockets.

There were white-cross belts visible, and someone yelled at the sentries to hold their fire. Another moment, and the nervous marines would have poured a volley into the boat.

An officer stood in the sternsheets and cupped his

hands, pausing between each roar of explosions to make himself understood.

'*Sir Richard Bolitho!*' A pause. 'The Admiral-Commanding sends his compliments, and would you join him in the flagship?'

'What a time to choose!' Bolitho glanced round and saw Jenour with Allday close by. To Keen he said, 'I will go across in the guardboat. It must be urgent not to keep until dawn.'

They hurried to the entry port where the boat had eventually been allowed to hook on.

Bolitho said tersely, 'You know what to do, Val. Cut the cables if you are attacked—use the boats if necessary.'

Then he was down in the guardboat and pressed between Jenour and the officer-of-the-guard.

As they pushed off from *Black Prince*'s massive, rounded hull someone thrust his head through an open gunport and yelled, 'You get us out o' this, eh, Our Dick?'

The officer snapped, 'Damned impertinence!'

But Bolitho said nothing; he was too moved for words. It was like being pulled across liquid fire, with anonymous pieces of charred wood tapping against the hull, and falling ashes hissing into the water.

Admiral Gambier greeted him in his usual distant manner.

'Sorry to drag you over, Sir Richard. Your squadron may be sorely needed tomorrow.'

Bolitho's hat was taken away and replaced by an ice-cold glass of hock.

Admiral Gambier glanced aft towards his quarters. All the screen doors were open to the warm air, and smoke drifted in and out of the gunports as if a fireship were already alongside.

The great cabin seemed to be packed with blue and scarlet coats, and Gambier said with obvious disapproval, 'All congratulating themselves—before the Danes surrender!'

Bolitho kept his face impassive. *The Danes* again.

Gambier jerked his head. 'We are using my captain's quarters. Bit quieter.'

In the cabin, similar but older than Keen's in the *Black Prince*, all but one lantern were extinguished. It made the stern windows burn and spark like the gateway to hell.

Gambier nodded to a midshipman and snapped, 'Fetch him!' Then he said, 'Damned glad of those vessels you managed to poach from Good Hope. The Captain of the Fleet never stops talking about it.'

There were footsteps on the outer deck and Gambier said quietly, 'I must warn you, this officer's face is most hideously wounded.'

Bolitho swung round. 'James Tyacke!'

Gambier muttered, 'Never mentioned that he knew you. Odd fellow.'

Tyacke came into the cabin, ducking beneath the deckhead beams until Bolitho gripped his hands warmly in his.

Gambier watched. If he were impressed he did not reveal it. He said, 'Give Sir Richard your news, Commander.'

As Tyacke described his sighting of the French ships, and his later meeting with Herrick's convoy, Bolitho could feel the anger and dismay crowding in from the flashing panorama beyond the ship.

Gambier persisted, 'You are certain, Commander?'

Tyacke turned from the shadows and momentarily displayed his ravaged face.

'A second-rate, possibly larger, and another sail-of-the-line astern of her. There were others too. I had no opportunity to linger.'

Gambier said, 'This is a small-ship war now that the army is ashore, Sir Richard. I did not anticipate that Rear-Admiral Herrick would need further protection. It seems I was wrong, and should have left your squadron on its station until—'

Bolitho interrupted sharply, 'Do you think they've found the convoy?'

Tyacke shrugged. 'Doubt it. But they will, if they maintain their course and speed.'

Bolitho looked at the admiral. 'I am asking you to allow me to order my squadron to sea, sir.'

Gambier eyed him severely. 'Impossible. Out of the question. In any case, most of your ships are to the east'rd in the Baltic approaches. It would take two days, longer, to get them in pursuit.'

Tyacke said bluntly, 'Then the convoy will perish, sir, as will its escorts.'

The admiral frowned as a gust of laughter came up from his quarters. 'People are dying over there! Do they care for no damned thing!'

He seemed to make up his mind. 'I will release your flagship. You can have one other—*Nicator*, as she is moored with you. Poor old girl will probably fall apart if she is called to battle!' Then he exclaimed, 'But there is no one to guide you through the Sound.'

Bolitho said desperately, 'I did it before, under Nelson's flag, sir.'

Tyacke remarked calmly, 'I'll lead the way, Sir Richard. If you'll have me.'

411

Gambier followed them to the side and said to his own captain, 'Would you say I am an easy man to serve?'

The captain smiled. 'Fair, sir.'

'Not the same.' He watched the guardboat speeding across the water, one minute in total darkness, the next illuminated so brightly in the falling Congreve rockets that he could see every detail.

Then he said, 'Just now, in my own flagship, I felt that *he* was in command, not I.'

The flag-captain followed him aft towards the din of voices. It was a moment he would savour all his life.

Back aboard *Black Prince*, Bolitho rapped off his orders as if they had been lurking there in his mind.

'Send a boat to your old ship, Val. She's to weigh and follow without delay.' He gripped his arm. 'I'll not have any arguments. *Larne* will lead us out. I *said* this might happen, damn them!'

The great three-decker seemed to burst alive as calls trilled between decks and men ran to their stations for leaving harbour. Anything was better than waiting and not knowing. They would not care whatever the reason. They were leaving. Bolitho thought of the unknown wag who had called out in the darkness.

The capstan was clanking busily, and he knew that the kedge-anchor would soon be hoisted inboard.

A lantern moved across the water, and occasionally Bolitho saw the brig's sturdy shadow as she made ready to take the lead.

Two great rockets fell together on the city, lighting up the sky and the ships in a withering fireball.

Bolitho had been about to call for Jenour when it happened. As the fire died away he took his hand from his injured eye. It was like looking through clouded water, or a misted glass. He lowered his head and murmured, '*Not now*. Not yet, dear God!'

'*Cable's hove short, sir!*'

Keen's voice was harsh in the speaking-trumpet. 'How does the cable grow, Mr Sedgemore?' Then he paused until the next flash so that he could see the angle of the lieutenant's arm. There was not much room, especially in the darkness. He needed to know how the ship, *his* ship, would perform when she tore free of the ground.

Cazalet bellowed, '*Loose tops'ls!*' A few paces aft. 'Stand by, the Afterguard!'

Black Prince seemed to tilt her lower gunports close to the black water as the cry came drifting aft.

'*Anchor's aweigh*, sir!'

Bolitho gripped the tarred nettings and tried to massage his eye.

Jenour asked in a whisper, 'May I help, Sir Richard?'

He cringed as Bolitho swung on him, and waited for the stinging retort.

But Bolitho said only, 'I am losing my sight, Stephen. Can you keep a secret so precious to me?'

Overcome, Jenour could barely answer, but nodded vigorously, and did not even notice a boat pulling frantically from under the black figurehead while the ship continued to swing round.

Bolitho said, '*They must not know*.' He gripped his arm until Jenour winced with the pain. 'You are a dear friend, Stephen. Now there are other friends out there who need us.'

413

Keen strode towards them. 'She answers well, sir!' He glanced from one to the other, and knew what had happened. 'Shall I send for the surgeon?'

Bolitho shook his head. Maybe it would pass; perhaps when daylight found them, it would be clear again.

'No, Val ... too many know already. Follow *Larne*'s sternlight and put your best leadsmen in the chains.'

Allday materialised from the darkness, holding out a cup. 'Here, Sir Richard.'

Bolitho swallowed it and felt the black coffee, with a mixture of rum and something else, steady his insides so that he could think again.

'That was more than welcome, old friend.' He handed him the cup and thought of Inskip. 'I am over it now.'

But when he looked at the burning city again, the mist was still there.

CHAPTER NINETEEN

TRUE COLOURS

With her great yards braced so hard round that to a landsman they might appear to lie fore-and-aft, *Black Prince* steered as close-hauled to the wind as was possible. For most of the previous night they had clawed their way up the narrow Sound from Copenhagen, pursued all the while by the continuous thunder of the bombardment.

Somehow *Nicator* had held station on the flagship, but for *Black Prince*, a powerful three-decker, it had been a trial of nerves as well as skill. Urgent voices had passed each sounding aft from the leadsmen in the forechains, and at one time Bolitho had sensed that only a few feet lay between the ship's great keel and disaster.

Dawn had found them heading out into the Kattegat, still comparatively shallow, but after the Sound it felt like the Western Ocean. Later, when Bolitho watched the pink glow on the choppy water, he knew that darkness would be upon them early that night. A glance at the masthead pendant assured him that the wind was holding steady, north-east. It would help them tomorrow, but had he waited until daylight as Gambier had suggested, the wind's sudden veer would have bottled them up in harbour. He thought of Herrick for the hundredth time. *Lady Luck.*

Keen crossed the deck and touched his hat, his handsome features raw from a full day on deck in chill wind.

'Any further orders before nightfall, sir?'

They looked at one another, like friends across a common garden wall at the close of an ordinary day.

'It will be tomorrow, Val. Or not at all. You know what these supply convoys are like, the speed of the slowest vessel in it, necessary for mutual protection. Rear-Admiral Herrick's convoy apparently numbers some twenty ships, so if there *was* a battle, some of the fastest must surely have reached the Skagerrak at least by now?' He forced a smile. 'I realise you think me morbid, even mad. Herrick will probably doff his hat to us at first light tomorrow, and sail past full of noble contentment!'

Keen watched him, the man he had come to know so well.

415

'May I ask something, sir?' He glanced round as the calls twittered in the endless daily life of a man-of-war: *Last dogwatchmen to supper!*

'Ask away.' He saw the gulls pausing to rest on the pink water like flower petals and thought of the dead Captain Poland, who had seen nothing but the path to duty.

'If you were in Rear-Admiral Herrick's position, what would *you* do, if an enemy second—or even first-rate as it now appears—and other vessels hove in sight?'

Bolitho looked away. 'I would scatter the convoy.' He looked at him again, his eyes dark in the strange glare. 'Then I would engage the enemy. A waste of time . . . who knows? But some might survive.'

Keen hesitated. 'But you do not think *he* would order them to break formation, sir?'

Bolitho took his arm and guided him a few paces past the big double-wheel, where Julyan the tall sailing-master was speaking to his mates in his deep rumbling tones. *Worth his weight in gold*, Keen had claimed several times; he had certainly proved his skill with wind, tide and rudder when they had struggled up the Sound.

'I am concerned, Val. If the enemy is searching for his ships, he will see it as something . . .' He groped for the word but saw only Herrick's stubborn eyes.

'A personal thing, sir?'

'Aye, that's about the strength of it.'

A sickly smell of pork came from the galley funnel and Bolitho said, 'After both watches have eaten, have the ship cleared for action. But keep the galley in use until the last. More warm bellies than

416

steel have won battles in the past, Val!'

Keen gazed along the broad length of his command, seeing it probably already enmeshed in the chaos and destruction of close-action.

'I agree.' He added suddenly, 'Your Mr Tyacke could be right about the largest Frenchman, but then precious few know about *Black Prince* as yet—she is far too new.'

The officer-of-the-watch glanced at Keen and cleared his throat impressively.

'A chill, Mr Sedgemore?' Keen grinned with easy humour. 'You wish to have the watch relieved?'

They both turned, startled, as Bolitho interrupted sharply, *'What did you say?'*

He stared at Keen's bewilderment. 'About *Black Prince*'s unknown strength?'

'Well, I simply thought—'

'And I did *not*.' Bolitho glanced up at the ensign curling above his head. 'You have a good sailmaker?'

The watch was changing, but they stood quite alone in the midst of its quiet disorder.

'Aye, sir.'

'Then please ask him to lay aft.' He watched the soft light of a northern dusk. 'This needs to be quick. I must pass word to Captain Huxley before we adopt night-stations!'

Keen sent a midshipman off at the double. Bolitho would explain. Perhaps when he had decided for himself what he intended.

Black Prince's sailmaker's name was Fudge. He was so like the many of his profession that he might have been cut from the same bolt of canvas. Bushy grey hair and sprouting eyebrows, and the familiar leather jerkin which was hung about with tools, thread, needles and, of course, a palm or two.

'This is he, sir.'

They all looked at him in silence. Keen, the officer-of-the-watch, midshipman and master's mates.

Fudge blinked his watery eyes.

'Aye, sir?'

Bolitho asked, 'Can you make me a Danish ensign, Fudge—full-scale, not some trifling boat-pendant?'

The man nodded slowly, visualising his stocks, neatly stored in one of the holds.

He answered, 'Foreign, then, Sir Richard?'

Lieutenant Sedgemore opened his mouth to add a sharp comment of his own, but Keen's glance left it unspoken.

Bolitho said, 'Foreign. White cross on red ground, with two tails like a commodore's broad-pendant.'

Fudge said, 'I was in *Elephant* with Nelson at Copenhagen, Sir Richard.' The bent back and stiffness of his trade seemed to fall away as he glanced around at the silent watchkeepers. 'I *knows* what a Danish flag look like, sir!'

Bolitho smiled. 'So be it. When can you provide it for me?'

Fudge showed his uneven teeth, surprised at being asked.

'No more'n a couple o' days, Sir Richard!'

'This is very important, Fudge. Can I have it by dawn?'

Fudge studied him feature by feature, as if to find an answer to something.

'I'll begin now, Sir Richard.' He looked around at the seamen and Royal Marines, as if they were of

418

some inferior race. 'Leave it to me!'

As Fudge bustled away Keen asked quietly, 'Some deception, sir?'

'Aye, mebbee.' He rubbed his hands together as if they were cold. 'A favour, Val.' He glanced at the shimmering reflection on the water, the first hint of sunset. He held his hand over his left eye and said, 'I would like to walk through your ship with you, if I may?'

It was like sighting a signal from a far-off frigate. An end to speculation. *It was tomorrow.*

Keen said, 'Of course, sir.'

'But first, please signal *Larne* to close on us. I shall have a written instruction for your old ship, Val—there will be no time later on. *Larne* can then haul up to windward. If the French do come, they will surely recognise Tyacke's brig and may decide to stand away. Whatever that French ship is, *I want her.*'

'I see, sir.' He beckoned to Jenour. 'A signal for you!'

It was a short note, which Bolitho wrote in his own hand while Yovell waited in the pink glow, ready to apply the seal before putting it into an oilskin bag for *Nicator*'s captain.

Then he said to Keen, 'It is fair that you should know a part of what I wrote. Should I fall, you will assume command; and if *Black Prince* is overwhelmed, Captain Huxley is to take *Nicator* out of the fight and return to Admiral Gambier.' He watched Keen gravely. 'Did I forget anything?'

'I think not, sir.'

Later, as the last dogwatchmen were finishing their evening meal, Bolitho and Keen, accompanied by the ship's junior lieutenant and, of course,

419

Allday, went slowly along each deck and down every companion ladder into the very bowels of the ship.

Many of the startled seamen at their mess tables started to rise at the unheralded tour, but each time Bolitho waved them down.

He paused to speak to some of them and was surprised at the way they crowded around him. To see what he was like? To assess their own chances of survival; who could tell?

Pressed men and volunteers, hands from other ships, dialects which told their own stories. Men from Devon and Hampshire, Kent and Yorkshire, 'foreigners' too, as Fudge would describe any one from north of the border.

And of course a man from Falmouth, who said awkwardly before his grinning messmates, 'O' course 'ee won't know me, Sir Richard—name o' Tregorran.'

'But I knew your father. The blacksmith near the church.' For a brief instant he laid his hand on the man's shoulder while his mind sped on wings back to Falmouth. The man Tregorran stared at the two lines of gold lace on Bolitho's sleeve as if he had been mesmerised.

'He was a good man.' The mood left him. 'Let's hope we'll all be back home soon after this, lads!'

The overcrowded messdeck was stuffy now with the gunports sealed to contain the familiar smells of tar, bilge and sweat; a place where no tall man could stand upright, where their lives began and too often ended.

He climbed up the last of the companion ladders and some of the men stood to cheer, their voices following him, deck by deck, like other men he had known and commanded over the years; waiting perhaps for him to join them in that other world.

Allday saw his face and knew exactly what he was thinking. Roughknots, thieves and villains, alongside the innocent and the damned. England's last hope. *Only* hope—that was what he was thinking right now.

A midshipman's grubby breeches caught the lamplight on the ladder and there was a quick, whispered conversation, before the lieutenant who had accompanied the unorthodox tour said, 'Mr Jenour's respects, sir!' He was looking at Keen but was very aware of his vice-admiral. 'The signal-bag has been passed to *Nicator*.'

He licked his lips as Bolitho remarked, 'All or nothing.' Then he said, 'You are Lieutenant Whyham, are you not?' He saw the youthful officer nod uncertainly. 'I thought as much, but did not wish to lose the use of memory!' He smiled, as if this were a casual meeting ashore. 'One of my midshipmen in *Argonaute* four years ago, correct?'

The lieutenant was still staring after him as Bolitho and Keen climbed into the cooler air of the upper deck. After the sealed messes it tasted like wine.

Keen said, uncertainly, 'Will you sup with me tonight, sir? Before they pull the ship apart and clear for action?'

Bolitho looked at him calmly, still moved by the warmth of those simple men who had nothing but his word to hold onto.

'I would relish that, Val.'

Keen removed his hat and pushed his fingers through his fair hair. Bolitho half-smiled. The midshipman again, or perhaps the lieutenant in the

421

Great South Sea.

'What you said in your instructions to *Nicator*'s captain. It makes one realise, but not accept, how narrow that margin is. Now when I think I have everything I ever wanted ...' He did not go on. He did not need to. It was as if Allday had just repeated what he had said before. *'An' then you dies...'*

Keen could have been speaking for both of them.

*   *   *

At the very first hint of life in the sky *Black Prince* seemed to come slowly into her own. Like men from forgotten sea-fights and long-lost wrecks, her seamen and marines emerged from the darkness of gundeck, orlop or hold, quitting that last pretence of privacy and peace which is the need of all men before a battle.

Bolitho stood on the quarterdeck's weather side and listened to the awakening thud of bare feet and the clink of weapons around and below him. Keen had done his work well: not a pipe given, no beat of drum to inflame the heart and mind of some poor soul who might imagine it was his last memory on earth.

It was as if the great ship herself was coming alive, her company of eight hundred sailors and sea-soldiers merely incidental.

Bolitho watched the sky, his eye at ease in the darkness. First light was not far off, but for the present it was only anticipation, a sense of uneasiness like the sea's deceptive smile before a raging gale.

He tried to imagine the ship as the enemy would gauge her. A fine big three-decker with her rightful

422

Danish ensign flying directly beneath the English one, to announce her true state to the world. But it needed more than that. Bolitho had used many ruses in his time, especially when employed as a frigate captain, and had been caught out by almost as many triggered against himself. In a war which had lasted so long and killed so many men on all sides and of all beliefs, even the normal could not be accepted at face-value.

If the day went against them, the price would be doubly high. Keen had already passed his orders to the boatswain—no chainslings could be rigged to yards and spars to prevent them from falling to the deck, to cripple the ship or crush the men at the guns. It would put an edge to their spirits when the time came. There had been no protest from the boatswain about keeping all the boats stacked in their tiers. Bolitho had expected none. For despite the real danger from flying splinters, some like saw-toothed daggers if tiered boats were caught in an attack, most sailors preferred to see them there. The last lifeline.

Keen came up to him. Like all the officers who would be on the upper deck he had discarded his tell-tale captain's coat. Too many clues. Too many easy targets.

Keen stared at the sky. 'It's going to be another clear day.'

Bolitho nodded. 'I had hoped for rain—cloud at least with this nor'-easterly.' He looked towards the empty blanket beyond the bows. 'We shall have the sun at our backs. They must sight us first. I think we should shorten sail, Val.'

Keen was peering around for a midshipman. 'Mr Rooke! Tell the first lieutenant to pipe the hands

423

aloft, to take in t'gan'sls and royals!'

Bolitho smiled in spite of his dry tension. Two minds working together. If they were sighted first, any enemy would be suspicious of a prize-ship being driven under full sail when there was nothing to fear.

Keen looked at the vague shapes of men rushing aloft up the shrouds, to take in and fist the heavy canvas to the yards.

He said, 'Major Bourchier knows what to do. He will have marines on the forecastle, aft here, and up in the maintop, just as he would if he were controlling a prize with her original company still aboard.'

There was nothing more they could do.

Cazalet called, 'Sailmaker, sir!'

Fudge and one of his mates came through the shadows and held out the makeshift Danish flag between them.

Bolitho said, 'True to your word. A fine job.' He beckoned to Jenour. 'Help Fudge to run up our new flag—*his* should be the honour!'

It would have been something to see it, he thought. But even in the raw darkness, with the spray occasionally pattering over the decks like rain, it was a moment to remember. Men crowding inboard from the guns to peer at the strange flapping ensign as it mounted up to the gaff beneath the ship's true colours.

Someone called out, 'Yew musta used all yer best gear fer that 'un, Fudge!'

The old sailmaker was still staring at the faint, curling shape against the black sky. Over his shoulder he said dourly, 'Got enough to sew you up in after this day's over, mate.'

Keen smiled. 'I've put one of our master's mates in the masthead, sir. Taverner—used to be with Duncan. Eyes like a hawk, mind like a knife. I'll see him made sailing-master even if it does mean losing him!'

Bolitho licked his dry lips. Coffee, wine, even the brackish water from the casks would help just now.

He shut it from his mind. 'We shall soon know.'

Keen said, 'Rear-Admiral Herrick could have taken another course, sir. He may have turned the convoy towards England where he could expect to meet with the patrolling squadron.'

Bolitho imagined he could see Herrick's round, honest features. Turn the convoy? Never. It would be like running away.

Tojohns, the captain's coxswain, was kneeling on the deck to secure Keen's curved hanger, the lightweight fighting sword he always carried in battle. As he had when *Hyperion* had gone down under him.

Bolitho touched the hilt of the old family sword at his hip and shivered. It was like ice. He felt Allday watching him, caught the heady scent of rum as he released a great sigh.

Keen was busy again with his master and lieutenants, and Bolitho asked, 'Well, old friend, what say you about this?'

For just a few seconds the darkness was gone, the night torn apart by one great, searing explosion which laid bare the whole ship, the men caught at their guns like statues, the rigging and shrouds sharpened by the glare like the bars of a furnace. Just as suddenly the light vanished, as if snuffed out by a giant's hand. Then, it seemed an eternity later, came the volcanic roar of the explosion, and with it

425

a hot wind which seemed to sear the canvas and throw every sail aback.

Voices called out in every direction as the silence, like the darkness, hemmed them in once more

Allday said harshly, 'One o' the vessels carryin' powder an' shot, I've no doubt!'

Bolitho tried to imagine if any one had known, be it only for a split second, that his life was ending in such a terrible way. No last cry, no handshake with an old friend to hold back the scream or the tears. *Nothing*.

Keen was shouting, 'Mr Cazalet, send midshipmen to each gundeck to tell the lieutenants what has happened!'

Bolitho looked away. Keen had managed to remember even that, as his ship sailed blindly on . . . into what?

Keen was heard to say, 'God, they must have felt that like a reef on the lower gundeck!'

A small figure emerged from somewhere, groping past the helmsmen and officers, the men at the braces, as if he did not belong here at all.

Allday growled, 'What th' hell are you doin' on deck?'

Bolitho turned. 'Ozzard! What is it? You know your place is below. You were never a Jack Tar like poor Allday here!' But the old joke fell flat as he realised that Ozzard was quivering like a leaf.

'C-can't, s-sir! In the dark . . . down there. Like last time . . .' He stood trembling, oblivious to the silent men around him. 'Not again. I c-can't do it!'

Bolitho said, 'Of course. I should have thought.' He glanced at Allday. 'Find him a place close to hand.' He knew the words were not reaching the terrified little man. 'Near to us, eh?' He watched

426

their shadows merge with the greater darkness and felt it like an old wound. *Hyperion* again.

Allday returned. 'Snug as a bug, Sir Richard. He'll be all right after what you just said.' *If only you knew the half of it*, he thought.

There were whispers as the upper yards and masthead pendant suddenly appeared against the sky, as if caught in another explosion, or even separate from the ship.

From the foremast cross-trees the master's mate's voice: 'Deck there! Land on the larboard bow!'

Keen exclaimed, 'Excellent, Mr Julyan—that must be The Skaw! Be prepared to alter course to the west'rd within the hour!'

Bolitho could share the excitement in many ways. They would soon be out and into the Skagerrak with sea-room which had no bottom, where it was said that wrecks and drowned sailormen shared the black caverns with blind creatures too terrible to imagine.

Be that as it may ... when the jib-boom pointed west again, nothing stood between them and England.

The light was spreading down on them to reveal each deck like a layer of a cake. Following astern, the seventy-four *Nicator* was completely laid bare in the weak sunlight, when minutes earlier she had been invisible.

Taverner the master's mate, who was sharing the lookout, yelled, '*Deck there! Ships burnin'!*' He seemed choked for words. '*God, sir, I can't count 'em!*'

Keen snatched a speaking-trumpet. '*This is the Captain!*' A pause, to give the slender link time to fasten, the months of training and years of

427

discipline to reassert themselves. 'What of the enemy?'

Bolitho walked to the quarterdeck rail and watched the upturned faces, the stark contrast with the almost cheerful air when Keen had explained what he had intended for this very moment.

'Two sail-of-the-line, sir! One other dismasted.' He broke off and Bolitho heard the master murmur, 'That's not like Bob. It must be bad then.'

The speed with which daylight was ripping away their defences made every moment worse. The enemy must have stumbled on the convoy before dusk yesterday, while they had been crawling out of the Sound with no thought but rescue in their hearts.

They must have taken or destroyed the whole convoy, leaving the clearing up to do until daylight. Until now.

Keen said in a tired voice, 'Too late after all, sir.'

The sudden echo of cannon fire vibrated over the sea and sighed through the masts and flapping canvas like an approaching squall.

Taverner called, 'Dismasted ship has opened fire, sir! She's not done in after all!' Discipline seemed to leave him and he yelled, *'Hit 'em, lads! Hit th' buggers! We'm comin'!'*

Keen and Bolitho stared at one another. The mastless, helpless ship was *Benbow*. There was no other possibility.

Bolitho said, 'Hands aloft, Val. Full sail. Just as we would if we were a prize and escort.' He saw the eagerness and despair in Keen's eyes and said, 'There is no other way. We must hold the surprise, and we must keep the wind-gage.' He felt his

428

muscles harden as a responding broadside overlapped another and knew that the enemy would divide *Benbow*'s remaining firepower, then board and take her. The ship could not even be manoeuvred to protect her stern from a full broadside. He clenched his fists together until they ached. Herrick would die rather than surrender. He had already lost too much.

Black Prince leaned steadily under the mounting pressure in her sails, and began to turn towards the western horizon beyond the blurred finger of land, a sea where the darkness still lingered.

With every minute the daylight revealed the awful evidence of a lost fight. Spars, hatch-covers, drifting boats, and further out, the long dark keel of a vessel which had capsized under the bombardment. As the darkness continued to retreat they sighted other ships. Some were partly dismasted, others outwardly undamaged. All flew the French Tricolour above their English flags, mocking patches of gaiety in a panorama of disaster.

Of the second escort which Tyacke had described there was no sign at all. Under Herrick's flag she would have gone down, too, rather than strike.

Taverner's voice was controlled again. 'Deck there! They've discontinued their fire!'

Keen raised his speaking-trumpet almost desperately. 'Have they struck?'

Taverner was watching from his private eyrie. All his years in ships under every kind of captain; but always learning, stowing it all away like rhino in a ditty-box.

He called, 'The big ship's standin' away and makin' more sail, sir!'

Bolitho gripped Keen's arm. 'They've sighted us, Val. *They're coming!*'

He saw his nephew, Midshipman Vincent, staring wildly over the nettings as far-off screams ebbed and flowed through the lengthening pall of dense smoke from one or more of the wrecks.

Tojohns said between his teeth, 'What's that, in Hell's name?'

Keen looked at him and answered flatly, 'Horses. Caught below decks when their ship was torn apart.'

He saw Bolitho touch his injured eye. Remembering too. The awful cries of army mounts dying in terror and in darkness until the sea finally ended it.

Bolitho noticed some of the seamen staring at each other with anger and sick dismay. Men who would barely turn a hair when they saw an enemy fall, or even one of their own if the time was wrong. But a helpless animal—that was always different.

'May I, Val?' Then all at once he found himself at the rail again, his voice surprisingly level and controlled as every man turned aft towards him.

'That ship is coming for us, lads! Whatever you may think or feel, you must stay your hand! Behind each port is a double-shotted gun with Englishmen to use them when I give the word!' He hesitated as he saw Ozzard's tiny shape scurrying along the starboard gangway towards the forecastle with one of the big signals telescopes over his shoulder like a mace.

He dragged his mind away from what it must have been like here. Helpless ships; Herrick standing like a rock between them and impossible odds. Perhaps Herrick was dead. In the same

430

breath he knew he was not.

'*Stand together!* This is our ship and those people yonder were our kin! But this is not revenge! It is justice!'

He fell silent, exhausted, empty. He said quietly, 'They don't have the heart for it, Val.'

'*Right, lads! Huzza for Our Dick!*' The ship seemed to shiver to the sudden wild burst of cheering. '*An' huzza for our Cap'n whose bride's waitin' for 'm in England!*'

Keen turned, his eyes full of tears. 'There's your answer—they'll give you all they have! You should never have doubted it!'

Allday seized Ozzard and cursed the men for cheering when they had no minds for what they were facing.

'What the hell were you doin'? I thought you'd run dizzy like them natives do in the sun!'

Ozzard put down the telescope and stared at him. He seemed very composed. More so than Allday could ever recall.

He said, 'I heard what Sir Richard just told them. That it's not revenge.' He looked at the powerful telescope. 'I don't know much about ships, but I know *that one* right enough. How could I forget?'

'How d'you mean, matey?' But the throbbing pain in his chest had already warned him.

Ozzard glanced towards Bolitho and the captain. 'I don't care what they call her or what flag she flies. She's the same one that destroyed our *Hyperion*. It will be revenge all right!' He peered at his friend, his courage gone. 'What shall we do, John?'

For once there was no answer.

* * *

Midshipman Roger Segrave pressed his palms on the quarterdeck rail and took in great gulps of air, as if he were being suffocated. His whole body was like taut wire, and when he looked at his hands and arms he expected to see them shaking uncontrollably. He glanced quickly at the figures around him. The master and his mates by the compass, the four helmsmen, with extra hands standing by but pretending to look like men with nothing to do. It was like a madness. The larboard gangway, the one which was nearest to the tall enemy three-decker, was packed with sailors, all unarmed, apparently chatting to each other and occasionally pointing at the other ships as if they were not involved. Segrave dropped his eyes and saw the lie revealed. Beneath the gangway and matched by the two decks below that, the gun crews were crammed against their weapons. Handspikes, rammers and sponges were close to hand, and even the breechings were cast off to avoid even a second's delay.

He looked at Bolitho who was standing with Captain Keen, hands on hips, sometimes pointing at the other ships but mostly keeping his eyes inboard. Even without their uniforms they stood out from the rest, Segrave thought wildly. The lordly Midshipman Bosanquet was speaking with the flag-lieutenant and Segrave saw signal flags rolled and ready to bend on, partly hidden by some hammocks stretched out to dry in the sunshine. Only the marines made no pretence of hiding their true identities. Their scarlet coats filled the maintop by the depressed swivel guns, and two more squads were properly deployed with fixed bayonets on the forecastle and aft near the poop.

Segrave heard Bolitho say, 'Mr Julyan, *you* are supposed to be the captain today!'

The tall sailing-master gave a broad grin. 'I feels different already, Sir Richard!'

Segrave felt his breathing and heartbeat steady. He must accept it, as they did.

Bolitho added in the same easy way, 'I know that our Danish opposites dress somewhat more soberly than we do, but I think a hat might make all the difference.'

More grins as Julyan tried first Keen's cocked hat and then Bolitho's, which fitted him perfectly.

Bolitho glanced around the quarterdeck and Segrave tensed as the grey eyes rested momentarily on him. 'The waiting's over. *Stand by!*'

Segrave looked again at the enemy. The second large ship, a two-decker, was falling downwind and changing tack, flags rising and vanishing from her yards as she exchanged signals with her superior. She would confront *Nicator*, which was making full sail as if to head off any attack on her 'prize'.

Keen watched his former ship and murmured, 'She was a good old girl.' *Was.*

Segrave jumped as the first lieutenant's harsh voice smashed through his thoughts.

'Lower gundeck, Mr Segrave! Report to the third lieutenant there!' He glared round the darkly shadowed deck. 'That bloody Vincent should have been here by now! Tell him I want him if you see him!' His eyes fell on Segrave and something perhaps from an old memory made him say, 'Easy, young fellow. Men will die today, but only if chosen.' His hard features cracked into a smile. 'You've proved your worth—it'll not be your turn

433

yet!'

Segrave ran to the ladder and suddenly remembered the rough kindness shown to him in Tyacke's *Miranda* before she had been blown to pieces. He was a year older. He had lived a full lifetime since then.

He paused for a last glance before losing himself in the hull's darkness. A captured scene, which he would never forget. Bolitho, his frilled shirt blowing in the fresh breeze, one hand on the old sword, with his coxswain just behind him. Keen, Jenour, Bosanquet, master's mates and seamen, people now, more real than any he knew at home.

As he turned he felt his mouth go dry. Beyond the larboard gangway was a solitary flag, like a lance-pendant above an armoured knight in one of his old storybooks.

As close as that. He knew it was the foremast truck of the enemy ship.

Someone shouted, 'She's luffed! She wants to speak!' There was no defiant response, no ironic jeers such as he had heard from sailors in danger. It was like a single animal growl, as if the ship were speaking for them.

He found himself hurrying down, deck by deck, ladder by ladder, past wary marine sentries posted to prevent men from running below, and ship's boys as they ran with fresh powder for the guns which had yet to be fired.

He saw a midshipman cowering by the carpenter's extra stock of wedges and plugs, and knew it was Vincent.

He said, 'Mr Cazalet wants you on deck!'

Vincent seemed to shrink into the heap of repairing gear and sobbed, 'Go away, damn you to

434

hell! I hope they kill you!'

Segrave hurried on, shocked more than anything by what he had seen. Vincent was finished. He had not even begun.

The lower gundeck was in total darkness, and yet Segrave could feel the mass of men who crouched there. In places chinks of sunlight probed down the gunports to touch a naked, sweating shoulder, or a pair of eyes white and staring like a blind man's.

Flemyng, the third lieutenant, commanded here. This was the main power of *Black Prince*'s artillery, where twenty-eight thirty-two pounders and their crews lived, trained and waited for just this moment.

Flemyng was a tall man, and was crouched over with his face pressed against the massive hull by the first division of guns. Only when he looked inboard did Segrave see the small round observation port, no bigger than a sailor's basin, where the lieutenant could watch the nearness of an enemy before any one else.

'Segrave? Stay with me.' His voice was clipped sharp. He was usually one of the easiest of the lieutenants. 'Gunner's mate! See to Mr Segrave!' He dismissed him and turned back to his little port.

Segrave's eyes were getting used to the darkness and he could see the individual guns nearest him, the black breeches resting on the buff-painted trucks, men crowded around them as if in some strange ceremony, their backs shining like steel.

The gunner's mate said, ''Ere, Mr Segrave.' He thrust two pistols into his hands. 'Both loaded. Just cock an' fire, see?'

Segrave stared at the closed gunports. Would the enemy come swarming in here? Into the ship

435

herself?

The gunner's mate had gone, and Segrave jumped as somebody touched his leg and murmured, 'Come to see 'ow the poor live, Mr Segrave?'

Segrave got down by the gun. It was the man he had saved from a flogging, the one Vincent had discovered in the hold below them at this moment.

He exclaimed, 'Jim Fittock! I didn't know this was your station!'

A voice barked, 'Silence on the gundeck!'

Fittock chuckled. 'You got yer pieces then?'

Segrave thrust them into his belt. 'They'll not be allowed to get that close!'

Fittock nodded to his mates on the opposite side of the great thirty-two pounder. It said that this young officer was all right. The reasons were unnecessary.

'Aye, we'll rake the buggers after what they done!' He saw a sliver of sunlight glance off one of the pistols and gave a bitter smile. How could he explain to such an innocent that the pistols were for shooting any poor Jack who tried to run when the slaughter began?

A whistle shrilled and a voice piped from the companion ladder, 'Right traverse, sir!'

Someone growled. 'She's that close, eh?' Handspikes rasped across the deck to move the guns to a steeper angle; this division would be firing directly from the larboard bow.

Lieutenant Flemyng had drawn his hanger. '*Ready*, lads!' He peered through the darkness as if he were seeing each of his men. 'They've been calling to us to heave-to!' His voice sounded wild. '*All nice and friendly!*' As he turned back to look

436

through his observation port, the sunlight, which had held his face suspended against the darkness like a mask, was cut off. It was as if a great hand had been laid across the port like a shutter.

Fittock hissed, 'Keep with us!'

Segrave heard no more as the whistles shrilled and Flemyng yelled, *'Open the ports! Run out!'*

The air was filled with the squeak of trucks as the seamen threw themselves on their tackles and ran the great, lumbering guns up to the waiting sunshine. Gun-captains crouched and took the slack from their trigger-lines, faces, eyes, hands in various attitudes of hate and prayer while they cringed and waited for the order; it was like one vast incomplete painting.

Segrave started with disbelief at the high beakhead and ornate gilded carving—a ship's tall side already smoke-stained from bombardment and conquest.

It was like being held in time. No voice, nor motion, as if the ship, too, was stricken.

Flemyng's hanger slashed down. *'Fire!'*

As each gun came lurching inboard to be seized, sponged out and reloaded in the only fashion they knew, Segrave stood gasping and retching, the smoke funnelling around him and blotting out everything. And yet it was there. Frozen to his mind. The lines of enemy guns pointing at *him*, some with men peering around them, watching their latest capture until the massive weight of iron smashed into them at less than fifty yards' range.

The ship was swaying over as deck by deck the full broadside was fired across the smoky water. Men were cheering and cursing, racing one another to run out the guns and hold up their hands in the

437

swirling mist of powder smoke.

'*Run out! Aim! Fire!*'

A ragged crash thundered against the side and somewhere a gun rolled inboard and overturned like a wounded beast. Men screamed and fell in the choking mist, and Segrave saw a severed hand lying near the next gun like a discarded glove. No wonder they painted the sides red. It managed to hide some of the horror.

'Cease firing!' Flemyng turned away as another midshipman was dragged towards the hatchway which would take him to the orlop. From what he could see he had lost an arm and a leg. There was not much point . . .

Segrave also tore his eyes away. The same age as himself. The same uniform. *A thing*. Not a person any more.

'*Open the starboard ports!*'

Fittock punched his arm. 'Come on, sir! The Cap'n's comin' about and we'll engage the buggers to starboard!' They scrambled across the deck, stumbling over fallen gear and slipping on blood as sunlight poured through the other ports and the enemy seemed to slide past, her sails in complete disorder. Unless engaged on both sides together, the gun crews usually helped each other to keep the broadsides timed and regular.

'Ready, sir!'

'On the uproll, lads!' Flemyng was hatless and there was blood splashed like paint on his forehead. '*Fire!*'

Men were cheering and hugging each other. ''Er bloody foremast's comin' down!'

By one of the guns a seaman held his mate in his arms, and frantically pushed the hair from his eyes as he babbled, 'Nearly done, Tim! The buggers are dismasted!' But his friend did not respond. Together they had lived and yarned by this one gun. Every waking hour it had been here—waiting.

A gunner's mate said roughly, 'Take that man an' put 'im over! 'E's done for!' He was not an unduly hard man, but death was terrible enough without seeing it lingering on.

The seaman clutched his friend closer to him so that his head lolled across his shoulder as if to confide something. *'You won't put 'im over, you bastards!'*

Segrave felt Fittock's hard hand helping him to his feet as he called, 'Leave them, gunner's mate!' He did not recognise himself. 'There is enough to do!'

Fittock glanced across at his own crew, his teeth very white in his grimy face.

'Told you, eh? Right little terrier!' Then he guided Segrave to the curve of one great timber so that the others should not see his distress. He added, 'One of the best!'

Throughout the ship men stood or crouched at their tasks, bodies streaked with sweat, ears bandaged against the deafening roar of cannon fire, fingers raw from hauling, ramming and running-out again and again.

It took time for the marine's trumpet call to penetrate each deck, and then the cheering clawed its way up towards the smoky sunlight, that other place where it had all begun.

Bolitho stood by the quarterdeck rail and watched the enemy ship. As she drifted downwind she turned her high stern towards him, the name *San Mateo* still so bright in the sunlight. He had

439

thought it would never stop, and yet he knew that the whole action, from the time the Danish flag had been hauled down and his own run up to the fore, had lasted barely thirty minutes.

He said, 'I knew we could do it.' He felt Allday near him, heard Keen yell, 'Stand by to starboard!'

There had been casualties. Men killed when seconds before they had been waiting to start the game.

'*Nicator*'s signalling, sir!' Jenour sounded hoarse.

Bolitho raised a hand in acknowledgment. Thank God. Jenour was safe too. *Black Prince* must have fired three broadsides before the enemy had gathered wits enough to return a ragged response. By then it was already too late.

He said, 'Signal *Nicator* to close with the convoy. Make certain that she tells the boarding parties that if they try to scuttle our ships or harm the crews, they will have to swim home!' He heard men muttering with approval and knew that had he so much as suggested it, they would have run every French prisoner up to the mainyard.

It was what war dictated. A madness. A need to hurt and kill those who had brought fear to you.

He thought suddenly of Ozzard. So innocuous, and yet he had known, had recognised that it was that same ship which had so brutally destroyed *Hyperion*. Maybe it was the ship, and not the men who crewed her? French flag, Spanish, and now if she surrendered, an addition to His Britannic Majesty's fleet. Would she, the ship, remain unchanged, like something untamed?

It still sickened him to recall how *San Mateo* had poured her broadsides into *Hyperion*, regardless of the destruction and murder she was causing to her

440

own consorts, which were unable to move clear. *The ship then.*

Keen walked round to face him.

'Sir?' He watched quietly. Feeling it. Sharing it. There was pride too. More than he had dared to hope for.

Bolitho seemed to rouse himself. 'Has she struck yet?' *Is that me? So cold, so impersonal ... An executioner.*

Keen answered gently, 'I believe her steering is shot away, sir. But their guns are still, and I think many of her people are dead.'

Bolitho said, 'A glass if you please.' He saw their surprise as he crossed to the opposite side and levelled the telescope on Herrick's flagship. Unmoving and heavy in the water, her masts and trailing rigging dragging from either side. Thin scarlet threads ran down from the upper deck scuppers to the littered surface and the ship's unmoving reflection. As if she herself were bleeding to death. He felt his heart leap as he saw the tattered ensign still trailing from the poop where someone had braved hell to nail it there. Beyond *Benbow*, the other vessels drifted to no purpose. Spectators, victims; waiting for it all to end.

He called sharply, 'Prepare all divisions to fire, Captain Keen!' There was no reply, and he could almost feel them holding their breath. 'If they do not strike, *they will die.*' He swung round. *'Is that clear?'*

Another voice; another still alive. Bosanquet called, 'Brig *Larne* is closing, sir!'

Perhaps his meticulous interruption helped. Bolitho said, 'Call away my barge and ask the surgeon to report to me. *Benbow* will need help.

Your first lieutenant would be a great asset.' He shook himself and walked to his friend. 'My apologies, Val. I had forgotten.'

Cazalet had fallen to the first exchange. A ball had all but cut him in half while he had been sending men aloft to attend repairs.

They were cheering again; it went on and on and Bolitho believed he could see men in *Nicator*'s yards waving and capering, their voices lost in distance. Like great falling leaves the two French flags drifted down from *San Mateo*'s rigging and men stood back from her guns, silently watching like mourners.

Keen said harshly, '*She's struck!*' He could not contain his relief.

Bolitho saw his barge lifting and then dipping over the nettings, and knew that Keen had been dreading the order to re-open fire, flags or not.

Allday touched his hat. 'Ready, Sir Richard.' He studied him anxiously. 'Shall I fetch a coat?'

Bolitho turned to him and winced as the sunlight pricked at his eye.

'I have no need for it.'

Julyan the sailing-master called, 'What about your hat, Sir Richard?' He was half-laughing, but almost sobbing with relief. Men had died right beside him. He was safe—one more time. Another step up the ladder.

Bolitho smiled through the smoky sunshine. 'You have a son, I believe? Give it to him. It will make a good yarn, one day.'

He turned away from the surprise and gratitude in the man's face and said, 'Let us finish this.'

It was a silent crossing, with only the creak of oars and the bargemen's breathing to break the stillness.

As *Benbow*'s great shadow loomed over them, Bolitho did not know where he would find the strength to meet whatever lay ahead. He pinched the locket beneath his filthy shirt and whispered, '*Wait for me, Kate.*'

Followed by the others, he clambered up the side. Shot holes pitted the timbers from gangway to waterline, rigging, some with corpses trapped within it like weed, tugged beneath the sea, pulling her down.

Bolitho climbed faster. But a ship's heart could be saved. He saw faces staring at him from open gunports, some driven half-mad, others probably killed at the outbreak of the battle.

He reached the quarterdeck, so bare now without the main and mizzen to protect it.

He heard *Black Prince*'s surgeon calling out orders, and another boat already hooking alongside with more willing hands; but at this moment he was quite alone.

The centre of any fighting ship, where it all began and ended. The shattered wheel with the dead helmsmen scattered like bloodied bundles, even caught in attitudes of shock and fury when death had marked them down. A boatswain's mate who had been kneeling to fix a bandage to the flag-lieutenant's leg, then both of them killed together by a hail of cannister shot. A sailor still bending on a signal when he had fallen, and the halliards were torn from his hands as the mast had gone careering overboard.

Propped against the compass box with one leg bent beneath him was Herrick. He was barely conscious, although Bolitho guessed that his pain

443

was deeper than any gunshot wound.

He held a pistol in one hand, and raised his head, holding it to one side as if the broadsides had rendered him deaf.

'*Ready, Marines!* We've got 'em on the run! *Take aim*, my lads!'

Bolitho heard Allday mutter, 'God, look at it.'

The marines did not stir. They lay, from sergeant to private, like fallen toy soldiers, their weapons still pointing towards an invisible enemy.

Allday said sharply, '*Easy*, sir.'

Bolitho stepped over an out-thrust scarlet arm with two chevrons upon it and gently took the pistol from Herrick's hand.

He passed it to Allday, who noted that it was in fact loaded and cocked.

'Rest easy, Thomas. Help is here.' He took his arm and waited for the blue eyes to focus and recover their understanding. 'Listen to the cheering! The battle's o'er—the day is won!'

Herrick allowed himself to be raised to a more comfortable position. He stared at the splintered decks and abandoned guns, the dead, and the scarlet trails which marked the retreat of the dying.

As if speaking from far away he said thickly, 'So you came, Richard.'

He uses my name and yet he meets me as a stranger. Bolitho waited sadly, the madness and the exhilaration of battle already drained from him.

Herrick was trying to smile. 'It will be ... another triumph for you.'

Bolitho released his arm very gently and stood up, and beckoned to the surgeon. 'Attend to the Rear-Admiral, if you please.' He saw the dead marine corporal's hair blowing in the breeze, his

444

eyes fixed with attention as if he were listening.

Bolitho looked at Jenour, and past him to the waiting, listless ships.

'I think not, Thomas. Here, Death is the only victor.'

It was over.

EPILOGUE

The relentless bombardment of Copenhagen by day and night brought its inevitable conclusion. On the fifth of September, General Peyman, the governor of the city, sent out a flag of truce. Terms were still to be agreed, if possible with some honour left to the heroic defenders, but all fighting was to end.

While Bolitho and his ships took charge of their prizes and did what they could for the many killed and wounded, the terms of Copenhagen were decided. The surrender of all Danish ships and naval stores, and the removal of any other vessel not yet completed in the dockyard, and the occupation by Lord Cathcart's forces of The Citadel and other fortifications for a period of six weeks while these tasks were carried out, formed the basis of the armistice. It was thought by some that even the skills and experience of the English sailors would be insufficient to complete this great operation within the allotted time, but even the most doubtful critics were forced to show admiration and pride at the Fleet's achievements.

In the allotted span of six weeks, sixteen sail-of-the-line, frigates, sloops and many smaller vessels were despatched to English ports, and the country's fear that the blockade of enemy ports would collapse due to lack of ships was ended.

The various squadrons were returned to their normal stations and some were disbanded to await further instructions. Perhaps, after the glory of Trafalgar, the second battle of Copenhagen was slow to catch the imagination of a public hungry for victories. But the results, and the severe setback to Napoleon's last hope of breaking the line of wooden-walls which stretched from the Channel ports to Biscay and from Gibraltar to the shores of Italy, were real enough.

The New Year arrived, and with it some of the victors came home.

For late January it was deceptively mild and peaceful in the little Cornish village of Zennor. Some said it was an omen for such a special occasion, for this part of the county was not noted for its placid weather. Zennor lay on the north shore of the peninsula, as different from Falmouth and its pastoral landscape of low hills, silver estuaries and lovely bays as could be imagined. Here was a savage coastline of cliffs and serried lines of jagged black rocks like broken teeth, where the sea boiled and thundered in constant unrest. In normal times, a bleak, uncompromising shore where many a fine ship had made its last and fatal landfall.

Zennor was a small place, owing its existence mainly to the land, as only the foolhardy sought to live from fishing, and there were many stones in the church to confirm as much.

Despite the chill, damp air, not a villager missed this particular day, when one of their own, the daughter of a respected local man who had been wrongly executed for speaking out on the freedoms of farm workers and others, was to be married.

The village had never seen such an occasion. At first glance there were more expensive carriages and horses than residents. The blue and white of sea officers rubbed shoulders with a few Royal Marines and some of the local garrison, while the gowns of the ladies were of a quality and style rarely seen in this proud but humble place.

The little twelfth-century church, more accustomed to farming festivals and local weddings, was packed. Even with extra chairs and stools brought from the dairy, some of the congregation had to remain outside in the timeless churchyard—as much a part of their heritage as the sea and the rolling fields which surrounded the village.

A young lieutenant bowed to Catherine as she entered the church on the arm of Captain Adam Bolitho. 'If you will follow me, my lady!'

An organ was playing in the background when she reached her allotted place; she had noticed several heads leaning forward to watch her pass, then moving together for a quiet remark, or more gossip perhaps.

Strangely, it no longer mattered. She glanced across the church and thought she recognised some of Bolitho's captains. It must have been difficult for a few of them to reach this remote village, she thought. From Falmouth it was some forty miles, first north and through Truro on the main coaching road, then westward where with each passing mile the roads became narrower and more rutted. She smiled to herself. Nancy's husband, 'The King of Cornwall', had performed magnificently, living up to his name by obtaining the full co-operation of the local squire, willingly or otherwise. He had offered his spacious house, not only for many of the guests to stay overnight, but had also joined with Roxby in providing such a spread of food and drink there that it would be talked about for years to come.

She said quietly, 'I am so glad it is a fine day for

them.' She watched Adam's profile and remembered what Bolitho had told her, that he seemed troubled by something. 'Look at poor Val! He would rather face another battle than stand and be still like this!'

Keen was standing by the small altar, with his brother beside him. Like his two sisters in the church, the other man was fair; and it appeared odd, in this gathering, for him not to be wearing uniform, but Catherine knew he was a distinguished barrister in London.

Adam said, 'I shall have to leave soon after the wedding, Catherine.' He glanced at her, and she felt her heart leap at the resemblance as it always did. So like Richard; or perhaps all the Bolithos were cast in the same mould.

'So soon?' She laid her hand on his sleeve. The young hero who had said that he had all he had ever dreamed of; but for a few moments he had looked quite lost, like the boy he had once been.

He smiled at her—Bolitho's smile. 'It is the burden of every frigate captain, I'm told. Turn your back and the admiral will poach your best men for some other captain. You find only the sweepings of the press if you stay away too long.'

It was not the reason, and she knew that he realised she understood as much. He said suddenly, 'I want to tell you, Catherine.' He gripped her hand. 'You of all people—I know you—care.'

She returned the pressure on his hand. 'When you are ready, you will share it perhaps.'

There were more whispers by the altar. She sat silently, studying the ancient ceiling of Cornish barrel vaulting, recalling the famous legend of this place. It was said that a mermaid had once sat in the back of the church and lost her heart to a chorister here. Then one day she had lured him out to the little stream which ran through the village and down into the sea at Pendour Cove. They were never seen again; but even now it was claimed by many that you could hear the lovers singing together when the sea was calm ... like today.

She smiled wistfully as Keen turned and gazed up the aisle, a brave, distinguished figure in the cool winter light reflecting against these old stone walls. Theirs was a role reversed, surely? Zenoria had been his mermaid, and he had plucked her from the sea to make her his own.

She saw Tojohns, Keen's coxswain, proudly dressed in his best jacket and breeches, wave a signal from the door. It was almost time. Beyond him she had seen Allday's familiar figure. Did he feel a little neglected, she wondered? Or was he, like herself, trying not to think of that other marriage that could never be? She touched her finger where Somervell's ring had been. They must not waste a day or an hour, whenever they were together. All those years which had been denied them could never be lived again.

There was a sound of distant cheering, and someone ringing a cow bell. Then carriage wheels on the rough track, and she felt a burning pride as the cheers grew louder, not for the bride this time but for her man. The hero whom even a stranger could recognise and make his own.

She wished they could be alone afterwards, escape back to Falmouth after the wedding, but it was impossible. Forty miles on these roads in the darkness was a sure way of ending everything.

Catherine turned and watched their shadows shut

out the bright sunlight in the ancient doorway, and put her hand to her breast.

'What a lovely creature she is, Adam.' She turned to speak further and then made herself face the aisle, as Bolitho with Zenoria on his arm moved slowly into the body of the church.

It was no imagination. Perhaps another woman might have been mistaken; and Catherine found herself wishing it were so.

But she had seen the look on Adam's face before, on Bolitho's in those difficult, reckless days...

Adam was in love all right, with the girl who was about to marry Valentine Keen.

Richard Bolitho looked down at the girl and said, 'A promise kept. I said I would give you away. It is a coming-together of so many hopes!'

What had she been thinking on the endless journey by coach, and now along the aisle's weathered stones where so many generations had trod? There seemed only happiness.

He saw familiar faces and smiles, his sister Nancy already dabbing at her eyes as he had known she would. Ferguson and his wife Grace, people from the estate side by side with officers high and low. Even the port admiral from Plymouth had made an appearance, and was sharing a pew with Midshipman Segrave—a suddenly older and more confident young man who would be standing for lieutenant when he returned to the ship.

He smiled at Allday and knew he would have liked to be in charge today as was Keen's own coxswain, organising a carriage decked with ribbons, to be drawn on boat ropes by some of Keen's midshipmen and petty officers to carry them to the squire's house.

He saw a dark shadow slip along the wall and enter the pew shared by Adam and Catherine; he sat among other shadows with his face half averted and the collar of his boat-cloak turned up. He did not need to be told it was Tyacke, paying his respects in his own special way, no matter what the cost to himself. A true friend, he thought with sudden affection and admiration.

He touched his injured eye and tried to ignore it. It was pricking painfully in the smoke of the many candles which lined the church.

There were many others in the shadows today who would remain equally silent. Friends he would never see again; would never be able to share with Catherine.

Francis Inch, John Neale, Charles Keverne, Farquhar, Veitch, and now poor Browne ... with an 'e'. And so many more.

He thought too of Herrick, who would be at his own home recovering from a flesh wound, but with a far harder disablement to endure forever.

He gave his place to Keen as the clergyman, whom he did not know, opened his book and beamed nervously at the unusually illustrious congregation.

Bolitho stood beside Catherine and they clasped hands as the familiar words were spoken and repeated, and the ring was offered and received to seal their vows to one another.

Then the ancient bells were chiming overhead and people were leaning out of the pews to call their best wishes to the bridal couple.

Bolitho said, 'Wait a while, Kate.' He saw that Adam had already gone, and of Tyacke there was no sign, although almost lost in the joyful clamour of the bells he heard the beat of hooves as he galloped away; like the devil's highwayman, he thought.

'Young Matthew will bring the carriage for us after the others have left.'

He looked past her at the empty church, a child's glove fallen between some stacked Bibles.

'What is it?' She watched him, waiting, believing he had seen and recognised Adam's despair.

He said quietly, 'This is for you.' He raised her hand and held the ring above it, a glistening band of diamonds and rubies. 'In the eyes of God we *are* married, dearest Kate. It is right that it should be here.'

Allday watched from the porchway. Like young lovers.

He grinned. And why not? A sailor and his woman. There was no stronger bond.

And he shared their joy: and somehow, it dispelled his own envy.

Photoset, printed and bound in Great Britain by
REDWOOD PRESS LIMITED, Melksham, Wiltshire